A Dusk Forever Waning

Book One from Torrenth

By Adam Nathaniel Davis

Dedicated to:

Salima, for all of your amazing love and support

And to John, for riding my ass like a rented mule

Chapter 1 – A Brutal Proposition

The alert rang through his mind. He reached into his pocket and produced a small, yellow, diamond-shaped pill. The corporate logo of LiveLong rose from its surface. Popping it onto his tongue, he waited a few seconds for it to completely dissolve. He found it difficult to define the taste. Nothing else on Torrenth tasted quite like it. But he savored this time every day when he took his Telomore. In fact, he had enjoyed this moment every day during each of the 1,878 years of his life.

As the last grainy pieces evaporated in his mouth he felt a surge of confidence. It was a silly emotion. Telomore produced no high. In fact, it produced no conscious, measurable indications of its use. Its effects were far subtler – yet far more important. This pill added, quite literally, another day to the relentless stream of days that comprised his life.

The scaler moved along suspended rails. Pontius stared through murky glass to the endless skyscrapers beyond. The compartment accommodated 30 people but there were more than 60 onboard. The ever-present patter of rain created a backdrop that never failed to soothe him. Most of the passengers gazed at the inner projections from their Universal Neural Implants. They traversed their own private worlds. Pontius preferred the kabuki theater of the real.

Despite the crammed preponderance of bodies in the cabin, three dogs found room for themselves. He wasn't sure if they had come in recently, in the last stop or two, or if they were of more of a permanent presence. One perched on high, curled into the luggage bin. How it managed to get there was anybody's guess. Another crouched behind the row of seats opposite him. The third was sitting at his feet. All three were staring at him. He told himself that this was some kind of optical illusion, like the eyes in a painting that follow you no matter where you go in the room. But as he scanned the other passengers he realized that none of them had the dogs' attention.

He made a brief attempt to win a staring contest with luggage bin dog. Before he could engage the beast in earnest, the automated transit voice announced that they had reached the Argus 50 platform. Most of the stoic passengers still stared at their own internal projections. The dogs watched him with renewed attention, as if to ask if this was his stop. He rose and shook some of the rain off his coat. As he made his way to the exit, he wondered if the dogs would follow. But they stayed riveted to their positions, watching him as he left.

The wind on the platform was forceful. It was always forceful 150 meters from the surface. Although the air at this height was cooler than ground level, it was still warm and heavy. A depressing layer of humidity blanketed the island and thwarted any attempts at relief. Pontius stood on the platform for several minutes and watched the lightning raging in the distance. Random bolts illuminated the smooth surfaces of buildings as it sought out one target after another. He knew the dampness would irritate him later, but the rain dancing down his face felt good for the time being. He was loathe to abandon the sensation.

A Dusk Forever Waning

He sighed to himself and turned around to resume his journey. Covered corridors led in both directions around the outside of the building. His destination was deep in the bowels of the Argus complex. He spotted the grand hallway leading straight into the structure and began wading through the people.

The Argus complex was a group of seven structures, with the smaller six emanating from the main like spokes on a wheel. Argus Prime was 350 stories tall and represented some of the finest architecture on the whole planet of Torrenth. Walls and doorways throughout the building featured intricate patterns inlaid in chrome and alabaster. The floors were solid but had an odd springiness that forgave his tired soles.

Dynamic murals danced across the ceiling. They offered a dramatic and ever-changing display of sea monsters, gods, and ancient dramas. Pontius felt he was walking through a brooding, melodramatic atmosphere in an alien theater.

Walking through the bustling hallway, he scanned the faces of those who passed him. Although he believed his target to be in the central marketplace, he knew he wasn't far from his goal. He could never tell when someone might slip right under his nose. Some of his most critical stops had happened outside or near the target's presumed location.

Her name was Felencia and she worked for a sauce shop. This particular shop sold a myriad of products dredged up from the depths of Oceanus. Given this simple fact, he assumed that she must smell bad and look worse. He couldn't imagine anyone even halfway attractive wanting to work for an eel monger.

She was young – not even 200 years old - and bi-racial, having a clear mix of Felosian in her. She was single – or at least, there were no state records of a cohabitant. She had worked at this particular sauce shop for more than 75 years. Pontius presumed only dimwitted people could work in a sauce shop for 75 years. Crucial to his investigation was the fact that she had just given birth.

She had no formal maternity records, but the intelligence reports were unmistakable. Surveillance caught her on many occasions ferrying a suspicious bundle. She recently missed a lot of time at work. Acquaintances observed her as exhausted and irritable. She experienced rapid weight gain, followed by drastic loss. Worst of all, neighbors had sold her out. She was the confirmed mother of an unlicensed baby.

He worked under the Department of Population Control. He was a tactical agent for a specialized task force - the Newborn Corrections Unit. He couldn't remember any of his early days in NCU, but they had just thrown a 1,500-year anniversary party for him. He was the most decorated agent in the entire unit, although there were plenty who had been there much longer than him. It was not an exaggeration to say that he had achieved almost mythical status in PC. He never turned down an assignment. He completed the most challenging of assignments. He was as reliable as rain.

Far ahead in the grand hallway, he saw light and could hear the unmistakable sounds of the atrium. His heart quickened and his pace increased. Yet he pulled back the reigns and ducked off into a side hallway to collect his bearings and check his notes.

He closed his eyes and began sifting through his UNI. He could access it with his eyes open. But he found it disorienting to have the virtual displays of internal computing overlaid onto reality. It worried him to think that if he projected UNI imagery onto his reality he could lose the basis of what is real and what is overlaid. There were many people who had tried, or would continue to try to kill him. He couldn't afford to have any distrust in his natural senses.

He pulled up Felencia's records and began reconfirming her data. He checked agency records to ensure the she hadn't somehow, in the last minute, acquired a Vitapass for her baby. No one ever acquired a Vitapass in the last moments before he arrived, but it was protocol to check nonetheless. He retrieved all messages from the office to ensure that directives remained changed. Directives always remained unchanged, but it was protocol to check nonetheless. He downloaded the termination license into virtual memory for easy access. Desperate parents always demanded to see a copy of the termination license. The Grand Court ruled, years ago, that termination licenses were unnecessary. But it was policy to generate them anyway. It avoided any hint of impropriety.

Reaching under his shirt, he could feel the necklace that carried a totem for each member of his Priori. One by one, through all six of these Priori, he held the totem, ruminated on the task before him, and prayed. He felt that some of the Priori were better for different qualities, so he prayed to his first Priorus for initiative and agility. He prayed to his last Priorus for wisdom and fairness.

With his meditation complete, before he stepped back into the grand hallway, a haggard beggar stumbled by. He asked if Pontius wanted to feel good. Pontius paused for a moment, perplexed. Pointing to the atrium down the hallway, he looked at the old man and explained, "I can get all the drugs I want right there. Clean. Powerful. Legal."

The old man kept his gaze downward, shaking his head. Then he lifted his head to reveal a gaping maw of toothless gums encased in a broad, wild smile. "I no have, 'Drug'. I have, 'Feel goooooooood'."

He swiped the cretin's grasping paw away. He reentered the bustling fray of pedestrians in the grand hallway. Although it was mere minutes since he was last in the hallway, he believed that the traffic had doubled. Men darted to and fro in front of him. Sometimes women would bunch behind him, leveraging his ability to part crowds. He was not a large man, but he was tall, and his tanned, sinewy features gave him a presence that tended to make lesser men get out of his way.

Ahead he could see the warm glow and hear the chaotic sounds of the marketplace. Walking about a hundred meters further, he spilled into the edifice with a gaggle of people bunched around him. The market was a broad circular atrium more than 500 meters in diameter. All around the circumference there were other major hallways that emptied into the atrium. A brief observation gave the impression that all traffic flowed into the atrium and nothing flowed out.

The most breathtaking aspect of the atrium was the ceiling. It comprised a grand dome displaying an endless series of rich, moving images. The images themselves were indistinct and ever-changing, like impressions gleaned from cloud gazing. But staring at them long enough made it clear that definite artistic images were arising. The brightness, color, and tone of the images would shift every 5-10 minutes. It happened in a gradual manner, such that one might wonder how the ceiling had changed if he weren't paying close attention.

The marketplace below was a study in detail. Every vendor crammed an ever-greater array of wares into ever-tighter spaces. The larger vendors had permanent storefronts around the atrium. They deployed smaller tents in front to snag passersby. Minor vendors had nary but a tent hunkered down at random spots throughout the concourse. The tents were often chained together to maximize space. It had the effect of creating streets and pathways between them.

For a moment, he stood his ground and stared at the ethereal images on the ceiling. They carried a sense of wonder for him that he couldn't quite explain. He remembered being here before, but he also knew that he had been here far earlier than his memory stretched. He couldn't help but wonder if he had been here hundreds of years before, or as a young man, or even as a child. Had his path today been a repetition in an endless cycle leading him down the same rut, through the exact same locations? He considered searching his UNI for long-term images, but he knew this to be a poor use of his time. It was more efficient to guess.

He noticed that the traffic flowed around the circumference in a clockwork direction. Wanting to be as nondescript as possible, he slipped into the traffic like a leaf on a river. He allowed the current to take him past all the potential vendors. He floated past drug vendors – half of all the vendors were hawking drugs. He floated past those selling crafts and home wares. He floated past fish mongers. The creatures pulled from Oceanus and offered up as "food" never ceased to amaze him. He floated past textile vendors and craftsmen who were working their magic right there in their booths. He even floated past pimps who offered nothing but the finest of whores. The ladies sat on stools. They were available for all the poking, prodding, and licking anyone could desire before making a decision.

After perusing the menagerie, Pontius found himself in front of Centrian Sauces. It was a larger enterprise than he had imagined. They had a wide storefront on the circumference. There were no fewer than four tents in front of the store offering specialized sauces. Inside the main store he could see long rows of shelves offering an incredible array of multicolored bottles. He had no idea that there could be so many sauces peddled in a single store.

The four tents upfront were all manned by men. That made his targeting simpler. He proceeded to wade into the main store itself. Once inside he found there were only three main attendants. There was a man in authority, a blonde woman working the checkout, and a raven-haired woman in a yellow frock at the back counter. The woman at the back counter was Felencia.

He walked up to the counter and proceeded to observe. She was working with other customers. His presence qualified as just another individual waiting for service. He leveraged the situation to soak everything in.

Felencia was more attractive than he imagined. He found it hard to believe that anyone attractive would make their living processing eel guts. He listened to her interactions with the other customers. She had a light, easy-going demeanor that put everyone at-ease. Her hair wasn't just black. It had a healthy sheen and it hung with uniformity around her shoulders as though it resided in a well-oiled sheath. He assumed this was some trick of cosmetics, but it still caught his attention. She was slim with slight features. She wore a baggy sweatshirt under her yellow frock that had the effect of concealing her midriff. He was familiar with this as a common feature of women who had just given birth.

The store was open to the central concourse and the popularity of their wares made him cautious about his work. Although he had no doubt about his legal authority, experience taught him that stealth always won the day. The counter she commanded was also open. There was, however, an inviting door behind the counter that led to a backroom with some kind of fish butchering station. He could see no other doors leading off the main store, so he assumed that all backrooms connected to this area.

When she had processed all customers in front of him, Felencia made her way over to Pontius. She flashed him a dazzling smile and asked if she could help him. He was a bit stunned by the sheer whiteness of her teeth and took a moment to reply. Collecting himself, he motioned around the store and said, "So what kind of sauces do you have?"

She paused for a moment at the silliness of his question and then let out a carefree laugh. "We have *thousands* of sauces, sir! What exactly are you looking for?"

"I've heard that eel sauces are your specialty. Are those made onsite?"

She motioned to the backroom behind the counter and said, "Absolutely! We are preparing fresh sauces at this moment. Our fish is cleaned and cooked right here, but eel has always been our specialty."

"Show me."

And with that, Pontius made a rather abrupt dart around the counter and into the backroom. Stunned, Felencia didn't know how to react. She hurried after him with a look of nervousness and angst.

The backroom was larger than he expected. Designed for sauce preparation, a long cooler against the north wall held a variety of species on ice. They stared at the absurd man who had just burst into the room. Against the east wall there were a series of shelves with glass doors. Behind each door was an arrangement of pots, pans, ingredients, and cutlery. At the end of these shelves were two large ovens. In the middle of the room were two long tables with troughs running lengthwise on each side. On one of the tables there was an assortment of minced fish bits. On the other table lay three massive, whole eels stretched to full length and gaping at the ceiling. It smelled of ingredients that have been sautéed, roasted, and burnt, all in the previous day. Along the south wall there were various supplies for bottling and labeling product. On the ceiling there was a series of large industrial fans. They sputtered along, cutting thick swaths of air as they creaked and wobbled through each revolution.

Everything looked clean and logical for a business of this nature except the raggedy mutt that sat next to the ovens. Bare patches riddled its coat and one of its eyes was weeping. As Pontius barged into the prep room the dog made no attempt to protect its territory – if indeed, this was its territory at all. It sat upright, a little startled at the intrusion, but then began to return to a weary, relaxed posture.

Along the west wall there were two doors. One led to a tiny employee restroom. Through the other he could see a Spartan desk and chairs – the makeshift business office for this bustling retail outlet. He began striding toward the office when he heard Felencia calling after him in a shaky voice.

"Sir! You're not allowed back here. What are you doing? Where are you go..."

As he reached the door of the office her voice halted. He stopped in his tracks and looked back across the room at her. She was trembling and starting to cry. She knew why he was here. As soon as he saw that look in her eyes, he knew that the baby was here. He turned away from her and stepped into the small office.

In the corner under a blanket he could see the rough shape of a cradle. He snatched the blanket and peered inside, revealing a new infant, no older than four or five weeks. Despite his carelessness, the child was fast asleep, sucking on an empty bottle and dreaming. The child had a good head of hair for a baby its age and it poked out of its papoose-style bundling.

He turned around to find her standing in the doorway to the tiny office. She had a violent shake and it was all her fragile legs could do to keep her upright. Every ounce of her body looked like a gelatin mold. She wanted to say something, anything, but the sounds escaping her mouth betrayed her. Her words devolved into nothing more than shapeless desperation.

He barged past her and made his way back to the prep room door. He shut the door and pulled from his inner pocket a small hand-held welder. With one hand against the door and the other hand holding the welder, he began to seal the door shut.

Just as the welder began liquefying bits of door and frame, someone on the other side attempted to barge in. It had to be the owner. Pontius had firm leverage against the door, but the owner was insistent and making an all-out attempt to open it. Pontius realized that he was never going to get the door sealed with this kind of disturbance.

He relaxed his weight from the door, took a step back, and waited a half second for the owner to make another attempt. As soon as he saw the owner's arm come around the door, he launched his shoulder with the full weight of his body into the portal. He could hear the satisfying snap of bone as the owner screamed and fell to the floor, dragging his useless arm down with him. Pontius stepped to the opening and kicked the mangled arm back into the main store area. Looking down at the crippled man he said, "This is not your concern."

There were no more disturbances while he spot welded the door shut. When he turned around again, he couldn't see Felencia but he could hear her whimpering in the office. The scene he saw when he returned to the room was one with which he was all too familiar. She was cowering in the corner with the baby clutched to her chest.

He had done this too many times - thousands of times - for sentimentality. He marched into the corner and grabbed the baby in one hand. With a swift motion of the other hand, he managed to wrap a broad switch of her hair around his palm like a reign. He dragged her, screaming, across the floor and back into the prep room. She became hysterical.

Once they were back in the prep room, he tossed her into a corner and placed the baby on the table that was devoid of eels. A large cutting board traversed half of the table and he laid the baby square in the middle of it like he was framing a picture. He surveyed the available toolset with lightning quickness and snatched a filleting knife. In one fluid motion he raised the knife above his head and brought it down with savage efficiency.

The power of her scream impressed him, given that he had dispatched her so easily to the corner. She felt a minor sense of relief when she realized that he had not killed, nor had he even harmed her baby. Rather, he had pinned it to the cutting board. He had driven the fillet knife through the cocoon-like fabric of the papoose and deep into the board. The baby started to fidget, but it was otherwise in good health.

He walked the length of the cutting table and sat on its corner. She was despondent, muttering over and over again, "Don't kill my baby. Please, don't kill my baby." He had learned long ago that there was no real sense in trying to calm someone once they had reached this point. They would just have to let it out of their system. He had a few minutes before any semblance of sanity could return to this scenario. Making use of the time, he pulled a cigar from his pocket and proceeded to enjoy a smoke.

For the next ten minutes she cowered in the corner, shook, and told him, "Don't kill my baby." During those same ten minutes, he puffed his cigar and watched the trails of smoke as they became caught in the slow updraft of the fans. Every time he replied, "I don't have to kill your baby." For the first five or six minutes, he was certain that she didn't even hear him say this. For the next several minutes, it started to seep into her consciousness. They must have repeated this cycle at least 30 times. The mutt stared at both of them during this whole process.

During one of these cycles, he said, "I don't have to kill your baby," and she became quiet for a moment. Her shaking seemed to subside and she somehow garnered the courage to look up at him. She couldn't bear to look into his face, but she raised her head a little and said, "What do you mean?"

That was his cue. It was time to make a deal. He jumped off the table and began pacing around it, all the while facing her and watching her reactions.

"First, let's get the legalities out of the way. You are in violation of at least 12 different statutes governing the birthing, housing, and protection of unlicensed humans. What I'm about to transmit to your UNI is the termination license for your baby. Since your baby has no Vitapass and is therefore not a *real* person, it has been assigned the legal identifier of G829POG19. I'm also transmitting all of my licenses to operate as an NCU agent anywhere in the nation of Centrian. You don't need to accept any of these transmissions. In the Grand Court case of Hakkernon vs. Centrian, it was ruled that my transmission of these credentials establishes my legal authority, whether you accept those transmissions or not."

Looking down he could see that she was starting to resort to panic mode again. Her breathing was erratic and her shaking returned. While keeping a reasonable distance, he knelt down to her level, looked her in the eye, and said, "But I don't have to kill your baby." He waited a moment for that to sink in again, then he stood up. He resumed his speech and his march around the table.

"I don't have to kill your baby. I don't even *want* to kill your baby. Over thousand years, I can't even count the number of babies to which I have granted life. It's not an exaggeration to say that every time you walk through that marketplace, every time you ride the scaler home, every time you go to the doctor, every time you pay your taxes, you are walking past someone to whom I have granted life. All of those people out there who shouldn't be. All of those people are there, because of *me*. All of them – my progenies. Your baby can be one of those people – one of the chosen, one of the lucky. And it's all in your hands now."

The light was starting to come on for her now. Although her voice was still feeble, she looked up at him and said, "What do I have to do?" In a much meeker voice, she said, "I'll do anything..."

He grew silent for a moment and returned to his cigar as he paced the table. The fans made odd shadows that danced against the walls. It forced him to keep jerking his head to one side, then the other, as he could swear that he had missed another person in the room. He took another long puff on the cigar and then, with the smoke wafting from his mouth, he said, "You have four options. Your first option is already known to you – and it's a nasty option. Let's not talk of that option any longer."

He took another long puff on the cigar and this time exhaled in the direction of the mutt. He had this impression that the smoke would somehow stick to the dog, as everything else had apparently done over the last several months.

"Your second option is a very simple one. I release that door and I walk out of here. It is done. I don't come back, but I can't guarantee that someone else will not. I will report to the NCU that your baby is dead, but it will continue to live the miserable life of an unlicensed human. It will fear every scanner and hide in the shadows of every government office."

She stared up at him now, knowing that this was too good to be true. She was waiting for the catch, and the catch did come.

"The second option will cost you 100,000 squalem."

She began sobbing again - this time, while shaking her head. "I don't have 100,000 squalem."

"Understood. So few people do. Besides - who wants to damn their child to an eternal life without a Vitapass? They would be forced into an existence in the shadows. So let's discuss your third option. As with option two, I could leave here for good. But before I do, I could grant your baby a Vitapass."

Now he had her attention. The mere suggestion of a Vitapass had a transformative effect. Her head lifted, her eyes brightened, and her face became a melting pot of hope, skepticism, and confusion.

***

The Vitapass was the lynchpin of life on Torrenth. With it, one could expect to lead a productive and immortal life. Without it, one would live as a ghost, always fearing termination from PC. Every significant activity in life required a Vitapass. One could not hold a job, buy property, receive healthcare, or perform any legal functions without a Vitapass. Unlicensed humans, if they could even manage to avoid termination, led perpetual lives "off the grid".

Vitapasses were not tangible items – at least not in the traditional sense. A Vitapass came with no card or token to confirm its identity. Rather, the pass was a unique code imprinted through the reprogramming of specific sequences of junk DNA. Once issued and injected, this unique ID would propagate through every new cell in the human body. The Vitapass was, quite literally, a part of the owner's being.

Specialized nubots, injected into the body, installed the passes. They targeted the appropriate strands of junk DNA across most of the various cell types. The nubots could never reprogram all the cells in the human body, but there was no need to. Once the body was "seeded" with this new sequence of junk DNA the natural cell replication process took over. The unique code continued spreading throughout the body. Within two weeks of injection, the Vitapass was readable on specialized proton scanners.

PC issued and controlled the individual IDs for each Vitapass. There was only one official avenue to acquire a new Vitapass – through the presentation of a Tombstone. A Tombstone was a verified record of someone's death. The Tombstone carried with it the unique Vitapass code owned by that individual. Once PC authorized a Vitapass, they destroyed the Tombstone. Then they reused the same code from the old Vitapass when issuing the new one.

The reuse of Vitapass codes was a critical control mechanism meant to be an absolute cap on population growth. Nine thousand years ago, PC issued a single set of codes - five billion of them in total - and there had been no new codes issued since. Recycling meant that some of the codes saw more than a dozen owners. The official population of Centrian hadn't risen by a single person in all those nine thousand years.

The only means of acquiring a Vitapass was with a Tombstone. Only heirs received Tombstones after someone's death. Citizens could not buy or sell them. Each Tombstone came imprinted with the identity of its heir. Tombstones and the resulting Vitapasses were the most coveted commodities on the entire planet.

For those wanting a Tombstone, prospects were bleak. They could wait for a loved one to die, which could take tens of thousands of years. Or they could orchestrate someone's death and hope that they weren't caught. Pontius was not bound by these constraints. He had one of the rarest assets on Torrenth – an inside connection at PC.

***

She wiped some of the tears from her eyes and looked at him with a new sense of practicality. "So how do I get a Vitapass for my baby?"

"I issue that baby a Vitapass, imprint it right here before I leave, and I walk out of your life forever for a half million squalem."

"Are you deaf, asshole?! I already told you that I don't have 100,000 squalem. What makes you think I can pay a half million?"

She began fidgeting as if to rise and she had a clear look of irritation on her face. Pontius held his hand out like a traffic cop and shook his head. With the cigar still smoldering in his other hand, he whispered, "There is still option number four."

He paused for a moment to listen to the slow creak of the fans above. The shadows now seemed livelier, edgier. Something thick hung in the air and it had nothing to do with eels. He was about to explain the fourth option but he noticed a sneer rising on her lip. She wasn't listening. She was reaching her own conclusions.

"Option number four? I know about your options. You want me to suck your dick? Fine. I'll suck your dick. You want to fuck me? Let's get it over with. Fuck me right here. Do what you want with me, but don't hurt my baby."

Her Felosian tendencies were showing through. She would do whatever was necessary to save her child, but she wasn't going to give him the satisfaction of subservience. This didn't bother him in the least. In fact, he rather enjoyed it.

He now stood in front of her and chewed on his cigar, rolling the smoldering end between his lips. He did not smile, nor did he show any emotion. He shook his head and stared into her eyes.

"You're not going to fuck *me*." He allowed a full five seconds to pass. "You're going to fuck *them*." As he said this, he motioned behind him to the table with the massive dead eels.

The initial look on her face was one of pure confusion. His statement did not compute. She looked at the table, then back at him, then back at the table again. His expression, or lack thereof, did not change in the least.

"What in the hell are you talking about? Who is *them*?"

"Don't make me draw you a picture. I don't stutter. You're going to fuck those eels, all three of them, and I want you to make it good. None of this in-out-and-I'm-done crap. You're going to make love to those eels."

Felencia cut off a momentary gag reflex and sprung to her feet with surprising agility. In the same fluid motion she hurled an impressive volume of spittle that landed in his left eye.

"Filthy pig! This is how NCU gets their little cocks hard?"

He didn't even bother to wipe the spittle from his face. Again he grabbed a thick handful of her shiny hair and converted it into a binding that he could use to control the placement of her head. With his hand putting constant pressure on the back of her head, he drew her face all-too-close to his. The lit end of his cigar was mere millimeters from her tiny, upturned nose. She could feel its heat emanating up her nostrils. The smoky stench of his breath engulfed her face and reinvigorated her gag reflex. She launched another volley of spittle, this time covering his entire face in a voluminous spray. He again showed no direct reaction, instead managing to drive her face even closer to his.

He lowered his voice to little more than a whisper and said, "Don't be a hero, Felencia. In exchange for a few brief moments of... discomfort, your baby will live a long, full productive life. Your child can go to college, become a professional, own a nice house, eat at the best restaurants. Or your baby could die, right now, pinned to that cutting board like a fucking piece of sushi. I can grant that child an eternity. What's it going to be?"

He pulled his face back and turned her head to face her baby. The child was still fidgeting, but was otherwise quiet on the cutting board. It was making a mild attempt to talk, or coo, or sing, or something – but it was not crying. He held Felencia's head still and allowed her to soak in the image of her baby on the cutting board. The scene before her said more than words ever could.

They both stood in a state of absolute tension. His arm flexed to ensure her immobilization. Her entire body was strung tight like a violin. Beads of sweat formed on her brow so fast that one could almost watch them form in real time. Her body trembled, mitigated only by her fear of Pontius and her desire to hide from him her true emotions.

The fans sped up. This was no figment of their imaginations. The amperage throughout the island was notorious for occasional fluctuations. They were still creaking along, but at least now there was the physical sensation of an updraft in the room. As their velocity increased, the slow creaking transformed into a rhythmic pulse. It reminded Pontius an atmospheric nightclub. The rhythm made for a timer that was more effective than any hourglass.

"If I do this – *thing*. How do I know you'll deliver the goods?"

"If I wanted to kill your baby, it would already be dead. If I left your baby alive with no Vitapass, I would have to answer to NCU."

"Ok," she said, swallowing hard.

He relaxed his grip. He gave her a firm push toward the eels while he himself backed off about a meter. He activated the recording feature in his UNI and he began framing the scene like a film director. This was going to live in his memory banks many hundreds of years from now, long after his natural memory had erased the imagery.

She walked to the table and surveyed the carcasses. Her eyes darted to him, then to the eels, then to her baby, then to the other features of the room. Staring at the eels for a moment, she placed a hand on the tail end of one and looked up again to him.

"Nuh-uh," he said, shaking his head. "Head first."

She began removing her pants in a slow and deliberate fashion. He knew that she was stalling but he didn't care. This was part of the show. After a belabored display of undressing, she stood before him naked from the waist down. She was trembling in an almost uncontrollable fashion. Raising her hand toward the first eel, she spent no time looking at the creature itself. Her eyes continued to dart to Pontius and then about the room. Her palms were so sweaty that he began to wonder if she would be able to hold the slimy beast at all.

She calmed herself, looked straight at him, and then made one swift move to grab the eel's head. But she didn't grab the eel's head. Instead, she grabbed a knife that had been sitting in a water-filled bin beside the eels. Without thinking to threaten or aim, she flung the knife at his head with impressive velocity. It was by luck, and a small degree of agility, that he managed to avoid catching the knife in his eye. He ducked and could feel the blade rustle the long blonde hair on his head. He popped back up, but that was a significant mistake. The second knife found its mark deep in his left triceps. While he was reacting to the shock of such a direct hit, the third knife launched with even greater mortality. It would have been more damaging than the second, but he made a wild swipe at the blade which sent it spinning upward. It ricocheted off one of the fan blades.

He was preparing to fend off the next projectile when he realized that she had no more to expend. He gazed straight into her eyes as he yanked the bloody knife from his arm and showed it to her. The look on her face was the desperate expression of a caged animal. She tried to look for more ammunition but she dared not take her attention from him and his horrifying expression of rage.

Without saying a word, he took the few steps toward the baby pinned to the table and a blood-curdling scream arose from Felencia. Without even stopping to listen to any of her protests he drove the knife straight through the head of the bundle on the table. As he did so, Felencia turned limp as though her bones had been vaporized. The bundle commenced an unsettling sequence of vibrations. The little energy she had left was that required to scream and cry as she lay in a heap on the floor.

While she wailed at the base of the table, Pontius contacted headquarters with a simple message.

"Target acquired. Unlicensed human eliminated." Headquarters responded with, "Confirmed, Pontius. Good work."

He took a few moments to attempt to clean himself up. Kitchen towels made for a makeshift bandage on his arm. He was trying to ensure that the blood didn't ruin his coat. As he tended to his wounds, Felencia wailed from the floor, "My baby is more than you will ever be. My baby is what you could never see."

Having cleaned himself for the trip home, he moved to the door and began to undo his welding handiwork. As he released each bead of metal on the door, he could hear her screaming ever louder. "My baby is the life you were meant to be! My baby is always a part of me!"

When the door was free he swung it open and took one last look at her cowering on the floor. He looked straight at her as she stared back into his eyes for a moment and he said, "Your baby - was."

With that, he exited the sauce shop and headed for home.

Chapter 2 – Atop a Stormy World

The Nighthawk raged through the watery blackness of Centrian's sky. It plunged, climbed, and weaved in a heated dogfight against no one in particular. Although fastened to her seat, Conti had a death grip on the arm rest. She searched in vain through the murky windows for any sign that they were nearing their destination. The random lights of skyscrapers and traffic blurred past her rain-drenched windows. The vehicle made an impromptu racecourse of the steel jungle all around them.

Cruisers were rare over Centrian. Public scalers so efficiently carried pedestrians from one public place to another. Few people had the means or the motivation to forgo them. Caspian was one of those few, because he was in no particular hurry to reach any specific destination. The rush of independent flight was one of his few remaining thrills in a life that had spanned more than 3,300 years. If he had to, he would compete with the winds, and the lightning, and each individual raindrop for air superiority. And he would do it while he was mind-numbingly high.

Much to Conti's relief, Caspian leveled the cruiser and engaged the autopilot. He searched through his UNI for contacts. With a uniform flight pattern and a reasonable speed, she might be able to see some of the passing landmarks and gain her bearings. Yet somehow the rain pounded ever harder against the transparent shell. Even as their relative speed calmed to a mere sprint, everything outside the cabin lay obscured behind a wall of water.

Caspian's countenance brightened against the dim glow of the instrument panel and it was clear that he had found that for which he was searching. He paused for a few moments in stilted anticipation and then let out an elongated, "Captain!"

There was a long pause over the cabin speakers before Pontius's weary voice returned serve, "What is, brother?"

Caspian made no notice of Pontius's tone. Pontius could have been desperate and screaming amidst the sounds of a prison riot. Caspian would not have cared.

"Indiarium is happening tonight. I have decided to assemble the crew. I'm thinking that we should be starting hors d'oeuvres in about two hours."

There was a long pause, much longer than Caspian expected. He looked over to Conti, raised his eyebrows, and shrugged his shoulders. Against the eerie underlight of the instrument panel, it made him look like a malevolent poltergeist. Conti had no idea how or if she should respond.

"I don't know, Caspian. I think I'm going to sit this one out."

"Captain – not an option! This isn't just you and me tonight. I have a new friend I need you to meet. She has *connections*." He allowed the last word to slide from his maw, escaping and hovering in the cabin like an unwelcome guest.

Caspian turned to Conti and grinned. To most people, it would have been a creepy grin. To Conti, it was rather endearing. Pontius groaned as though

Caspian had just twisted the honorable blade of seppuku deep within his bowels. After the graphic events of his day, he could think of few more detrimental – or unhealthy - activities than a night out with Caspian.

"Really, Caspian, I think I'm out tonight."

Hearing this second rebuttal, Caspian grabbed the controls of the Nighthawk again. He dodged raindrops and phantom winds. The cruiser dipped and climbed and dipped again. Conti resumed her white-knuckled grip on the arm rest. Caspian leaned forward over the controls and pressed his dry, sandpapery nose to the glass before him.

"Dania is joining us." Caspian lied. He had no idea if Dania was joining them.

There was another long pause, then a sigh, then a reply. "OK, I'll be there. Can you please get me a bottle of nanimax booster? I won't have time to stop off on my own."

Caspian pulled his nose back from the glass and asked, in a tone as close as he ever came to concern, "Is all good? Nanimax doesn't sound encouraging…"

"Nay big deal. I just had an assignment that went a bit awry. You know the drill. And don't bring me any of that generic crap. I want the real LiveLong stuff."

Caspian nodded and said, "Sure yes, Captain. I'm on it. I'll see you at Indiarium. You know where we'll be."

***

Nanites were one leg of the Torrenthian triumvirate of life. Centrian scientists introduced them more than 9,000 years ago. They were artificial life forms that could procreate. They served two purposes – ridding the body of toxins and repairing damaged tissues. There were several different "species" of nanites. Some of them fed on dead and dying tissue. Others fed upon naturally (or unnaturally) occurring toxins in the body. A third class fed upon the body's own energy reserves. Their byproduct was a nutrient-rich scaffolding used to create new tissues.

They were not self-sustaining. Although they could proliferate, their rate of reproduction failed to keep pace with their rate of entropy. This meant that they would die out if left to their own devices – but they were never left to their own devices. 11,000 years ago, the federal authorities began injecting them into the water supply. They were cheap and easy to cultivate. Their continued reintroduction into the wild was a public utility, like the water supply itself.

Nanites had an amazing, almost magical ability to heal the body. They could not cure traumatic or catastrophic wounds. Nor could they cure the gravest of unnatural toxins. But their self-replicating nature meant that their response rate could scale almost exponentially.

This meant that while it was easy to become intoxicated, it was almost impossible to drink yourself to death. While it was simple to acquire scrapes and bruises (and even stab wounds), it was difficult to die from such a traditional injury.

While organs could fail, it was difficult to expire from something as basic as appendicitis or a ruptured spleen.

The second leg of Torrenthian immortality was Telomore. Telomore was the miracle pharmaceutical manufactured for millennia by LiveLong. Telomore had one simple effect on the human body – it extended telomere length after each cycle of mitosis. This meant that Torrenthians arrested the natural process of cell entropy. Human cells no longer entered a state of senescence. Skin no longer wrinkled and grew papery. Neurons no longer withered. Arteries no longer hardened. Torrenthians no longer aged in any traditional sense.

The third leg was that of the organ farms. The term "organ farm" was a bit of a misnomer because they did not grow organs in advance. Rather, they held stem cells and DNA samples for every registered human. These served as the basis to grow replacements as needed. Even the term "organ" was a bit constrictive. With enough lead time the farms could produce new arms, legs, digits, etc.

These technologies meant that Torrenthians were not mortal in the traditional sense of the word. They could still die through sudden, tragic means. Murder, suicide, and violent accidents still claimed lives every day throughout the islands. But no one had died of a natural cause on any of the central islands in more than 5,000 years. Disease and old age evaporated millennia ago.

***

Caspian continued his hectic dogfight in the Nighthawk as he proceeded to strain his UNI for one contact after another. He convo'd Indiarium and ensured that his favorite waitresses were available for the sky room. One particular cutie had a gorgeous scar that ran all the way from her left temple down to her clavicle. The original cut was so severe that not even the nanites could clear its aftermath. It was a scar that Caspian had given to her.

He looked at Conti and asked if she had ever been to Indiarium. She replied that this would be a new experience for her. She had been there several hundred years ago, but she no longer had any recollection of the experience. She was telling him the truth for as far as she knew.

Staring back into the blurry torrents outside the cruiser, he sat back and convo'd Dania.

"La Signora! You have plans tonight. The crew is assembling at Indiarium. Your presence is required."

There was a sigh heard over the cabin speakers that held within it the tale of a thousand restless nights. Caspian heard many expressions throughout his life, but more than anything else, he heard sighs. He sat waiting in anxious anticipation of her response, but he received silence – and a shorter sigh.

"Dania – what is the word?"

Another long pause ensued.

"I'm not interested, Caspian. You need to stop convo'ing me."

"Signora! You hurt my feelings." He lied. The smile on his face was unnatural and it permeated his voice with saccharin. His shiny teeth sparkled in the blue light of the instrument panel as he spoke. "This isn't just me and my lonesome. Pontius will be joining us…"

Having set his hook, his voice tailed off as he turned to Conti and grinned. There was another unnatural pause but it was one for which he would make Dania answer. There was an awkward silence overlaying the warm hiss of the speakers – a silence he found comfortable.

"OK. What time will you be there?" she said.

"A few hours! Ask for me at the door." And with that he cut the convo.

Caspian spent the rest of the journey convo'ing an eclectic assortment of LiveLong officers, government officials, drug dealers, whores, gamblers, entertainers, and media types. They wouldn't all show up, but they would all know that a Caspian gig was in full swing tonight.

Arriving at Indiarium was as abrupt to Conti as waking from a nightmare. One moment she was gripping her armrest and battling the omnipresent urge of nausea in the gray soup of Centrian's night sky. The next moment the Nighthawk shot above the upper limit of the clouds and the cruiser was floating in a dream-like atmosphere. The scene was difficult to grasp for Centrian citizens so far below in the gritty streets and buildings of the inner core.

At this altitude there were a handful of buildings peaking above the clouds. The Icarus building was the tallest structure on the planet – more than 400 stories high. Its upper reaches were always above the cloud cover, even on the worst of stormy nights. Indiarium was the most exclusive nightclub on the entire island. It perched in the uppermost outcrops of the Icarus.

It was not enough to be above the clouds - the absence of rain was sufficient to shock some citizens upon their arrival at such heights. But the nocturnal shine of India was a breathtaking sight that few Centrians ever laid eyes upon. The single Torrenthian moon glistened with a most unusual layer of indium. It made the entire sphere shine like a chrome ball bearing. The resulting silvery glow over the cloud tops of Centrian was both luminous and brilliant. It gave the entire night sky an eerie sheen.

No scientist had proven how India became covered in a metal as rare as indium. Popular convention held that aliens paved it millennia before the arrival of man. More respectable theories posited a supernova. Poisoned with various nuclear cocktails, it spewed forth in its final days great globules of rare metals. In a contiguous star system there may lie entire moons of platinum, rhodium, gold, iridium, and palladium.

Pulling up to the VIP platform aside Indiarium, Caspian exited the cruiser. He led Conti through the various stages of the club. The lowest level was a posh restaurant with a 360 degree view of the night sky. The second level was a series of interconnected miniclubs leading from a central atrium. Each club was distinct from its brethren, including its own décor and music. The third level was an überclub – a single edifice that stretched the entire breadth of the Icarus. The interior was dark and decadent. Random windows of Indian light danced across the floor. Off to one corner there was a discrete entrance that led to a fourth level – the Aerie.

A Dusk Forever Waning

The Aerie was a private level perched above all other floors of the Icarus. It was about an eighth of the breadth of the total Icarus but it was not positioned in in the building's center. It jutted out in such a way that a full 75% of its floor area extended outside the walls of the Icarus itself. The entire outside shell consisted of translucent materials. Even the furniture featured milky composites that gave the guests the impression of sitting on clouds. The translucent walls held an ever shifting fiber optic display. Changing colors worked their way across the walls, interacting with India's brilliant light. They made an ethereal display as they danced across the exterior.

Caspian led Conti to the extreme outward edge of the Aerie and pulled up a pair of chairs. They were not the kind of chairs designed to make someone comfortable. They were set at a 45 degree upward angle and they swiveled according to UNI input. Their responsiveness made it effortless to pivot as the lounger gazed at the sights all around them.

In Conti's mind, a fierce battle raged between amazement and discomfort. She had no recollection of anything so breathtaking in her entire life. But the sheer weight of the sensory overload before her was not just overwhelming – it was overbearing. The first thing she noticed when they entered the Aerie was the shear volume of the music. It wasn't just loud – it was shrill to a point that it almost hurt her ears and it made her wince with every high note. And the beats were deep – so much so that they made her chest cavity vibrate in an uncomfortable way.

The shifting lights of all the exterior surfaces were at once beautiful and affronting. The dancing optics would at times shine powerful beams into her line of vision, causing her to squint and shield her eyes. Just when they receded into a sea of ambiance, a new brigade of beams would drive in and assault her optic nerves again.

Perfumes permeated the room. There were subtle and enjoyable tones that she tried in vain to enjoy. But there were more overpowering aromas that seemed to muscle out the others and assault her nasal passages. Just when she thought that she could relax with the soothing smell of a tropical breeze, a wave of vicious cologne overtook her.

Even her sense of touch was under attack. The chair, although positioned to allow a panoramic view of all that was around her, was also unforgiving. The footrest provided some kind of vibratory feedback that she found discomfiting. The armrests alternated between hot – to the point that her arms would sweat – to a chill that left her skin prickly and numb.

They were not the first ones to arrive. When they walked to their seats, there was a woman waiting for them. She looked at Caspian with an odd sense of anticipation, but he did not address her unspoken questions. While she looked no older than anyone else in Indiarium, she had a matronly aura about her. Her hair was not of the most recent style. Her clothes were perhaps a bit frumpy. But worst of all, she just looked *nice*. She wore a pleasant smile as the two approached and she sat with a posture that was too prim for the environment.

Sensing that he was not going to escape cursory introductions, Caspian motioned toward Conti.

"This is my new friend, Conti. She's a Telomore dealer."

The woman flashed a broad smile, looked at Conti, and said, "So you work for LiveLong?"

Caspian's face curled in disappointment as he shook his head. Conti paused for a moment, then broke into a gentle smile and said, "Not exactly."

The logistics of that statement sunk into the woman's head. She just said, "Oh." Then she sat for a few more moments and the light clicked on for her, and she said, "Ooooh, I see. Well, welcome to the Aerie."

Conti nodded and turned away from her as fast as possible, looking to avoid further questions. Caspian motioned back to the woman and said, "This is Moria. She works for PC."

Conti's attention snapped back to the woman. She was a bit startled by this revelation.

"PC? And what do you do for them?"

Moria waved a dismissive hand and said, "Oh I'm just an admin – pushing papers. I work in Trenchtown. Nothing special." Moria flashed a warm smile at Conti and Conti lost interest.

Three waitresses descended upon the trio and began taking orders. Moria ordered a cocktail. Conti ordered two. Caspian launched into a protracted process of ordering food. He was ordering dish after dish, but he seemed less concerned with the food than with how they prepared it. Every dish he requested came with explicit instructions to be as spicy, as hot, as cold, as cooked, or as raw as possible. He didn't just want tentacles. He wanted tentacles simmered in three of their oldest brines. He didn't just want drinks. He wanted cocktails made with the strongest and the oldest of the available liquors. He wanted extra dishes of spices and dipping sauces made available. He ordered some of the sauces boiled down to increase their potency. The waitress – the one with the face-long scar – nodded in an annoyed fashion indicating that she had heard this all before.

Once the waitresses left, Moria became anxious again.

"Pontius is coming, right? When will he be here?"

He looked through the translucent walls at the brilliant luminescence of India and made no attempt to give her eye contact. "I don't know. He didn't answer my convos." Caspian lied much more often than he wiped his ass – and he was much better at it.

Moria said nothing. She just sat back in her chair, closed her eyes, and absorbed the music as it flowed over her. Conti couldn't help but wonder if closing her eyes would help her deal with the visual assault. Caspian sat in his chair with a painful alertness. He stared at the natural and unnatural lighting. He gripped the armrests, intensifying every temperature fluctuation and vibration coursing through his body. From time to time he would inhale every last iota of the aromas that encompassed him. With a restless air he spun from side to side as he tried to take in ever more of his surroundings.

For the next 30 minutes there were at least a dozen of Caspian's guests arriving. He introduced each one of them to Conti – and none of them to Moria. Conti had a difficult time concentrating on the details of anyone's names or faces.

Every new person that arrived served to further muddy the sensory landslide in which she found herself. There was a male dancer, a politician, a restaurant owner, a singer, an owner of fishing fleets, and a "club owner" whom she was certain made his money from something other than owning a club. There were several other people whose introductions she missed. They began talking to other guests upon their arrival.

When the food arrived it took almost a half dozen waitresses to deliver all the dishes. They positioned each on singular stands of varying height. Some dishes were sunken almost to foot level, while others perched so high that one had to stand to partake. The stands consisted of polished chrome and sparkled as the light show continued its dance across the walls. The aromas stung her nostrils. There were smells of mustard, cayenne, vinegar, wasabi, horseradish, ginger, salt brine, cumin, and curry - amongst others. Although some dishes were saucy or granular, they were all consumed as finger foods.

Famished, Conti wanted to scarf down the offerings but she moved gingerly from one dish then to the other. She reached, stopped, withdrew her hand, and then pensively reached toward another. With every few inches that she moved in either direction, a new aroma drove up her nose and several made her eyes water. She looked sheepishly to Caspian, hoping that he might provide some guidance on how to navigate this minefield. He paid her no mind. He was staring out at the night sky and tossing morsels from random dishes into his mouth like a happy child munching on popcorn.

She settled on some minor crustacean-like creature that stared at her as she closed her eyes and plopped it into her mouth. It had a creamy coating that appeared mild and savory, but the creature's revenge was swift and unrelenting. She spat the intact shell across the room and retched. She swallowed nothing, but that mattered not. Its fiery attack marched right down her esophagus and into her stomach where she could swear that it began to smoke. Luckily, there was nothing in her stomach to expel. Her dry heaving exhausted itself after several minutes and she slumped back into her chair. Her unsatisfied appetite was now slain.

Moria stared at her in silent concern, but made no motion to rise from her seat. She knew that there was no cure for Caspian's food but time – and tears. Caspian was oblivious to the opera. He noticed none of her despair. He plunged his long fingers into a deep narrow vessel and withdrew an entire handful of black tendrils. Yellow sauce dripped from them. He devoured them, slurping and chewing as rogue juices streamed down either corner of his mouth. It was at this point when Conti realized that no one else was touching the hors d'oeuvres.

After a significant recovery period, Conti saw that two new guests had arrived. A stunning woman with long black hair stood arm-in-arm with a short, scruffy-haired man. He looked the part of a sergeant with better clothing. He made a significant contrast to her regal air. She had olive skin with a subtle iridescent undertone that made her hair sparkle. Their arms were not entwined as partners, but as friends.

Upon their arrival, Caspian forgot his food and jumped to his feet. "La Signora! I knew you'd come! It's so good to see you."

A Dusk Forever Waning

Dania flashed a smile at Caspian – the empty smile of a denture model – as she looked through him like glass. He made a motion to step forward and embrace her. As soon as he advanced, and without losing her acid smile, she stepped backward. She parried his affections and spun her friend almost halfway around.

Unfazed, Caspian turned his attention to her friend, introducing him to Conti. "This is Telarus - an honored member of the crew! He works for LiveLong." He placed an unnatural emphasis on "LiveLong" and he stared at Conti as he said it in a way that was obvious to anyone paying attention.

Dania's arrival marked the first time in the evening that Moria looked rather uncomfortable. Moria's gaze kept returning to Dania, even though Dania was oblivious to the attention. Dania carried herself with a general fluidity that made her impervious to the attention of most observers.

Dania sat down and began corralling drinks. Between her attempts to flag down a waitress, her lip curled as she surveyed the half-eaten cuisine strewn about her. Telarus began a conversation with Caspian that was loud and demonstrative – but no one could catch a single word they were saying. Moria sat alone, trying to act as though she enjoyed the atmosphere. And Conti sat in wonderment at the menagerie of characters around her. Before she could solve the riddle of how to interact – or with whom – Pontius arrived. Everyone's attention marked him as a unifying force in the group.

As soon as Caspian caught sight of Pontius, he rushed across the Aerie to meet him. Pontius embraced him, wincing from the pressure placed on his arm. The difference between the two men was striking. Although Caspian had not aged in the traditional sense – no wrinkles, liver spots, or grey hair – he carried a great deal of weathering. Pontius showed no such signs.

***

Weathering was the Torrenthian term for the tell-tale signs of age that still manifested in the ancient. While they may not have looked elderly in the traditional sense, over time they took on the weathered look of an old leather bag. Their skin would darken into a permanent tan. Worse, it looked and felt like a saddle. Some aspects, like eyes and teeth, tended to maintain their natural sheen. This gave them the rather odd effect of looking almost fake in contrast to the rest of their features. Some ancient Torrenthians were even mistaken for androids. Although Caspian was far from an elder statesman on Torrenth, his lifestyle led him to an advanced state of weathering. He looked more artificial than 3,309 years would suggest. This made him look like a stiff, animatronic version of Pontius.

***

Caspian led him back to the group and they offered warm greetings. Moria gave him a long, intimate hug that had the others wondering how long it would last. She kissed him on the cheek before releasing him and stared into his eyes as she stepped away. Telarus gave him the age-old man-hug and the friends smiled at each other. Dania just extended her hand and he shook it. He gave her a fleeting glance. It was their traditional greeting, and something of an inside joke.

Before Pontius could conjure up a seat, Caspian was yanking him by his good arm to the balcony where they could talk. The balcony annoyed Caspian for its relative solitude. But it was one of the few places in the Aerie conducive to a normal conversation.

On the balcony, Pontius could feel every wind of Torrenth railing against his face. The rains of the lower altitudes hid beneath the ever-present blanket of clouds, so far beneath their feet. But they could never escape the winds. The piercing reflections of India made him squint and cower. The updraft of Centrian's storms bolstered his presence on the precipice and he towered above the world.

Caspian stood next to him in an unnatural silence, blowing fire from his nostrils like a dragon lording over his horde. Pontius strained to find breaks in the clouds, fleeting windows in which he could peruse the vibrant life of the masses. Caspian stared off to distant lightning storms, pondering in vain what wonder must lie in an electrical strike. He pulled a yellow vial from his vest and held it in front of his friend. Pontius grabbed the vial, jabbed the tapered end into his bloody arm, and breathed deep as the nanites coursed into his veins. They both stood in silence for an extended period. They heard nothing but the howling winds and the muted bass of the club rising up through their feet.

"Do you ever wonder what it's like?" Caspian was gazing into the distance but Pontius's attention stayed on the clouds below.

"No." Pontius knew where his friend was going, but he refused to indulge him in this fantasy.

"Think it about it, brother," Caspian continued. "Imagine the sensation of a million volts coursing through your muscles. Your brain. Your genitals. What do you think goes through someone's mind at the moment they're struck? How alive do you think they feel?"

"They feel crispy." Pontius was in no mood for Caspian's philosophical musings on pain, suffering, and death. Caspian fell silent but continued staring at the distant lightning. A static expression of joy and wonderment painted his face. The two enjoyed the bracing wind and the night air in solitude until they became aware that Conti was standing behind them. She had a partner that Pontius didn't recognize.

The perma-grin on Caspian's face shifted from the atmosphere to his guests. He grabbed Conti's hand and draped his arm over her shoulder as he introduced her to Pontius. Pontius tried to be cordial but he could not hide his bewilderment whenever he met one of Caspian's new women.

She didn't seem tall so much as she seemed long. Her fragile features felt like a dangerous match for Caspian's sadistic fantasies. Pontius made a quick note in his UNI that she could last no longer than two weeks. She had a casual yet sophisticated air. Her clothes were new, expensive, stylish - but not trendy. Her auburn hair was long and arrow-straight. It was woven down the length of her back into an intricate tapestry. One could discern different images from it when viewed at varying angles. The rising slit in her skirt revealed polished legs that captured India's light and spewed it forth in all directions.

Even after 1,500 years of knowing Caspian, Pontius was still surprised by the women that would flock to him. He respected Caspian. He admired Caspian. Somewhere in the forgotten recesses of his mind, he wished that he could *be* Caspian. But if he had a daughter, or any woman whom he cared about, he would not allow her within a thousand meters of Caspian. And yet they came, one after the other, drawn to the daring and recklessness of a playboy with money and power.

He may have spent more time perusing Caspian's latest toy, but his attention wandered to her colleague. He was a man who could never qualify as inconspicuous, even in the most audacious of crowds. Her friend was tall – one of the tallest persons Pontius had ever seen – and yet he couldn't have been half the weight of an average man.   His bony fingers protruded from his gaping sleeves like the slivery tendrils of a jellyfish. His clothes hung on him, so much so that Pontius found himself wondering if they would, at some point, fall off. He wore a long black trench coat – common fare on Torrenth. But on him it was so long and so ill-fitting it seemed as a super-villain's cape worn by a play-acting child. His head rose from his shoulders on the soaring pike of his spindly neck.   Every ounce of blood throbbing into his brain visibly pulsed through his carotid arteries. His eyes were wide, almost luminescent, and he did not appear to blink. His skin was a dark brown and had the complexion of a saddle bag that had never seen oil or shelter. His papery lips were insufficient to cover his prodigious smile. They revealed teeth that were a brilliant and unnatural silver. His cranial movements were irregular – spastic – even as he stared straight at you.   This gave his audience the uncomfortable feeling that they were somehow adrift. Atop his desiccated head rode a shock of hair trimmed uniformly to 10 centimeters in length. The color changed through a span of many minutes. It was so slow that it was hard to tell that anything was happening by direct observation. His hair was not spiked, but rather it seemed to be fleeing from his scalp. Every hair reacted in time to his audible environment. It pulsated with the undulating beats of the nightclub. Then it arched to and fro with the higher-pitched sound of voices in the immediate vicinity. This made his hair seem alive, like some modern day Medusa. From the moment Pontius laid eyes upon him, he recognized him as one of the worst cases of meth addiction he had ever seen.

Pontius felt compelled to stare at the stranger but he managed to force his gaze back to Conti. Caspian was trying to do the cute-couple-thing, standing next to her and tracing circles on her shoulder. Pontius found this to be both reprehensible and hilarious all at the same time. He knew where Conti would end up and he knew that Caspian couldn't care less.

Conti proceeded to make small talk for the next 30 minutes. She had been waiting as Caspian exposed her to his kaleidoscope of associates and it seemed that she was now determined to let loose. Pontius wasn't interested in her but he wasn't inclined to interrupt her either. She was a Telomore dealer - or to be more accurate, a knockoff dealer. The market was rife with Telomore knockoffs and dealers of Telomore knockoffs. She also had some "regular" job bartending at the Skyskimmer Lounge in the Titan complex. He couldn't help thinking that she didn't seem like a Skyskimmer bartender. She met Caspian at the launch party for the latest model of the Invictus shuttle pod. Caspian attended all the launch parties for all the new shuttle pod models. She had heard much about Pontius from Caspian. She knew that Pontius was a decorated NCU agent. She knew that he lived in the Bowery. She knew that he was single. She seemed to know many things – too many things. She could spew a great volume of minutiae of which Pontius cared not at all. She would have talked for another hour if Pontius hadn't decided to commandeer the conversation. While she was in mid-sentence, and apropos of nothing, he motioned to her colleague and said, "Who's your friend?"

"How rude of me," she replied, "this is Kryx. But others know him as *The Middleman*."

Throughout Conti's diatribe, Kryx stood still. He stared at India and paid no attention to the people around him. As Conti babbled on, Pontius watched out of the corner of his eye as Kryx often scratched all around his neck and cheeks. He dug his spindly claws into his taut skin with such a rabid fervor that he left bloody stains behind. They would fade over a period of 15 or 20 minutes as the nanites in his system went about their healing business.

Pontius allowed a wry grin to escape his lips. With the confidence of a formal introduction already granted, he surveyed Kryx's bizarre countenance. Kryx broke his gaze from the brilliant moon and turned to face Pontius, extending a hand in proper greeting. Pontius wondered if Kryx's hand might crumble in his own. But the shake revealed a shocking and sneaky power hidden in that bony grasp.

"So you're a..." Pontius allowed the sentence to trail into the distance. Kryx leaned forward to catch the final word which wouldn't come. "Middleman? And what exactly does a *middleman* do?"

Without hesitation, Kryx replied. He had a voice much deeper than Pontius expected, "I balance the scales. I am the conduit through which vital business flows. Every buyer requires a seller. Every commodity requires a marketplace. I am the matchmaker for those in need of a transaction."

"So I suppose that makes you something of a public servant?"

Kryx gave no heed to the obvious sarcasm and answered, "On my better days, I'd like to think so."

"And *middleman* means that you're Conti's supplier?"

Kryx sighed and gazed off again at the brilliant light of India. "*Supplier* is such a menial and limiting term. If she needs to buy more Telomore, I can arrange the transaction. If she needs to sell more Telomore, I can arrange that, too. Telomore is but one commodity in an ocean of goods and services. I know buyers and sellers of Telomore – sure. But I also manage the flow of countless other..." Both men locked eyes while still fighting to appear casual. "Products."

"*Products* is a broad term."

"My business is a broad endeavor."

Pontius wasn't certain where to take the conversation from there. From his posture, it was clear that Kryx felt he had passed the verbal baton back to

Pontius. Pontius had no desire to hear more about these *products*. He shot a glance at Caspian, but Caspian shrugged, signaling that he hadn't expected this guest and knew not what to make of him. He shot a glance at Conti and it was clear that she wasn't comfortable with the conversation. At last, the pangs of sobriety overtook him and he headed back downstairs to the Aerie, announcing that he needed a drink.

The Aerie sported a single bar in the middle of the edifice. It was irregularly shaped – akin to an amoeba; its various tentacles offered an extended array of seats. Pontius sat on one of the translucent stools. The stools bore special transducers. These transducers transferred the musical vibrations right up one's rear. From there the rhythm continued through the spine and into the cranial cortex. The drink he received was not ordered. The bartenders at the Aerie did not ask you for your preferred drink. They served you the drink they felt you deserved. Pontius's drink was dark and frothy, roiling itself against the confines of its container.

In the stool to his right sat a dog – a hairless dog that hovered over a dish of some teal liquid placed before it on the bar, but it did not drink. The dog bobbed its head to the bass line in the current track. Pontius stared at it, and it felt like hours, but the dog would not acknowledge his presence. It just kept bobbing its head and hovering over the bowl, as though it were threatening to drink at any moment.

He abandoned any attempts at the mongrel's attention and allowed himself to drift back to the events of the day. He had no qualms about the spike he drove through that infant's skull. But he could never fathom the parents who refused his wondrous gift of life. There were 99 other agents in NCU. Every other one of them was nothing more than a government-sponsored exterminator. No one else had his unique connection. No one else could offer something so beautiful, and so valuable, as a Vitapass. The department was rife with agents who would take bribes in return for some child's life. But those bribes could only offer temporary reprieves. Those bribes, even at their most successful, would buy nothing more than a life spent lurking in the shadows. Those bribes bought lives devoid of legitimacy. Unlike any of his colleagues, he was an angel of life, and he granted that life for free. For no out-of-pocket cost whatsoever, these parents could ensure their child a future – an immortal future. All they had to do was endure a few awkward moments of degradation and their baby could live forever. And yet he sometimes found parents who could not set aside their own childish pride. They could not think beyond themselves in return for something that they loved so dearly.

On cue, Pontius felt a tap on his shoulder and turned around to find Moria standing behind him. She threw her arms around him and planted an affectionate kiss on his cheek. She embraced him for an extended period that he found to be awkward, but he knew better than to push her away. She stared into his eyes and smiled for a bizarre period of time. Backing up, she attempted to sit in the chair occupied by the hairless dog. She presumed that the feral beast would vacate when he saw her ass approaching. Instead, it held its ground like an obstinate younger sibling, refusing to capitulate. Without missing a beat, and without removing her gaze from Pontius, she plopped down. The two of them – woman and mongrel - awkwardly coexisted on the seat.

"It feels like I never see you anymore," she said while coddling the milky orange concoction placed before her.

"You saw me two days ago at headquarters, right after my morning briefing." Pontius's voice was simple and matter-of-fact and he gazed past her as he spoke.

Moria took his attitude as affectionate. She took any attitude Pontius offered as affectionate. "I know that, silly. I mean that I never see you out of the office. I feel like we've grown so distant."

Pontius now trained his gaze upon her, trying to discern if this was a joke. It never was, but sometimes he still felt compelled to categorize her delusions. As he stared through her, she smiled and soaked in his attention.

"You know we have an assignment next week, right?" He was asking to shift the subject. She always knew what was on their agenda.

"Of course! What kind of team would we be if I didn't know that?" She reached forward to touch his hand but he held tight to his drink and moved his gaze to the dance floor.

* * *

Moria was an administrator in Population Control. In fact, she had one of the most critical and sensitive jobs in the entire unit. She was one of a handful of individuals who governed the reassignment of Vitapasses. She verified the legitimacy of existing Tombstones. She then reassigned Vitapasses for the newborns who inherited those Tombstones. She was like a mild-mannered bank clerk who works with vast amounts of currency. She was powerful far beyond her natural demeanor – although she had no natural proclivity to leverage such power.

The two of them did not work together in the traditional sense. She worked for the broader Population Control department. He worked for its subunit, Newborn Corrections. In the completion of his normal duties, he would have no need to interact with her, or with anyone outside the NCU. The children he removed had no Vitapass and should never have them. They were unlicensed, illegal, unregulated – and it was his job to cleanse them from a bloated and overgrown society. But little about the two of them was traditional.

Long ago, Pontius married her. They were together for almost 500 years and Moria saw him as the absolute love of her life. She was uniquely qualified to make such a statement. She remembered much more of her life than the typical Torrenthian. She belonged to a class of individuals called the *memoriae*.

As the Torrenthian lifespan began to dramatically increase, there were still some natural limits. The body – and the mind - were not immutable. Telomore could keep the cells of the brain reproducing without entropy. Nanites could keep it free of toxins and plaques. But the brain itself had certain computational limits. During a man's natural lifespan he would never reach those limits.

A Dusk Forever Waning

Through empirical evidence, people found they remembered few life experiences after about 400 years. They maintained some pieces of critical data – like learned skills – much longer, especially if they were in constant use. But the true quality of memory, the sense of an experience owned by the one doing the remembering, eroded after 400 years.

Memories older than 400 years could disappear as they were overwritten by newer ones. They could also live on inside a person's Universal Neural Implant. While UNI-assisted memory was a great boon to the civilization in general, it was not a substitute for natural memory. UNI-assistance came across to the user as being a distant fact from a database. It felt foreign and impersonal. By harvesting your UNI for past memories, you could come up with all sorts of data about your past – images, names, narratives, etc. – but the information did not feel like yours. Rather, it was just one more piece of information in a world overflowing with information.

UNI memories also harbored a dangerous flaw. Recorded as the user remembered them – not as the event actually happened – they came with all the inconsistencies of real memory. An objective person might understand the failings and idiosyncrasies of their own recollection. But UNI-assisted memory felt like codified fact. It felt like something referenced from a library.

This mental barrier gave rise to the planet's dominant religion. Most Torrenthians did not worship gods in the traditional sense. Rather, they venerated prior periods in their own lives. They tended to view these prior periods as related, but different people. As other societies have chosen to venerate their ancestors, Torrenthians venerated themselves. The longer one lived, the more of these prior periods existed. They viewed these periods almost like separate lifespans, separate people. Torrenthians called each of these prior iterations a Priorus. In aggregate they worshiped them as the Priori. They would pray to their own Priori the way a Catholic would pray to the saints. They felt that each different version of themselves still lived somewhere in their subconscious. They prayed to this subconscious for guidance and lost abilities.

Of course, the 400-year barrier was not a hard line, but rather a rule of thumb. Some cursed individuals had even shorter memories, as brief as 200-300 years. But there was a genetic variation found in about three percent of the population. It allowed them to maintain memories for far longer. These individuals – the memoriae – could maintain a personal association to their memories far longer. In some cases, these memories lasted thousands of years. Even memoriae had upper limits on their long-term abilities. But there were some who had been alive for several thousand years and had not yet reached such a barrier.

Memoriae were not supposed to marry common folk (they pejoratively referred to such people as blanks). Even if the marriage began well, the blank would begin to lose the connection over time. The highlights of their relationship would fade from the blank's memory. All the while, the memoriae still felt the same bond with the blank. The blank would start to see their partner as a roommate, and even further on, as a stranger living in their own house. With pairings between normal people, they accepted this process as the natural life cycle of a marriage. But with pairings between blanks and memoriae, it always ended with the memoriae being heart broken.

When Moria first met Pontius 2,300 years ago, she fell hard for him. She worshiped him. She was so enamored with him that she decided to lie about her status as a memoriae. She convinced herself that she could keep their love fresh and create new memories with him. She planned to remain as a loving couple for many thousands of years. Her plan failed.

Pontius understood, on an academic level, that their marriage occurred. He could access UNI-memories. He would sometimes run across the detritus of their failed relationship. But he could no longer find any of the feelings that had made him love her. Nor did he care to. He had long since moved on to other romantic interests.

While this may have been the end of a tragic story for most memoriae, Moria was far more dedicated and cunning than most. She determined, through any means necessary, to keep a connection with Pontius. She strove to rekindle in him the feelings that he once felt for her. But to do this, she had to find a way to stay in his inner circle. To that end, she managed to work her way into Population Control.

When she captured her coveted position in PC, she alerted Pontius. She made it known that she now had the amazing power to reissue unclaimed Vitapasses out of the system. This often happened when solitary people committed suicide, and there were always a handful of them on standby. This arrangement intrigued him. In those cases where he extracted a bribe, he would split the proceeds with her. Well, "split" was a generous term — he would often give her a small percentage of the money extracted, but she didn't much care. In those cases where he extracted nothing more than the degradation of his victims, she gave him the Vitapass for free. She wasn't concerned about the equity of the relationship. Her true payoff was the ongoing partnership with the man she loved.

***

She would have continued to talk to Pontius for as long as he allowed. But soon Caspian and Conti walked up to the bar, with Conti making a conscious effort to draw Moria away in conversation. Moria was not pleased to have her attention diverted, but she was far too polite to resist. She turned her focus to Conti and trailed off into a sidebar with her new acquaintance. Seizing on the opportunity, Caspian slid next to Pontius at the bar.

"So what do you think of the lovely Miss Conti, Captain?"

Pontius took a long, deep drought from his frothy drink and paused for a moment as the liquid swirled its way into his gut. "I think she's... fragile."

Caspian conjured one of his rarer tricks — a frown. Placing his hand on his friend's shoulder, he feigned concern.

"Really, Captain? I'm not accustomed to such concerns from you. She's a grown woman and I'm a man of many qualities."

Pontius couldn't help but chuckle. "Qualities, eh? Yay right, my friend. What woman wouldn't be drawn to your *qualities*?" He took another drink of the brown liquid, which seemed to grow more delicious with each gulp as he pondered the dissonance he felt in Conti. "So you met her working at the Skyskimmer?"

"Not exactly. I ran into her at the Skyskimmer during the launch party for the Invictus. But she wasn't working that night."

"And you've been there when she was working?"

Caspian lingered on the question for a moment. He wasn't sure what Pontius was angling at, but he wasn't concerned about it either. "Nay. I don't go there often."

"Hmmm..."

The two sat for a few minutes. Out of nowhere Caspian blurted, "You know, Captain, I think she might have a potential business deal for you..."

This caught Pontius off guard. He swiveled on his stool and looked straight at his friend. "What kind of business deal could she possibly have for me?"

In a childish display of cloak-and-dagger-ism, Caspian leaned over and spoke into Pontius's ear. No one could hear what they were saying anyway above the cacophonous rancor of the nightclub's sound system. "She's looking for Vitapasses."

Pontius sprang to his feet, startled. This news from Caspian made him immediately irritated.

"You talked to her about Vitapasses? What, by India, is wrong with you? You broach these subjects in casual conversations with your transient flings?? What have you told her about me? What have you offered her?"

Caspian sprung into immediate damage control. He guided Pontius back to his stool and motioned for another round of drinks. The smile on his face was extensive and forced.

"Relax, relax, old friend. I've told her nothing. I've promised her nothing. I haven't even given her your name in connection with such a transaction. She just mentioned that she was interested in acquiring Vitapasses and I just replied that I might have such a connection."

Pontius's annoyance was waging an epic battle with the brown frothy liquid that continued to flow down his throat. If caught in some of his activities, they would sentence him to life on a penal island. Life sentences on Torrenth were the longest, most brutal punishments one could earn. There were convicts on those islands who had been enduring hard labor for more than 9,000 years. Immortality took on a whole new meaning when one was condemned for life. Pontius was always wary of Caspian's mouth. Caspian's mouth was far too loose, and connected to far too many dangerous people.

"I don't know why you would even consider me in such a conversation. And I don't know why you would engage in such folly with a bartender."

"Dealer, Captain. She's a dealer. Everyone has their facades. Hers just happens to be bartending."

"Why wouldn't she just go through her, her... middleman? He seemed quite anxious to facilitate any transaction that she might desire."

Caspian shrugged his shoulders and gave Pontius a knowing smile. "Apparently, even The Middleman has his limits. You can't trade goods that you can't acquire."

"So just talk to Moria. You know damn well that I can't do anything to issue a Vitapass. She is the wizard behind the curtain."

Caspian laughed and shook his head. "Moria has never been an open commodity. She is your source, and a source that only you can tap. She only does what she does because she longs for you."

Pontius sat for a moment in awkward silence, refusing to acknowledge Caspian's words but knowing them to be true. He understood that Moria was once his wife. He understood her deep love for him. But he always found it painful to be in her presence knowing that he could no longer conjure any feelings for her. He had no natural memories of her from a time when he shared her passion. He preferred to maintain his own internal delusion of Moria as a simple business associate. He didn't appreciate when someone pointed out the folly of that delusion.

"Well forget about it, Caspian. When she mentions Vitapasses, you have forgotten my name. When she is looking for connections, you can't remember my face."

Caspian smiled, made a flourishing gesture with his hand, and said, "Then it is done. We shall speak of it no further."

Upon hearing these words Pontius relaxed. He turned his attention once again to the brown liquid, which now had some type of swirling maelstrom within it. Watching the patterns of this miniature tempest somehow enthralled him like a cat eyeing a laser dot. After several minutes of relative calm, Pontius blurted out, "This middleman – Kryx – where in the world did you meet that freak?"

Caspian shook his head and said, "I have never met him before. Conti brought him."

"Hmmm…" replied Pontius, and they both trailed off in silence.

The next several hours flew by with all manner of people introducing themselves to Pontius – none of whom he cared one ounce about. Every new face met a drunker version of Pontius. They enjoyed the entertainment of seeing him in an ever-more carefree state. The various drinks given to him worked ever deeper into his brain. Although he did not enjoy the company of anyone he met that night, each of them served as a sort of shield to keep Moria at bay. He knew that she would keep her distance as long she saw him in conversation with someone else.

Caspian was ready to leave. Conti had already traveled through several states of consciousness. She had been up, and down, and up again, soaring through the night on a wave of chemicals and neural boosters. By the time Caspian motioned for them to exit, she was ready to ravage him right there on the dance floor. She couldn't wait to explore every inch of his 3,300-year-old body. She thought she was a kinky woman. She thought she was going to teach him a few things that night. She was wrong.

Once they reached his apartment he commenced an extensive lesson in Caspian sex. When she was kinky, he was rough. When she was rough, was sadistic. Sex for him wasn't just an exercise in pleasure – it was an exercise in sensations, all manner of sensations. He was not satisfied that night until he had put her through a wringer of explosive and excruciating sensations. She had never experienced most of those sensations and had no desire to experience them again.

Chapter 3 – Balancing the Scales

Kryx was in a broad underwater roundabout 100 meters in diameter and 40 meters below the surface. The distant ceiling offered a panorama of the inky soup of Oceanus. An ocean view would often be murky, at best. But the aquapod housing this roundabout featured brilliant floodlights. They exposed a great menagerie of Torrenth's indigenous ocean life. The creatures cruised outside the pod's exterior at all times of night and day. The gentle whir of electric scalers filled every centimeter of the edifice.

Centrian was an archipelago of 12 major islands on which 99% of Torrenth's population lived. The largest of these islands was 700,000 square kilometers. The smallest was 15,000. A million square kilometers for a population of five billion - crammed, to say the least. Engineers first resorted to their most comfortable convention – building upward. The Centrian skyline was breathtaking - and crowded. Only in the last thousand years had economic pressures led to large-scale underwater development. The aquapods created a deep sea halo around Centrian, no more than several kilometers from land. They offered the greatest opportunity for spatial expansion.

The entire underwater biome was a collection of pods and transit tubes. The larger transit tubes accommodated scaler traffic. Between smaller pods were minor tubes designed for several side-by-side pedestrians. In some places, one pod joined another like caviar eggs. In other places, the pods interspersed with various transit tubes like the bonds in a molecular model.

Kryx had already docked his transporter and was heading to an indiscreet programming shop on the outer edge. When he walked through the front door, no one in the shop acknowledged him. A casual observer might wonder if they had seen him at all. As he walked through the office he could sense the grid signal in his UNI waning.

He walked through three contiguous pods. They comprised the front office, middle cubicles, and executive suites. He went through a small door that led to a pedestrian tube, 100 meters long. The dim tube was lit by two side rails of guide lights. They led him to the opposite door that granted access to a large manufacturer of ship parts.

As he walked through the machine shop, none of the dozens of employees paid him any attention. He strode through the manufacturing floor with the confidence of a duke. Reaching the other end of the machine shop, he opened the door to a second pedestrian tube. Before entering he could once again sense his grid signal dissipate further in the murky depths.

The second transit tube was much longer than the first, extending a full 450 meters into the bowels of Oceanus. When he reached the far side, he opened the hatch to find an edifice of brilliant office lights. Inside, at least 100 random individuals sat at monitors pecking out trades in any one of nine different markets. None of the traders bothered to acknowledge his presence. When he had traversed the entire trading floor, he slipped into the break pod. Half a dozen burnt-out traders were drinking Caffeinate like it was water and staring at the news feeds. In the restroom, he walked into a stall, rapped on the wall with a particular code, and watched as the polymer wall fell away before him. It revealed yet another transit tube. Stepping into this corridor, he received UNI confirmation that he had exceeded the range of the grid signal. He had at last escaped the surveillance of Centrian.

He walked the remaining 200 meters down this last transit tube, cherishing a silence he could not find anywhere else. There were no warnings, no alerts, no bulletins – nothing pumped into his brain. It was, for any Centrian resident, an amazing, almost breathtaking feat of stillness. After traversing this last pathway, he reached the far hatch which granted him access to his personal office.

His office was an impressive edifice. He owned each business through which he had walked. The revenue from those businesses allowed him to extend his empire ever further into the blackness. The aquapod was 60 meters in diameter and there were no central walls to obfuscate the view. Equipped for business, it was clear that this space was also suited for extensive habitation. Aside from the usual office furniture, fold-away accouterments allowed for sleeping, cooking, and lounging. Most items in the enclosure were back-lit with dim, multicolored track lights. They imparted an eerie glow across their surroundings.

Although the lighting seemed dismal, it enabled a grand panorama as sea creatures skirted the outer edges of the pod. Bioluminescence was a primary strategy deployed by a great many of the planet's creatures. In the vast expanses of Oceanus, many of those creatures grew to Leviathan proportions. Staring upward through the pod's shell looked like a brilliant meteor shower. The tail of a 50-meter creature might slither by with an impressive array of glowing spots across its entire length. A school of brilliant fish might sail by, each one darting in unison and shimmering like a diamond in the blackest of caves. The glowing performance never ceased.

At the far end of the pod were three hatches leading to clear chambers. The first chamber harbored a simple Amphibian at the other end – Kryx's personal vehicle for traversing the open sea. The second chamber was identical to the first, but harbored no vehicle – this was a docking station for his associates. The third chamber was smaller and did not appear equipped for docking a vehicle. It gleamed inside with brilliant metal appendages. It had an opposite door that seemed too small to accommodate any open-ocean transport. It also had polymer walls much thicker than the other two chambers.

Calon sat behind one of the desks with a physical grid jack plugged into the base of his skull, too engulfed in his numbers to greet Kryx. While Kryx savored the network silence of this room, there were still times that called for official business. The various jacks littered throughout the pod ensured this was still possible.

It was difficult to describe Calon in any terms that would leave a lasting impression. His greatest assets were that he was prim, efficient, and average. It was possible to spend hours talking with him and then forget anything specific about the discussion after he had left. Hundreds of years ago he practiced law, but he laid that aside to serve as Kryx's personal attaché. On his better days, he was an accountant, a broker, and a powerful conduit for Kryx's business. On his worse days, he was little more than Kryx's messenger and mouthpiece.

Kryx reclined in a utilitarian chair and bathed in the iridescent glow of Torrenth's ocean life. Despite his silent and detached UNI, he could hear Calon convo'ing multiple clients on the other side of the pod. One after the other, Calon arranged payments, shipments, meetings, and negotiations. Although Kryx desired to swim in the blissful silence of the sea, the Middleman in him would not allow him to completely shut down.

As Calon's voice rose and fell from one convo to the next, Kryx heard names that he did not recognize. He wondered if these were new associates or partners that he had dealt with hundreds of years ago and could no longer remember. As he gazed at the fluorescent light show above him, he wondered how many of these species he had consumed in his many thousands of years. He had no idea. As he looked around the spacious pod, he wondered how many times he had been here before. Without querying his UNI, he had no way of knowing.

The relaxation of this underwater mecca overcame him and he began drifting into sleep. The telltale signals of withdrawal yanked him back and quickened his thoughts. His heartbeat skipped and small beads of sweat began to form on his weathered brow. His hair, so vibrant and responsive, began to sag and sway on his mantle. The shake was returning to his hand and he thrust it into a drawer wherein lie hundreds of empty capsules. He frantically pulled out one, then another, then yet another, realizing that each was empty. After sorting through more than a dozen, he started to feel a true sense of panic. He retrieved a full capsule and admired it just briefly in the dim light before holding it to his neck. Upon contact the internal liquid evaporated and within ten seconds there was nothing left in his hand but a shell. He threw the spent husk back in the drawer to be part of another desperate future dance.

Although he had been using meth for millennia, it no longer had a traditional effect on him. Where typical junkies might enjoy a "buzz" or a "high", at this point it did nothing more than calm him. It smoothed out a jagged world ill-equipped for mortal men. And while the effect was something he perceived as benign, it was nonetheless a fix that he could not do without.

Nanites removed the physical scourge of overdoses and addiction. Yet they did nothing to alleviate the crutches of the mind. Drug addicts were still forced to contend with the debilitating effects of dependency. Most Torrenthian addicts prayed to their Priori for death. Yet their overriding desire for another fix kept them from ever consummating suicide. With the counteracting effects of nanites in their bloodstreams, junkies often ingested epic doses. They would do anything to offset the real-time cleansing powers of technology. Torrenthian drugs had a frightening potency. They would kill anyone who didn't have a full complement of nanites coursing through their system.

Centrian addicts were sad specimens. The technology kept them in a perpetual prison of addiction. They lingered for hundreds, even thousands, of years while living an endless existence as a ghost. They were twitching, feverish waifs searching for any way to satisfy their desires.

He was one of the heartier and more functional examples of this. He enjoyed an impressive constitution that would baffle any standard physician. He was an addict – make no mistake about it – but he had been an addict for far longer than even he could remember. He was far more productive than lesser men who had never ingested such substances.

With the soothing effects of the chemical coursing through his veins, he slunk back into his chair. He stared once again, agape, at the aquatic show above him. He might have nodded off again if he had not heard Calon slip the name of "Sirin" past his lips. Kryx's ears perked up. His posture stiffened. He eavesdropped with impunity on his business manager's conversation. After a few moments, once it became clear that Calon was indeed talking *to* Sirin, Kryx wove his arm and spoke with authority.

"Calon! So you've reached our man, Sirin?" Facetiousness dripped from Kryx's voice. He already knew that Sirin was on the line.

Calon paused and asked his audience, "One moment, please."

He then raised his visage to Kryx across the room and said, "Yes-un. I have Sirin on the line." Calon halted in anticipation of Kryx's instructions.

"Well I'm so glad that we've reached him! I was afraid for a moment that something ill had befallen him. Please let him know that I need to see him right away. Tonight!"

Kryx relaxed back into his chair with a smug happiness and awaited the inevitable reply. He already knew his retort. Calon relayed the request to Sirin, listened to Sirin's reply, and then reported back to Kryx.

"He's on the other side of Majorus-un. He'd like to know if he can come in next week." Calon spoke the words without passion, but a wry smile was on his lips. He was the mouthpiece in a drama he had facilitated far too often before.

"Of course, of course! That's an impractical journey. He can come by next week, that's fine. Let him know that in the interim, I can simply get the information I need tonight – from his *mother*."

Once again, Calon relayed the information and, on cue, there was a long, unnatural silence. While Kryx fished in the drawer for another capsule, Calon reported back, "He says he can be here in a few hours-un."

"Excellent!" Kryx feigned relief, even though his audience was a close consort who knew this game inside and out. He enjoyed the theater. "Let him know we'll be waiting."

Kryx slid back in his chair and allowed his impending slumber to overtake him. Calon continued working the convo's, but Kryx was already satisfied in the prize that would soon be awaiting him.

***

Kryx was an ancient soul, even by Torrenthian standards. He was more than 9,000 years old. His exact age was unknown because he would need to reference his UNI to discern such a number and he had no interest whatsoever in the number. Age, holidays, milestones – they were all meaningless digits that flew past him in a blur of history. It was not cliché to say that he had forgotten more in half his lifetime than most men could ever remember.

For the first couple millennia, he was a world-class software engineer. His specialty was the creation of processes and operating systems based on neural networks. He was the lead engineer on the team that created the core operating systems for all species of nanites. His logistics software, even today, was the basis of 80% of the planet's shipping. He created autonomous medical systems that could complete some of the most complex surgical procedures. He was, without a doubt, an unmitigated star in his field.

He had records of a time when a mere three billion souls roamed the planet. He had records of times before PC or the NCU. He could almost remember with his natural memory a time before man had delved into the great sea of Oceanus. He was, in some respects, a walking talking library.

At his perigee he was one of the highest paid intellectuals on the planet. And like most men who care about their legacy, he yearned to have children. Or just, to have a child.

His first wife was barren. No degree of Centrian technology could save them from their childless fate. So after decades of excruciating trial-and-error, he made the painful decision to leave her. His second wife was a different sort. She seemed to have no problem conceiving children – but she was incapable of bringing them to term. After an agonizing series of five miscarriages, he consigned her to the same fate as his first wife.

By the time he met his third wife, the political atmosphere of Centrian had changed for the worse. With the end of death by natural causes, rampant population growth led to a critical breakdown of societal norms. Cannibalism was rampant in the streets. Death matches littered the arenas. Looters went on weeks-long binges, burning entire complexes to the ground. The situation required something drastic – and thus, Population Control was born.

He found himself in an awkward situation. For all his wealth and power, he had no living relatives. Neither did his wife. This meant that they could not sit back and wait for someone to will a Tombstone to their yet-unborn child. He had no legitimate means by which he could father children.

At first he believed that he could save their family through his own technical prowess. He had, after all, programmed many of the central systems that used to tag and track humans throughout Centrian. It stood to reason that he could create the software conventions necessary to legitimize his own children. And to this end, he and his wife proceeded to conceive three children.

What he failed to understand was that the innate desire of most people to procreate spawned a technological arms race. He built the systems designed to track licensed and unlicensed humans. But by the time he was fathering his own children those systems had grown exponentially in complexity. There was no way he could hope to keep up. He stood by and watched the slaughter of his first three children by NCU agents – two of them within 48 hours of birth, the third after six months.

Undaunted, he decided to take a new approach. He began genetically engineering his own children in utero. He believed he could beat the DNA scanners. The scanners had become ubiquitous on every corner of every public thoroughfare and in every public office. He came exceedingly close to his goal. His first three engineered children lasted only days. His next three made it six, seven, and nine months respectively. He was triangulating toward what he saw as the ultimate solution.

His next three children were the most long-lived – and the most crushing. He had a son snuffed out at seven years. His daughter made it to 12. His next child – another son – graduated college with Centrian-wide honors. NCU exterminated him on the first day of his first job.

This last extermination destroyed his resolve. His son was a shining light following in his father's footsteps. He invested so much precious time and energy in him. His loss was too much for him to bear. He abandoned his own self-sufficient, technological approach. He was a man of means. He was a man who could bring great resources to bear. Perhaps his solution was not in advanced technological innovation, but in plain-old human motivation.

For his next two children he became much more practical. He decided to outright bribe the NCU agents who came to remove them. He would bribe anyone he had to, at any time of the day or night, until he was broke or dead. The problem was that bribing was a temporary and clumsy solution. A bribed NCU agent could ensure that his child would live today. But that unlicensed child would continue to trip every scanner he passed and every checkpoint he traversed. There were not enough hours in the day, nor enough money in anyone's bank account, to bribe the endless stream of officials. They came knocking at his door with their hand out, stating that he should either pay or his child would die. After four years of struggling with this equation, both of his latest children were dead.

He was at wit's end, and he was on the brink of giving up, when his wife accidentally became pregnant again. He had grown tired of the cat-and-mouse game. He didn't know how he was going to save his latest child. But he was as determined as ever to keep this newest child – a daughter – alive.

The NCU agent shocked him when he arrived at their door. He had taken so many precautions. He had hacked into so many core systems. He had reprogrammed so many critical sequences of her DNA. He believed this was his one shining chance to save his own child. This was his opportunity to live the rest of his life, as he had always wanted to live it, as a father.

He thought too many times about the events of that night. He could no longer relate to those events as personal memories, but he had them all saved in easy-to-access nodes. He replayed them through his UNI with a stunning frequency.

When the NCU agent burst through Kryx's door it fostered mass confusion. Even after watching 11 of his children die at the hands of these agents, there was no way to steel yourself against this. He knew the drill. Or at least, he thought he knew the drill, but this NCU agent offered something he had never heard from their ilk. This agent offered them a Vitapass – an eternal chance at long life, fatherhood, and legitimacy. All they had to do was submit to the temporary torture and degradation of his wife.

Against the pained, screaming protestations of his beloved he implored her to take the deal. This woman had endured so much heartbreak and pain for the sole purpose of making him a father. And now he stared into his wife's eyes and convinced her that she should do whatever the NCU agent asked. It would be worth it. It would secure the life of their child. It would make them a family. And he watched with riveted eyes as the agent dragged her into the other room to be gang raped by a mob of street thugs.

What happened next would change him forever. The thugs deployed by the agent – brought in for his own sadistic satisfaction – had no guidelines and no discipline. The agent watched as they brutalized her again and again – and, being new to this game, he did not know when to call them off. Inevitably, they killed Kryx's wife, watching her slip away as she stared into the wicked eyes of her own defilers. Realizing that plans had gone terribly wrong, the agent burst from the room. He shot Kryx's daughter through the chest, and then attempted to take out Kryx as well. But despite the genteel disposition of a software developer, Kryx was no wilting daisy. He killed two of the thugs and was damn close to killing the agent. The telltale alert of support agents started sounding throughout the corridors. Realizing a win here would be a Pyrrhic victory, Kryx fled. He ran through the corridors and the scalers of the city. He ducked off the traditional grid.

He could no longer remember the exact sequence of that night. It was several thousand years ago and the only remaining records lived in his UNI-assisted memories. He reviewed them, over and over again, every single day of his life. Yet he still wondered what it had done to him – and where he was going from here. What he did know, beyond any shadow of a doubt, and without any receding of passion, was that he hated the NCU. He would do anything he could to destroy anyone who carried that badge.

For the next several hundred years, Kryx slipped into drug addiction – a condition from which he would never recover. He abandoned the formulaic world of the software engineer. He withdrew himself from all formal aspects of society. Over the course of centuries, The Middleman was born – a man who had no greater interest than to balance the scales. He had no desire to side with one party or the other. He had no desire to align himself with any cause. His motivations were, 1) to kill NCU agents, and 2) to place himself in the middle of any transaction. This allowed him to feel uncommitted and unaligned with either party. It was his way to disconnect from a world he had come to abhor.

***

Calon was tapping him, interrupting his slumber. He wiped the drool from his chin and plastered a smile on his face as he surveyed Sirin standing before him. Sirin had been through many tight spots. His experience allowed him to hold his composure. But Kryx's keen eye could spot the ever-present wobble in Sirin's knees.

"So, Sirin, undoubtedly you have brought me my shipment of babies?" Kryx knew damn well that Sirin had no shipment of babies. Sirin worked for NCU. Rather than kill his unlicensed targets, he had been stockpiling the children for delivery to Kryx. But one of Kryx's rivals stole Sirin's shipment and he now had nothing to show for the advance he'd already received.

Sirin did not respond, but instead began to shake his head and weep under his breath.

"So, Sirin. No babies! Then certainly, you have come to return my half million squalem?"

Before Sirin could venture a response, Calon interjected, "Nay-un. Sirin's bank account contains only 128 squalem. A scan of his living quarters reveals only 3,000 squalem worth of fungible goods. He is carrying nothing of value."

He sprang to his feet and his already wide eyes took on a new sheen that left even Calon unsettled. He rushed to within centimeters of Sirin's face and said, in a deceptively quiet demeanor, "So, my good man. What's it gonna be?"

Sirin began to stutter. The pungent aroma of urine wafted up as the liquid trickled down his leg. He started to shake and Calon wondered if he would even be able to remain upright. Not missing a beat, Kryx yelled with deafening authority, "WHERE-UN, ARE MY BABIES?!"

Sirin made no attempt to reply. Rather, he lost all composure and crumpled into a limp ball at Kryx's feet. Kryx turned to Calon and commenced his diatribe.

"You see, Calon?! This is the problem with NCU agents! None of them – not a single fucking one of them – can be trusted to deliver on ANY promise they make! If you give them your money, they'll FUCK YOU! If you give them your dignity, they'll FUCK YOU! In fact, no matter what you do with an NCU agent, they will FUCK YOU EVERY TIME!"

Calon knew the drill, but sometimes he was still taken aback by the force of Kryx's anger. He almost wondered if Kryx's violence would shatter the translucent polymer all around them.

He looked back at the crumpled ball of stinking humanity at his feet and decided to give him one last chance. "Give me a reason – any reason – why I don't execute you right now."

The crumpled ball made no attempt at composure, but after several moments of rabid sobbing he managed to reply, "I- I- I- I… will get you the money." He was hyperventilating like a schoolyard kid punched in the gut.

"Calon!"

"Yes-un." Calon stood almost at attention.

"Did I ask this piece of shit for money?!"

Without hesitation, Calon replied, "No-un. You gave him a half million squalem in return for a standard shipment of babies."

He looked skyward through the murky haze of Oceanus. He said, to no one in particular, and in a more subtle tone, "What we have here, is failure, to communicate." Calon did not understand the archaic reference, nor did it matter.

And with that, he reached down and gathered the prostrate Sirin with a single hand. With a brute strength that belied his frame, Kryx dragged him the few yards to the smallest of chambers hanging off the aquapod. Realizing his fate, Sirin now struggled like a desperate madman – but it was far too late. With brutal force of will, Kryx overpowered every effort of his muscles. Kryx tossed him into the chamber and swung the door shut, listening as the auto-locks pressurized.

Sirin began to scream, but it was barely heard through the thick polymer walls of the pod. Kryx sat back in his chair and connected his UNI. He set the controls – a process that had taken him years to perfect. They worked in such a way that Sirin would remain alive and conscious for hours. The tiny razor blades of the swirling walls bled him dry. It took almost two hours for Sirin to die. In another 30 minutes the razors liquefied him. And once he became a bloody smoothie, his soupy remains jettisoned out of the chamber and into the sea. His final pleasure was watching the myriad of Oceanus scavengers slurp up the sinewy remains. The ocean waters scrubbed the liquefaction chamber clean and he smiled.

Chapter 4 – Access Denied

Pontius was enjoying all the benefits of a wonderful mood. There were times, as an NCU agent, that he could go weeks with little to do. Much of his work consisted of researching suspected babies or trailing their parents. The satisfaction of his work – or at least, what the public perceived to be his work – was something that came to him far too infrequently. Parents would often flee before he could pounce. Various underworld types would steal the unlicensed before he could get to them. Rogue bounty hunters would snuff out the children before he could close in. In rare cases, they were even killed by their own mothers in fits of despondent fatalism. But today, he had his mark and he knew how to proceed.

He had, at times, gone months between assignments. There were a mere 100 agents in the entire NCU to police an official population of five billion, but this was more than sufficient. The environmental pressures of Centrian had caused the natural birthrate to plummet of its own accord. The looming presence of PC provided an active disincentive for those who might choose to test the system. A constant barrage of government messages drove home the idea that unlicensed birth was a foolish endeavor. This could sometimes lead to bored NCU agents.

It pleased him to have a second assignment in such a short period of time. He was always optimistic about his work. He saw each unauthorized soul as an opportunity for him to be the grantor of eternal privilege. The majority of his clients acquiesced to his demands and they, in turn, received a full life, an eternal life, a legitimate life. None of his 99 peers in NCU could offer such a promise. No one but him could grant an enriching existence spent as a full-fledged member of society.

Torrenthia had given birth almost nine months ago. It was impressive that she had managed to evade PC for this long. It was no doubt in part due to the combined efforts of her and her performer husband, Malorus. He was quite the established acrobat. The show in which he performed was popular and long-running throughout Centrian. She traveled with him as he toured the islands as part of this circus troupe. It was this constant movement that had allowed them to evade detection for some time. They were now staying in a temporary apartment for the last couple of weeks. Several days ago, PC surveillance started to hone in on their whereabouts.

Pontius sat on the wide balcony of an expansive café situated on the 30th floor of the Colonus Tower. It may have seemed that few Centrian patrons would ever utilize an outdoor balcony. But the general populace was so accustomed, so numb, to the ever-present rain that it no longer registered with them. Some ignored it; some enjoyed it; but most failed to recognize it at all as a significant atmospheric condition.

If rain is a condition where drops fall in a vertical path from the sky, then this weather was something different altogether. Swirling updrafts combined with 99% humidity and a light precipitation. This created an atmospheric condition known as an aethyr. Tiny, almost imperceptible droplets swirled in all directions, dancing in the competing winds. It did not feel as though any moisture was falling from the sky. Rather, it was roiling in the very air itself. It danced and floated in intricate eddies as it gathered and then dispersed upon the whim of every frantic breeze.

This side of the Colonus Tower faced its twin, the Colonius Tower. They were a broad mixture of low-end temporary housing, middling retail establishments, and swarthy office spaces. From his perch at one of the outermost tables, he could gaze across at the outer windows of apartment 29-40. It was the temporary residence occupied by Torrenthia and Malorus. Looking up 10 floors he could also see the nearest connecting skyway that joined the twins.

The previous day, Pontius had planted a bug over the door sill of the apartment. It was now mid-afternoon. He knew that Malorus left each day about this time to prepare for that night's show. He now sat embroiled in the aethyr. He cradled a steaming Caffeinate. He watched passersby and listened to the feedback from his transmitter. He heard the opening of the door, the kiss at the threshold, pleasantries exchanged in departure, and the closing of the door. He knew it was time to act.

His first step was to convo Moria to ensure that she was on standby. She was, as always, on standby. Her thrilled and flattered voice came through the convo. He had to cut her off to avoid the risk of humoring her while his target left the apartment. Knowing that he had a Vitapass waiting, he finished his drink and initiated a UNI payment to settle his tab. He started a brisk walk to the skyway 10 stories above.

The inner edifices of the Colonus Tower were as ornate as they were decrepit. Every piece of molding, every flourish, every alabaster fitting sought to escape its moorings. The failing environmental controls allowed a fine sheen of algae to cover many of the smoother surfaces. The black refuse of microbiotic organisms oozed down the walls in slick sheets.

The skyway was more than 100 meters in length with a ceiling dominated by great fans. The blades seemed too long and too wide for placement in such a narrow berth. They swung in slow, magnificent arcs that cut the air with great whooshes, but somehow provided little in the way of airflow.

If the Colonus Tower was derelict, Colonius was its danker twin. He wondered how it could be that the inner walls were somehow wetter than the building's outer skin. The pungent sting of mold hung thick in the air, so much so that he wondered if this was what it felt like to live in a bayou. As he navigated the inner halls he had to swipe aside wallpaper or siding that had freed its moorings. It hung in great swaths through the central causeways.

As he approached 29-40, it stood out from its surroundings. The door was a brilliant yellow – not from paint or wallpaper, but some kind of shiny metal. It shone in the dim hallway like a beacon and it confused Pontius to the point of making him slow his stride as he took stock of his surroundings.

At the foot of the door sat a dog – a massive beast. Pontius froze upon spying it and assessed the potential threat. He relaxed when he realized that it was ancient – and toothless. It curled up at the apartment's threshold, taking an obscene amount of pleasure in a huge bone with great mounds of rotting flesh. Without the luxury of teeth, it was gumming the rancid meat with a fervor that bordered on pornographic. He approached the doorway, watching for any reaction from the uninterested mutt. It cared for nothing beyond the scope of its bone.

With the dog oblivious, Pontius stood before the apartment door and hailed its residents. There was a long pause, followed by rustling sounds from within, followed by another long pause, and finally an answer.

"Can I help you?" Torrenthia's reply came through his UNI.

"Yes-un. Centrian Health Inspector. An infectious bacterium has been identified on this floor and I have a warrant to inspect all apartments for signs of the contagion."

Via UNI, he transmitted his counterfeit health inspector credentials and his counterfeit warrant. There was another long pause on the other side of the door. It was followed by a frantic discombobulation of sounds and huddled voices.

"Miss?"

The noises continued for a short while and then another period of silence followed.

"Miss?"

There were a few more scurrying sounds and then the door opened. Torrenthia flashed a bright smile at Pontius and welcomed him in. She was trying to look relaxed, and would have accomplished the feat if it weren't for the giveaway beads of sweat on her forehead. She may have enjoyed some relief if Pontius wasn't reaching down and dragging the decrepit dog into the apartment. This had the effect of layering confusion on top of her stress.

"That's not our dog," she said with a nervous smile. Pontius offered no reply. He did not return the dog to the hallway.

The apartment was tidy. Effigies of their Priori decorated the walls. They made every attempt to flood the dank edifice with fresh air and natural light. The appliances were old but he could tell that they had put considerable effort into scrubbing them before they settled in. The seating was all covered with crisp, unmatched blankets that gave the room a motley, but tended-to feeling. Nestled between a couch cushion and the armrest, he could see the top of a baby bottle peaking up past the covering blanket.

There were two doors leading from the living room. According to the floor plan he'd studied, one led to the bedroom, the other to the bathroom. An open archway led to the kitchen on his left. The kitchen centered on an island that doubled as the dining room table. Several bar stools stood around the island. On one of those stools sat Malorus, staring at Pontius.

When his gaze fell over Malorus, he froze in quiet disbelief. He suppressed his shock – his panic – and made every attempt to look nonchalant about Malorus's presence. He was certain that he heard Malorus leave. He knew that Malorus had a show to perform in tonight. He knew that this was already 30 minutes beyond the time when Malorus should have left. And yet there he was, with a firm visage locked upon Pontius that bordered upon intimidating.

Malorus wore shorts and an undershirt. Even from his perch on the bar stool, it was obvious that he was a short man, at least 15 centimeters below average. But his muscled physique belied any confidence one might hold over him due to height. He sat with his arms crossed, his gymnast's biceps bulging against the pectorals. They strained the flimsy confines of his undershirt. His cropped hair made him seem almost militaristic.

Exterminations with both parents present were rarely attempted. It was hard enough to subdue a delirious mother without the worry of the father going ballistic as well. The presence of both parents also tended to belabor negotiations. Where one parent might acquiesce to Pontius's demands, the other might dig in against the inevitable outcome.

Pontius allowed his gaze to linger on the kitchen far longer than he would have in normal circumstances. He made a half-hearted attempt to move his head around, as though he were "inspecting" something in that room. But it was clear that Malorus held his attention. Malorus, in return, offered no reprieve, staring back at this odd intruder.

Feeling compelled to do something, Torrenthia asked, "Is there something you need to inspect-un?"

Pontius turned his gaze to her but remained silent. He was still trying to compute the miscalculation he had made. Malorus's presence made no sense to him – and it was destroying his ability to think. He looked at her, surveyed the room, looked back at her, then noticed she had leaned forward. She cocked her head in an anticipatory gesture. She expected him to provide some kind of reply.

"I just need to see the other rooms, then I'll be out of your way."

Without asking or waiting for her guidance, he moved straight toward the bedroom. He swung open the door and strode inward with a rabid eye. His target was easily spotted. Tucked in the far corner, nestled next to the bed, was a cradle. Abandoning pretense, he strode to the corner and stood over the cradle. He gazed inside at the child within, bundled in a bright yellow blanket with a matching yellow cap stretched over its round head. It was sound asleep.

He turned around to see both of them standing in the doorway. Torrenthia maintained her nervous smile. She was clinging to the naïve hope that this was just a health inspection. Malorus's grim expression had given way to a simmering anger. He was under no such delusion. Pontius could see Malorus's thigh muscles twitch as he pondered different options to defend his baby. Realizing that Malorus was not the type to take things sitting down, Pontius drew his blunderbuss and aimed it at the doorway.

The Centrian blunderbuss was an effective weapon for the cramped urban metropolis. It would spray hundreds of tiny pellets in a shotgun-like circumference. Those pellets did not have the momentum necessary to carry through walls. They did, however, have the momentum necessary to embed themselves in flesh. Once in their mark each pellet would explode with a payload of acid. The acid would overcome the healing effects of the nanites. It provided a lethality far greater than traditional ballistics while ensuring minimal collateral damage.

"You are in violation of at least 12 different statutes governing the birthing, housing, and protection of unlicensed humans. What I'm about to transmit to your UNIs is the termination license for your baby. Since your baby has no Vitapass and is therefore not a *real* person, it has been assigned the legal identifier of Q82RTP8BX4. I'm also transmitting all my licenses to operate as an NCU agent anywhere in the nation of Centrian. You don't need to accept any of these transmissions. In the Grand Court case of Hakkernon vs. Centrian, it has already been established that my transmission of these credentials certifies my legal authority, whether you accept those transmissions or not."

Torrenthia began shaking, great tears welling up in her eyes, but Pontius paid her no attention. He was staring at Malorus, ready to handle any threat presented by him. He could see every centimeter of Malorus's body tensing and throbbing with anger. Malorus's eyes darted around the room, then to his child, then back around the room again. He was trying to formulate a plan.

The next 15 minutes were a tense dance of strained communication and desperate bewilderment. Pontius struggled to lay out the terms of his deal. Malorus's presence multiplied his clients' natural outrage in this situation. At several key points, Pontius expected Malorus to launch himself across the room in a foolish and suicidal rage. The couple had no serious money to speak of. Their only real option was Pontius's offer of degradation-for-life. Pontius explained what Torrenthia needed to do with the toothless mutt. Every muscle in Malorus's body pulsed with a vicious adrenaline. Pontius explained that he expected Malorus to watch every moment of the festivities to seal the deal. His twitchy trigger finger was at its most aware. But somehow Malorus managed to keep himself together.

When he had laid out everything, and the forlorn couple was as calm as they were ever going to be, Pontius asked, "So what's it going to be?"

Malorus was about to spew a blistering invective. Before he could launch a single syllable Torrenthia shot out, "I'll do it." He shook his head at his wife, jaw agape, and mouthed, "No. No. No." But she placed her hand on his chest, managed to conjure up the most soothing of smiles, and said, "It will be OK. This is for our future."

Pontius gave no outward sign of relaxation, but inside he released a massive sigh of relief. It was the simplest of choices. It was the logical choice. And now he could proceed to close the transaction. He felt secure in the knowledge that he had once again granted a life where none should have existed.

He motioned for them to return to the living room, all the while keeping his blunderbuss poised and ready. He directed Malorus to sit still on the couch. He warned him that any sudden movements would void their deal and lead to the death of him, his wife, and their child. Malorus sat, shaking, and would not acknowledge the commands. But Pontius made it clear that they would not be continuing until Malorus had confirmed his understanding. Malorus glared at Pontius with a burning hatred but nodded in silence.

Pontius positioned himself on the other side of the room and made a quick convo to Moria. Once she confirmed that she had a Vitapass ready for imprinting, he cut the line, lit a cigar, set his UNI to record, and enjoyed the show. Throughout the grotesque proceedings, Pontius never recorded, or even bother to look at, Torrenthia. Her torture in this dance was secondary to Pontius. He focused his attention on Malorus. The contortions of Malorus's face as he witnessed the degradation of his wife fascinated Pontius.

When the disgusting act was complete, Torrenthia's amazing composure evaporated. She lay sobbing in a heap on the floor. Pontius sat in contented silence. He savored the last bits of his cigar and captured any remaining bits of drama for posterity. Malorus sat, stunned. When it became clear that Pontius was in no hurry to complete the transaction, he shot a look of rage at Pontius. He yelled with evil authority, "The fucking Vitapass!"

Without acknowledging Malorus's rage in any way, Pontius nodded his head and said, "Indeed."

He rose to his feet, ground his cigar into their flooring, and strode back into the bedroom where he moved toward the cradle. Standing over the baby, it surprised him to see that it was wide awake and cooing. As he moved overhead to peer upon the bundle, the baby flashed him a broad smile and began to giggle. Pontius felt startled at his own reaction to the child, believing it to be adorable. The baby's gleeful demeanor and festive yellow attire shone a light into the room that had just before appeared so dank.

Malorus again stood in the doorway. Pontius made it clear, with an efficient motioning of his blunderbuss, that he should come no closer. He looked at Malorus matter-of-factly and said, "This will only take a moment."

Pontius looked down at the child and began to daydream about the fruitful life it would enjoy. He couldn't help but wonder if he was now granting life to the world's next great scientist, or politician, or artist, or doctor. How many lives might this child save? How many people would this child touch? And it was all thanks to the magnanimity that Pontius was now about to display. The prospects made him almost giddy.

He pulled from his trench coat a cylindrical device about 40 centimeters in length. At one end was a bulbous fixture that he already began pointing toward the baby. At the other end was a display panel that provided video feedback but could also accept input from his UNI.

The device began to whir and a blue iridescent light, focused into a narrow beam, emanated from the bulbous fixture. Pontius just had to aim the light on any of the baby's open skin. While still eyeing the doorway for any rash movements from Malorus, he held the device steady over the baby. He awaited a confirmation signal. After several minutes of continual whirring, the light cut off and the display panel flashed a message. "Target DNA identified". Pontius then entered a command to transmit the DNA identifier to PC. The screen began flashing a new message: "Acquiring Vitapass". The blue light began blinking and the panel displayed a progress report. He looked up to Malorus again and flashed a knowing smile. Malorus did not return the gesture.

The process of acquiring the Vitapass took about 20 seconds. During grid congestion, it could sometimes take as long as 40 or 50 seconds. Pontius didn't notice that anything might be at all out-of-place until a full two minutes had passed.

He gazed down at the imprinter, then looked up at Malorus, then gazed down at the imprinter again. Once two-and-a-half minutes had passed, he wondered if he should reinitiate the process. After the three minute mark, the imprinter began flashing a red light. The display read, "Vitapass acquisition FAILED".

He stared down at the device in shock. In millennia of this activity he had never seen such a result. He turned the imprinter over in his hand, wondering if it was somehow damaged. It appeared as smooth and as functional as ever. Unsure of the proper course of action, he reset the device and reinitiated the DNA scan.

After the baby's target DNA was again identified, he repeated the process of transmitting the data. "Acquiring Vitapass" again came onto the display. This time around he was much more sensitive to the unusual passing of time. First 30 seconds passed, then 60, then 2 minutes, then 3, and then a flashing red light. The flashing message: "Vitapass acquisition FAILED".

As the blinking red light played off the edges of the cradle he looked up and caught the look of suspicion on Malorus's face. He wondered if it had been wise for him to reinitiate the process. He reset the imprinter again, clearing the red light and restarted the scan. This time, as it completed the initial scan, he convo'd Moria. When she answered, she met him with a simple and uncharacteristic, "Pontius..."

"The deal has been completed. I need that Vitapass now." It was not like Moria to be lagging with the Vitapass and he was walking a verbal tightrope. On one hand, he needed to let Moria know that this was beyond urgent. On the other hand, he was doing everything he could to look calm and collected in front of Malorus. He needed to communicate that this was all just part of the process.

"I don't know what's happening." He could hear a clear strain in her voice, buoyed by sincere confusion. "I've seen your transmission. In fact, you transmitted the DNA sequence twice. But each time when I've tried to issue the Vitapass I am told that my access is denied."

Those words – *access denied* - turned around in Pontius's mind for a moment. He had done this with Moria hundreds of times before. In all those times, he had never once experienced such a roadblock. In fact, he had long ago ceased planning on what would happen if the process didn't play out smoothly and perfectly – it always did.

"Moria, I need you to think, calm and clear. What exactly have you done in the system that was in any way different from the many times that you've done this before?"

He wanted to hear a calm, collected response from her. He needed to hear a response that indicated she was in control. Instead, what he received was a rising voice stained with the stress of accusation.

"There's nothing different! The process is always the same. You acquire the target's DNA. I receive the transmission and reissue one of the unclaimed Vitapasses. You imprint the Vitapass on the target. It's that simple." Moria was struggling to maintain her demeanor. He could identify the panic in her voice.

"To what areas of the system do you still have access?"

"All areas! I haven't been shut out. I'm still in the Vitapass Administration System."

"Yes, I know that, but clearly something is blocked. Can you still poll existing Vitapass holders?"

There was a long pause as she attempted a few trial queries. "Yes."

"Can you still access those areas not specifically designed for issuance?"

There was another long pause as she tried to access the more mundane features of the application. "Yes."

"Can you poll historical data?"

He didn't think this was leading anywhere. But he noticed that as he asked more questions in a methodical fashion, she seemed to calm down. "Yes, the data is all there."

"Is anyone else in the system?"

He waited while she arose and walked around the Vitapass Administration office. She was trying to determine who else might be issuing passes. Since the reissuance of a Vitapass was such a rare event, she had few coworkers and they were never in the system at the same time.

"There are only a few other people here. They're not even at their desks. They're standing in the hallway talking about last night's game."

"How many Vitapasses do you have in inventory?"

Pontius waited as she performed several queries, searching through the Centrian Vitapass database. "There are a dozen."

"And the last two denials we've received – were you attempting to reissue the same pass?"

There was an incredulous pause. "Well, yes, but I don't know what-"

"We're going to do this again. This time, when you receive the DNA signature, I want you to reissue a different Vitapass – any one, as long as it's not the same one that you tried to reissue those last two times."

"Pontius, if there's a hold on any given pass I would see it in the system."

"Do you have a better idea?" His voice was low, but sharp and accusatory. He was in no mood to debate the efficacy of his methods.

"No," was her quiet, reprimanded reply.

Pontius again initiated the process. He furled his brow and gazed hard at the baby. He was trying to give every impression that he was in the latter stages of a standard, but technical, process. As the excruciating minutes wore on, he stole another glance at Malorus. Every time he looked, Malorus appeared more agitated. After several minutes, the flashing red light returned with the message, "Vitapass acquisition FAILED".

"What the hell, Moria? Did you try to reissue a different Vitapass this time?"

"Yes! Of course I did. The same thing happened."

Pontius was incredulous. It was not like Moria to screw up basic details in the system. He could not understand how the process was now failing if she hadn't done something wrong. But he had no ability to look over her shoulder. He was limited to her description of the issue, and he was powerless to change the outcome.

There was another long pause as Moria struggled for words.

"What are we going to do?" Moria's voice was pleading, underscoring her mounting anxiety.

Pontius struggled to plot his next steps. He looked down at the baby and it afforded him another broad smile. He fought back the urge to return the smile. The baby was adorable in a way that he was not accustomed to. He told himself that it would have smiled at anyone standing above it. Yet he could not help but think that this innocent smile was for him and him alone.

He looked up again at Malorus. Malorus's broad features were apparent in the child, stretching the infantile smile in a way that made it even cuter. The resemblance was striking.

Malorus had done all he could to remain patient. He had experienced the degradation of his wife. He had suffered the intolerable smugness of Pontius. He had done everything asked of him in this macabre theater of torture. And yet it was apparent to him that his payoff was somehow delayed, denied. He searched his mind for recourse.

"The Vitapass! Where is the fucking Vitapass?!" As the words escaped his mouth he flexed his muscles and growled in a guttural display of might. This would have rattled any man who had not been through as many terse situations as Pontius.

Pontius raised his blunderbuss again to illustrate the ballistic power at his fingertips. Without removing his gaze from Malorus, he referred back to his convo with Moria and said, "What do we do now? I *need* that Vitapass."

The response from Moria was as pained as it was inevitable, "I don't know, Pontius. I'm sorry. I just don't know…" Her voice trailed off in his mind, echoing with a power that he had never afforded her before.

Pontius looked once more at the beaming smile of the infant and let out an audible sigh. His mind was now a jumble of disparate thoughts. He scanned the bedroom for escape routes, but he knew the single viable exit lay through the front door. He racked his brain for rational excuses. But he knew that after the trials through which he'd placed Malorus's wife, no excuse – no matter how plausible – would suffice. He tried to think of some story to relay back to NCU, but he knew that they tracked his progress to this point. They would not believe he had lost the target. For the first time in Pontius's remaining natural memory, he felt trapped.

"What are we going to do, Pontius?"

Resigning himself to the truth, he was in no mood to explore the possibilities so he cut the convo with her. With a firm grip on the blunderbuss, he stared at Malorus and attempted something he had never tried before – an escape.

Sensing the impending implosion, Malorus yelled with rising authority, "Where is our fucking Vitapass?!"

Pontius had never before felt true fear in the completion of his official duties, but he felt fear now. Malorus was displaying all the signs of a caged animal

– an animal that had endured an endless array of inhumane experiments. Pontius felt the flush of an emotion he could not remember having felt before – shame.

He tried to muster an air of legitimacy, but the charade held little sway with Malorus.

"Look, Malorus. This process is not always as smooth as we'd like to believe. We're having a lot of trouble capturing your child's DNA sequence. Without that sequence, there's no way to imprint the Vitapass, and without a proper Vitapass, none of us will be satisfied, right?"

He stared into Malorus's murderous eyes for some sign of confirmation, of acquiescence. Malorus was having none of it. With every word that flowed from Pontius's mouth, Malorus became more and more enraged. Pontius tried to trick himself into thinking that somehow Malorus was digesting these words. The evidence showed otherwise. Undaunted, Pontius still tried to soothe this agitated beast.

"This actually happens on a fairly frequent basis." Pontius lied. "DNA is a tricky substance. You've paid for the right to this Vitapass. You've paid in full. To ensure you get what you've paid for, I need to head back to NCU headquarters. They can rectify this. They can make your baby whole."

Pontius probed for a sign of acceptance from Malorus – a sign he knew he had no right to expect. The rage in Malorus's eyes shone bright, making Pontius aware that there would be no such acceptance provided. It was clear that an official line of malarkey was not going to satiate Malorus, so he tried a different tack.

"Look, I understand that this looks… awkward."

He walked cautiously toward the doorway, all the while keeping his blunderbuss aimed at Malorus's chest.

"This is not part of my standard operating procedure. You have done everything that was required to give your baby a Vitapass and, by all my Priori, your baby *will* receive a Vitapass. There is nothing that will keep me from fulfilling that promise. But right now, at this exact moment, nothing will be rectified until I get back to headquarters and investigate the glitch in our systems."

Pontius had no reason to expect the slightest bit of understanding. Yet he found himself praying that somehow logic would prevail in Malorus's mind. He continued his labored march across the bedroom, hoping that Malorus would concede. With each step forward, Malorus's muscles bulged tighter against the bounds of his skin. When Pontius was almost a meter from Malorus, he stopped and glared into his eyes.

"I need to leave this place so I can get your baby the Vitapass that I promised." His voice was low and deliberate. "There is going to be no Vitapass issued while I remain here. One way or another, I'm going to walk out your front door and head back to headquarters so I can rectify this situation. If I have to kill you to complete this transaction, I will do it."

Malorus didn't move. He wanted to speak. He wanted to scream. But his rage was crippling in its intensity. Pontius inched forward and stuck the blunderbuss right against Malorus's chest.

"So what's it going to be?"

His reply was to stumble backward into the living room. Pontius allowed him to clear some space between the two of them and then began to step into the room himself. The decrepit dog, unconcerned with the previous activities, had returned to its obsession with the bone. Torrenthia was absent. This initially gave Pontius pause. Then he noticed the light emanating from under the closed bathroom door, accompanied by the hush of shower water.

He paused for a moment near the center of the room and allowed Malorus to continue backing away toward the kitchen. When he felt there was sufficient distance to allow for an escape, he turned toward the front door. Before he could initiate another step something crashed down upon his back. Before he could register the situation, a cord wrapped around his neck. It wrenched upward with slicing force. With his free hand he struggled to get so much as a knuckle between the cord and his skin. He could already feel the sting of blood welling out from under its bounds. Even in the chaos of this moment, the pungent smell of wet dog on his attacker made him realize that this was Torrenthia. She now rode his back and was strangling him from behind. This realization was further confirmed when he heard her release a guttural scream. She poured every ounce of her strength into her desire to sever his head.

"Pontius? Pontius!? What's going on??" Moria had initiated a new convo and was now trying to make sense of the sounds he was transmitting.

He arched his head backward and launched himself against the wall behind him with all his might. He could feel the force of the wall transferred through her and into his back, but it seemed to have no effect on the veracity of her attack. She was still pulling upward on the cord with both hands and all her will, riding him like a bull. He bucked several more times but found her too entrenched on his shoulders. With each attempt he grunted hard as he tried to launch her through the wall.

"Pontius!!!" Moria screamed through the convo. Her panicked voice did nothing to help him in this scenario. Yet somehow, hearing her on the line gave him the presence of mind to turn his gaze downward. When he did so, it was just in time to see Malorus charging hard from across the room with a massive butcher knife in his hand.

Pontius still had the blunderbuss in his right hand. He raised it and pulled the trigger. It was not the cleanest of hits. But a volley of acid capsules tore through Malorus's shoulder and face. It dropped him like a stone and forced him to release an agonizing scream. His head began smoking and melting away.

This temporary victory gave him no opportunity for relief. Seeing Malorus's gruesome demise forced a terrifying scream from Torrenthia. She began to yank wildly on the cord around Pontius's neck. He held his weapon aloft, trying to aim at his attacker. She was bucking with so much power that he could not hope to shoot her without taking out a good portion of his own head at the same time. He made a few more clumsy attempts to steady the blunderbuss. He aimed above and behind him but finally dropped the weapon altogether. He needed both hands free to oppose the cord as it edged ever deeper into his throat.

A Dusk Forever Waning

The next several moments were a frenetic haze for Pontius. His field of vision started to narrow. The sounds of his screaming attacker drew fainter, muffled by the pounding of blood vessels. Those blood vessels struggled to transport blood to his brain. His lungs burned with spent air and his attempts to draw in fresh replacements became futile. The pungent smell of Malorus's burning flesh grew distant. Pontius found it ever harder to draw any type of breath. A strange relaxation washed over him, receded, and then washed over him again. While this tide was back at sea he realized he was on the verge of passing out.

He was incapable of removing the cord from his throat. He tried first with one finger at a time, and then with all his fingers in concert, but he could not provide any purchase. The harpy riding his shoulders held a demon grip around the cord. Every ounce of her soul ensured that it would only tighten. Even his decision to tear into the flesh of his own neck provided no means by which he could lever the garrote free.

He wondered how much time he had left. He tried to scan the floor for the knife that was in Malorus's hands, but he saw no sign of it. The other knives that must reside in the kitchen now seemed like they were many kilometers away. There was no time for rummaging through drawers. The living room was devoid of any blunt objects that might fill the role of an effective club. He no longer had the strength to continue wrenching her back against the wall. And when he had done that earlier, it did not seem to have much effect.

His knees started to wobble – violently. In the misguided fog of his distress, he dropped all attempts to pull the cord from his throat. He gave his full attention to strengthening his stance, even as Torrenthia renewed her attempt to fell him by swaying to and fro. Even with his refocused attention to stability, the shaking remained in his knees. He was resigning himself to failure when he once again heard Moria screaming through the convo.

As it had done before, his acknowledgment of her voice somehow sparked him to widen his gaze. As he did, the first thing he saw was the doorway to the bedroom – the bedroom where the baby lay. The door was still open and the doorway was not high – maybe 15 centimeters taller than Pontius. An idea exploded in his burning mind. With no luxury of planning, he gathered his scant remaining strength and ran full speed through the doorway.

As he passed the threshold, Torrenthia's head collided with the doorway, making a thunderous crash. The force of the collision pried her from his shoulders. As she hit the floor he heard a sickening thud as her head met the unyielding hammer of the synthetic flooring.

The force of the sequence, coupled with the sudden loss of weight on his shoulders, led Pontius to fall forward into the bedroom. Lying prone on the floor he gasped for breath. Each gulp of air provided just a portion of the relief he desired. The garrote, while no longer connected to choking force, had been brutally applied. It was still embedded deep within the flesh of his throat. He was aware of it but made no attempt to remove it from the bloody pulp of his neck.

He laid face-down on the floor and tried to suck in all the remaining air in the room. As he did so, he had to fight back the urge to vomit. He could feel blood and mucus congealing into a sickening mixture in his gut. Any attempt to expel it would keep him from drawing in more oxygen, so he fought the urge with all his will.

He may have stayed there on the floor for many minutes, maybe even hours, if he hadn't felt the sting of a blade. It wrestled deep under his shoulder blade. Such a blow delivered even a few moments earlier would have been a simple precursor to death. But he had managed to recover just enough that he squirmed himself around. Torrenthia attempted to resume her position on his back. As he spun from under her his motion threw her off balance and torqued her into the nightstand, sitting just inside the doorway. The corner of the nightstand found its way into her temple with a crunch. She fell into a heap on the floor beside Pontius.

He made no attempt to rise. He had never felt fatigue like this. He turned his head to his right as he lay on the floor. Torrenthia lay crumpled up in an unnatural position. Her head and torso slumped over the rest of her body as though she could fit into a suitcase. Her chest expanded in irregular motion. The disquieting sound of gurgling permeated her breathing. She spent the next 10 minutes breathing in fits and starts. She took a few sporadic breaths, then sat still for long periods of time, then erupted in a few more belabored breaths.

She never raised her head again. As Pontius stared at her in these final moments, he felt that she was fighting not to defeat him, but to save her baby. Her neck twitched as though she was trying to look upward, but the only response she could muster was to pull another gurgled breath. It took him a while to realize it, but she was trying to speak. After 10 more minutes of this agony, he could make out but one word from her – *Vitapass* – and then she died.

Pontius spent a full 15 minutes laying on his back and staring at the ceiling. The cord was still embedded in the bloody skin of his neck. He had regained a small portion of his natural strength. A rivulet of Torrenthia's blood streamed from her fractured skull and found its way to his hand. He made no attempt to clear it. He felt that somehow he deserved its stain.

The blade that had found the back of his lung had come free when he turned around underneath her. Its damage was still felt as he struggled to breathe. He blacked out twice, maybe three times – he wasn't sure. Each time he would come back to consciousness only to wonder again how this scenario had gone so wrong.

He could not be sure how long he laid there. It might have been a few minutes or it might have been a few hours – he was not feeling any direct sense of time. He may have laid there for much longer. But he responded to the gentle sound of cooing emanating from the cradle above and behind him. This sound provided to him a strange alertness – an energy that jolted him back to reality.

With a pained countenance he managed to bring himself to his feet. He had killed many people in his past, but this carnage disturbed him. Malorus's shoulder and head now formed a puddle in the living room. Torrenthia was a sad pile in the bedroom doorway. The dog was gone. The quiet between the baby's occasional sounds was jarring. He stared all around him and felt a lump in his

A Dusk Forever Waning

throat. Something here had gone wrong in a way that he had never seen. After surveying the gruesome scene for many minutes, he initiated a new convo to NCU.

"Target acquired. Unlicensed human eliminated." Headquarters responded with, "Confirmed, Pontius. Good work."

"I also had to eliminate the parents. Malorus and Torrenthia are dead. Their Vitapasses can be reissued. They gave me no choice."

There was a small pause on the convo. Headquarters responded with an understanding acknowledgment. "Confirmed. We will handle their records accordingly."

There was another long pause as Pontius waited for them to end the convo.

"Pontius, are you alright? Do we need to summon medical attention?"

"No. I'm fine. It was a nasty fight – the usual. I might need to take the next several days off, but I'll just go home and sleep it off." Pontius was struggling to speak with clear, even breaths.

The operator chuckled. "Understood. We will see you around next week. There are no pressing assignments right now anyway."

Once the line was clear, Pontius moved back into the bedroom and stood above the baby. It was looking somewhat agitated, but it did not cry out or fuss in any way. It was still wrapped in its papoose and the constraints of the cloth seemed to provide it with comfort. He stared down at it in befuddlement.

He convo'd Moria and before he could begin any kind of conversation she began weeping.

"Oh my gosh, Pontius, are you OK?"

"Moria – "

"I didn't know if you were dead. I heard all kinds of awful sounds and then you must have passed out because the convo just terminated."

"Moria – "

"Were you able to get out of there? Where is the child? Did you eliminate it?"

"MORIA!"

He finally had her attention. She ceased talking and sat still, awaiting his instructions.

"Moria, we have a serious problem."

Chapter 5 – A Journey Under Watchful Eyes

Pontius stared down at the baby and soaked in its innocence as he struggled to draw each painful breath. It was alert and active. It pushed gently against the bundled constraints of its yellow papoose. It had learned the trick of spitting bubbles and they were frothing from its mouth at a prodigious rate. He reached down and gathered the yellow cloth in his hands, lifting the child from the cradle. Carrying it like a small duffel bag, he turned and made his exit from the apartment.

As he made his way through various floors of the Colonius Tower, passersby viewed him as quite the spectacle. He had ripped the bloody cord from his neck but he had made no attempt to wash up. The drying blood made for a macabre necklace. His collapsed lung gave him a labored gait that caused him to bob and weave as he struggled to maintain a normal stride. He carried the baby, hanging under his hand, in a way that belied any parental instincts. The more he tried to blend into the crowds, the more he became aware of his conspicuousness.

He had no concern for the attentions of the masses. At this point, his solitary goal was to return home and regroup. He asked Moria to meet him there. He hadn't told her about the child. He just told her that there was some disturbing, unfinished business. They needed to discuss what had gone so wrong at the assignment. Under normal circumstances, Moria's Vitapass failure would have been his primary concern. But given the new arrival in his hand, the access problem was a distant second in his mind.

His mind swam with unsolved mysteries. Why was Malorus still in the apartment? What in the world was wrong with Moria's Vitapass access? And was Moria's problem a temporary glitch? What if something fundamental had changed in the system? What if he could no longer grant life as he had magnanimously done for so many years? And what was he now to do with this, this – *child*?

The 50th floor of the tower accommodated a broad retail walkway. It featured an assortment of thrift shops, strip clubs, convenience stores, whorehouses, drug stores, and fish markets. At the other end of this walkway he could reach the scaler terminal and then be on his way home. Across the roof of the walkway was strewn a long array of massive fans. Their blades spun in creaking, whining strokes as they slashed the air. He couldn't help but notice that, despite their whirring, they provided no air flow. The atmosphere was a thick stew and he felt condemned to slog through it with a depressing inefficiency.

As he began to traverse the walkway a tiny red light caught the corner of his eye. Stationed next to the doorway of the first establishment, he wondered if it had always been there. Despite the mental incongruence it caused, he continued walking.

Ten meters down the walkway he saw another red light at the door of the next establishment. He swore that it had not been there before but now it shone through his mind like a lighthouse. He stopped, turned toward the light, and inspected it from a safe distance. It was a light embedded in some sort of discrete scanner. It swung back, then forth, then back again as it perused the harried pedestrians. He resumed his progress toward the terminal. This time he stepped slowly, one foot in front of the other, as he kept his eyes trained toward the shops on this right. As he reached a point parallel to the next shop, like clockwork, a tiny red light lit up next to the shop's doorway.

He stopped again and looked back down the walkway from whence he had come. He could see the first two red lights starting to dim as though they were flares that, once lit, would spend their fuel and fade out. He then turned back toward the terminal at the far end and renewed his trek, this time with a more urgent gait. As he did, he noticed that lights went off like red dwarfs cluttering an astronomer's telescope.

As he reached the expansive terminal at the other end of the walkway, he looked back. He saw a wide array of fading red lights – dimming, cooling in the thick Torrenthian air. And when he turned his gaze back to the wider edifice of the terminal that was when he saw it. For the first time in his life, he could see the fnords.

He stood still in the sea of people and started scanning every aspect of the terminal. At first it was like finding a hidden needle in a cluttered haystack. He stared at the walls, the shops, the people for many minutes and only occasionally would his mind latch onto one of the scanners. They were small, black, and discreet. Although they seemed to be shielding themselves from his gaze, the more he looked, the more he found. In 1,878 years of life, he couldn't ever remember seeing them before, and now here they were – everywhere. Their ubiquity stunned him – a ubiquity so complete that he had never made conscious note of them before.

Across the terminal he saw the platform. Scalers were lining up to dump their payload of busy passengers and board new ones. A 30 meter stroll – one which would have been so simple and carefree mere hours ago – now filled him with dread. Those lights – those damn penetrating lights – were set to go off like sirens. They announced to the world that he was carrying an unlicensed human.

He felt a sense of awe, thinking of the many children he had intercepted after they had survived for many months – in some cases even, years. How had their parents managed to keep them from such a broad net of penetrating surveillance? The tactical realities of living off-grid now struck him with brutal force.

He looked at the 30-meter expanse and it felt to him like a sea of magma – an impenetrable field that led to certain doom. He stood motionless and scanned his surroundings. It seemed that there was no path to the scalers that would evade the scanners. The scanners covered the terminal in such a way as to cover every angle, every potential path. The clammy sensation of sweat bathed his palms and his forehead. His breathing, already painful and laborious, quickened as he considered his options. Finally, with a desperate resolve, he broke into stride and walked across the terminal. As he did, the red lights illuminated all around him like a Christmas tree.

A Dusk Forever Waning

No one else in the terminal or in the walkway before this made any notice of the lights. Pontius was a neon sign shining in an inky expanse. But the mindless travelers around him made no notice of his conspicuous condition. As each light blinked on it made no impact on the minds or faces of those who passed before it. It was as though the scanners didn't exist to them. They could not see the fnords.

He made his way to the scaler that would take him home. The scanner above the scaler's doorway clicked on with a light that appeared brighter and redder than any of the others. The scanner itself locked onto Pontius and he made every attempt to look anywhere else. He stared at the floor, then at the baby still hanging from his hand, then back to the floor again. He gazed at the feet of the other passengers. He looked anywhere he could that would allow him to avoid the penetrating visage of the scanner.

He sat down in the cramped compartment and tried to be calm as he waited for the journey to begin. But it did not. He sat for several minutes, hoping that the trip home would be as quiet and uneventful as possible. As he waited for the scaler to begin moving he noticed that the doors were not closing. He also noticed that the red scanner light above the scaler door was not dimming, but instead was blinking. Some of the other passengers showed clear signs of confusion and impatience as they waited for the scaler to move.

A slew of unformed plans flew through his mind as he wondered if the scaler would ever begin its journey. Before he could consider his next steps, an abrupt alarm began beeping in a low monotone. The red light flashed with an even greater frequency. The other passengers did not know what was happening, but they now had a sense that something was going wrong. They started to display their irritation. Feeling that the situation was turning critical, he lept out of his seat and darted out the door. He plunged back into the cacophony of the terminal. Moments after he did so, the scaler doors closed and it resumed its route unhindered.

Back in the terminal atrium, he began to plot his fastest course to the residential levels. He had seen no scanners – no red lights – when traversing the hallways of the apartment levels. This may be a haven from the scanners. He wasn't sure how he was going to get home but he was already growing weary of the scanners' watchful eyes. If he could escape their gaze he could think.

After rising two levels he was once again in the dingy hallways of the apartments. The moldy air stung his dysfunctional lungs in a way that he never noticed before. In a wandering haze he staggered his way through the residential levels. He passed a door leading to a maintenance stairway. He opened it to find a quiet, empty set of stairs that led to several different storage rooms on floors above and below him. Feeling that this was as safe a haven as he would find, he sat down with the bundled baby on his lap and began to collect his thoughts.

He queried his UNI for floor plans of the twin towers. He was quite familiar with them but he never had to traverse them with the avoidance of public places in mind. There was plenty of residential space across most levels of the towers, but none of that space provided open access to a cruiser. Public, retail, or commercial enterprises crowded all the accessible platforms. After agonizing for several minutes over the blueprints, he settled on a risky plan of action.

"Caspian." Pontius initiated a new convo.

"Captain! We were just talking about you. You have plans tonight! It's going to be one for the ages."

Caspian was Pontius's best friend, but at times Caspian's careless voice could grate on him. He suppressed his own annoyance and waited for Caspian to calm down.

"I need your help." There was a long pause as he struggled to take in another breath. "Do you have your cruiser?"

The pained nature of Pontius's speech would have shocked a normal person. Caspian was oblivious.

"We're in the Nighthawk right now. Should we meet you somewhere?"

Pontius was not pleased with the inference of "we" but he was in no condition to dictate terms, so he carried on with his instructions.

"I need for you to pick me up at the Colonus Tower."

Pontius could hear Caspian's scowl coming through the convo. There were few things more affronting to Caspian than low-rent districts. He again waited for Caspian's inevitable response.

"Colonus Tower? Slumming, are we? Why don't you just meet us in Aerondale? It's not far and they have some fabulous restaurants. Are you hungry?"

"Caspian, you're not listening to me." He paused again as he drew in another breath through the quagmire of his lungs. "I can't travel on my own right now. I need for you to pick me up."

"Well, ummm, sure, Captain. What level should I dock at?"

"I need you to pick me up on the roof."

There was a new, awkward pause as Caspian searched his UNI for schematics. He couldn't remember there ever being a docking station atop the Colonus Tower. Querying public records confirmed what he already knew.

"There's no public landing on that roof. Where else can I pick you up?"

"I can't explain now, but you can't pick me up at any of the public platforms on the Colonus Tower." Caspian tried to interject but Pontius continued with his instructions. "You can't pick me up at any of the public platforms on the Colonius Tower either. In fact, you can't pick me up in any public place." He sat for a moment while those words sunk into Caspian's brain. "Do you understand what I'm saying?"

"Yay, I believe I do."

"So I need you to get to the roof as soon as possible and take me home from there."

Caspian's withered mind was racing with the possibilities. He wanted to delve right into an inquiry but he could see that this was not a time for joyful conversation. He decided to turn toward the practical.

"Colonus Tower is 150 stories tall. With no public platform on the roof, that means there are no wind stabilizers in place. Do you have any idea what the winds are like at an altitude of 500 meters?"

"Are you afraid that you can't pilot in those winds?" Pontius knew how to sting Caspian's pride.

"No, Captain!" Caspian lied. His piloting skills had been eroding for years. "But I'm afraid that you'll blow off the roof before I can pick you up."

"Let me worry about that. I just need you to get here as fast as you can."

"Yay-un. We're over Bull Run right now. It will take us at least 45 minutes to get there."

"Confirmed. I'll see you on the roof."

Pontius lingered for a moment on the thought of Caspian attempting stable flight in hurricane-force winds. It was a plan that was far from ideal but he could think of nothing better at the time being.

***

Caspian had once been a world-class pilot of anything that flew either terrestrially or in space. He spent the first thousand years of his life building a commercial empire out of several aviation companies. Under the ancient model of Howard Hughes, Caspian was a pilot first, a businessman second. There were few things he enjoyed more than being in the command seat of a cockpit.

His companies first built cruisers. They were avian toys allowing Centrian's elite to shuttle across the islands of the archipelago. He later acquired shuttle pod companies. They built the jump ships that shuttled goods and passengers to Torrenth's sister planets. These companies grew to be commercial behemoths and Caspian was the face of the burgeoning industry. He was always the first to test-pilot the newest models. He was always the spokesman highlighting the features of those models to the press. He was the closest thing that the industry had to royalty.

There was little that he could now remember about his companies. He knew that they were his. He enjoyed the ongoing revenue that continued to buffet his bank accounts. But he could remember little of the day-to-day operations. After a few thousand years of growing his domain he reached a point of boredom. Once the boredom took hold his descent was swift and thorough.

Having accomplished all he could in business, he found himself unable to set a new course. This malaise, accompanied by the gradual and literal dulling of his senses, led him to withdraw from his empire. He committed himself to the relentless pursuit of new sensations. Over the course of several hundred years, he became a poster boy for the "zombie class".

The zombies were old souls who had lost their sense for the flavor of life. The older they became, the more that all the events of their lives unfolded before them as something viewed from a distance. They could see things happening around them. They understood that they were an active participant in the proceedings. Yet they no longer felt involved in the events of their own lives. For them, the pure carnal ability to feel had become dulled over time to the point where they no longer enjoyed the act of living.

Like most zombies, he pined for death. He prayed daily to his Priori for death. He dreamed about it. He fantasized about the sensation of dying. But despite this overt desire to end it all, he could not overcome his own survival instinct. He could not bring himself to commit suicide. He wished for death, but he took his Telomore daily. He abhorred the monotony of his being, but he kept the nanites active and flowing through his system. He would not take any steps necessary to end his life. He found himself locked in a perpetual state of no longer feeling alive but not being able to affect his own death.

While he counted the days of his endless existence, he concocted elaborate attempts to defeat the nothingness. He could barely taste his food or drink. Even the sensations of hunger and thirst were mute impulses in his calloused mind. So he ate and drank the most affronting concoctions he could get his hands upon. He did everything faster, harder, and with more fervor than his colleagues. But the irony was that in the midst of this zeal he felt everything so much less.

His innate sexual desire still drove him to pursue all manner of women but he did not gain any true pleasure from the act. He was more intent to experiment with thresholds of pain than to pursue an orgasm. He had long ago found an orgasm to be unattainable. At first, he was able to satiate his carnal desires by trying everything he had eschewed in his youth. He exhausted every avenue of BDSM. He paid for every disgusting pleasure. For a time, he found that men could bring him back to orgasm, but that novelty wore off long ago. He had pioneered new sexual techniques with virtual reality and androids. He tried animals. But at this point in his long life he could no longer even remember the last time he had achieved a true sexual release.

While some looked down on Caspian as a depraved and degenerate playboy, Pontius admired him. He had an annoying charm with women that Pontius could never emulate. Pontius was envious of the endless financial means afforded to him by his prior enterprise. Perhaps more than anything, Pontius envied the fact that Caspian had built so much and had created such a legacy. Caspian may not have been able to remember the building of his empire, but everyone understood that he had indeed built an empire. He designed those shuttles. He created those businesses. He grew those markets. Those were immutable historical facts, even if they were little remembered by Caspian himself.

Although it seemed improbable, Pontius still wondered if or when Caspian might work up the nerve to end his life. He found cruiser rides with him both exhilarating and terrifying. He felt at any moment that he might choose to plunge the cruiser deep inside the bowels of a Centrian skyscraper. And as his skills in the cockpit eroded, this possibility seemed ever more likely.

***

While he bided his time in the stairway he found himself gazing down at the child. For the first time it struck him how serene this kid was. It had at times fussed, cooed, gurgled, and even giggled, but he had yet to hear it cry. While he was carrying it through the walkway to the scaler terminal his labored gait lulled the child to sleep. It was only now, as they both sat in the stillness of the stairway, that the child awoke and looked up into Pontius's wide eyes. The two engaged in a bizarre staring contest for several minutes until the child broke out in a broad grin. When he found himself smiling back at the baby, it shocked him.

When the time was right, Pontius gathered as much strength as he was ever going to have under the circumstances. He rose with the child and left the stairway. Still carrying the baby like a duffel bag, he made it to the nearest elevator and ascended to the top floor. On the 150th floor, he found the maintenance stairway to the roof and a locked door. The lock was primitive and, even in his diminished state, his NCU training allowed him to make quick work of it. Ascending the final flight of stairs, he reached the last door. It broadcast safety warnings and screamed of restricted access.

As he opened the door, the blast of wind shocked him, despite the warnings he had received earlier from Caspian. Much to his relief, the Nighthawk was waiting on the roof. It wasn't parked because to do so would have left it to blow off in the hurricane winds. Rather, it was hovering 1-2 meters above the roof. It flew into the wind at a variable speed allowing it to remain almost stationary. When Pontius first saw this he was rather impressed, as this took a great deal of manual skill on the part of Caspian.

Caspian maneuvered as close as he could to the door, but there were still at least five meters to traverse on the open roof. Pontius convo'd Caspian to make it clear that he was going to make a dash for it and to be ready. He stood for a moment in the doorway with his shoulder wrenched against the door. The winds, while unpredictable, were at least coming from a standard direction. They would rise, and fall, and rise again in rough cycles. By timing these cycles Pontius was able to make a dash for the cruiser at the most opportune time. With a death grip on the papoose, Pontius sprinted through the driving rains and lunged at the Nighthawk just as the hatch opened. After an awkward and painful shuffling, he found himself in the back of the cruiser with the hatch safely closed. The cruiser ascended to escape the danger of the building.

As soon as Pontius felt situated, he looked up to find an entire cabin of people staring at him. Caspian had gone into autopilot and had turned all his attention to Pontius. Sitting beside him upfront was Conti, who openly gaped at Pontius. Next to Pontius in the backseat was Telarus and just beyond him sat Kryx. Telarus and Kryx stared at him.

Children were so rare on Centrian – even licensed children – that it was a shock to even see one in their presence. For anyone who knew Pontius, this was outright unsettling. His friends would have bet money that they would never see a baby in his arms.

Pontius felt a pang of annoyance at the crowd assembled around him. This was too much attention for such a delicate situation. He was also annoyed by the presence of Kryx and, to a lesser degree, Conti. But he knew that he had neither the ability nor the right to demand the terms of his rescue. So he bit his lip and tried to gain his bearings. He had not expected Conti to stay with Caspian for more than even a few days. He was more surprised that Caspian was myopic enough to keep this Kryx character in their company.

"What..." Caspian's voice stalled for a moment in an uncharacteristic display of confusion, "is that?"

This was not the audience Pontius would have picked for such a revelation so he parsed his words with care.

"That's a baby." He thought that a mere statement of the obvious might allay their curiosity until they could at least arrive at his apartment. He was wrong.

"And whose baby is it?" Caspian allowed the inquisitiveness to drip from his voice like honey.

The simplicity of this question took Pontius by surprise. Its parents were dead but he wasn't sure what that meant now for this baby's ownership. The scenario was such a surprise to him that he hadn't thought this far ahead. He couldn't even answer whose baby this was.

"Its parents are dead." He looked around the cabin and allowed those words to sink into the minds of the recipients.

"So you're..." Caspian's voice stalled again. He struggled for the proper way to define this scenario. "Watching this child for someone else?"

"Not exactly."

All four of his audience members stared at him with a pleading look that screamed, "And?"

"Look, I'll explain more about this when we get back to my place. I'm in some distress here."

Caspian shot a grim expression at Pontius and nodded, assessing his friend's predicament. He then turned back to the instrument panel and checked a few notes in his UNI. While he did this, the other three made no attempt to avert their stares. After a few minutes, Caspian leaned his head back and said, "When we get to your building, we can dock on the public landing, yay?"

"Nay!" Pontius's reply was sharp and instinctive. The forcefulness caught everyone off guard, including him.

"Captain, there's no roof access at The Bowery." He sat and stared straight ahead into the rain pelting the windshield, allowing the reality of his words to seep into Pontius. Pontius knew Caspian was right. The building sloped into an ever-finer needlepoint. It stabbed into the heavens with no horizontal surface. There were, of course, several public landing docks for cruiser access. There were many scaler platforms. But there was no roof to speak of and Pontius had no desire to trip an endless lineup of scanners as he walked into his own building.

"I need to stop and buy a suitcase."

This would normally have given Caspian pause. But given the already surreal nature of the proceedings, he instead said nothing. He changed course to descend to the nearest department store. It was no more than 10 minutes before the Nighthawk was pulling up to a landing dock on the side of just another anonymous skyscraper. Several minutes later the cruiser was resting on the platform. Caspian turned around to give an inquisitive look to his friend.

"Everyone wait here. I'll be right back." With little forethought, Pontius thrust the yellow bundle at Conti in the front seat and opened the hatch. Before he closed the hatch on the confused crew, he looked back inside and said, "Whatever you do, do not leave this cruiser until I come back."

As he walked across the platform he found himself wondering why he had thrust the child at Conti. He supposed it was an ingrained assumption that the woman in the cruiser would be best equipped to hold the child. The more he thought about it, the more he realized that Conti was non-matronly – edgy, raw, and not who you would trust your kids to. Nevertheless, he would only be gone for a few minutes and there would be no real parenting skills required.

After he reached the inner marketplace he identified the store most likely to carry the best selection of luggage. When he found the proper aisle he was relieved. They did indeed carry a wide array of bags, although the majority of them were ill-suited to his purpose. They were all constructed from the tanned hides of various sea creatures. Each one was polished, oiled, and stretched to provide the best protection in such a deluged environment. None of them was appropriate for his task.

He was starting to feel antsy and was wondering if he would have to move to the next store when a salesman walked up to help. Before the salesman could utter a single word, Pontius blurted out, "Metal. Where are your metal suitcases?"

Pontius feared he was wasting his time. He had confused the salesman. But then a spark lit in the salesman's eyes and he said, "You need a *briefcase*, not a *suitcase*."

He led Pontius to the other end of the store where a smaller aisle offered a collection of briefcases. Most of these, like the luggage, consisted of sea hides. But in the corner he could see several shiny metal briefcases standing out like diamonds. The first two models he picked up were too narrow – maybe 10 centimeters in width. But the last one was almost double that, a hardy case that provided ample interior room. He purchased it and moved as fast as possible back to the cruiser.

Back in the Nighthawk, Pontius's first instinct was to grab the baby back from Conti. He wasn't sure why. She wasn't doing anything *wrong* with it – or to it – but he just wasn't comfortable with it in her lap. He then set the briefcase under his feet and told Caspian that he was free to head back to The Bowery and to dock at the public landing.

The remaining ride home took a full 30 minutes. Caspian flew with his normal reckless abandon. He offered no deference for the presence of an infant or for Pontius's degraded physical state. Pontius didn't want to complain. He was just happy to return home as fast as possible, even if that meant dealing with the nausea of Caspian's piloting.

About halfway home, Caspian leaned his head back. He wanted to clarify some of the lingering confusion in his mind. "So now that you have that suitcase, you don't mind using the public landing?"

"Nay." Pontius was still trying to escape with sparse responses.

"Then why couldn't you have bought that magical suitcase before we risked life and limb to pick you up on the top of the Colonus Tower?"

Caspian now had everyone's attention. The words he spoke were on everyone's minds and they were anxious to hear the answers.

"I couldn't get the suitcase because I was carrying the baby."

"Since when do luggage merchants refuse service to customers carrying babies?"

"Since those babies are unlicensed." Pontius's words rang throughout the cabin like a shotgun blast. Conti stared straight ahead into the watery windshield, not saying a word. Telarus had a look of shock on his face, buoyed by genuine concern. Kryx made no attempt to conceal a wide grin – a grin that made Pontius want to pummel his face.

The remaining 15 minutes passed in total silence. When they reached the public landing, Pontius told them that he was going to go ahead on his own to open his apartment. He was moving slowly at this point and he didn't want his own handicap to become a liability as they moved from the landing to his apartment. Before he left the cruiser, he opened the briefcase and placed it on Telarus's lap. He then picked up the baby and placed it inside. Before he could close the top, he looked at it squirming in its bright yellow papoose and said, "I'm sorry."

"There's at least 15 minutes of air in there. Give me a few-minutes head-start so I can get to my apartment and get it unlocked. Then come behind me. Move swiftly, but don't run. I don't want you banging the poor kid around in this coffin."

Caspian nodded his head but was also confused.

"Why is the kid in the briefcase?"

"The metal casing will block the bioscanners."

Caspian's expression portrayed more confusion. "Bioscanners? What bioscanners?"

"Trust me. I don't have time to explain right now. Just come behind me with the baby."

As he walked through the public landing – a landing he had traversed thousands of times – he looked all around him and saw the scanners. They were everywhere and he had never before seen them during any of his commutes. He left the landing and traversed the shops that fronted his residential entrance. Each shop in turn featured its own scanner at each doorway. It was a spectacle that now baffled him.

As he slogged through the public areas, at one point he looked back. He could see Telarus and the rest of the crew making their way through the far end of the landing. He scanned around the periphery for any sign of red lights. There were none. He breathed a pained sigh of relief and he continued on to his apartment.

Moria tried to fling herself against Pontius as he came in the door. He held his left hand out like a traffic cop, making it clear that she should come no further. He hunched over and asked her to prop some pillows up on the couch. With no care for his stained clothing, he plunked himself down in convalescent exhaustion.

The last thing he saw before passing out was Telarus walking through the door with the briefcase in hand, followed by the others.

Chapter 6 – The Commitment Stands

The muddled sounds of conversation came wafting back to Pontius like voices heard through a waterfall. He laid there for quite some time with his eyes closed, gradually returning to consciousness. As he did, the voices became clearer, but they didn't comprise a cogent discourse.

The constant, throbbing pain of his journey had left him. In a few restful hours the nanites had already managed to repair any of the acute damage that would have caused him immediate pain. If it weren't for the elephant he felt sitting on his right lung he may have believed himself recovered. The nanites performed many medical wonders but they were incapable of repairing entire structures. They could not re-inflate a lung. They could not replace an organ. Their healing powers were impressive, but still limited. He realized he would require surgery.

As he began to pry his eyelids open he moved his gaze around the room without bothering to turn his head. The previous cast from the cruiser was still there. They sat idly in his living room and passed thoughts between each other as to what was happening and how he had ended up in this situation.

Kryx was sitting in the large chair in front of Pontius's desk. Pontius would not have appreciated anyone – least of all, Kryx – sitting in his desk chair, but he was not going to protest at the time being. More annoying to him was the fact that Kryx had removed the effigy of one of Pontius's Priori from the altar in the hallway. He was tossing it between his hands - from one hand to other and then back again like a juggling ball.

Telarus, Conti, and Caspian sat around the dining room table. Caspian was voraciously eating an array of foods arranged before him in small bowls. Conti and Telarus were playing a game of Battlefield. It was clear from the initial glance that the game was a secondary diversion to the conversation. Even from across the room, Pontius could see that Telarus held a commanding position. But he did nothing of consequence with it as the two played out their moves.

Although perturbed by Kryx's presence, Telarus's participation in this impromptu conference comforted him. Pontius rarely said anything to Telarus, but it wasn't because he held any ill will toward him – quite the opposite. Telarus often struck Pontius as being so upright, so logical, so consistent in his actions that they never had much in common. Yet somehow Telarus was a frequent member of Caspian's inner circle and Pontius was grateful for it. During some of their more delicate adventures, Telarus was the only person in the room that Pontius could trust.

Telarus was a lieutenant in the Live Army, a quasi-militaristic brigade maintained by LiveLong. Its sole purpose was policing the market for counterfeit Telomore. The government granted LiveLong carte blanche to enforce its patents anywhere in Centrian. LiveLong found that funding this army was a small price to pay to enforce its exclusive patent. It was much more effective than trying to rely on public authorities.

A Dusk Forever Waning

Telarus lived in LiveLong barracks where he led a small squadron of enlistees. Although he dressed in civilian attire today, it was not uncommon to find him in the informal Live Army uniform. It consisted of black pants with long black boots, form-fitting blue t-shirts with the LiveLong logo (a double helix twisted into the shape of an infinity symbol), and a black baseball cap also sporting the same logo. Even when he had his cap off, his dense, cropped black hair almost seemed like an extension of the uniform itself.

He had a quiet air about him and he never spoke for the novelty of hearing his own voice. He could listen for hours in an intense situation before offering a few sage sentences that solved the matter for everyone. Like Moria, he was also a memoriae. During his long periods of silence he searched through years of memories for the proper experience to draw upon. The scarcity of his words ensured that when he did speak, he had the attention of those around him. His militaristic bent meant that he would try, whenever possible, to work within the confines of the system, but he was not naïve. He understood the practical realities of this world. He offered valuable advice even when his colleagues engaged in questionable or dangerous activities.

If Telarus had any blind spot it was in his undying, almost irrational support for his employer. He didn't view his work at LiveLong as a profession – it was a lifestyle. He didn't view LiveLong as just an employer. They were the pharmaceutical engine by which billions were magically granted an endless life. Everyone respected his opinions on a wide array of topics. But it was impossible to have a balanced conversation with him regarding his employer. He was an unabashed LiveLong evangelist. Caspian had warned Conti not to make any mention of her dealings in counterfeit Telomore in Telarus's presence. There was no way that such a conversation could end well. As far as Telarus knew, Conti was just a bartender.

Pontius made a conscious effort to sit upright on the couch, a move that grabbed everyone's attention. Although Telarus and Caspian urged him to lie back down, he felt determined to get off his back. Even with the full support of the couch, he felt a dizziness rush to head. He assumed the dizziness to be temporary, but did not feel it subside.

He surveyed the room and asked, "Where is it?"

Caspian had a blank expression on his face. "Where is what?"

"The child – where is the child?"

Conti did not raise her head from the Battlefield board but instead nodded toward the bedroom. "Moria has been trying to get him to sleep."

Pontius nodded. As though on cue, Moria emerged from the bedroom with the baby on her arm. "I changed him using one of your hand towels. It's all we had to suffice for a diaper. I can't get him to sleep – he's hungry. Pontius, what are we going to feed him?"

He made a weak attempt to motion his arm toward the kitchen and said, "I have a freezer full of food and the pantry is full of dehydrated snacks."

Moria frowned at him. "Should I just fry him up a filet? You ridiculous oaf. What do you have that I can feed a baby?"

He stared straight ahead and provided no direct reply. It was a simple enough question but he realized for the first time that he didn't even know what babies ate. There would be no breast milk for him here, and beyond that he was clueless to a baby's dietary needs. He performed a mental inventory of his sparse food stores. He could latch onto nothing that would be palatable, or even digestible, for the child. Faced with Pontius's non-reply, Moria walked into the kitchen and rummaged through the cupboards.

A long moment of silence passed amongst the group before Caspian decided to take the reins. "So, Captain... What is going to become of this new, ummm, crew member?"

Pontius made little attempt to reply, furrowing his brow and shaking his head. "I..." He looked around the room again and could see that he had everyone's undivided attention. "I'm not exactly sure."

"Hmmm..." Caspian put his food down and stared at his friend. "This child – this child is... unlicensed, correct?"

"Aye."

Caspian made no attempt to parse this confirmation, instead letting it settle upon the other group members like a fog.

"As an NCU agent, it is your job to kill unlicensed humans – typically, babies – correct?"

"Aye."

"So you're going to kill this baby, correct?"

"Nay." Pontius's reply was quick and decisive.

"Hmmm..." Caspian grabbed something from one of the bowls in front of him and began nibbling on it hungrily. "So how is it that a decorated NCU agent – a man whom I happen to know has performed his job in a stellar fashion for many hundreds of years – finds himself in possession of a baby such as this one?"

"The baby has been paid for."

Caspian seemed to relax a bit at this news. "Oh! So you need to deliver it to someone else?"

Pontius shook his head again. "Not exactly."

"Then who paid for the baby?"

"Its parents. They paid handsomely for this baby to live."

"Then shouldn't you bring the baby back to its parents?" This line of questioning intrigued Caspian and the vague nature of Pontius's replies did not seem to bother him in the least.

"I can't. They're dead."

This last statement set off the computing alarms in Caspian's head. He put his food down again and shook his head as though he were trying to clear a physical roadblock from his neural pathways. "So the parents paid you for the life of this child, but now those parents are dead? And if those parents are dead, then the payment they made no longer matters, correct?"

Pontius now stared at Caspian with a look of true bewilderment. He understood the nature of Caspian's words, but he could not abide by their logic.

Coming from his friend, this line of reasoning confused him. He furrowed his brow again and looked into Caspian's eyes from across the room.

"Its parents paid a price – an extreme price – for the legitimate life of their child. That baby is supposed to have a Vitapass and the payment they made was supposed to ensure the delivery of that Vitapass."

"So give the baby its Vitapass and be done with it."

This line of discussion had Conti sitting at full attention. She made some weak attempt to appear nonchalant but she could not hide her interest in the subject. Caspian's tone was one of pure matter-of-fact simplicity. The equation was easy to solve in his mind.

"You don't understand. I wasn't able to secure the Vitapass."

At this point Kryx jumped in with an unwelcome and smiling response, "Then why didn't you just return the payment and leave?"

"For some payments, there is no refund. Some things cannot be undone."

This last statement left Telarus in a state of confusion. He was not privy to all the inner workings of Pontius's deals. Caspian said nothing but nodded grimly, understanding full well what this meant. Pontius assumed that Kryx was just as oblivious as Telarus, but Kryx just smirked at Pontius and said nothing. Moria was still rummaging through cabinets, unable to hear the gist of the conversation.

Kryx grasped Pontius's Priori in one hand and squeezed it until he could hear the plaster starting to crumble under his grip. He leaned forward and stared at Pontius. The hair on his head throbbed as though it was keeping time with his chemically stimulated heartbeat. "So because you could not provide the Vitapass, and you could not return the payment, you chose to murder the parents instead?"

Most of the room missed the irony of Kryx passing moral judgment. The word murder hit Pontius's mind like a hammer and brought within him an angry, defensive reaction. He held his emotion in check and returned Kryx's gaze in kind. "I have murdered no one. I am often required to kill parents in the course of my normal duties. Removing unlicensed humans is not an activity that spawns placid compliance from the average parent. I had no intention of killing anyone when I arrived at their apartment. This was supposed to be a simple deal. Sometimes," and here Pontius paused to collect his thoughts, "things get complicated."

He thought he had done sufficient work in rebutting Kryx's inquiries, but Kryx was not satiated. "You are an NCU agent. Your job – one that I'm told you excel at – is to eliminate unlicensed humans. So you tried to consummate a deal, and that deal turned sour. The simple fact is that deals turn sour every day. There's nothing so unusual in that. In this botched deal, the parties were so affronted that it ended in violence. Am I tracking things properly so far?"

Pontius had no desire to feed Kryx's line of questioning but it was clear that Kryx was waiting for a reply. "Yes, that's correct."

"The botched deal is done. Over. As you so gracefully explained, the terms of the deal cannot be undone. But the deal itself was between you and two deceased individuals, meaning that the deal is no longer valid. So I place it to you now, Agent Of The State, why would you not just do your job and eliminate the unlicensed child rather than smuggling it around in cruisers and briefcases?"

Pontius became agitated. His agitation was not only with Kryx, although he was a convenient target. He could see from the expressions around the room that Kryx was voicing what was already on everyone's mind. It was annoying that no one else could see the basic tenets of this equation.

"Look. Those parents may be dead, but the deal was made nonetheless. I received full payment for that child to have a long, legitimate life and the unfortunate death of its parents does nothing to change that commitment. It's not that child's fault that it has no Vitapass. It's not that child's fault that it has no parents. It's not the parents' fault that I wasn't able to immediately deliver on my commitment. But damn it, I *will* deliver on my commitment. I will honor my word. A price was paid and I have received that payment. I will give that child the life that was paid for."

His voice had risen and the abrupt end of his statement left an awkward silence ringing throughout the living room. Moria now stood on the threshold of the living room. She hovered over the dining room table and soaked in his words. The baby munched on some sticky substance she had spread over her fingers as a crude feeding mechanism. The others soaked in the veracity and the finality of his words. They took turns looking at each other, then at Pontius, then at each other again. Pontius was catching his breath after the speech he had just delivered.

Kryx looked out the window at the rain pelting the glass. Without turning his head or his chair, he asked the basic question, "Then what exactly will you do?"

Caspian was more than a little dumbfounded by Pontius's position but he was not going to abandon trying to parse the meaning. "You can't honestly tell me that you're going to try to *raise* that child? An *unlicensed* child?"

Pontius somehow managed a faint chuckle and shook his head. "No. Absolutely not. No one understands better than me the foolhardy nature of trying to raise an unlicensed human. Besides, there's no way that I can be terminating unlicensed humans on one hand and raising one on the other."

This bit of logic relieved Caspian. However, he was still annoyed by Pontius's inability to do the obvious task and just kill the baby. Pontius was telling only half the truth, though. It was easy enough to hide behind the logical excuse here.

No one could fault an NCU agent who didn't want to raise an unlicensed human on his own. But the simple fact was that Pontius had no desire to raise a child even if he thought he could do it safely. He had never fostered any paternal instinct.

During his lifetime he had received three separate Vitapasses via legitimate means. One came from each of his parents when they passed away and another from an uncle who committed suicide. On each occasion he opted to revert the Vitapasses back to the state. There was no mechanism by which one could sell a Vitapass on the open market. If you couldn't, or wouldn't, use one willed to you it went back to the state. After a life spent killing children he could not imagine one in which he might raise one.

Upon hearing these words, Moria began walking across the room and sat down on the couch next to Pontius. Her head was down, avoiding his gaze. The baby bounced on her knee and drooled at everyone, and at no one, all at the same time.

"I can raise him."

An incredulous pause filled the room. Pontius looked agape at every person in the room, as if they could explain the logic in this statement. He received nothing reassuring or explanatory in their eyes. He returned his sight to Moria but she looked down at the baby, refusing to make eye contact.

"How in the world – nay, *why* in the world would you ever want to raise an unlicensed?"

She sat for a moment, searching for the proper response that would sway him.

"You sold this child a life. You made the commitment. I can give it that life."

"And how exactly would you propose to do that? Are you going to flee to the sewers to raise it amongst the stench of the street walkers?" Although she was trying to offer a helpful alternative, Pontius's tone was only scornful in return.

"I'll give him a Vitapass."

Pontius gripped the pillow next to him in frustration and hastily motioned for the others to give them some privacy. Even after the others had filed out and into the kitchen, he lowered his voice as though he were sneaking past a military checkpoint. He leaned in closer to bridge the distance.

"Certain things are not easily discussed amongst friends."

She had a saddened air, but stoicism steeled her face as she continued to stare downward. "I know, but we don't have many options here. We have to do something."

"And what makes you think that you can issue more Vitapasses? Have you determined what went wrong?" Pontius's sternness gave way to inquisitiveness as he started replaying the events that led to their current situation.

"No."

"And this – this, glitch. Was this temporary? Will you be able to issue Vitapasses again?"

"I don't know. When I realized you were in trouble I headed over here as fast as I could. I didn't have time to further investigate what took place."

"You realize this is bad, Moria? This is so very bad."

She sat for a moment as she considered what was going to become of her job – and her life – if she could no longer issue Vitapasses. She looked up at him, then back at the baby, then back at him again.

"I'm acutely aware."

Pontius now looked around the empty room. It was as though he expected the furnishings to answer the questions flying through his mind.

"Let's assume for a moment that this is not a temporary obstacle. Let's assume for a moment that there is no Vitapass forthcoming." He paused while he allowed the gravity of those words to sink in for her. "And let's also assume for a moment that we are not both sent off to a penal island for the next 10,000 years."

He paused again as the fear of this proposition swept over her countenance. "How then do you propose to grant this child a life?"

Although his tone was antagonistic, this was not a rhetorical question. He wanted to know how she would propose keeping the baby free from PC for millennia. He now stared at her and resolved to wait through any length of awkward silence. He would wait until she could provide some kind of meaningful answer. After just such a pause, she shrugged, saying, "They're out there, Pontius. He wouldn't be the only one. There are unlicensed all around us – all around Centrian. They find a way. They escape the authorities. They survive. I can raise him. I can keep him safe."

At this, he attempted to throw up his arms in dismay at such a ridiculous notion. He would have succeeded were it not for the searing pain in his chest. "Oh hell, Moria! You can't be serious. I've been killing these people for as long as I can remember, and you think that this baby will be the one exception?"

She now affected a pleading tone. "Come now. You know it to be true. There are those who evade such a fate. Surely you know that every soul on this planet isn't sanctioned through Population Control?"

She believed this to be a salient point but it just annoyed him further. "Aye, of course I know that. They ghosts - the revenants of the underworld. They eat from the compactors. They burrow underground. They dare not show their faces for fear of being exterminated. They lead the lives of vermin."

She tried to interject – to convince him that she could save the child from this fate. She tried to muster the words that would at least allow her to try. But before she could make any progress he stared at her with fierce eyes and said through his teeth, "That is *not* the life we sold his parents."

And with that she knew it was useless. She rose and walked back to the kitchen. As she did, she motioned for the others to return. They all resumed their positions as though nothing of real consequence had taken place.

Caspian was now hovering over a drink, ruminating over the bits and pieces he had caught from their conversation. "So if you're not going to raise this child, who is? And how do you ever hope to provide it the legitimacy to which you've committed?"

Pontius gazed out through the same window that hypnotized Kryx. When he was lacking answers to life's questions, he found it soothing to watch the random patterns. Water smashed or drizzled down the large bay window, depending upon the direction and force of the wind. This was now his life's largest question and he had no good answers.

"I don't honestly know. But I do know this – I have to figure something out soon. That baby can't be transported through public spaces and it will be extremely difficult to maintain its existence in the normal Centrian environments."

"Why do you say that?" Conti was confused.

"There are bioscanners all around the public areas. I never noticed them before, but when I was trying to reach the scaler they were going off all around me as I traversed the public walkways, and when I finally boarded the scaler with the baby in my hands, it wouldn't move until I had gotten back off. I suspect that they are widespread all around Centrian."

"Bioscanners? Where? I've never seen any bioscanners." Conti's voice was incredulous but Telarus countered.

"I've seen them myself. They're ubiquitous – so much so that you've probably never even noticed them. Most of them look like basic security cameras but they scan DNA signatures and they turn red when an unlicensed human passes. They communicate with headquarters. They monitor the movements of the licensed and the unlicensed. They are the eyes and ears of Population Control."

Conti may have objected further, but Telarus always had the effect of quelling any potential debate when he chimed in.

Kryx began tossing the mangled Priori effigy in the air again, staring at the ceiling as it rose, then fell into his hand, then rose again. Without averting his gaze he stated, "Vitapasses can be acquired."

Everyone knew to what Kryx was referring. The nation was replete with desperate individuals. Some of those individuals took part in unauthorized death matches. Both participants signed the contract necessary to will their Vitapass to a given beneficiary. The beneficiary was contractually bound to rip up the will of the winner. This ensured that the winner would still keep the right to their Vitapass and earn a huge sum of money in return for their victory. The loser's Vitapass went to the beneficiary. For those who lived in squalor and were willing to fight to the death in return for a chance at great wealth, it was a golden ticket out of the slums. The matches were illegal but it was easy to subvert any regulatory stricture. All that was necessary was to find two desperate souls and one wealthy benefactor who desired a Vitapass.

Caspian and Conti perked up at the hopeful thought of such a solution, but Pontius's lip curled into a sneer at the suggestion. He had a special hatred for those who would sacrifice their lives for a gambling shot at wealth. He had his share of carnal desires. But he could not fathom someone so enamored with financial ease that they would put their life on the line. Furthermore, he could not justify purchasing a Vitapass at the expense of an innocent. He did not promise those parents a Vitapass by arranging the slaughter of some vagrant. He promised a Vitapass in return for a temporary act of degradation. That act was transient and it would allow for the continuation of full, normal lives.

Moral concerns aside, Pontius had a much more practical reason for dismissing such an idea. To get a man to commit to a death match, even a desperate man in a horrific state of life, it took a fabulous sum of money. That sum was well beyond even Pontius's comfortable means. Even if a man offered participation in return for a modest sum the price would still skyrocket. Those who brokered these matches – working on commission - would drive up the price. The beneficiary was basically buying a Vitapass from whichever participant ended up losing. The market for those Vitapasses was exceedingly tight. So with two participants identified, a bidding war would ensue for the right to be the beneficiary in the match.

A Dusk Forever Waning

The only man in the room who would be capable of footing such a bill was Caspian. Although he was free with his money when hosting others, he was tight – even with friends – whenever someone would ask him for funds. Besides, Pontius was far too proud to ask Caspian for the money anyway.

"I'm assuming that all we'd need to establish a death match would be someone with enough contacts to broker the deal – a, ummm, *middleman*. Am I correct, Kryx?" Pontius made no attempt to disguise the scorn in his voice. As a reply, Kryx swiveled his chair around to Pontius and flashed him another smile.

"Forget it. The child will not be purchasing life at the cost of someone else's."

"That's a high road to take for someone who murdered the child's parents."

Pontius put a death grip on the pillow to his side. He wished in vain that he had the physical stamina at this moment to dispatch of Kryx. By Pontius's way of thinking, he had never in his life murdered anyone. He had never struck another in anger. He had never initiated a physical altercation. He had never taken a life for which he was not already authorized by PC. But every word that dripped from Kryx's bitter maw made Pontius re-evaluate the utility of an outright murder.

He knew that he could subvert this whole line of discussion by pointing out the fiscal infeasibility of the solution. But he was never comfortable talking about his personal finances. He was also uncomfortable with any implication he was asking for Caspian's direct assistance.

So he decided to hold tight to the moral argument and flatly reiterated his position, "I don't orchestrate death matches, nor do I participate in or facilitate them. You can talk about this all night if you please, but it's a complete non-starter."

Without acknowledging Pontius, Kryx made a waving gesture above his head. This indicated a dismissal of the topic. Conti and Caspian, who had once appeared so intrigued by the idea, now slumped in their chairs. They were mentally spelunking for alternate solutions. Telarus sat and stared through the Battlefield board, no longer giving it any attention.

While the group sat in thought, Moria blurted out a logical question that Pontius found ridiculous. "What is his name?"

The question annoyed Pontius. What did it matter what the child's name was? He had never seen an official name for any of his targets. These unofficial children never had any registered name with the state. They never had any formal records or birth certificates. To have had such records would have implied legitimacy. That would have precluded Pontius's participation in the situation.

He wanted to avoid the question altogether but he could see that the innocent query intrigued the others in the room. Not considering the tactics of Pontius's typical engagements, he could see that they were all looking at him. They actually thought that he knew the child's name. He blathered incoherently for a moment. He waved his arm in a discombobulated gesture that meant nothing at all. Then he looked back at the baby stuck to Moria's arm still glomming onto the sticky mess on her fingers. For all its adorable characteristics, he couldn't help but think that it looked like some amorphous chunk. It latched to her arm and was now feeding off her in a bizarre parasitic dance.

"Chunk."

"*What??*" Moria was confused.

"I said, *Chunk.*"

"The kid's name is Chunk?" Moria was beyond incredulous. She began protesting but she could see the stonewall expression on Pontius's face. She knew that he was going to provide no further clarification or justification. She shot a pleading look around the room, hoping to feed off the others' indignation at such a ridiculous moniker. But the curiosity in their eyes drained away as soon as Pontius blurted out this "name". They gave no indication that they shared her disbelief. Feeling alone and outnumbered, she shrugged her shoulders and sat down at the table. Chunk still enjoyed the tasty mess on her fingers.

Another few minutes passed with everyone in solemn thought. Out of the blue, Conti said, "Centrian is home to more than 99 percent of the planet's population."

Everyone looked at her, not understanding the point of her statement. Kryx stared at her mockingly with wide eyes that begged for a continuation in the thought.

"Where does the other one percent live?" she asked.

Caspian piped up. "Oh, there are other islands, some of them are literally on the other side of the planet, but they are scant and absolutely tiny. I've flown over most of them at some point."

"But they're inhabited, nonetheless, right?" Conti was insistent with her premise.

"Yes, of course. They're technically, ummm, inhabited – but not in the same way that we see Centrian inhabited."

Conti didn't understand his direction. "How do you mean? How is a landmass inhabited differently?"

Caspian was dismissive but felt compelled to explain himself. "I mean that it's not a society in the way we all think of society."

"But are they *licensed*?" Pontius was intrigued.

Kryx jumped in before Caspian could finish his thought. "Yes, some of them are, and some of them aren't. There are refugees out there – the unlicensed, the criminal, the vagabonds – and there are some people who just don't fit in a civilized venue. I know some of those islands well. I trade with them."

"Who really cares if they are 'civilized'? I'm trying to think of some way to provide a positive future for Chunk." If Moria didn't know better, she would almost have mistaken Pontius's tone for one of caring paternalism.

"I go out to those islands, sometimes as frequently as every few weeks. They have access to some commodities out there that you just can't find in Centrian." Kryx was now refactoring himself in Pontius's desk chair and getting comfortable for an extended explanation. "Most of the islands are downright primitive. They only have electricity, in fits and starts that comes from generators. They are off the grid. They don't have UNIs. Their state of health – even their state of hygiene – can at times be shocking. Criminals take refuge there because there is no access to centralized law enforcement. The islands break into tiny tribes that are constantly warring. When one tribe defeats another, they override the village, rape the women, burn the men at the stake, and pillage whatever goods they can find. Very few of them can read and some of those tribes have been out there so long that they have their own dialects – dialects that are so severely branched from our language that they couldn't even communicate with you if they tried. The men participate in ritual homosexuality as a means of building inter-tribal bonds. Disease is rampant. Even those that seem 'healthy' have only learned to live in concert with the range of parasites that infests their bodies. Whenever I go there I have to barter with them because they have no centralized system of money. I have literally found myself trading shiny beads in return for goods and services."

Pontius was suspicious of these tales. He had heard such things of the outer islands, but he knew few people who had been there. Caspian claimed to have been to many of the islands long ago. But he could no longer remember much of substance with regard to their inhabitants or their state of life. The only person he knew that traveled to the islands with any regularity was Dania. She scoured distant atolls for spices and ingredients that formed the heart of her famous cuisine. He never remembered her telling any such stories of the inhabitants. Then again, he never remembered her telling any stories of the inhabitants, period.

He looked around him and began cataloging the accoutrements of a connected life. He could live without such niceties as manufactured furniture or a sturdy skyscraper over his head. But how could anyone persist without the grid? And how did one function without access to a UNI? With no computer-assisted memory, he imagined the savages as ignorant. They could keep no more than 400-years' worth of knowledge and memories around them.

As he pondered the consequences of that "savage" life, he became aware again of his belabored breathing. He was becoming exhausted, even though he had done nothing more than sit upright on his couch and talk. With every waking minute it seemed as though the weight on his chest grew and every breath became more painful. Pointing at his own chest, he looked at Kryx and said, "What would they do with something like this?"

Kryx replied with brutal deadpan, "They would die."

Pontius shuddered for a moment. As he shuffled through his UNI he could query every major injury he had suffered along 1,800+ years of life. Broken bones, sprains, and other minor orthopedic headaches had been often treated. But he had also replaced every major organ in his body – some of them multiple times. He had replaced both Achilles tendons. One of his anterior cruciate ligaments had been rebuilt. And then there were the acute illnesses.

"What does one do if, say, their appendix bursts?" Pontius was curious. He couldn't envision a scenario where medical care was not easily and quickly at hand.

"They suffer days of excruciating agony and, in some cases, they die of toxic shock."

Pontius had heard enough. "That is not the life that was purchased for Chunk."

No one in the room bothered arguing. His previous principled stand was so complete that it now seemed illogical to counter such a statement. If this was not the future he had promised for Chunk, then there was nothing that they could do to talk him out of it. Telarus experienced a pang of mild annoyance. He did not trust the stories given by Kryx. But he didn't know enough about the conditions on those islands to refute those stories either. Once he heard the verdict from Pontius he realized it was pointless to protest.

Pontius began to feel a wave of depression overcoming him. He was no closer to divining a solution and he was starting to wear down. Uncertainty was an uncomfortable state for him. There was nothing he could see as being more uncertain than the undetermined fate of Chunk or, for that matter, himself.

He sat listening to the rain battling the window. He wondered for the first time what might happen if his situation was to become known at NCU. He was confident that his word alone was good enough to keep anyone there from investigating Chunk's existence. But this assumed Chunk wasn't snuffed out by scanners, the narcs, or the rest of the surveillance apparatus stationed who-knows-where around Centrian. Would NCU fire him when they learned of his predicament? Would the Centrian authorities prosecute him? This was all uncharted territory. He was unaware of any precedent for an NCU agent harboring a known unlicensed human.

It seemed he would have to slip back into his quasi-coma and attack the problem after more rest. But Telarus's strident voice startled him.

"I have a solution." All eyes now focused on Telarus. "LiveLong has its own compound of unlicensed humans, right here in Centrian. I can get Chunk a home there."

This was stunning news to Pontius. "What? What do you mean by *compound*?"

"The LiveLong campus is vast, covering no fewer than twelve different towers in northwest Majorus. One of those towers is completely inaccessible to the public. It is solely dedicated to unlicensed humans. In LiveLong, we call them the *Diaspori* – they are people who we think of as the children of the LiveLong Corporation. They are almost all unlicensed and they are completely protected by LiveLong."

Pontius was flabbergasted. "How many of these 'children' are there?"

"Thousands."

"And you can get them Vitapasses?"

"Not exactly. They aren't issued Vitapasses – even LiveLong doesn't have the power to pull off something like that. But LiveLong has so much sway that we can give them essentially normal lives. They have UNIs and grid access. They have nanites and they enjoy the greatest health care in all of Torrenth. And of course, they have an endless supply of Telomore. They are, for all practical purposes, full Centrian citizens."

This stunned Pontius. It stunned everyone in the room. If this had come from anyone else's mouth they would have dismissed it as pure fantasy, but no one doubted Telarus's sincerity. Pontius looked at Caspian who just shrugged. Conti and Kryx were somewhat confused but could offer no dissent. Even Moria seemed relieved at the thought that Chunk might have a real home and a real life. Pontius smiled at Telarus. Telarus didn't return the smile. Instead, he nodded in reply, as if to convey that this alternative was safe, legitimate, and reliable.

After realizing that there was little else to discuss, Pontius gave a wave to the room and said, "I think Chunk just might have a home." And with that he fell back onto the couch and returned to his convalescent daze.

Chapter 7 – Live Long for LiveLong

It was one of the darker days in Pontius's recent memories. The cloud cover was so thick that it triggered the automatic lighting in every venue he passed. The rain came down not in droplets, but in great sheets crashing against every surface in their wake. With stunning regularity the skies exploded in grand bursts of lightning. It exposed a heavenly tapestry of clouds that were otherwise invisible to the naked eye. The bustling citizenry of Centrian was often immune to the annoying effects of wind and weather. But now they braced against the gales. They ducked for cover and sprinted from one sheltered edifice to another.

Pontius sat in a neon establishment. It catered to those who enjoyed drinking early and often. He just left the hospital that morning and he felt like a new man. The millstone weighing down his breath was now replaced with the efficient functioning of new lungs. The energy flowing through his system was well worth the days spent in stasis acclimating to his newest organs. He sipped his drink and waited for Telarus to arrive. Every rabid puff on his massive cigar was fuller and smoother than any in recent memory.

The two were meeting before the cross-island trek to LiveLong. Pontius trusted Telarus. He believed the explanation of the Diaspori. But this was still something that he had to see for himself. Telarus was going to expose something few non-employees ever saw – the inner workings of the LiveLong behemoth.

With impeccable timing, Telarus arrived just as Pontius was taking the final drags from his stogie. Although the bar offered efficient air filtration, an oppressive haze hovered over his table. Every thunderous crack rocked the bar. Pontius believed he could see the smoke itself shake and vibrate under the violent assault. Telarus sat at the table and greeted Pontius with a confused stare. Pontius said nothing.

"Where is Chunk?" Telarus's voice was calm but agitated.

The inquiry took Pontius off guard. "What do you mean? He's at the apartment with Moria. Where did you think he would be?"

Telarus paused for a moment while another volley of thunder rang through the enclosure. "I thought you understood our objective. I'm taking you into LiveLong."

He analyzed Pontius for some sign of recognition, but his search was fruitless. He gave Pontius a few more moments to compute the situation. When it was clear that this process was pointless, he leaned in closer to Pontius and lowered his voice.

"There are no public tours through LiveLong. We won't just be walking through the front doors and checking in with the receptionist. I can only get you in with the understanding that you have an unlicensed to join the Diaspori." Pontius was a little surprised, so Telarus paused again and waited for those words to sink in. "Do you understand?"

Pontius took the dying embers of his cigar and mashed them into the stone ashtray on the table. He ordered another drink and turned back to Telarus. "Look, friend. I have a baby, a human life, currently in my possession. You expect me – nay, LiveLong expects me – to just hand it over for the greater good of your vaunted corporation without so much as seeing these facilities? Without so much as meeting the people who will become his family?"

Telarus sat back again and tried to explain the tactical realities of his position. "That is exactly why we are going to LiveLong – you, me, and Chunk. It's already an incredible challenge to get an outsider through the gates. The security is fastidious. The technology is exquisite. This is highly unusual and I called in several favors to make this happen. They don't just welcome in the public on casual business."

Pontius placed his hand on his friend's shoulder and tried to comfort him. "My apologies. I guess I had a misunderstanding. I knew we were going to LiveLong today. I just didn't realize that you required me to bring Chunk. I've been in stasis for almost three days. My head is swimming. My wits aren't about me. I'm just a little groggy right now."

He lied. He knew exactly what he was doing. Although he trusted Telarus, he was also leery of Telarus's myopia for all things LiveLong. The deal offered to him seemed too good to be true. He was intent on investigating it before he saw his commitment as fulfilled. There was no proper inspection that was to happen while a slobbering kid was hanging on his shoulder.

Telarus began to relax somewhat, believing he understood. He sighed and said, "Good. Very good. Just call Moria and have her meet us here with Chunk then we'll be on our way."

"And how exactly do you propose that she does that?" Pontius withdrew another massive cigar from his trench coat and licked it voraciously. "We're 45 minutes from The Bowery and her only viable means of transportation would be via public scaler. How many bioscanners do you believe exist between here and The Bowery?"

Telarus tensed again, making no attempt to hide the agitated look on his face. "Then convo Caspian. His cruiser can bypass most of that."

Without saying a word, Pontius initiated a new convo with Caspian and patched in Telarus.

"Caspian!"

"Aye, Captain!"

"I need to ask a favor of you. Can you please pick up Moria and Chunk from my apartment, bring them here to meet me and Telarus at Executor, then ferry the four of us across Majorus to the headquarters of the LiveLong Corporation?"

The response was swift. "Nay, Captain! The fluctuator blew this morning. I'm confined to public transportation like a plebeian until it's fixed."

"That's too bad. I hope it's fixed soon. Out."

Once the line cleared Pontius looked at Telarus and said, "Well that's unfortunate." He lied. He had already coordinated this conversation with Caspian before he arrived at the bar.

Telarus shook his head with a quiet defiance. "Then this is over. We'll have to do this another day, another time."

Pontius sat up straight in his chair and pulled himself closer to Telarus. While still cradling his cigar he looked into Telarus's eyes and poured his soul into these next words. "There are 99 other agents out there just like me. An NCU agent could be knocking at my apartment door at this very moment. They've already picked him up on scanners. I don't know how much time he has. I'm asking you – I'm *begging* you – to just let me see this place first. You can blindfold me. You can handcuff me. You can ship me there in a crate if it makes you feel better. Just let me see what LiveLong does with these children and then we'll figure out how to get Chunk there."

The two men stared at each other for what felt like an hour. Telarus was tense, unhappy, and agitated. This was not part of his plan. Pontius stared back at him with an unyielding resolve. He provided no visual cue that his stance was negotiable or frivolous. Once half of his cigar had burned away in his smoky hands, Telarus leaned back in his chair and shook his head with an ominous chagrin.

"Let me make a few convos." And with that, Telarus stepped away from the table and left Pontius to his smoke.

Telarus walked to another set of massive windows some 20 meters away. His prim and muscular form created a dark outline against the raging skies outside. A few times every minute a brilliant blast of lightning bathed him in light. It turned his features crystal clear in this otherwise dark theater. Pontius could not hear any of the content of Telarus's discussions, nor did he make any attempt to eavesdrop. But Telarus's wild gesticulations made it evident that there was a great deal of debate taking place across the room. After 30 minutes of this pantomime, Telarus made his way back to the table and said, "I can get you in."

Pontius gave no acknowledgment of Telarus's pained nature. He gave a broad smile and nodded his head in relief. "Thank you."

Telarus offered no reply, opting just to stand again and motion toward the door. It was clear that he was ready to leave.

At the scaler platform, a crowd of harried travelers huddled under the nearest awning. When a scaler arrived, the mob sprinted across the open concourse and dove into the cabin with reckless abandon. Once in the scaler, everyone tried to scurry to relative dryness, only to realize the futility of their efforts. The scaler doors stayed open for a full 90 seconds. During this long period, the torrential winds blew into the cabin. They soaked all the passengers in a miniature maelstrom. The passengers had little choice but to sit and endure the dousing until the doors closed again.

The ride across Majorus was both long and silent. Pontius never expected much conversation from Telarus. But he assumed that he was especially quiet today in annoyance at the terms of this engagement. The translucent walls of the scaler offered nothing in the way of scenery. The angry blur of water pelted the transport as it made its way from one tower to another. They rode an express line, meaning that they skipped most of the menial stops at minor platforms. Still, every

15 minutes or so, the doors opened and the full rage of the Centrian storm spilled into the cabin again. This cycle repeated itself for a full two hours.

About 30 minutes out from their destination, the weather pattern subsided. The light drizzle that remained qualified for sunshine in the waterlogged minds of the travelers. This cessation allowed Pontius to better occupy his mind. He gazed outside the scaler at the various skyscrapers littering the Centrian skyline. After passing the Sinian Tower, the scaler made a sharp left and aimed itself down a massive alley. The alley was borne from the girding presence of skyscrapers on either side. The berth between these rows of towers was wider than usual. Pontius realized that the scaler was traveling down a grand aerial causeway.

At the far end of the causeway he could see the towers giving way to the LiveLong campus. In all Pontius's years he had never seen LiveLong's headquarters. Its presence was ubiquitous throughout the archipelago. It littered the commercial edifices with office spaces and retail centers. But he had never had any reason to visit their home base. He also never knew anyone to have gone inside who was not a LiveLong employee. The corporation was as insular as it was commercially dominant.

As the scaler moved closer to the campus the first thing he noticed was the barrier of empty land that ringed it like a moat around a castle. Only the wealthy on Centrian owned land. Only the audaciously, fabulously wealthy were so ostentatious in their riches that they would deign to leave plots of land empty. The barrier was several hundred meters in width and stretched out of sight in each direction around the campus. A dense canopy of trees covered the land – a sight rarer on Centrian than sunshine.

The campus itself was a glittering ring of a dozen towers. Each stood of its own right but it interconnected with the others in a way that made it clear that they were a part of a single cohesive whole. The outer towers formed an audience around a central skyscraper that was one of the tallest he had ever seen. The central tower was a twisted pair of skyscrapers. Walkways connected them at regular intervals. The entire unit mimicked a double helix stretching into the stratosphere. The towers in the outer ring were a deep, shiny black reminiscent of obsidian. The central helix shone in a brilliant white alabaster. The subsiding rain had coincided with a dramatic rising of the cloud ceiling. But the helix still darted well above the visible barrier of the cloud ceiling.

The isolation of the complex was striking. Centrian buildings connected to each other in a complex maze of scaler tracks and sheltered walkways. It was possible to walk across all Majorus – the largest island in the archipelago – without ever touching the ground. If walking was not desired, it was possible to take the many scalers that jumped from one elevated platform to another. Again, the traveler never touched the ground. There was a vast grid of streets at ground level, but those streets were ill-equipped for vehicles. The lowest castes of Torrenth crowded them – street walkers, the homeless, and petty merchants. A typical Centrian might go years without ever setting foot on the ground.

But LiveLong's campus was an island unto itself. The undeveloped land that surrounded it was not just for show. It isolated the campus from all other buildings. There were no walkways that spanned the divide. There were no scaler tracks that crossed over to the LiveLong towers. In fact, there weren't even any platforms adorning the outer walls of the LiveLong buildings. They were eerily smooth and Pontius realized there must be only a handful of entrances to the entire complex.

The scaler descended to street level – something that never happened on most scaler routes. As the elevation fell the grandiose effect of the LiveLong buildings escalated. The scaler slowed its descent until it came to rest at a ground-based station on the outer edge of the treed ring. They both exited and stood for a moment while Telarus waited for the bulk of the travelers to find their way around him.

Once the scaler departed and the pedestrian crush subsided, Pontius felt as though he was on the cusp of two different worlds. To the south lay the typical urban explosion of Centrian. Skyscrapers ranging from brilliant to dingy littered the sky and blocked his view as he gazed back at his world. To the north lay the forested outer ring of LiveLong. Rising above it in the distance were the awesome towers creating its framework. Cutting straight through the forest was a broad walkway leading to soaring gates at the far end. Hundreds of people traversed this walkway in both directions.

Telarus touched Pontius on the shoulder and motioned for them to head into LiveLong. Pontius paused for a moment, staring back at the Centrian side of the scaler station. Sitting in a long row at the edge of the station was a gaggle of dogs. They sat motionless and made no attempt to rise from their position. Each one of them portrayed an anxiousness, as though poised to fetch a stick or catch a scrap. They panted with long tongues sagging groundward. They seemed disciplined in their resilience, holding their position even as pedestrians pushed past. Pontius wanted to point this out to Telarus. Perhaps he expected an explanation. But Telarus motioned again with an impatience indicating that he was not interested in minutiae. Pontius turned and joined him on the brisk journey through the walkway.

From the heights of the scaler, he first assumed this jungle must be overrun with homeless vagabonds. Traversing the walkway, he now saw that this was impractical. The trees were all thick tropical species. They spread out to grab every ounce of sunlight that might somehow peak through the Torrenthian sky. The trees did not form a traditional canopy because there was no dearth of branches along the height of any given tree. They all featured branches and vines and tendrils that shot out in every possible direction from their bases to their tops. The result was that this forest was dense – so much so that he could not see more than a few meters through the undergrowth. He could not imagine anyone but the most desperate of miscreants trying to carve a home from such surroundings.

As soon as they entered the walkway, Pontius's ears filled with an unfamiliar din. He presumed it to be some kind of cacophonous sound pumped from speakers stationed in the underbrush. But the more he concentrated on its random components the more he realized that it came from an organic source. The noise was so loud that it made regular conversation impractical. He looked to

Telarus to see if this was unusual in any way. His scripted countenance conveyed that this noise was typical. After traversing half of the path, he realized that this discombobulated symphony was the song of thousands of birds. He could see precious few of them. But if he concentrated on a particular point in the undergrowth he could glimpse a few flitting from one branch to another.

As they approached the far end of the walkway the wall came into view. It was eight meters tall, black, and glassy-smooth. It formed a barrier between the forested ring and the LiveLong complex. At various points the wall gave way to one of the outer towers. The towers comprised part of the wall itself. There was a five-meter dead zone between the forest and the wall that consisted of nothing more than gravel.

All the hundreds of pedestrians were passing into and out of LiveLong through a central gateway. The gateway itself consisted of a dozen individual checkpoints. Two security guards manned each checkpoint and each checkpoint featured a turnstile. This gave the impression that these people were visiting a grand amusement park. But the guards at each checkpoint looked nothing like a concessionaire. The guards wore LiveLong uniforms. Each one featured a long pole slung across his back. The poles were capped with electrical charges used to coral a large crowd in a stampede. They also had several weapons displayed in holsters hung from their belts. They were all tall, grim, and fit.

Each arriving pedestrian stopped at one of the turnstiles under the watchful eye of the guards. A scanner – similar to those only recently discovered by Pontius – sat above each turnstile. After scanning each person, it paused for a second while it perused the internal database. Then the light would turn green and the pedestrian would walk through the turnstile.

He did not know how to proceed but Telarus motioned for Pontius to stand in line in front of him. Once it was Pontius's turn to move through the turnstile, the scanner stayed dark for about three seconds, and then turned red. The guards to either side of the turnstile started moving forward. Each placed a hand on a weapon in their belts, and Pontius looked back to Telarus for assistance. Before the guards could make any serious progress, Telarus held up his hand. The four of them stood still while he transferred access records to the guards' UNIs. After several more seconds, one guard nodded to Telarus and stepped beside Pontius. He transmitted an access code to the scanner and the light turned green.

Once they had cleared the gateway, both men stood in the center of a grand covered concourse. The dome above it stretched far into the sky, covered in magnificent frescoes. The scene in every fresco depicted various aspects of Centrian life. It struck Pontius that every scene portrayed the nation as a bright, sunny, and carefree environment. Ruddy men played sports under a bright sky and women nurtured hordes of children in garden environments. An omnipotent creator disseminated knowledge. The characters all seemed to rejoice in the mere act of living. The scenes illustrated nothing Pontius could relate to in any period of his long life.

He wandered through the bright confines of the concourse. Telarus nudged him toward a soup vendor stationed against one of the far walls. Pontius realized that he hadn't eaten anything since he emerged from stasis. His hunger, dormant up to this point, surged within him as soon as the aroma of the broths hit his nostrils. Both of them ordered and sat down at an impromptu table stationed around the vendor stand.

"We need to go over some ground rules." Telarus's countenance was stern and steady.

"Aye."

"We will be met in a few moments by Aria. She is a high-level executive and a friend of mine. She is the one who got you in here." There was no direct question inherent in this statement. But it became clear to Pontius that Telarus was expecting a confirmation.

"Aye."

"She is the chief executive in charge of Diaspori services." Telarus did not need another confirmation on this, but he paused for a few seconds to allow this to sink in.

"Aye."

"She is going to take us on a tour of the facilities. I will stay with you at all times, but do not make any attempt to stray from the two of us."

"Aye."

"If you do become separated, for any reason, find the nearest place to sit down and convo me immediately."

"Aye."

"If we were to somehow become separated, do not speak directly to any of the guards."

"Aye-un." Pontius felt as though he was in a military debriefing. The formality of the discourse caused him to start using the formal –un suffix even though he was talking with an old friend.

"You are to share nothing you see here with anyone outside LiveLong."

"Aye-un."

"If you disregard any of these instructions, I can make no guarantees about what will happen to you."

Pontius paused for a moment. He was about to tour various nooks and crannies of a corporate headquarters. *What could happen to someone just because they spoke about what they saw here?* He wasn't sure where Telarus was going with this, but he didn't want to further agitate his friend either. "Aye-un," he replied.

The two sat for about 20 minutes and ruminated on the soup. Telarus sipped the broth and gazed around the concourse at the anonymous passersby. Pontius focused on the food placed before him. It was in a huge bowl and it featured generous chunks of some meat that was unfamiliar to him – unlike any fish he had ever tasted before. The broth was savory and hearty and he relished every spoonful as it washed down his throat and warmed him from the inside out. While Telarus seemed unimpressed with the fare, Pontius found it delicious.

Pontius scarfed down his portion and Telarus still had plenty sitting in his bowl. A woman came up and introduced herself as Aria. The name Aria gave

Pontius visions of a tall, elegant, graceful woman with delicate features and a disaffected air. This woman was the exact opposite. She wasn't quite a meter-and-a-half tall. She wasn't overweight, but stocky with shoulders too broad for a woman her size. Her dark, cropped hair was so close to Telarus's in style that Pontius wondered if it was corporate-issued. She wore a loose, flowing robe so expansive that she could have weighed 45 kilograms – but she just as easily could have weighed 70.

She approached the men with a huge smile and both hands extended, desiring to clamp onto theirs. She gave Telarus a cursory handshake but turned the brunt of her attention to Pontius. She clasped his hand between hers and gazed into his eyes. Despite her portly and unattractive nature, her eyes shone bright with a blue-green hue like the bay of a tropical atoll. She motioned for both of them to sit back down as she sidled up beside them, her energy focused on Pontius.

"So I hear that you are currently in possession of an unlicensed?" The broad smile on her face belied the gravity of the question.

Despite the ease of her voice and the warmth of her smile, Pontius was uncomfortable with the direct nature of her query. He surveyed the concourse around them and then replied in a muted tone, "Aye-un."

Recognizing his hesitance, she renewed her smile and reached forward to grasp his hand in hers. "You're amongst friends here, Pontius. That child will have a good home." She lingered on the word *good* like it was an all-day sucker.

As warm and inviting as she seemed, there was something about hearing his own name across her lips that unnerved him. He was certain Telarus had already transmitted information to her. She was just working on the details she had at hand. But it still made him uneasy to think that this unadulterated fortress possessed his sensitive data.

She took no notice of his obvious fears, instead rising to her feet and motioning for them to follow. Pontius tried to catch Telarus's gaze, hoping to receive some visual cue that this was expected. Telarus just stood up and followed her lead, paying no attention to Pontius.

Aria spent the next few hours walking Pontius through areas of LiveLong that held no interest for him. She walked them through several of the outer buildings. They even glimpsed the first couple floors of the grand, central, double-helix structure. She was taking them on a tourist path. She walked them through public concourses in the human resources department. She gave them samples of some of LiveLong's newest trial drugs. They took an extensive tour of the marketing department. She handed them a plethora of LiveLong swag as though they were attendees at a pharmaceutical convention. She brought them onto a catwalk that skirted above the vast call center. She showed them a dizzying array of servers in the datacenter, the breadth of which Pontius had never witnessed. She showed them a shipping dock that was epic in scale. Hundreds of massive corporate cruisers loaded cargo destined for all corners of the nation.

Checkpoints girded every location. They were identical to those at the front gates. Armed guards monitored each one – guards who all looked identical. No one moved into any area of the LiveLong campus without authorization. They even scanned Aria at each checkpoint to ensure she was not wandering into unauthorized areas. At every checkpoint the same ritual repeated. Pontius failed the scan. Aria then transmitted the proper access credentials to the guards via UNI.

Although LiveLong's corporate business bored Pontius, he was in awe of the environments. Everything was larger, taller, and grander than anything else he could compare it to. From the corporate boardrooms to the public restrooms, there was no detail spared. The desks for the lowest of employees were intricately carved with ornate flourishes. Plastics were absent. Everything consisted of fine, and often rare, materials. Everything was polished to a high sheen.

He also became aware of a virtual army of menial staff that scoured all areas like termites devouring anything in their path. Some of them were scrubbing all manner of tiny architectural details. Some of them were ferrying Caffeinate and snacks to the regular employees. Others dragged great wheeled sleds behind them. They stewarded loads of office supplies from one location to another. Still others handled building maintenance. They wore belts with all manner of utilitarian tools.

Pontius came to realize they were of a different class – a different caste. This was evident by two basic facts. The first was their dress. They all wore black from head to toe. Men and women alike wore identical boots, pants, long-sleeve shirts, and headdresses. The headdresses left nothing visible except their hands and a small window into their faces. The cloth that covered these articles of clothing was curious in that it had an amazing ability to absorb light. As he watched them scurry around the open areas this didn't strike him at first. But when he caught a glimpse of one such person retreating into a shadowed enclave, he had to strain to see if the person was still there at all. It was as though the servant had disappeared – engulfed by the shadow itself.

A second fact identified them as part of a different, lower caste. None of the regular employees seemed to notice these people at all. Aria's tour continued, revealing more of LiveLong's inner workings. It became remarkable to see the extent to which these black figures did not exist in the minds of those doing their own work. Pontius wondered whether any of the employees could even see the black figures at all. So complete was their disregard of the men and women in these uniforms.

Pontius's astonishment at this black army peaked when he witnessed one of them pass through a checkpoint. They did not pause. They did not look at the guards – nor did the guards look at them. They did not stop in front of the scanners. They just marched through the turnstile. The scanner itself portrayed no color of acknowledgment. The turnstile offered no resistance. It was as if they floated through the checkpoint on an ethereal plane.

After a thorough inspection of the accounting department, Aria turned to Pontius and asked, "How are you holding up?"

The question caught Pontius off guard. Over the last several hours she had offered an unending stream of narration. She illustrated everything from the staff to minor details of the buildings' architecture. She urged them from one point of interest to another without ever asking for their feedback. Telarus remained silent – no doubt because he had seen all this before and knew it well. Pontius also remained silent. He had no window through which he could interject his own thoughts or questions.

"I'm doing well." He glanced at Telarus but received no acknowledgment. He was hesitant to say much more after Telarus's original briefing at the soup vendor. "Is there more to see?"

Aria chuckled and gave a dismissive wave. "We could go on for days."

Pontius feared this was a license for her to return to the tour, so he mustered the courage to blurt out, "The Diaspori?"

Her smile widened and her face took on an air of excitement. The way that she pounced on the query gave him the impression that she was waiting for this invitation all along.

"Well, Pontius, you have already seen some of them." With this statement she moved her gaze around the room in an exaggerated fashion. She made a point to pause whenever her sight fell over one of the black-clad figures.

"So that's what the Diaspori are? They are the janitors and the handymen of the LiveLong campus?" His tone was not dismissive or judgmental. He was asking a simple matter-of-fact question.

She chuckled again. She looked him straight in his eyes and moved closer. Once her chuckle had died away and she had returned to a mere grin, she said, "Those are only the ones who have chosen to work up-top."

Up-top? The thought caught Pontius off guard. What did she mean by *up-top*? "So the others work in the basement?"

She shook her head and began walking away down a far hallway, motioning for them to follow. Once they had a chance to fall in next to her, she turned to Pontius and continued narrating.

"The LiveLong campus you've seen is an iceberg, with just a portion of its mass protruding beyond the planet's skin. As impressive as it is to behold the wonders of our campus from above, the greater engineering achievement is what we've built below the surface. What you call a *basement* is instead a massive complex of housing, factories, administrative offices and a great many support facilities."

He was about to ask for clarification but she was already two steps ahead of him, both literally and figuratively. "You can't just house the Diaspori like boarders in a flop house. They have families. They have lives. They require all the accouterments of normal society. We have several schools. There is a world-class hospital. There are theaters, restaurants, and nightclubs. There is a stadium. We even have stores that cater to the Diaspori."

They stepped into an elevator. She did not press a regular button for one of the hundreds of floors in the helix. Instead, she transmitted UNI commands to the interface indicating that they would be going down. There were no normal functions in the elevator that would have indicated this was possible.

"It sounds like LiveLong has an entire city down there."

She made no attempt to fill the air with words. The elevator ride was swift. Rather than try to explain the environment, she chose to stand still and allow the doors to open. She watched the expression on his face as Pontius witnessed the undercity for the first time. He gasped.

They stepped out into a grand expanse. It was so wide and so bright. He would not have believed that he was underground if he hadn't just been traveling downward from the first floor. When she was describing this undercity he envisioned a dingy network of tunnels connecting one artificial space to another. But now he saw an open expanse the likes of which he had never experienced. The ceiling – or what he presumed to be the ceiling – was at least a few hundred meters above them. It emitted a light that was so natural – so sun-like – that it would be easy to forget that one was underground. The song of birds filled the air - similar to those he had heard on the walkway coming in. A refreshing breeze filled the space and made the flora that littered the public causeways sway to and fro. The haze of humidity from up-top was gone. The breeze was magnificent. It belied the oppressive winds that suffocated Centrian's citizenry like a wool blanket on a hot summer night.

He strained his eyes but could not see where this edifice ended in any direction. It seemed as though he could make out far walls obscured by a gentle haziness some kilometers off in the distance, but he couldn't be sure. For a moment he entertained the fanciful notion that this underworld extended under all of Centrian.

As he gazed through the warm-but-empty sky, he asked, "Where are the moorings? This space – it's *under* all the skyscrapers of the campus above. Where are the anchors for those behemoths?"

It impressed her that Pontius had the presence of mind to consider such engineering realities. "You are now standing near the center of the largest dome on the planet – a dome that most Centrians don't even know exists. It extends several kilometers in all directions. It is also the strongest structure on the planet. The skin of this dome is made of progressive layers of carbon nanofiber. Imagine a sphere made of pure granite, then imagine something that is several orders of magnitude stronger. The skyscrapers that you reference above are anchored directly into this dome. This dome is, quite literally, the foundation of LiveLong."

They all stood in silence, each one of them – even Aria – soaking in the magnificence of the scene. As they remained stationary, a sea of Diaspori moved all around them. It was a reversal of the equation from above. The majority of souls passing by wore the garb of the Diaspori. Occasionally Pontius would spy a "normal" person walking by. But this was the domain of the Diaspori and they held sway in this undercity.

Another incredulous thought arose in Pontius's mind. "If this dome is the foundation of LiveLong, that means that this edifice was built *first*. This city was not created as an afterthought. This was the basis of the entire campus."

Aria shot a wise nod at him. "Who owns LiveLong?"

He thought for a moment. Lame though it may be, he felt the need to search his UNI for public records. After a few brief seconds of query results, he answered, "Cassian Minian."

"Minian is the CEO. His office sits astride the helix towers above, but he's not the owner. Who *owns* LiveLong?"

He considered returning to his UNI but then he realized the folly of this line of questioning. "LiveLong is a public corporation. It's owned by countless shareholders."

She nodded again, not willing to concede the point. "Yes, it is certainly a public company, but one person owns a majority of all shares."

She paused for a moment while Pontius pondered this point. LiveLong was, by far, the largest, wealthiest corporation on the planet. No other company was even close. Its public valuation was in the trillions of squalem. It had never occurred to him that any one person could hold a controlling interest in the entire corporation. It would be akin to owning most of the planet's water, or air, or food.

He was about to resort to his UNI again when she decided to save him the effort. There was no way for him to know. "LiveLong was founded by a woman named Teressa Montava. She was the first person to synthesize Telomore. She created LiveLong and she still owns a controlling interest in the public shares."

Pontius tried to let that tidbit of information just flow past him but his bullshit sensors were tingling. He was never one for historical facts. He was certainly never a scholar. But the founder of LiveLong was a celebrity. Even hundreds of years after he had retired from the board of directors, Orith Sinian was still a worldwide brand unto himself. He was the public voice of LiveLong. He graced every stock market show. He dined with the political royalty. He was relentlessly hounded by the paparazzi. He was synonymous with LiveLong.

For the first time during their visit he caught an expression on her face that was unsavory. She could not contain the scowl that crept across her features. It dissolved her ever-present smile as she read his thoughts.

"Sinian is a puppet. He founded this company in the same way that you founded the NCU. He worked here. He proved himself to be an eloquent soldier for LiveLong. But he had nothing to do with the founding of this corporation, nor did he make any meaningful decisions behind the scenes. Montava is the guiding force for this company."

"Why does LiveLong need a *public face*? Why wouldn't Montava just show herself to be the puppet master that you claim she is?" Pontius was confused and had abandoned any pretense of compliance.

"Because she's unlicensed."

Those words struck Pontius with the force of a battering ram. This undercity – this world within a world – was built as the power base for a founder who could never be accepted by the general populace. This wasn't a refugee camp. This was Montava's home.

It all started to make sense, but Pontius still wasn't sure about the details. "That would make Montava, hands down, the richest individual on the planet. Why wouldn't she just buy her Vitapass like anyone else? She could arrange a death match in minutes. She could pay top dollar. She could be legitimate in a matter of days."

Aria shook her head as she realized that Pontius was still a long ways from any true understanding. "Are you going to tell a self-made woman – a woman who created the single greatest technological breakthrough in the history of this planet – a woman who has her hand in every transaction that takes places across Centrian – that she needs to arrange for the gladiatorial death of an innocent just so she can be *legitimate*? Do you think she will submit to your convention of licensure? What do you think happens when you tell someone who built all of *this*," and with that she raised her arms above her in a grand flourish, "that they are illegitimate? That they are unlicensed? That they need to come begging to your authorities for a Vitapass?"

She allowed the power of her words to trail off into the artificial sunshine of the undercity. Telarus was silent, as usual, but unbeknownst to Pontius, much of this information was new to him. Pontius was speechless. He had nothing to say to such a concept. He still harbored some degree of skepticism. But it was hard to put up much resistance when faced with the engineering brilliance that he witnessed today. He felt that if the corporation could accomplish all this splendor, then almost anything was possible.

Sensing that words had reached their limit, Aria began to guide them again through the vagaries of the undercity. At first she showed them the amenities of this place. She walked them through an empty stadium that would accommodate tens of thousands of people. She showed them numerous retail shops. She called out the nightclubs and entertainment establishments as they passed each one. But Pontius was still curious about two major concerns – the working conditions and the housing facilities.

Just when Pontius was on the verge of impatience, she led them into a huge complex of buildings. They formed a conglomerate stretching upward, almost to the edge of the artificial sky. These buildings – dozens of them – formed a tight-knit inner campus. LiveLong conducted the bulk of its business here.

The first building they entered was a manufacturing facility. In this cavernous edifice Pontius saw all manner of archaic devices designed for the creation of pills. He saw huge boiling pots. He saw Diaspori ferrying palettes across the factory floor. He saw manual assembly lines where workers poured hot goo into tiny molds designed to cut out individual pills. He saw other lines where the Diaspori furiously inspected each pill as it flew down the line. Further along they slaved feverishly to corral the pills into appropriate containers. The entire process, while mildly automated, still felt archaic.

She was intent on pressing through the facility but he decided on his own to stop and watch the proceedings. There was something amiss in this presentation. He determined to put his finger on it. The mass of people on the floor was crushing. There were so many of them that he found it amazing they could keep from running over each other. And yet they seemed to intertwine like dancers in an intricate ballet. They were always on the verge of overrunning each other, and yet they always managed to somehow avoid any such catastrophe. There were Diaspori to mix the pharmaceutical ingredients. There were Diaspori to fire the ovens. There were Diaspori to power the assembly lines. There were

Diaspori to pour the ingredients into the molds. There were Diaspori to inspect each and every pill as it rolled out of the furnaces. There were Diaspori to sort them by size – ensuring that rejects could not reach the market. There were Diaspori to handle every aspect of bottling and packaging. There were Diaspori everywhere.

The trio was standing on a catwalk above the main action on the floor. She motioned for them to continue but he held up his hand, indicating that he wanted information. She returned to where he stood, Telarus coming up behind her. He expected her to extend her narration, but she just smiled, awaiting his query.

"Does nothing here strike you as out of the ordinary?"

She smiled at him, perused the floor below them, then returned to him with the same smile. She was gracious, but confused by his query. Rather than prompt him for specifics, she continued her smile and waited for him to explain himself further.

"Doesn't all of this seem a bit... manual?"

He had read textbooks in his youth. They had long ago receded from natural memory but still resided in the depths of his UNI. In these textbooks, he recalled illustrations of Earth. He recalled the lessons absorbed about the Industrial Revolution. Men lost their lives to manual processes involving thousand-degree ovens and steam-powered machinery. The scene before him was reminiscent of such lessons.

"Ooooh. Aye. I see your point." She relaxed a bit once she understood the nature of his inquiry. "As you can imagine, LiveLong can bring tremendous resources to bear. When this factory was first laid out, it was automated to such a degree that 20 people could oversee the formulation of more than 70,000 tablets per hour. But the Diaspori keep coming. We have ever more of them that require homes, and jobs, and lives. First we decommissioned the androids. Then we started removing the factory equipment – one machine at a time. Over the course of a few hundred years, you could say that our manufacturing process has, quite frankly, devolved to its current state."

"How many tablets are manufactured on the surface?"

She shot him a confused look, not sure why he would offer such a bizarre question. "Nothing is manufactured up-top."

He offered no retort. He just nodded his head and scuttled up behind her, signaling that he was ready to continue. As they made their way off the catwalk, he looked down again at the manufacturing floor. He made a mental note of the fact that there were no workers there not dressed in the garb of the Diaspori. He, Aria, and Telarus were the only outsiders he could identify in the entire facility.

Their next stop was in accounting. As soon as he realized the function of this building, he asked her, "I thought we saw the Accounting Department up-top?"

She smiled and shook her head again. "The plebeians upstairs manage public contact. All public interfaces to LiveLong are through standard, licensed humans who work in the towers above. But nothing – and I mean *nothing* – gets paid unless it is accompanied by a valid purchase order generated from down here."

He allowed this to sink in for a moment and then asked, "So it sounds like Accounting is actually *run* from down here?"

She nodded and said, "But of course."

As he watched the hustle and bustle around him he noticed again that there was no one here devoid of the standard Diaspori garb. He also noticed that there was a ridiculous amount of paper – real, old-world paper – handed back and forth. Clerks carried file folders. Secretaries stamped physical documents with "Approved" or "Denied" labels. Minus the UNIs stationed behind every employee's ear, he found it hard to identify any aspect of modern day technology.

He paused again for a moment and considered hailing Aria again. Before he could do so, she cut short his train of thought.

"The entire department used to handle the billing for a population of five billion with 20 accountants. Now we employ more than 600 Diaspori in this one department alone, and that's in addition to the 'face people' we have employed upstairs."

Pontius nodded again and submitted himself to the next stop on the tour. Marketing was similar to the two departments he had seen before. The Diaspori did all the real work down here. The puppets upstairs were a showpiece. The work they completed was manual. He saw graphic artists mocking up advertising campaigns with grease pencils on broad easels. Every employee seemed to clutch a host of manila file folders under their arm as they scurried from one desk to another. The secretaries were taking messages with pens and paper. The notes were then stuck to bulletin boards for their superiors.

The next location was of particular surprise to Pontius. After taking a back way through a series of office buildings, she opened an emergency door. They spilled out into a broader arena. Metal tables blanketed the floor. Various animals occupied cages so numerous that they formed their own aisles. Beakers, microscopes, and a slew of unidentified machines littered the tables. It was a lab.

The Diaspori crowded each table. Some of them took notes. Others mixed concoctions. Others huddled around whiteboards where they brainstormed and debated ideas. A central board stretched across the entire north wall. Diagrams, equations, and notes, written by many different hands, covered almost every inch of it.

Pontius didn't remember seeing any labs upstairs. "The Diaspori help with research and development?"

"The Diaspori do *all* of the R&D."

"There are no public facing equivalents of this up-top?"

"R&D is typically an insular activity. We have no need to maintain a façade up there."

While her words were sensible, he was somewhat shocked to hear this revelation. It was all fine and good to put the basic, tactical operations of the company in the hands of this underclass. But he didn't anticipate LiveLong trusting something so critical as R&D to these *unlicensed*.

"What functions are not accomplished from down here?"

She shrugged and thought about it for a few scant moments. "Only those that, by their nature, require public interaction. Shipping. Security." And with this she gave an acknowledging nod to Telarus. "Retail sales. That's about it."

He couldn't help but notice that all the facilities were clean and well equipped. It appeared these Diaspori wanted for little in the completion of their duties. It also appeared they were happy.

They may not have been joyous but each of them seemed to attack their duties with relish. There was an industriousness that oozed from every environment in the undercity. It would not have surprised him if they had broken out into coordinated song. Their actions were so timed, so neat and orderly, that he felt they were marching to some kind of inner beat.

"Can I meet some of them?"

He had no idea what they would talk about. But the more he watched this theater play out before him the more he felt the need to reach out to some of them on a personal level. He wanted to know that they were real. He wanted to know if they were just marionettes levered by the massive power of LiveLong.

She perked up at these words, as though she had been waiting for the invitation. "I've already arranged for you to meet some very important people."

She lept back into a frenzied pace, almost leaving the two men behind. Pontius looked at Telarus, wondering if he had some clue to this next destination. Telarus returned a confused look that betrayed his passivity in this scenario. Pontius was thinking that maybe she would resume her narration of the upcoming events as they walked. She offered no such information. She led them by one building after another as she pressed on to her destination.

After passing many central business buildings, the party entered a new portion of the undercity. The bustle and formality of the LiveLong engine gave way to the casual environment of the residential area. A series of apartment buildings rose halfway to the false heavens, each one identical to the next. They stretched out in a long line as far as he could see. Between them lay the vestiges of suburbia. There were parks with athletic fields. There were retail shops at the ground level. They offered everything from groceries, to clothing, to restaurants, to prostitutes.

After passing four such buildings, she entered the ground floor of the fifth. Although the buildings were rather plain – almost utilitarian – from the outside, they were ornate inside. Intricately carved friezes adorned the lobby. They shifted dynamically before the onlooker's eyes. The flooring was a rare mineral found only in the deepest regions of Oceanus and prized for its forgiving nature on the human foot. The ceilings were overlaid with holographic images. They gave the impression that one was standing under a brilliant sky adorned with all the stars of the galaxy.

Passing through the lobby and into the upper floors, she made quick work of the journey. Within minutes the trio found themselves at the door of one of the apartments. She hailed the residents through her convo and the door flung open with gleeful anticipation.

A couple greeted them. They dressed in casual attire – the Diaspori were at least free of their uniforms in the comfort of their own homes. The man had a warm smile and a pot bell. He welcomed them into the home. A bushy, nappy beard dominated his gregarious face. It shook with his movements as though it consisted of wire brush. He shook the hands of Aria, then Telarus, then Pontius. The woman doubled his smile and seemed overly inviting, but she was also distracted. As she greeted each of them her eyes darted around them, anticipating the arrival of a fourth. She was much taller than the man. Her arrow-straight red hair extended almost down to her knees. Her skin was a faint shade of blue – a style that was en vogue for the wealthier Centrians.

Aria was now beaming. She stood with a nervous energy that rose with every word. "Pontius, this is Forthoran and his wife Lucretia."

Lucretia motioned for them to sit down in chairs arranged around a central table in the living room. She raced off to the kitchen but returned with a broad selection of sumptuous treats. Still hungry from his time in stasis and the vigorous tour he'd been through, Pontius dug in. The food was delicious and caused him to think again about the amazing soup he enjoyed after entering the LiveLong campus.

The apartment was plush. It shocked him to find that it was nicer than Caspian's. The furniture was of the finest make. The decoration was refined and tastefully done. Everything from the walls and ceilings down to the silverware on the table was ornately detailed. The walls and the furniture featured ivory inlays.

Pontius would have continued eating for quite some time, as the food was delectable and his hunger seemed to rise with each bite. But after several minutes it became clear to him that the others were waiting for him to finish before proceeding. After wrestling for a moment with his own ravenous desires, he returned his attention to the group. Recognizing that she was now free to continue, Aria commenced with explanations.

"Forthoran works in the information technology department. He's a data analyst. Lucretia works in the manufacturing facility. She's a quality control inspector." He wasn't sure what to do with this information, but he smiled and nodded anyway. "They have been married for almost a hundred years and they want nothing more than to have a child of their own."

Forthoran smiled and nodded in reply, his great beard gyrating as he did so.

"Unfortunately, Lucretia is completely barren. We've tried every avenue to help her, but she cannot conceive."

The light clicked in his head. Lucretia was smiling at him. As she did so, she looked around the room, as though another member of the party might magically materialize.

"This would be Chunk's home." Aria's words hit him with a thud. The thought did not displease him. But there was something about the abruptness of that statement that caught him off guard. As he looked again at Lucretia he could see the first sign of a joyful tear welling up in her eye.

She could contain herself no longer. In a burst of nervous energy she began talking. Forthoran chimed in on occasion, but Lucretia could not be quelled. She asked Pontius all kinds of questions. She walked the trio around their spacious apartment. She continued to bring out more food and drink. She started volunteering all sorts of details about her life, and Forthoran's. Some were so intimate that they made Pontius uncomfortable. She showed him the room they had decorated for Chunk, a room that featured everything that an infant could want.

For the next hour, she held sway over the proceedings. Pontius offered brief questions or offhand observations. But for the most part, he was happy to allow her to work off her anticipation in her own way. She told him all about her job. She explained how she and Forthoran liked to spend their free time. She told the story of how they first met. She talked a little about her family – some of whom also existed as Diaspori in the undercity. She expounded upon her hopes and dreams for their child – for Chunk.

Although Pontius was hesitant to acknowledge it in his own mind, he found her charming. Her joy at the thought of having a child was infectious. Her relationship with Forthoran appeared rock solid. The life they built together was, in so many ways, storybook. The one thing they were missing in this bucolic fairytale was a child and now she overflowed with the thought of having their own.

With the food cleared, she lost some of her steam. He sat back and drank in the reality of Chunk's future home. Forthoran gave every impression of being a gentle and caring father. Lucretia would be a doting mother. This world they lived in – this bizarre alternate world beneath the streets of an unsuspecting Centrian – was a fantasy land. Unlicensed vagabonds like Chunk could live long and fulfilling lives. It felt too good to be true. It also gave him an overwhelming sense of relief.

With a few drinks coursing through his brain, his quiet nature loosened a bit. Forthoran challenged him to a game of Battlefield – a game that Pontius enjoyed – and he could think of no good reason to deny. The two of them sat for another hour smoking and discussing much of the minutiae of Forthoran's life. Although she didn't participate in the game, Lucretia sat next to her husband. She added to the conversation whenever appropriate. Aria and Telarus retreated to the kitchen, engulfed in their own business.

After another hour of drinks and discussion, Aria returned to the living room with a satisfied grin on her face. Sitting across from Pontius, she had the look of someone anxious to close a deal.

"So. Pontius. It seems that we've found a home for little Chunk then?" She was nodding at him as she said this, willing him to accede.

He let out a relieved sigh and sat back in his chair, gazing at the tendrils of smoke as it drifted upward and outward. With this great burden lifted from his shoulders, he allowed himself to relax.

"Absolutely."

Lucretia let out a happy squeal and jumped into Forthoran's arms. Forthoran rushed over to shake Pontius's hand again. She ran to the kitchen to fetch a round of celebratory drinks.

When she returned he shared a toast and then looked straight at Forthoran. "I'm in a very delicate situation. An NCU agent with an unlicensed baby is a dangerous combination."

These words washed a somber mood over the group as they waited for him to continue. "It's extremely difficult for me to transport Chunk, given his unlicensed state. How soon can you pick him up? Can you get him tomorrow? I'm sure that you'd like to meet him as soon as possible, and I'd just as soon have this whole chapter behind me."

Lucretia's otherwise gleeful nature became sullied with confusion. She and Forthoran both looked into his eyes and said in unison, "We can't *leave*."

Pontius felt foolish for a moment. In seeing their lives he forgot about their unlicensed status. He was working off the ignorant assumption that they could just travel to his apartment tomorrow and pick up Chunk. Now, with their tactical reality articulated before him, it was obvious. And yet, it jarred him to hear these words spoken so plainly.

They could not leave. He turned that thought over in his mind. He allowed it to ricochet against the uncomfortable and often-silent areas of his conscience. It was a simple concept that for some reason was sticking in his throat as he labored to swallow it.

"Forthoran, how old are you?"

"I'll be 643 next month." Not knowing where this was going, Forthoran resumed his jolly nature.

"And Lucretia, how old are you?"

"I just turned 589." She was oblivious in her reply.

"When did both of you come here?"

Forthoran chose to speak for both of them. "I was brought here when I was two months old. Lucretia was actually born here. Her parents both work in Accounts Payable."

"When is the last time that either of you were outside the LiveLong campus?" He knew what the answer would be, but he had to hear it for himself.

"We have never been off campus." Forthoran pondered his own response for a moment and then added. "Why would we ever go off campus?"

Pontius ignored the question and sat still, formulating his next query. "How long do you think you will live down here? How many years will you live in the service of LiveLong?"

Lucretia looked at him with an empty expression and shrugged her shoulders. They both turned to him and spoke again in unison, "We live long for LiveLong."

This coordinated utterance sent a shudder down his spine. He said nothing in direct reply, trying not to betray his distaste for this new slogan.

"And what happens if you don't live long for LiveLong?"

The couple had no clue what this meant. They just stared at him, virtually begging him to elaborate.

"Surely in your five-or-six hundred years, you've known somebody down here that no longer wanted to work for LiveLong. Or at least, you must have known somebody who screwed up – somebody who got *fired*?"

This question relieved Lucretia. Now she knew what he was driving at. A perky smile returned to her face and she said in a cheery voice, "Oh yes. Those people are expelled." Forthoran happily nodded, as if to corroborate her reply.

A Dusk Forever Waning

There was a long awkward silence in the room. Aria sensed that something was awry but she couldn't quite identify it. Telarus, knowing his friend all too well, sat and observed the proceedings. Forthoran and Lucretia smiled and nodded long past the point that there was anything to smile or nod about.

Pontius stood up, signaling that he was ready to leave. Without waiting for anyone's acknowledgment, he looked past everyone into Chunk's future room. He said, "I'll bring Chunk back tomorrow. I'll figure out some way to get him here on my own."

Lucretia exploded in a new round of joy, springing out of her seat and throwing her arms around Pontius. Pontius tolerated the affection as a child tolerates the aggressive hugs of a smelly, overweight aunt. After another round of congratulatory handshakes, he nodded to Aria and said, "Let's go." As the trio left the apartment and proceeded down the common hallway, he could hear the repeated refrain of "Thank you! Oh, thank you!" coming from Forthoran and Lucretia as their voices receded in the still air of the building.

Aria made an attempt to resume their tour but Pontius made it clear that he felt tired and was ready to return home. He was polite but curt in his responses and at every turn he voiced his desire to take the most expedient path out of LiveLong. When the trio made it all the way back to the main gates, he made a point to thank her for her time, then he turned to make his way out.

"Pontius!" She wanted to complete one last piece of the deal. He turned to her and stopped, making no attempt to bridge the distance now between them. "When will you bring Chunk back? I want to ensure that everything is in order when he arrives."

"Tomorrow." He waited for no reply. He turned back toward the gates, with Telarus pulling up behind him, and made his way to the exit.

The friends traveled in silence through the forested walkway and onto the scaler platform. At the platform, Pontius seemed to take the wrong scaler. He chose a route requiring several transfers to return home. Telarus said nothing, choosing to follow Pontius on whatever path he might follow.

They sat side-by-side in the compartment. Telarus kept his gaze straight ahead and said, "You're not bringing Chunk here tomorrow, are you?"

"Nay." The response was crisp and precise.

"What are you going to do?"

"I don't know." His voice was somber and resigned. "I really don't know."

For the next 30 minutes, Telarus made a half dozen attempts to refute his friend's decision. Each time he welled up with a putative discussion point, only to swallow it before it could escape his lips. He saw where things broke down in the apartment, but that didn't mean he understood it. He felt compelled to somehow set this straight. But every time he deigned to engage the conversation, Pontius dismissed his points. He didn't know what was going through Pontius's mind. But he could see that his mind was already set – and once his mind was set there was little anyone could do to alter it.

Telarus knew of no greater future for an unlicensed than to join the Diaspori. A life spent wallowing in the underbelly of society – or worse, snuffed out by government terminators – could be traded for comfort and productivity. The Diaspori had the greatest gift that any refugee could hope for – the wealthiest of benefactors that was one of them. Without such a perfect arrangement, he knew of no other way for to solve this dilemma. In many hundreds of years of life he never saw anyone take so bold a step as to turn down this arrangement.

The scaler crept along at a horrid pace. This was a local line and it felt as though there were at least two stops at every building they passed. The evening rush was now in full swing and the cabin became more cramped with every platform they reached. Telarus grew tired of the parade of backsides continually crammed against his cheeks. He decided to stand. As he rose, Pontius made no attempt to join him. He sat in his seat and stared out at the watery blackness of the Centrian night.

After an hour of the sardine treatment, the scaler broadcast a UNI message indicating arrival at the Titan complex. Taking Telarus by surprise, Pontius rose and exited the scaler. Unaware their course had changed, he barely made it out of the scaler before the doors closed and the transport continued on.

Coming up behind Pontius amidst the sea of people moving in the opposite direction, he asked where they were going. Pontius replied, "I need a drink," as though this was evident for all to see. After traversing several retail walkways they reached an ornate edifice. The name *Skyskimmer Lounge* floated in bright space a meter above the archway marking its entrance.

Pontius headed straight to the bar. A service droid scanned his biometrics and whirred off to the kitchen. It would make a drink custom tailored to his biological makeup. Telarus pulled up a chair next to him and the cycle repeated. The two sat and observed the bustle. Horny people flitted from one table to the next, trying to strike up conversations and satisfy their desires. Telarus wasn't comfortable. He was ill-prepared for a night of partying and wondered how long they would be at this location.

He was about to start convo'ing others, hoping to liven up the crypt-like atmosphere offered by Pontius. A bartender came over offering an assortment of food and drugs. Pontius gave no attention to the offerings. Instead, he yelled above the club's sound system, "Is Conti working tonight?"

The bartender scrunched his face and shook his head. "There is no Conti that works here."

Pontius wasn't surprised, but he chose to delve a little deeper. "Really?" He asked in false surprise. "Did she recently quit?"

The bartender continued his look of annoyed confusion. "People don't quit this place. The money's fabulous. We haven't lost a bartender in three years."

Pontius ordered two variants of neural boosters, a plate of appetizers, and a refill of his drink. Telarus looked at him in bewilderment, but he only replied with, "Imagine that."

Chapter 8 – The Angel of Death

Moria spent the next several days trying to make Pontius's Spartan bachelor pad suitable for an infant. She made long forays to various shops purchasing supplies in stealth mode. She did not buy baby food. She bought items that she could cook into baby food. She did not buy toys. She bought items that she could fashion into toys. She became a master at acquiring the requisite items without ever having to buy them whole.

Before her first excursion she was distraught over leaving Chunk in the apartment. She could not afford to carry him around the public marketplaces as though he was legitimate. She could not complete transactions or traverse public transportation with him on her arm. But the thought of leaving him in Pontius's care petrified her. Pontius had the paternal instincts of a pimp.

She placed a few convos to some of her friends. She discretely asked if they could come to his place to provide "a favor" – but as soon as he received wind of this plan he killed it. It was far too dangerous to let others – anyone – know that they were harboring an unlicensed. He knew, better than anyone else on Centrian, how NCU could hone in on a mere handful of clues leading to a slaughtered child. He wasn't even happy knowing that Caspian and Telarus were aware of the situation. That Kryx and Conti were in on this drama annoyed him more. The last thing they could afford to do was to expand the inner circle. He felt he could trust no one in this situation. Thus, in her absence, he had no choice but to become a caretaker.

While they were alone, he spread out a blanket in front of the couch. This allowed Chunk to roll around between various makeshift toys and diversions. The entire time, he sat on the couch and stared at Chunk. When Chunk would fuss – which was rare – he threw a motley assortment of toys and snacks at the little fellow. At times this was effective. At other times it led to an epic mound of crackers, juice bottles, and diversions piled all around the disconsolate child.

He couldn't help but notice that Chunk always made a wandering path to him. He rolled, nudged, and grabbed his way to Pontius's legs. It appeared as though anything and everything was a candidate to insert into his mouth. Pontius considered his apartment to be quite well kept. But seeing objects consumed by the gumming beast made him aware of any shortcomings in his housecleaning.

He spent two full days laying around his apartment in an abject depression. Part of this came from his still-recuperating physical state. His new lungs, while efficient and powerful, still left him devoid of stamina at times. But more so than any physical malady, he was overcome by defeatist confusion.

Several long discussions with Moria did nothing to alleviate his fears about their situation. NCU put him on convalescent leave. She took a few weeks off in an impromptu "vacation" that gave her some time while they sorted things out. During this period, she tried repeatedly to connect to the PC systems. She found her access points intermittent – even, fleeting. Records she accessed would disappear from the system. They evaporated, then showed up as locked, then reappeared again. She feared she was being audited.

They were incapable of asking their superiors to explain what was happening. Corrupt employees can't simply ask their superiors why their hacks no longer work. There was no one in the organization who could be questioned about the change. The more they felt panicked about their place in PC, the more they were helpless to do anything about it.

They had several strained conversations about whether she should access PC systems at all. On one hand, her attempts to traverse the government databases were her only way to assess the situation. On the other hand, all access was traceable. Pontius directed her to stop all access at once, only to think about it for hours, relent, and then ask her to attempt new access.

When he wasn't thinking about their future in PC he was growing more paranoid about the safety of Chunk. He wasn't sure if the bioscanners from his initial journey had caught enough information to tie Chunk back to him. With every hour that passed he became ever more convinced that his NCU brethren were closing in.

During her first excursion for supplies, Moria came back with a small fork and spoon – something that would fit in Chunk's mouth. Although they weren't specifically *baby* utensils, it was enough to send Pontius into a panic. He flew out of the apartment and disposed of them in the first public disintegrator. He yelled random obscenities at her as he did.

His foray to LiveLong did not just disappoint him – it haunted him. Every part of his logical mind told him that he should bring Chunk there and finish this. The undercity was gorgeous. Those people looked so happy – and industrious. Lucretia and Forthoran were charming in every sense of the word. He had no doubt that Chunk would live a long and happy life there – and yet, he could not bring himself to cave to that deal. Despite the bucolic nature of their surroundings, he still felt that this was tantamount to slavery. He felt that this was something far short of the life that Chunk's parents had so painfully purchased for him.

Telarus paid a visit in each of the last two days. Each time he came under the guise of checking on Pontius's well-being and bringing any needed supplies. But this flimsy façade only existed to allow him to make his case. On each day, within minutes of his arrival, he launched into a logical case for why Chunk should be one of the Diaspori.

Each time, Pontius listened - impressed with the smooth and level demeanor of Telarus's argument. In almost any other matter, he would have bent to the desires of his thoughtful friend. Yet in this matter, whenever Telarus had his say and would wait for a verdict, he had a singular retort, *"They cannot leave."*

Telarus found the illogical nature of this refutation exasperating. *What difference did it make if they couldn't leave? Where would they go? Who in this world would treat them with the benevolence they could expect as part of the Diaspori? And why would they even want to leave?* The fact that they couldn't leave seemed to him like a complete and utter non sequitur. Yet it was the immutable pillar upon which Pontius based his decision. Telarus could speak eloquently for days about the myriad benefits afforded the Diaspori. But on this single point he had no retort.

With LiveLong no longer a viable alternative, Pontius felt confounded about what to do next. He couldn't live like this for long. Soon he would have to return to his normal lot – and along with it, they would have to find out what was happening with Moria's access. His colleagues in NCU would learn of his peculiar situation. He would face one of his own peers striding through his front door with the express intent of killing Chunk.

On his fourth day of Chunk's care, he awoke from a fitful and chaotic slumber on the couch. Through the first half of the night, he dreamed about being in an interrogation room. His superiors grilled him and forced him to watch as Chunk hung from a meat hook behind them. Various colleagues walked over and abused the child in full view of him. Yet he was powerless to move, paralyzed. His colleagues yelled at him with vitriol but he could not make out anything they were saying. After experiencing these horrific visions thrice, he disabled the region of his brain responsible for R.E.M. sleep. This ensured he would experience the sleep of the dead – deep and thoughtless, yet unsatisfying.

When he came to, it was late morning and Chunk was cooing on the blanket in front of him. Oblivious to most of the items strewn about him, Chunk focused on a flat panel propped up beside him. The panel displayed nothing coherent. It presented a barrage of shapes, colors, and sounds that all reacted to the thoughts and actions of the person in front of it. Its precise reactions confounded him. But Chunk learned in short order that the items shown before him were somehow tied to his own actions. The combination of light and sound before him was something that could almost be "played" – like an instrument.

Moria was a few rooms away in the gym, trying to mask her own stress through physical exertion. Through several open doorways Pontius could see the top of her head. She punched, kicked, thrust, and weaved to the sounds of some soundtrack playing through her UNI.

He sat up from his seat on the couch and resumed his standard routine of staring at Chunk. Chunk was too preoccupied with the screen in front of him to bother making his way over to him. This left him to gaze for quite some time. Then the convo came in.

The alert flashing across his vision startled him. For the last several days he had accepted no convos. He had everyone – even Caspian – set to receive a message of unavailability. There was only one source that had the override privileges necessary to convo him in this state – NCU.

The flashing indicator caused an immediate biological response. He shivered and his palms became clammy. His throat tensed into a tight wad of muscle that threatened to constrict his breathing. His Adam's apple – a feature he had never consciously pondered before – now sat in his airway with obstructive force.

He considered ignoring it. For a typical convo this might have been acceptable. But if NCU was overriding his blocking directives, they were going to keep convo'ing him until he answered. Then a more jarring thought occurred to him. *What if, by not answering, that would serve as the catalyst for sending an NCU agent to meet him in person?*

"Aye?" Pontius was never so terse with his own coworkers, but he wanted to articulate as few syllables as possible.

"Pontius, this is Tenarrin."

Tenarrin was the unit captain – the same man who briefed Pontius on all his assignments. There was a long moment of silence as he awaited a response, but Pontius was recalcitrant. After a period of awkwardness, Tenarrin proceeded.

"I'm terribly sorry. I know you're still recuperating and we hate to call on you like this."

There was another period of awkwardness while Tenarrin awaited a response that would not come.

"Are you feeling better? How are the new lungs?"

"I feel awful. I might need to have another pair implanted. Something went wrong." Pontius lied. He wanted to cut this conversation short.

With no pause and no care for his statement, Tenarrin conceded a cursory, "That's horrible to hear." And then he proceeded straightaway into the crux of his convo. "We have an emergency situation. We've been monitoring a most unusual group of mothers. They're holed up in a fish packing plant with their babies and we have reason to believe they're about to flee."

Again, another long and awkward pause.

"Aye?" Pontius had no idea where this was going.

"We need you to take this assignment – today – before these women get away."

He experienced the beginning stages of something he assumed was a panic attack. As he looked up he could see Moria's head bobbing back toward the living room. Chunk was still mesmerized by the kaleidoscopic display. Somewhere, somehow, he felt the desperate need to escape this scenario altogether.

"Why would you need to use me for this assignment?"

"Everyone else is out." Tenarrin's tone was so cool and matter-of-fact that he found it unnerving. Tenarrin said it with logical simplicity. He was stating the obvious answer to an elementary question.

"What do you mean that everyone else is out?" He allowed this last word to escape his mouth with a certain degree of scorn. "There are a dozen other agents in our office."

Tenarrin then gave a five-minute breakdown of the staffing crisis. A few others were on vacation, but each of the remaining team members were hunting down other cases. There was no one within a reasonable distance that could hope to make it to the packing plant before the women fled. By an odd stroke of circumstance, the plant in question was only a few kilometers away from his home in the Bowery.

He heard all of this streaming through his mind, but he listened to none of it. As soon as Tenarrin started going through the roll call of other unavailable agents, he knew he was screwed. NCU would not have overridden his convo block if they weren't adamant about getting him into the field.

"Captain-un, I'm not in the physical shape required to complete an assignment." This was his Hail Mary. He expected Tenarrin to reply with the scolding retort of a drill sergeant, berating his troops into battle. Tenarrin's chuckling surprised him.

"Pontius, you have completed assignments when you were missing an arm!"

A moment of incredulous silence followed as Tenarrin continued to chuckle. This sounded like a bluff. He knew that his arm had been replaced, but he couldn't remember ever completing an assignment in such a decapitated state. After performing a UNI search, he realized that he had completed an assignment in this condition. In fact, he completed several assignments while awaiting the growth of his new appendage.

The realization of this ancient fact quieted and depressed him all at once. Without taking his eyes off Chunk, he sighed and said, "Transmit the details."

Thirty minutes later, the convo was complete. Tenarrin transmitted the data while Pontius sat on the couch. Moria came back into the room with her hair still drying from a shower. She had fresh attire. Her breasts bounced under a loose-fitting t-shirt. He noticed that she looked more attractive – less prim and matronly.

Seeing his face alarmed her. He was ashen. The sweat from his palms spread over many parts of his tense body. He stared at her – but more accurately, he stared through her. He focused on something different, distant.

"What's the matter?"

Without the courtesy of refocusing on her, he said, "They have just given me an assignment."

She did not reply but the gravity of those words did not escape her. Her first instinct was to check the PC systems again but before she could do so he raised his hand, shook his head, and said, "Stop."

Confused, she asked him, "What do you mean? We have to know if I have access."

He continued shaking his head. "Did you have access a few hours ago?" He saw her trying to access the records this morning. He already knew the answer.

"No."

"Then what makes you think you can issue a Vitapass, or even access those records, now?"

She picked up Chunk and sat down in a chair opposite him. "Nothing makes me think that. But what else would you have me do?"

"Nothing. Don't do anything. I have a feeling that anything we do now only digs this hole deeper."

She did not disagree with him, but she did not understand how he was proposing to deal with the immediate issue at hand. "So if you can't acquire a Vitapass, what exactly are you going to do?"

He rose from the couch and allowed the full extent of his extensive frame to stretch toward the ceiling. Without looking at either her or Chunk, he started walking toward the door and said, "I guess I'm going to do my job."

He knew that she wanted to discuss this further. She wanted to lodge some form of protest. He grabbed his trench coat and exited such that an argument was impractical. As he fled the apartment he made a conscious effort to not turn back. He strode through the spacious hallways of his building and made his way to the nearest restaurant.

A long night of restlessness had left him famished. He knew that nothing productive was going to happen without sustenance. In the next tower over there was one of his favorite dives. It was open around the clock and served little else other than breakfast. It served dishes with generic names. It didn't offer buttered, sautéed bereia. It offered fish. It didn't offer toasted whole-grain English muffins. It offered bread. The Caffeinate was some of the strongest he had tasted and the servers were surly. This was a place where he stopped to collect his thoughts before attempting an assignment.

As he sat in his booth he gazed out at the aethyr swirling outside. Although the constant cloud cover swirled throughout the sky above, it was thin today. At random intervals bright rays of sunshine darted through the clouds. They illuminated the tumultuous moisture dancing through the Torrenthian air. This caused sheets of raindrops with rainbow hues to dance amongst the towers like butterflies.

For the next hour, he sat and munched on his fish. He reviewed the assignment's details in his mind. He presented a serene exterior. But his inner soul consisted of two wildly different, and at times confrontational, personas. He was at once the dutiful employee – the decorated agent who was about to embark on yet another successful mission. Yet he was also a caged animal searching for some plan, some scheme, that would solve this equation.

The details of the assignment were unique. He could not remember encountering more than one unlicensed child at a time. He often confronted a single individual – the mother – in the completion of his duties. On occasion, he had to deal with a couple, or a mother and her parents, at the same time - but there was only ever one baby. This assignment was different.

The Plethora Packing plant was several kilometers away. It was a sprawling facility. It processed and packaged ocean products for distribution and resale throughout Centrian. Great cargo ships hauled metric tons of raw materials from Oceanus into the facility around the clock. The plant processed organic materials – fish, rays, serpents, seaweeds, dragons, corals, etc. – but also had another division that processed mineral deposits mined from the ocean floor. He was quite familiar with the plant. On a bad day, he could smell its rotting industrial processes from his own apartment.

There were three Midlian women who worked in the factory processing a wide array of shellfish. According to NCU intelligence, they had all somehow managed to give birth within weeks of each other. They housed the babies somewhere inside the facility itself.

Midlians were an ethnic minority characterized by pale skin, a complete lack of body hair, and a short stature. They stood about half the height of an average Centrian citizen. They spoke the common language but had accents that made them difficult to understand. Like many minority communities, they tended to work and live in close-knit groups. It was rare to find only one of them residing in a given area.

They also had a unique ability to delay or accelerate, to a certain extent, their own gestational periods. With this in mind, it was not shocking that these three women managed to give birth at nearly the same time. Nevertheless, it was exceptional that the NCU found three women who had all borne unlicensed children.

With a solid meal in his gullet, Pontius left the restaurant and began the short trip to the packing plant. The temporary brilliance of the technicolored sunlight was now replaced by heavier cloud cover. With it came a driving, horizontal wind. It left him wondering if any of the drops completed a full vertical path to the streets far below. He walked through a grand concourse and made his way toward the nearest scaler platform. He couldn't help but notice the scanners positioned all around him. Although he had no logical reason to fear their presence at this exact moment, he couldn't help but watch each one as he passed. He almost expected them to alert the authorities to his now-criminal presence.

A few short stops later, he exited the scaler and made his way to the grounds of the sprawling Plethora complex. When the scaler door opened, the full brunt of processed fish guts assaulted his nose. The platform itself was still outside the Plethora grounds. But it was clear from the pedestrian traffic that this stop was primarily for the service of Plethora employees and clients. Various people en route sported thick leather aprons. They were stained with the entrails of thousands of sea creatures. Other individuals handled the shipping of the processed materials. From the scaler platform itself, almost everyone went to or from Plethora.

At the plant's gates, he presented an easy ruse as a health inspector. The guards asked him to sit in the gate station while they made numerous convos to their superiors. After having presented the proper (false) paperwork, he sat down and waited.

While he was awaiting authorization, he studied the individuals entering and exiting the plant. It was clear that there was an upper class of "normal" individuals. They wore the uniforms of managers. They garnered the respect of passersby. Some of them were in the act of managing others even as they traversed the gates. They barked orders through their convos. They transmitted notes to the assistants who walked alongside.

Midlians dominated the underclass. They wore the garb of the brutalized. They had filthy clothes. Scars adorned their arms and faces. The look in their eyes was that of hypnotized servants who had lost their zeal for life.

After 20 minutes, a plant representative came to the gate and shook his hand. He was a swarthy creature, not Midlian, but almost as short, with a portly build and a hirsute complexion. He smiled profusely and shook his hand with a false vigor. Improbable as it seemed, he found that this man somehow smelled worse than his surroundings.

"How can I help you-un?" His gaping maw revealed a set of teeth as brown as the eels processed within the factory. He seemed to have a nervous tic that consisted of half-bowing, so fervently as to resemble an awkward dance move.

He looked down at him and said, "Shellfish."

He learned long ago that subterfuge was one of the easiest ways to gain access to his targets. Yet he never took much relish in the acting aspect of his job. His officially-issued false documents meant that he never needed to be convincing in his ruses. This was convenient because he would have made for an awful thespian if his life had taken a different path.

The swarthy man's smile diminished as he attempted to process this order. "Ehh, processing, packaging, or shipping?"

"Processing."

The man nodded, made a one-eighty back to the plant, and began scurrying off. Pontius realized that he should follow. The round little man had surprising speed. He waddled off into the bowels of the plant.

The plant had its own internal transit system. Rails skirted either wall. Along each rail traveled small open platforms just wide enough for several people to stand upon. The little man hoisted himself onto one of the platforms and motioned for Pontius to join him. Although the platform accommodated several people, it was difficult to find stability without leaning on or over the little fat man. A small panel rose from the center of the platform, housing a single joystick. Once satisfied that Pontius had gained purchase on the platform, the man pressed the joystick forward. The duo whisked forward.

The rail-bound platform sped through many buildings. Occasionally, the rail would split in two-or-more directions. The joystick action of the fat man guided it down the proper path. On several occasions, Pontius nearly fell as the platform abruptly changed course.

The two sped along the rail for a full 30 minutes; such was the scope of the entire campus. After 20 minutes, Pontius stopped counting the number of buildings they had traveled through. A few of these buildings held the upper class administrative or managerial workers. The majority of the buildings housed the literal guts of the enterprise. Hundreds of workers, many of them Midlian, worked along assembly lines. They hacked and sliced all manner of ocean fauna. Some of the buildings housed the later-stage processing. This included handling various animal bits that were no longer identifiable. But the most fascinating buildings dealt with the initial processing of whole creatures. At one particularly boisterous processing line, workers disassembled the legs of sea dragons. Each one was more than six meters in length. Each massive leg started at one end of the assembly line. At the other end, various offshoots led to huge bins of scales, claws, bones, and myriad cuts of muscle and tissue.

In another building – a separating center – they dumped huge containers of various sea creatures onto a central stage. From that stage, ceiling mounted cranes plucked creatures off the pile. They placed the creatures onto their appropriate processing lines. These led off to other buildings. Although they sped through the building in less than a minute, he noticed many creatures he could not identify. Some of them had more appendages than he knew to be natural for anything in Oceanus. Others came sheathed in a thick, viscous layer of slime, such that it was hard to make out the fish (?) lying within.

The prevailing theme of all the buildings – indeed, of the entire company – was grey. Nothing was black. Nothing was white. Everything – from the employees, to the machines, to the buildings, to the fish themselves – emitted its own unique shade of grey. The effect was complete. He wondered if there was some economic advantage to constructing an entire facility from a single grimy color.

He also wondered why they didn't change the name of the company to Greyhound Packing. Every surface oozed grey and every building swarmed with packs of dogs. One couldn't swing a hammer without hitting at least two mutts. They crowded in packs along the processing floors. Some of them where almost run over as various wheeled machines moved about the processing floors. Still others perched precariously close to the intakes for some of the automated machinery. He saw that some of the processing stations emitted a spray of fish bits as they went about their butchering business. The dogs positioned themselves in such a way to ensure that no scrap ever hit the floor.

The shellfish processing building was like none of the others. Before the platform even made it into the building, a dull roar emanated from within its grey walls. Once they passed inside, the roar rose to a deafening cacophony. It was more felt than heard. At one end of the building they fed shellfish, some of them larger than a horse, into a series of violently shaking contraptions. With their inner workings obscured, it was easy to imagine the crushing and hammering inside. Each machine emitted a continual stream of pulverized shells and chunks of meat. Workers stationed along the exit picked the meat off the conveyor belt and throw it into bins wheeled behind them. The bins in turn found their way to other stations across the floor. From there, employees continued the long task of disassembling, flaying, dicing, and sorting the foodstuffs.

Great fans dominated the ceiling. Their incredible blades interlocked. They moved with such ferocity that they formed nothing but blurred visual discs. The discs heaved and swayed as they strained their moorings. While they were spinning with great velocity, he felt no iota of breeze emanating from them. In fact, he wondered if they were for airflow at all. Every so often a piece of mangled beast escaped one of the crushers and shot toward the ceiling. The fans served as just another butchering device.

When the platform came to rest, he was almost unsettled by the lack of motion. He had braced himself against the swift directional changes. Now the presence of stability was, in its own way, destabilizing. Giving no notice of his condition, the little man hopped off the platform. He turned back toward Pontius and motioned for him to follow.

Once they were both on the plant floor, the man made a grand motion all around him. He turned back to Pontius, smiled half-heartedly, and looked at him wide-eyed. His expression seemed to say, *"Well?"*

A Dusk Forever Waning

The continual pounding of the shell crushers made any form of traditional discussion pointless. Pontius found himself wanting to ask questions, but he wasn't sure how to accomplish the feat. He considered commencing the arduous task of UNI-mailing his questions to the man standing in front of him. He thought better of it. With no direct facility for conversation, it was a convenient excuse to snoop around and survey the situation. Pontius nodded as though he knew what he was doing. He then proceeded to stroll across the floor. He cautiously picked his path between scurrying vehicles, a host of line workers, and the swarm of fetid dogs. The swarthy man followed behind him.

It took him mere minutes to identify the entire coven of mothers. All three of them were stood side-by-side on one end of a conveyor belt. They lifted large chunks of claw meat, slicing them with amazing efficiency. They released the butchered pieces to continue down the line. He recognized all three of them from the records he downloaded earlier. He did not expect to find them literally working next to each other. Yet here they stood before him, paying him no attention and swinging their impressive blades. They carved up an endless stream of meat that had moments before escaped its protective shells.

He paused for a moment before the three women, not wanting to tip his hand. They never noticed his presence and the little man saw nothing out of the ordinary. NCU intelligence indicated that the children were living somewhere on the Plethora grounds. But it was obvious that the babies were not right here. He risked their escape if he alerted them now. He turned and continued his "health inspection".

Although he was not here for reasons of public safety, he could not help but notice the ecosystem throughout the plant. The dogs were a form of biological sanitation. The floors were clean to the eye, as the beasts lapped up any stray scrap. When not receiving adequate sustenance they licked fish bits off the massive machines – or off the coats of their brethren.

While the machinery itself looked clean, the dogs were another matter altogether. Huge insects, some of them as large as a man's fist, swarmed around the dogs with an angry persistence. It was clear that they fed not only on the random scraps from the machines, but also on the dogs themselves. Many of the mutts sported festering sores upon which even more insects intersected. The dogs themselves were in fierce competition. Every several minutes a new duel broke out between two or more of the canines. These often ended in nothing but feral bravado, but their scars made it clear that these contests were not just for show. Under one of the shell crushers, he saw a dead dog rotting. Many thousands of insects caused its skin to bubble like a pot of boiling water.

The sea creatures fed into the giant machines were beset by insects. They clung to the shelled carcasses, refusing to budge even as they were thrust into the crushers. When the pulverized creatures emerged, there were still insects clinging to any remaining foothold. New swarms joined the attack as the mangled crustaceans exited the machine.

Several meters past the crushers, the remaining shellfish pieces passed under a nozzle. It rained down a continual spray of clear liquid. This liquid had a repulsive effect on all insect life. None of them would come near the shells or the meat thereafter as it continued its processing journey. The dogs, however, still followed the assembly line. They searched for any stray scrap that might escape the conveyor.

Having seen his fill of the processing floor, he stood in the very center. He turned in a tight circle, surveying his surroundings, and wondering where he might search next. He considered asking to interview the coven under some pretext about health conditions. But he wasn't sure how to work that into his hunting expedition. As he raised his gaze, he saw a ring of second-story offices looking out upon the whole operation. Several metal stairways stationed around the outer walls of the expanse led to a gangway that circled the entire floor. That gangway was a vantage point. The managers could step from their spacious offices and survey the activities below.

He made a beeline for the nearest metal stairway and arrived on the upper gangway. When he reached this upper level, he pointed down to the mothers, some 30 meters away. He sent a message to his escort stating that he would like to speak with all three of them – and their supervisor. His escort maintained his smile but hesitated, unaccustomed to such a request. He was about to protest, but Pontius shot him a look indicating that this request was not up for discussion.

Without further messaging, the host nodded and scurried down the gangway. He motioned for Pontius to follow. Above the mothers working on the plant floor stood the entrance to one of the spacious offices. The host opened the door and motioned for Pontius to enter.

Entering the office was an abrupt entree into another world. Shutting the door behind them silenced almost all the raging sound from the plant floor. The violent smashing of the shell crushers was nothing more than a soft hum. It soothed like the white noise of a refrigerator running in the background. The office itself was huge, featuring almost 200 square meters in floor space. One entire wall consisted of glass. It looked out across the gangway and the expanse of the entire processing floor below. The room was fully furnished. It featured couches, chairs, and tables that were reminiscent of a residential setting. Like a studio apartment, one corner of the space was an efficiency kitchen, complete with a sink and a stove. Pontius saw a small bathroom through a door on the far wall. A closed door stood next to the bathroom.

There was some kind of perfuming and filtration system in place. The air inside the office was cooler and smelled somewhat better than the rest of the plant. While no place in Plethora could qualify as fresh, the room tried hard to cover the usual stench. He experienced an epic nasal battle between sage, cinnamon, and putrefying fish guts.

He couldn't help but notice the lived-in feel of the space. The couches were well-worn. There were some minor pieces of clothing crumpled amongst corners of the furniture. Some of the clothing was female. Gaming accoutrements sat on several of the end tables. There was a small pile of dishes in the sink.

Against the wall closest to the entryway was an impressive desk carved from the bleached, polished bones of a grand beast. A man of considerable stature sat behind it, but rose to greet Pontius as he entered. He smiled profusely, like Pontius's filthy host. Yet the manager had a far cleaner and more professional demeanor. The manager shook his hand and introduced himself as *Carian*. He motioned for Pontius to sit in one of the chairs hovering in front of the desk.

Carian was above-average height with a slight build and a ruddy complexion. This implied that he spent a great deal of time in the tanners. Given the overcast conditions in Centrian, a tan was one of the ultimate status symbols. His black hair flowed like a mane and danced upon his shoulders. His most remarkable feature was his brilliant jade-green eyes that shone with their own inner light. He wore a long, flat-grey tunic that flared from his waist and stretched just past his knees.

With the men situated, the manager smiled again at Pontius.

"I trust that you-un are having a pleasant tour of our facilities?"

Pontius did not answer. Rather, he turned to his host, who was floating haphazardly in his chair, and asked, "The women – where are the women?"

The little man was somewhat shocked. He assumed that the discourse from here forward would be between Carian and Pontius. When he realized that he was serious in his request, he jumped off the chair, scurrying out of the office and back to the plant floor. Carian pointed out that the plant workers were filthy. Pontius gave no indication that this bothered him at all.

With the two of them in the room, Pontius swiveled around and continued absorbing the details of the office. Carian began to make small talk but halted when Pontius held up his hand to signal for silence. After a full two minutes of this survey, he finally broke the tension.

"This is quite the spacious office you have here."

"I have worked for Plethora for almost a thousand years. They treat me quite well."

He swiveled such that his back was facing Carian. He made no attempt to reestablish eye contact.

"It seems as though you spend a great deal of time here."

"Some men choose to take their work home with them. Me – I tend to bring more of my home to work. It just makes everything so much easier."

"You must have a very understanding wife."

Carian chuckled and replied, "Thankfully, I'm a single man."

"And your children?"

This was a deliberately awkward question. The birthrate was so low that there was no natural reason to assume anyone had a child, let alone *children*, waiting for them at home. He did not turn to face Carian but listened to the painful pause in his voice.

"I am childless." Carian's response was terse.

Another full minute passed before he spoke again.

"Where does that door lead?" He pointed to the door situated right next to the bathroom.

"Those are my private quarters."

"The furnishings in this room already feel quite... private to me."

Carian didn't miss a beat. "I do spend a great deal of time in this office – even *private* time. But on those nights when I absolutely must sleep at the office, I have a bed and a few changes of clothes in the back room."

"I see." Pontius didn't see, but he wasn't inclined – yet – to push the issue. He sat in silence with his back to Carian and allowed another awkward three minutes to tick off the clock.

The little man returned with the confused women. They were less than half way through their 14-hour shifts. They were not accustomed to leaving the processing floor. A thick layer of shellfish detritus covered all three of them. Their broad leather aprons bore the bodily fluids of every kind of shellfish ever pulled from Oceanus. Their hairless heads hid under a slimy toupee of guts. Although they stood rigid, their eyes darted about the room.

The coven stood before the great white desk. They were shoulder-to-shoulder, like soldiers in formation, facing Carian. Pontius rose upon their entry and stood behind them. Feeling no need for explanations, he barked, "Turn around." They all complied.

For the next four minutes, he did nothing but watch them. He gazed around the room but often returned back to them. He watched their faces. He watched their faces as they watched his face watching their faces. He watched their reactions as he gazed around the room. He watched the involuntarily twitches in their knees as he feigned a movement toward one part of the room or the other.

Carian sat patiently, given that he he had no idea where this was leading. But after some minutes, the uncertainty and strain started to wear on him and the expression on his face soured. After several more minutes, he felt compelled to speak.

"Beg your-un pardon, but is there something you'd like to ask these women?"

Pontius returned his gaze to Carian but made no immediate attempt to reply.

Carian tried again. "Is there something you'd like to ask *me*?"

Pontius thought for a moment, struggling to put the pieces together.

Carian kept pressing. "Have you seen something here that needs to be addressed? Does it have something to do with these workers?"

Pontius was not inclined to hear the next question. He had a new plan of action.

"I need to use the restroom." And with that, he walked across the room toward the small bathroom, awaiting no invitation.

Once in the bathroom he closed the door tight and made no attempt to relieve himself. Standing in the narrow space between the toilet and the back wall, he pressed his ear hard against the smooth surface and waited. There was a muted background hum of the shell crushers. It provided a masking layer of white noise, but he closed his eyes and tried to listen to any sound above the dull baseline. He stood and listened first for a minute, then for a second, then for a third.

He was about to abandon this line of thinking and return to the main office area when he caught the faint sound of bells. He heard some kind of elementary music played with the automated staccato of a wind-up toy. He lowered the pressure of his face against the wall. Doing this had the effect of stunting the shell crusher vibrations transferring into his skull. Yet it allowed him to hear the faint report of the bells with greater clarity. He stood in this position for another 30 seconds before he heard the faint muffle of a voice. It was a single voice providing comfort in cooing tones.

Pulling away from the wall, he banged his fists fiercely and violently against its surface. This created an explosive series of vibrations that shook the tiny bathroom from within. After a full 10 seconds of this racket, he stopped abruptly. He heard the clear sound of babies' cries cutting through the stifling factory air.

He flew out of the bathroom. As he did, two of the Midlian women reflexively made their way to the backroom. The third woman was still frozen in front of the great desk, now shaking. Carian barked at the two women to come back but they paid him no mind. Pontius marched to a position in front of the desk. He turned toward the swarthy little man, and said with a seething menace, "Leave." He did not need to ask twice. The little man fled the office with impressive haste.

With the little man gone, he strode to the glass wall and banged it with his fist. He knew this would have the effect of turning the entire wall opaque. The glass surface became as grey as all the others in the office space. He removed his spot welder and sealed the door.

When he turned around he saw that two of the women had opened the door to the backroom. Having rushed in, they now worked to calm their babies, even in their filthy states. Standing beside them was another Midlian woman who had been in the backroom all along – he took her to be a nanny. Looking back again at the desk, the third woman was still frozen in front of it. She shook and wept. She didn't know what was going to happen, but she was afraid. Carian stood behind his desk but looked calm, almost serene, and showed no sign of curtailing the proceedings.

Pontius now strode into the backroom. This action was enough to draw Carian from his position. When he reached the room, he stood in the middle and surveyed his surroundings. Less than half the size of the front office, it appeared to have been a storeroom. They converted it into a makeshift nursery and play center. Three cribs stood against one side. Toys littered the floor. A rocking chair was off to one side where the nanny whittled away many hours in the overview of these children. Opposite the crib wall, three cots aligned in an almost military fashion. An open shower stood in one corner.

When Pontius turned back toward the entrance, Carian stood in the doorway, observing. The frozen Midlian woman had not followed. The two women who had originally darted into the room were now comforting babies against their slimy bosoms. The nanny was doing her best to quell the third child.

The babies – all three of them – shared common traits. They each sported sparse tufts of black hair, which made it clear to him that they were not pure-blood Midlians. Their complexions, while pale, were not the stark white of a typical Midlian child. Most telling, he could see through their squinting protests that they all had brilliant green eyes.

With robotic certainty, Pontius launched into his ritual. "You are in violation of at least 12 different statutes governing the birthing, housing, and protection of unlicensed humans. What I'm about to transmit to your UNIs are the termination licenses for your babies. Since your babies have no Vitapasses and therefore are not *real* people, they have been assigned the legal identifiers of AJ2903G33, X8B57J213, and Y921P5GTT. I'm also transmitting all my licenses to operate as an NCU agent anywhere in the nation of Centrian. You don't need to accept any of these transmissions. In the Grand Court case of Hakkernon vs. Centrian, it has already been ruled that my transmission of these credentials establishes my legal authority, whether you accept those transmissions or not."

While this ritual was much older than his natural memory allowed, the utterance of those words now felt bizarre. It felt foreign. He started the memorized speech with the same vigor that he always employed. But he became aware less than half way through the statement that the words were flowing from him in an automated fashion. It was as though he wasn't consciously speaking them, but instead was playing a recording. In fact, by the time he finished the statement, he could hear his own words coming back to him as though they were foreign. They sounded like an entity with which he no longer identified or understood.

The feeling invoked by these words was not the only foreign aspect to this engagement. He was well accustomed to the traditional signs of panic. He was always prepared for the potential threat of violence. But he was quite taken aback by what transpired around him now.

Carian stood in the doorway. He wasn't just smiling. He was smug. Pontius had the feeling that he was just putting on a show and that Carian was soaking it up. The women in the room paid no attention to Pontius. He understood their focus on calming their babies. But he could never recall a mother – let alone, two mothers and a nanny – so nonchalant regarding the recitation of his legal rights. The cold reality of an NCU agent's legal authority almost always reduced parents – especially mothers – to tears.

He experienced a most profound sensation – he didn't know what to do next. He was the most decorated agent in the department. He did this thousands of times before – and he did it better than anyone else before him. Yet now, he found himself at a complete loss.

When he left the apartment, the initial panic of this assignment subsided. He was never able to formulate a viable alternative plan of action – but he didn't need to. While at the restaurant reading through NCU records, his mind unconsciously flipped into autopilot. His worries about Chunk, Moria, the NCU, and Vitapasses melted away. He descended into the mindless and satisfactory function of completing yet another assignment. By the time he left the restaurant, he was as carefree as any skilled craftsman about to embark upon another day of productivity. It wasn't until now – until he spoke those plaintive words establishing his legal right to kill these children – that the reality of his own situation rushed back into his mind.

The perverse and nonchalant reaction he received from these people was even more unsettling. Here he was, threatening to slaughter not one child, but three, and no one in the room seemed stressed about the situation. This combination of factors had the unforeseen effect of sending Pontius into a panic. If these people responded violently, or even desperately – or just responded in any manner – it would give him some basis to act. He could work through a prescribed set of actions as a scientist works through similar steps every time he conducts an experiment.

He looked to the babies, then to the mothers, then to Carian, then back to the babies again. The mothers paid him no attention. Carian was waiting for something –exactly what, Pontius could not be certain. His mind raced as he considered his next steps.

It was at this point that his script became useless. He so wanted to move them along to his ultimate barter. It was at this point that he wanted to assure them that he could *grant life* – legitimate life – if they would only cooperate. This was the point where he could reveal his benevolent nature and save all three children in one charitable gesture. And yet, he knew that he had nothing to barter – no Vitapasses, no legitimacy, nothing that would make a deal worthwhile. Without his key to life, he was nothing more than a common agent, a carrier of doom.

The obvious conclusion was to kill the babies. This was his last possible course of action. The ideal solution was to work his deal with them for a Vitapass – a Vitapass to which he now had no more access than the common man. The middle ground was murky and he knew not where it led.

He looked back and forth between the actors for several painful minutes. He realized that he would have to spark a course of action. He began moving toward the nanny and said, "I will now exterminate these babies."

As he did so, he was looking at Carian, and Carian responded with the gesture for which he had been searching. Carian raised his hand, to signal a pause in the action, and his smile gained a renewed vigor. He started walking toward Pontius with hand extended. The hand held a transfer card.

"Now-un, there's no reason to be so brash. We are businessmen, and we conduct business every single day of our lives. There is no reason why today should be any different."

Carian stopped a safe distance away with his arm extended outward. Pontius grabbed the transfer card, pulled it back to his face, and inspected it. It contained a transfer of one million squalem. Pontius was dumbfounded.

His salary put him in the top two percent of Centrian wage earners. He made 120,000 squalem per year from the NCU. The reason he asked for a half million squalem when he negotiated his deals was because no one ever had a half million squalem to give. He never saw anyone come close to offering a half million squalem. So to see someone handing him a transfer card now for a full million was staggering.

He flipped the card over in his hand. He scanned the transaction signature on the bottom of the card and a cursory search confirmed that it was legitimate. It was a million squalem – more money than he had ever seen in his life – for the service of walking back out of the Plethora plant.

Before he could even consider accepting the offer, his natural curiosity forced him to ponder the source of such funds. Carian had a position of privilege in this plant, but Pontius assumed that the two of them earned a nearly identical salary. He expected that no one but the top executives in the company could afford such an audacious bribe.

Perhaps sensing the confusion, Carian nodded and said, "It's that simple. You just walk out of here and you're a million squalem richer."

Then it hit him. His ruse had been more apropos than he had imagined. There were many health inspectors – *actual* health inspectors – who came through the plant on a regular basis. It was quite possible that many of them ended up in Carian's office. Plethora authorized Carian to spend a great deal of funds to keep the inspectors at bay.

"This is Plethora money, isn't it?" He now looked at the transfer card with suspicion.

Carian moved forward and grasped Pontius's hand in his. He wrapped Pontius's fingers around the card. He looked into Pontius's eyes and said, "It's your money. Take it. Enjoy it. And leave us here in peace."

Carian's tone was not threatening or exasperated. He sounded almost reassuring. He was smiling at Pontius as he placed his other hand on Pontius's shoulder. This confused Pontius. It left him at a loss for words. But he wasn't moving toward the door either.

The two men stared at each other for a full minute before Carian reiterated, "Take it."

Something snapped in Pontius and he withdrew, staggering back as though breaking free from hypnosis.

"Nay. Nay. NAY. This doesn't make any sense."

Carian was bewildered, but didn't break character. "Why? What do you mean?"

"If I take this money, if I leave this place now, it's not done. *It's never done.* There are 99 others out there like me. There are scanners littered throughout this sodden planet. There are bounty hunters. There are all manner of miscreants who would prey upon someone of unlicensed status. If I take this money now, what's next? Where do you and these refugees go from here?"

The strain in his voice betrayed his perplexed state. With a potential future offered to Chunk at LiveLong, he was now incredulous that anyone would place the life of a refugee on a child. He could not see the utility of such a transaction.

He expected Carian to blanch at such a retort, but Carian's demeanor was calm and still reassuring. "I appreciate your concern, but we're not too worried about that."

But he was not allayed. He shook his head furiously and tried to reiterate his position, "Do you know how many of these babies I've killed? Do you know what happens to them even when they survive for a few more months or years? If I don't kill them today, another agent will be here – maybe next week, maybe next month, but trust me, they will be here. And what do you do then?"

Carian's grin turned impish and he reached inside his tunic, pulling out another transfer card. He waved it around with a flourish, saying, "There's always more where that came from."

Pontius had no doubt that Plethora's pockets were deep. Carian seemed to think this was a brilliant reply, but the smug nature of this reasoning annoyed him further.

"So that's your answer? Every week, every month, you'll dig up another million squalem to throw at the next headhunter who comes along? You can't honestly think that's sustainable? What happens if Plethora notices that your bribery money is growing exponentially? What happens if someone catches one of your Midlians here when you're not around to buy them out? What happens when you simply don't have a transfer card in your pocket?"

His tone grew every more impatient. The ignorance of Carian's solution dismayed him. He saw it as flawed and only buying a few more months before the slaughter of these babies commenced.

Carian shrugged, indicating that he did not consider these consequences to be viable. Pontius was not satisfied. He walked to the baby held by the nanny and snatched it from her grasp. For the first time, the nanny and both mothers looked somewhat alarmed, but they gave no overt signs of dismay. Carian affected a different posture. He struggled to keep his smooth demeanor. This turn of events began to agitate him.

"Two million." Carian flung the next transfer card at Pontius. Pontius managed to catch it, but was again annoyed by this reaction. He could not understand the logic of buying a few more hours of life.

"This is folly,. You don't understand the forces that will rain down upon these children."

Carian bit his lip and scowled, now growing exasperated by Pontius's recalcitrance. Pontius started raising the baby above his head. Carian dug into his breast pocket and flung another three cards at Pontius's feet.

"Five million! Surely you cannot sit in your ivory tower and scoff at five million? What kind of man so foolishly disregards his own future in such a way? Have you ever had five million in your account? Have you ever even seen a balance half that high? What could you do for the next *thousand years* with that much money in your account?"

Carian's voice escalated to one of outright anxiety. Pontius's knees were weak and shaking – almost as fast as his head was shaking.

"Damn it, you fool! You're missing the point. You're buying hours, days, maybe weeks. There are others like me. I don't want to eat your money just to watch these children slaughtered by the next man who follows me."

Carian swung his head to the ceiling and let out a wicked growl of frustration. Flummoxed and at a loss for words, he tried to solve this scenario. His equation, so carefully laid out many months ago, was now crashing to the ground before his eyes. There was no measure by which he could understand Pontius's foolhardiness. He could not imagine someone so stupid as to scoff at five million squalem.

"Fine! Then what exactly is it that you want? What shining jewel is the proper price for you to just exit this place and leave us the fuck alone? Take the money! Take whatever you want! Just take something and leave our family in peace!"

Carian screamed with a violent rage. Yet he made no signs of closing the gap. Even in his anger, he understood confrontation to be foolish. Pontius now held one of his babies precariously over his head. He searched his environment for some key that would send the assassin on his way.

"Do you want to fuck them? You can fuck all of them if you like! Marin – the one out by my desk – she can suck dick like no other. We'll clean them all up, we'll set you up here for the night. You can record the whole affair. You can jerk off to it every night when you're alone. You can do anything to them you want." There was a long pause as Carian began weeping, his voice cracking and his stature breaking down. "Take whatever you want, do whatever you want, but please, please don't hurt our children!" Carian sobbed uncontrollably.

The irony of this offer was not lost on Pontius. If he could get his hands on those Vitapasses – those fucking Vitapasses – this would all be so easy. A few days ago this offer would have been his ultimate goal – and now it seemed pointless. What was the point of such prostitution and humiliation if he offered nothing lasting and meaningful in return? What was the point of degrading this man's Midlian harem if it only stayed the execution for a few weeks or a few months? The whole endeavor seemed so worthless to him that he couldn't fathom accepting such an obscene offer.

Through his tears, Carian stared at Pontius, looking for some kind of reprieve, some sign of acceptance of his offer. He found it impossible that anyone opted for wanton violence when offered such wealth. It was the most shattering moment of Carian's two-thousand-year existence.

He watched helplessly as Pontius thrust the child to the floor. It landed with a sickening thud. The baby didn't cry. It didn't even move. Its soft skull and bulbous brain crushed on impact.

This tragedy was the first action that brought a sustained response from anyone other than Pontius. Carian screamed in agony and lept forward to the dead mass on the floor. All three women – two of them still holding their babies - flung themselves at Pontius. Their actions were not an attack so much as a pitiful attempt to drag him down from the knees. The wailing of Carian and the three women stung Pontius's ears and made him nauseous.

He wanted them to fight him. He was waiting – hoping – they would attack him in any way. Yet all they could do was cling to his legs – crying, yelling, sobbing.

With a trembling arm he reached down and plucked the second baby from one of the women. She screamed anew and the screech of her voice unsettled him like nothing he had ever heard before.

As he pulled the baby to his chest, he became aware that he was crying. There was no part of his natural memory that had ever remembered crying – not for anyone, not for anything. And here he was, in the middle of his sworn duties, sobbing like one of the women clamoring for their unlicensed refugees. The tears streaked down his cheeks in great torrents. The knot in his throat made it almost impossible to breath. He felt pain in his chest and he wondered if this was the sensation of a heart attack.

As he raised the baby above his head, it took on an impossible weight. He couldn't remember ever having lifted something so ponderous. He was vaguely aware that the baby – like everyone else in the room – was screaming wildly, but he could hear nothing. It wriggled and fussed and had its mouth open in a wailing fashion. Yet the more he looked at it, the more he struggled to hear anything emanating from it.

With the child raised above his head just like the first, he found himself surveying his surroundings. Carian was cuddling with the dead mass of his child and screaming incoherently. The three tiny women at his feet flailed and pulled at his coat but they could not find the strength to rise. The entire room was a solid mass of death, sorrow, and tragedy.

He had to steel his legs again, for he was almost certain he would faint. He became sick, vomiting down the front of his shirt even while both arms remained raised above his head. The pain in his chest grew sharper and he wasn't certain how long he could maintain this pose.

At that moment everything froze around him. The screams, while echoing throughout the room, did not register in his mind. The flailing of the women seemed to be stuck in molasses. He had the distinct impression that he was watching the entire scene. He stood above himself, outside himself. He saw the carnage already wrought and the carnage about to rain down. It was at this moment, for the first time ever, that he understood. He was the Angel of Death.

He had nothing to offer these people. He had no access to Vitapasses and without them, anything he accepted as a bribe would only delay the inevitable. He was now nothing more than an instrument of the state. He was an executioner with no thought and no morality about the actions undertook.

How long he stood there he could not tell, for his sense of time disconnected from reality. He was watching this horrific scene play out the way a teenage boy replays the penultimate scene in a horror movie. Unlike that boy, the scene sickened him. After some indeterminate period, he lowered his hands. He dropped the baby back into the waiting arms of one of the disconsolate mothers.

The significance of this act was not apparent to anyone else in the room. Carian didn't even see it. He was sobbing so powerfully over the corpse of his child that he was oblivious to anything else in the room. While the women may have felt relieved, they were still so hysterical that there was nothing to do but to continue wailing. They did not understand if this was some temporary reprieve or a true change in direction. It wasn't until he began shaking them off his legs that they first understood that something had shifted.

After a great effort on his part, he freed the women from his legs and managed to step clear of the train wreck. While Carian and the women were still beside themselves, a strange calm came over him. The pain in his chest subsided. His nausea fled. His knees felt firm and strong. He took one last look at the room, soaked in the destruction he had brought to bear, then strode toward the office.

As he walked through the office, the third mother was still standing there, shaking but frozen in place. She made no attempt to move. Yet she stared into him as he walked past her, freed the door, and escaped to the plant floor below. He wanted to flee, paying her no attention, but her face burned in his mind as he made his way out of Plethora.

Chapter 9 – Throwing It All Away

The whole of the Centrian sky rained down upon him as he trudged through the sodden surface streets. It had been decades since he had set foot on what was colloquially referred to as *base level*. The term was a deliberate double entendre. It indicated not just the lack of elevation, but also the mindset in which its inhabitants operated. Most citizens never had any reason to sink to this level. They would do anything in their power to avoid contact with an actual street. The aerial environments of skyscrapers, cruisers, scalers, skywalks, and elevated platforms comprised what most Torrenthians viewed as their natural environment. The streets so far below were a forgotten rung on the evolutionary ladder.

If one stood at base level and looked upward, he would see more than torrents of rain. A constant snow of debris descended from the platforms, vehicles, and pedestrians so far above. For this reason, no one at base level was stupid enough to look upward. In fact, a fair number of them chose to don protective headgear. Discarded waste papers were an annoyance, but a bolt sprung from its scaler mooring could be deadly.

A good number of the streets were not even streets in the traditional sense. Most of them were permanent avenues of runoff water. This water danced through the gutters. Some avenues served as meeting grounds where multiple streams merged into greater rivers. Some of these rivers commandeered entire streets. As much as a meter deep, they raced between the towering skyscrapers with a vicious current. They swept along with them all manner of detritus from the environs above.

The street fauna was a dark and fascinating menagerie of suffocating fish, scavenging amphibians, and resourceful crustaceans. Some had wandered too far upstream and now hoped to make their way back to the warm and turbulent waters of Oceanus. Most of them had come to set up permanent colonies here. The waste dropping down from above was more than enough to maintain an impressive array of species. Many Oceanus creatures relied on phosphorescence as an evolutionary trait. On dark nights (or even some days) the glow of these creatures was an eerie but reliable form of illumination on the streets.

In those areas where the streets were not overtaken by sea life, packs of feral dogs held sway. The beasts fed on any crustaceans they could catch or any edible scrap falling from above. If they could find a lone traveler without sufficient protection they were not above attacking a human. For this reason, most people at base-level carried stun guns or spray cans of repellent.

Base level was not just the place where Centrian's physical trash fell. It was also the home of its human trash. There were few establishments there that did not cater to some form of vice. These vice shops were often facades. They fronted seedier underworld activities that took place in back rooms and quiet corridors.

Pontius reveled in the filthy water that now poured over him. It may have filtered through several layers of Centrian's upper crust, but it still felt refreshing. It revitalized him. It washed the vomit from the front of his coat. It washed the embarrassing tears from his eyes. It washed the fish guts from his boots. But much deeper than that, he felt that it was washing away the memories of what he had just experienced in Plethora. It was cleansing the stench of an entire life spent as an officer of the state.

When he exited the processing plant he assumed he would be making his way back home. Yet he knew he could not bring himself to skip along the public pathways he knew so well. He walked home as men had done so many thousands of years before him. He walked home through Centrian's streets and alleyways. He needed to clear his mind with the bromide of the real.

As he waded through one waterlogged street after another, his boots and pockets filled with water. This didn't bother him much, but he reached inside his pockets to see if there was anything worth protecting. As he did, he felt the smooth surface of two transfer cards resting in his right hip pocket. He did not mean to keep those, but they somehow landed in his pocket during the nightmare in the Plethora office. As soon as he felt them he came to an abrupt halt. He turned around and considered returning to the office so he could return them to their rightful owner. Just as quickly, he thought better of the return trip. He could not imagine facing Carian or any of those women again. He never wanted to set foot in Plethora for as long as he lived. Maybe he would destroy them. Maybe he would give them to someone else. At this point, he couldn't be certain.

After making his way through several more blocks he came to a broad street given over to a sizable river. It flowed to his right – south - toward Oceanus. Its breadth and depth made him realize that this street had been submerged for quite some time. Although he was confident in his ability to cross the flow, he stood for a moment in awe at the volume of items floating with it. Most of them were too grimy or disintegrated to identify. Yet he shuddered at the sight of a human arm sailing along with the rest of the debris.

With the river cleared, he found himself in a tight alleyway between two twin towers, a mere 15 meters apart. A series of walkways and platforms situated between the towers above meant that this alley was free of rainfall. In this environment, rain-free translated into a marketing opportunity. The base level street overflowed with a kaleidoscope of competing storefronts and street vendors.

At the far end of the alley, about 100 meters away, he could see the tight space opening into a broad marketplace. This was where the filthiest of Torrenthian merchants operated. He had never been through that marketplace, but he knew that its position at base level was less than a kilometer from the Bowery. With this in mind, and knowing that he was not in a mental condition to face Chunk, he ducked into a side bar to kill time and collect his thoughts.

What the bar lacked in taste it made up for in size. It was spacious. The main floor consisted of black metal tables. Black metal benches surrounded each table. There were at least 20 of these tables strewn about the establishment. Each table was capable of accommodating at least 12 customers. The bar, made from the same black metal, stretched for 15 meters along one wall. There were at least 100 patrons in the bar.

A Dusk Forever Waning

He was lucky to find a seat at the bar. The bartender placed a large vessel of frothy liquid in front of him. He never bothered asking what he wanted. He didn't need to ask. This wasn't due to posh biometric scanning that determined the perfect drink for your mood and physiology. Rather, the bar only served one drink. You either consumed the beverage or you drank nothing at all. He didn't need to ask the brand of the beverage. He was certain they concocted it right here on site.

Paying for the drink was an act that almost got him thrown out. He tried to transmit payment by UNI but the bartender shook his head. This was a cash-only establishment. He could not even remember the last time he held cash in his hand. It was a concept as antiquated as the buggy whip, yet the bartender was adamant in his demands. Unwilling to resume the journey home, he pulled a ring from his finger and waved it at the bartender.

"I paid 500 squalem for this many years ago."

The bartender snatched it from his hand. He ignorantly inspected it (for he had no idea what it was worth) and dangled it in front of Pontius.

"Looks like it's worth 50 to me."

He was in no mood to barter. "Fine. But I expect you to just keep bringing me drinks while I'm here."

This was amenable to the brute behind the bar. He put the ring in his pocket, snorted his approval, and left to attend other customers.

The patronage of the bar was an odd assortment. There were no women; this wasn't surprising to Pontius. Most of the men were fabulously drunk and they were perfect fits at base level. However, there were several men who stood out like a beacon. In a far corner sat a man of obvious wealth surrounded by several friends of similar means. He was unclear as to why such men would be here. At another table next to the rich man sat a slick character in a shiny red jacket. While not wealthy, he had means and seemed to be coordinating various activities. At odd times over the next 90 minutes, it seemed that almost every patron in the bar made at least one trip over to the red-jacketed man. They talked. At times something changed hands between them. The red-jacketed man seemed to take mental notes.

Pontius tried to ignore these activities. He wasn't interested in the machinations of a base level slime pit such as this one. Yet somehow he found himself surveying these events and wondering about their origin.

His primary objective was to chemically erase the memories of the Plethora plant. The frothy liquid before him was quite apt for that purpose. The entire drink consisted of foam but it was oddly satisfactory on the tongue. Interspersed throughout the foam were various unidentifiable bits. He found the bits in the first drink to be unpleasant. They had a meaty quality and if he bit down on them they offered a sour taste. But after his third mug of the liquid, he no longer minded them at all.

When he had polished off six of these drinks his fuzzy attention was thrust toward the back of the bar. Two large doors swung open. They were previously unnoticed because they matched the surrounding walls. As they did, a sizable crowd poured out. Some of them were content to remain in the main bar area, but most of them filed back out into the streets, having seen what they came for. The crowd was in a frenzy. The men were abuzz with some riotous activity. About half of them seemed elated. The other half seemed depressed, even angry.

The crowd exiting the backroom displayed two significant features. A small group carried a bruised and bloodied man on their shoulders. He was striking the victorious poses of a prizefighter. He was one of the base level men. It was obvious that he had experienced a great triumph.

Near the rear of this crowd came a rich man with a group of friends in tow. He looked nothing like the wealthy man already in the bar area. Yet it was striking to Pontius to find two such men in this dank establishment.

Once the crowd from the backroom made their way out, a bell rang. All the patrons in the front bar area began making their way to the bottleneck of the double doors. Unbeknownst to him, everyone in the front bar had been waiting for their turn to go into the backroom. With a full dose of liquid courage coursing through his veins, he rose and took a place near the rear of this crowd. Against his better judgment, he decided to see what was happening in back.

It took 20 minutes to make it to the double doors. All the patrons in the front bar were trying to squeeze their way in. It was apparent that a few burly bouncers were screening entrants before they could make it into the back room. The drunken revelers herded into the funnel of the double doors like cattle corralled into a pen.

As he waited in the back of the constricted crowd, he realized how severely he was out of place. He looked like none of the other base level participants. He could hear them talking amongst themselves, and he talked nothing like them. He didn't even smell like them. He was the definition of conspicuous.

When it was his turn to pass the doors, he made a concerted effort to stroll into the inner chamber. As he did so, a bouncer on his right extended a beefy paw and barred his entrance. The bouncer didn't grab his clothing. He grabbed his entire chest in the palm of his hand as a professional athlete palms a basketball. He had no immediate reason to believe he was in danger, but it was clear that he would not simply traipse into the venue. The bouncer wore clothing made for a man of epic proportions and yet it stretched across his muscles like spandex.

"This is no place for a skylander."

The bouncer to his left, identical in size, took note of the situation and moved closer to box him in. He thought for a brief moment. He raised his right hand, palm open, in a gesture indicating that he was holding nothing threatening. With an identical dose of caution, he then reached back down into his pocket, keeping eyes locked with the bouncer. Slowly – painfully slow – he pulled from his pocket the transfer cards. Once he had raised them to shoulder level he waved them to and fro before the bouncer's eyes. The bouncer, unimpressed, released a guttural growl and began pushing him back into the bar. But before he could make any progress, the red-jacketed man barked an order to halt. He approached Pontius with a squinting skepticism. After a full 30 seconds spent inspecting the transfer cards, he ordered the bouncer to allow his entry.

Being cleared for entry, the doors slammed shut behind him with a forceful echo that rang over the crowd. As it did, the crowd responded with a raucous cheer. He tried to find his bearing, moving forward as his eyes strained to conquer the darkness. The red-jacketed man placed a firm hand on his shoulder and restrained his progress from behind. He spun back around to face his host.

He was still trying to find his bearings. Many colors of smoke fused throughout the inner sanctum. They melded into a grey haze so thick that it was difficult to determine the true dimensions of the room. The air was hot and thick, clogging his lungs and stinging his tongue. Several spotlights shone down upon the center of the room, an arena situated at the bottom of a steep pit. The remainder of the room was pitch black. All around the pit the spectators crammed into narrow walkways. These walkways skirted the upper edges of the pit, but some of them also traversed it. Brave souls clinging to the steel frameworks could look straight down onto the impending action below. The walkways themselves were little more than ladders, with no handrails and no safety features. The zealous patrons commanding these perches hung precariously to either side of the ladderways. They constantly threatened to fall into the pit below.

The pit featured a thick floor of sawdust. Although there was no one on the pit floor, the activity from the previous session was apparently vibrant. The sawdust from the floor floated amongst the smoke and made the entire atmosphere of the enclosure stifling. At random places on the pit floor, the sawdust clumped into mounds of red, yellow, and clear liquids. From afar, it looked like putty.

The red-jacketed man smiled at Pontius. His clothing was audacious and it could not hide the fact that he belonged on base level. An impossible maze of silver, green, and purple thread crisscrossed the jacket. It screamed ostentation.

The man underneath was frail, somewhat dirty, and alert. His knee-level jacket tried to remove any attention from his personal features. His long, black, stringy hair hung in oily clumps to the middle of his back and obscured his face. Pontius couldn't be certain what his face looked like or what color his eyes were.

The red-jacket's smile transfixed him. It was a smile that showcased gleaming and finely chiseled teeth.

"Where is your money tonight, skylander?" Although the man smiled unendingly, his tone was vicious and cynical.

Pontius turned back toward the pit and scanned his surroundings. He realized where he was and what was about to happen but he wasn't prepared to stake anything on this ritual.

As he did so, he noticed a most peculiar activity amongst the crowd. All around him men were swapping great wads of cash. Some of it was so plentiful that they couldn't even corral it as it passed from one man to another. Mixed between the smoke and sawdust one only had to wait a minute to see a stray note floating along in the oppressive atmosphere. The notes sailed around before other bystanders snatched them up.

This was remarkable on two levels. The first was the fact that cash had become such an antiquated concept in Centrian. He saw it in random places —

stashed away in someone's desk drawer or mounted on a wall as a souvenir. But it was no longer considered a true form of currency. Aside from the front bar, he could not remember the last time someone asked him for physical currency in return for any debt. Cash on Centrian long ago became an anachronism — an antique kept in vaults and passed along to heirs as a souvenir of a bygone era. And yet here were a few hundred men passing it around in piles like it was junk mail.

Odder than the presence of the cash itself was the men who were passing it around. These weren't men exchanging a few squalem on friendly wagers. These were men — poor men, desperate men — exchanging sums of money that made Pontius outright uncomfortable. While he couldn't count exact sums, he saw thick stacks of notes denominated in thousands. He could not imagine how these men — these base level men — could manage to transfer this volume of money between themselves.

He was in awe, staring at the transactions taking place before his eyes. He might have stood here for the duration of the event if it weren't for the man in front of him. He was still smiling, but becoming ever more agitated at the delay.

"Your *money*, skylander? Where is your money?"

The jacketed man still smiled but now twitched in a way that Pontius found unnatural. The more the man twitched, the more that Pontius could make out no feature other than the bright, chiseled teeth. He realized he was not going to escape this scenario without a response.

"I'm just trying to get the lay of the land. I think I'm going to sit this one out."

In an impressive display of naiveté, he thought this utterance would gain entry to the festivities. He learned immediately just how wrong he was. The red jacket grabbed Pontius's arm with a strength that both alarming and confrontational. He felt the red jacket's sharp nails digging through the thick leather hide of his trench coat. He looked back at the massive bouncers standing in front of the metal doors. He realized for the first time that he was in an environment that he might not be able to escape if he needed to.

"This is no spectator sport, skylander." The red jacket poured his heart, soul, and malice into *skylander*. He lingered on it in a way that sounded almost serpentine. "This is not a broadcast performance. You tell me where your money lies, or I will show you where you lie."

He was in an unfamiliar position. He was normally so calculating. He was normally so measured. He rarely found himself in any situation in which he did not feel in total control. And yet, he felt nervous. It wasn't just the red-jacketed man digging into his arm — it was the entirety of this unholy betting den into which he had stumbled. He did not know where his escape route lay. He did not know how quickly he could pull his blunderbuss in this crowd. He did not know if anyone in this base level jungle would aid in his escape. He realized that his fate was now in his own hands.

"Where are the combatants?"

A Dusk Forever Waning

He did not care about the combatants. He certainly did not want to bet on the them. But he needed at least some basis upon which he could make his arguments. And he needed some excuse to buy at least some modicum of time.

The red jacket did not speak, but motioned down to opposite sides of the pit. Where he had seen nothing but sawdust, he now saw two "combatants". They were, perhaps, better defined as *participants*.

One man was large. It was difficult to find obese men in Centrian. The nanites, while not self-sufficient, procreated prodigiously on fat reserves. This meant that a fat man was someone who ate in obscene proportions. One could not become overweight just by eating a bit too much of the wrong types of food over time. Obese people were those who gorged on every food item they could get their hands on. A fat man on Centrian was the worst kind of glutton.

He was unusually tall. He was unusually wide – and not just because of his weight. It was clear that he had never spent a day in physical exercise. Yet he was also someone with great physical gifts, if only he had buttressed his genetic gifts with hard work.

The opponent was the first man's polar opposite. He was thin, even by Centrian standards. Folds of skin hung off his arms and his legs like so much over-allocated tent cloth. But this is not to say that he was weak. Underneath his flaccid skin an observant spectator could discern his wiry muscles. They strained and pulled against his skeletal frame.

Each man wore a cloth thong best described as a diaper. They wore nothing else. Pontius expected them to dance inside the pit. He envisioned someone preening and showboating for the victory they envisioned. Yet they both sat downtrodden and motionless on opposite sides. The harried protestations of the mad spectators did not affect them. Neither man looked at each other. Neither man looked upward around the boundaries of the pit. Each man did nothing but sit and stare at his own feet, unaware of the chaos taking place above them.

The red jacket held his smile and stared at Pontius. Pontius thought that he might be able to hold out. He thought that he might be able to stall until the real action began. But the longer they stood here, the more convinced he became that nothing in this arena was going to begin until he had cast his lot. After a long silence, he turned to the red jacket and said, "I want to bet on the first man to fall."

The red jacket's smile did not dissipate, but neither did he relax in his target's company. There was a long pause. The smile almost faded, but before it could disappear, it came back with a furious vengeance. With a nodding that bordered on epileptic, he grinned from ear to ear and responded, "So your winner – he is the first man to fall in the ring?"

"Aye."

A sickening knot arose in Pontius's throat. He wasn't sure what he was committing to. He felt helpless to forecast the outcome of such a gruesome contest, but he had more than a hunch about how such things should play out. He had seen struggle. He had seen death. This was a script with which he was familiar.

The smile continued nodding and reached for a transfer card. As he reached, he chanted words to no one in particular, "The first to fall shall win. The first to fall shall win."

The red jacket snatched one of the cards from Pontius's hand. In a lightning-fast motion, Pontius seized upon his hand like a bear trap. The red jacket, accustomed to such bold motions, seemed unfazed, yet he was also confused. He waited for further instructions.

"Odds."

The ever-present smile started wilting on the red jacket's face. He stopped. He looked at the bouncers. Then he looked back at Pontius again. There was a look of true confusion on his face. Receiving no guidance from Pontius, he redeployed his plastic smile and asked, "Odds?"

Pontius was in no mood for debate. He didn't welcome questions on this point. He grabbed the red jacket's arm and made it clear that his grip was just as strong.

"I'm betting that the first man to fall wins the match. I want *odds*."

The red jacket ripped his arm away with a paranoid convulsion. He stared at Pontius for an unnatural period of time, then made an awkward attempt to regain his composure. Without explanation, he turned in a flourish and scurried off to a smoky corner beyond Pontius's purview. In less than a minute he returned and grabbed Pontius's arm. He whispered in a pseudo-confidential tone, "Two-to-one."

Pontius said nothing but nodded in satisfaction. With a seeming agreement between them, the red jacket held out his arm, reaching for one of the transfer cards. Pontius responded by extending a card and saying, "A thousand squalem."

The red jacket turned ashen. Before Pontius had the chance to respond, the red jacket had already summoned the bouncers. He motioned for them to make a quick end of him.

"The skylander! Remove him! He came for folly."

Each of the bouncers wrapped their massive hands around his arms. He didn't feel as though they were going to kick him out. He felt as though they were going to remove his arms. They lifted him like a rag doll and applied a tension to his torso that was terrifying in its insistence. At this moment he replied with an emotion that was foreign to him – he responded in fear.

"A million. A million squalem."

The grip of the goons receded and the red jacket reacquired his familiar smile. The bouncers released their grip and he felt his respiration drop at least 30 heartbeats per minute. He stood in silence as the goons receded and the red jacket made a full circle around him. He tried to convey a countenance of full composure.

"A million. On the first to fall." The red jacket smiled and chuckled to himself. He turned and scurried off to some unseen master.

Before he had put 10 meters of space between them, Pontius yelled after him with renewed vigor, "With odds!"

The red jacket stopped, turned around, then bowed in a facetious manner.

"Two-to-one, skylander. Thracius, here, judges a fall."

Pontius surveyed the bouncer, Thracius, and realized that this man would be judging the efficacy of his bet. Thracius provided no acknowledgment of his attention. He stared into the depths of the pit. He was beyond uncomfortable with this arrangement. Yet given the circumstances, he deemed it to be his most viable path.

He considered trying to find a seat, or some post for better viewing amongst the teaming crowd. He thought better of it and retreated back to the wall to the side of Thracius. He noticed that the sawdust had settled somewhat between the combatants. The haze had cleared as much as he would expect it to, given the chaotic conditions. The betting action of the men had not quelled in the least, but the visual clarity allowed him to better survey the arena.

The enclosure was circular, about 25 meters in diameter. The pit encompassed the lion's share of the room. If offered a meter's clearance at the top edge where observers crammed into every possible station. The steel ladders criss-crossed above the pit. They looked like an inverted bird nest stationed above the activities. Although men clung to all rungs of the ladders and blocked his view, he spied the rich man underwriting this endeavor. He and his entourage occupied a central location along the upper wall that gave him a superior visage of the impending combat.

The pit itself was at least three meters deep. Smooth metallic walls enclosed the pit. He saw no door or ladders affixed to the walls, leaving him to assume that the combatants were lowered in. Aside from the fighters and the thick sawdust floor, the pit contained nothing else. There were no weapons, no referee, and no viable means of escape.

After 15 minutes of aggravating delay, a hush overtook the crowd. They keyed on some unseen sign. The two men in the pit rose to their feet, both wheezing and looking resigned to a binary future they could not predict. With no visual or audible cue, the men advanced toward each other and the crowd erupted in approval.

The large man lumbered. He was in no shape to affect the stance or the vigor of a warrior. When he rose it became difficult to see the front of his thong, as it was obscured by his prodigious, hanging gut. Each of his steps released a small cloud of sawdust that eddied in the stiff air. It was apparent that even reaching the center of the ring was an act of considerable effort.

His opponent affected a different stance. As soon as the contest began, he hopped and weaved. His wiry feet stirred the dust, but he moved them to and fro with surprising agility. The stoicism he displayed while sitting in the sawdust vanished. He was now intent upon outworking his opponent.

The first several minutes of the fight were unsatisfying. The fat man stood in the center of the pit and spun in circles. He adjusted his stance to face the flitting, dancing opponent circling him. For all his energy, it was clear that the wiry man was hesitant to engage in close-quarters combat. He was unable to draw the fat man from his settled stance in the middle of the pit.

It took no more than 30 seconds before the crowd rained boos down upon the fighters. It took a few more minutes before the red-jacket nodded and winked to the bouncers. This led to the flipping of several switches on the wall by the door. The walls of the pit began moving and constricting, shrinking the effective size of the pit. The walls moved slowly but steadily. This effectively removed several square meters of floor space from the pit every 15 seconds or so.

The obese man showed no reaction to these events. In fact, it was unclear whether he was even aware that the pit was shrinking. His opponent, however, reacted with a sense of panic when he realized what was happening. He didn't know this could happen and when the reality settled on him it intensified his actions. Seeing his strategy of evasion thwarted, he resolved to move faster, with renewed energy.

This led to the first crowd-satisfying action. In a move of remarkable boldness, the wiry man ran straight toward his opponent. He launched himself into the air with a straight-legged kick to the head. It shocked the spectators with its technical brilliance. His foot landed squarely against the fat-man's head. It released a thwack that elicited a raucous roar of approval from the crowd. The kick, while tactically sound and hitting its mark well, appeared to do no damage to the fat man. Rather, he just stood there, absorbed the blow, and watched his opponent fall into the sawdust.

Seeing the wiry man fall to the floor, Pontius gave a quick glance to the bouncer. He wasn't sure if this satisfied the terms of his bet. Thracius responded with a frown and a shake of the head. This response made it clear that Thracius would wait until one man was actively taken down by the other.

The frail combatant recognized his compromising position. He scurried through the sawdust before the fat man could pounce upon him. Regaining his footing, he came straight back to the attack, this time charging at the legs of his massive opponent. The glutton shocked all the observers by backing away from the attempt. This left the wiry one to writhe through the sawdust to gain his footing.

This scenario played out several more times over the next few minutes. The smaller man kept trying to perform a take-down. He was repeatedly thwarted and found himself scurrying back to his feet before the glutton could pounce upon him.

The action that had at first appeased the crowd was again growing tiresome. The pit stopped shrinking, having reached a size about half its original. The fat one showed little inclination, or ability, to attack. The small one, while active, showed little skill in affecting a take-down. And so the lunging and weaving continued for several more minutes as the bettors grew ever angrier.

Pontius turned to Thracius and said, "How long can it go on like this?"

Thracius shrugged. "Sometimes minutes, sometimes hours."

He allowed that to sink in for a moment. He had assumed that these matches ended fast. Once an advantage is in hand, it shouldn't take long for one to leverage that advantage. Then again, he had also assumed that the combatants would be fit, viable fighters. He had no idea how long it should take for an obese pig and a scrawny mouse to dispatch of each other. Yet he found it incredible to think that such a struggle could go on for hours.

While he pondered the prospects of hours spent struggling in vain to wound an opponent, he noticed a change in strategy. Rather than trying to take the glutton's legs from under him, the wiry one decided to unleash a series of kicks. The kicks landed on the knee and thigh of his larger opponent. He darted in, unleashed a few well-timed kicks to the glutton's leg, and then darted back out to the walls of the shrunken pit. This strategy was frustrating to the bettors. The kicks seemed to do little damage, they showed no signs of felling the fat man, and they did nothing to goad the glutton into action. But while the boos again cascaded over the fighters, Pontius could see that this strategy bore some fruit.

This pattern repeated for a full five minutes. As the time wore on and the boos grew ever louder, he saw that the glutton's thigh was growing red and irritated. Each kick that landed against the fat man led him to wince in ever-greater pain. After several minutes of this activity, the large man's thigh was rose-red from hip to knee. He released an audible grunt with each new blow received.

The red jacket grew ever twitchier. He became agitated by the perceived lack of action and the growing unrest of the raucous crowd. He looked back to Thracius and began nodding and twitching frantically. Thracius in turn swiveled to the panel of switches on the wall. He was ready to spark the action, as had happened when they shrunk the pit. In a move of foolhardiness, Pontius intervened. He stepped toward the panel, held up his hand, and yelled, "Wait."

With the red jacket annoyed, Thracius swiveled back to the pit to discern why he intervened. No sooner had he returned his attention to the pit than the wiry one swung a kick with amazing speed dead on the glutton's knee. When his foot crashed into the leg of his opponent, the glutton crumbled to the ground with the crash of a collapsed skyscraper. A great cloud of sawdust rose to the ladders and the crowd roared a raucous approval.

As the crowd climbed to a crescendo, he noticed the dogs for the first time. Several dozen of them perched throughout the room. They squeezed into any space they could find between the onlookers. When the action was at a lull they seemed to blend into the typical rabble of base-levelers. They lounged as the spectators grew more impatient. When the excitement swelled the languid posture of the canines stood out in stark contrast. They sat and gave no mind to the crazed cheering in their midst.

The small one jumped on his opponent's back like a bull fighter. Although the glutton writhed and bucked, it was clear that the wiry combatant was hanging on for dear life. He was not focused on landing more blows to his opponent. Rather, he focused on wrapping his arms around the fat man's neck and worked his hands up to the eyes.

Pontius shot another glance at Thracius. This time, Thracius responded with a nod. He understood that he had now placed his bet on the glutton.

The next several minutes were as exhilarating as they were brutal. Nothing the glutton did could free the persistent opponent from his back. His sore leg and his cracked knee impaired his movement. Once he abandoned the struggle to free his back, he focused on keeping the wiry one's hands from his eyes. His sausage arms did little to extricate the probing hands of his opponent. He buried his head in the sawdust and worked to protect his face. A few minutes later, a terrifying shriek split the arena as the wiry fighter's thumb drove deep into the glutton's eye socket.

The panic of this vicious loss spurred the glutton into action. Although he could not remove the wiry pest from his back, he released a grunting roar and managed to bring himself back to his feet. Even as his opponent clung to his back, he was now in an all-out rage, oblivious to his fractured knee or his ruined eye.

Blood covered the glutton's face, having taken numerous blows the head. The blood clung to him in a coagulated mix of sawdust and mucous. His dead eye, still attached, hung from his socket and swung as his head moved. With little regard for tactical implications, he began spinning. He tried again to remove his unwelcome rider.

This spectacle played out below him. The crowd whipped into an ever-ascending frenzy. He became aware of the situation not as a participant or even as a spectator, but as someone who is experiencing the events from afar. He had the impression that he was somehow watching himself as he watched the fight. He felt disconnected from the environment in which he now found himself. Everything seemed so unreal – so *surreal*.

This dissonance had been growing in him almost from the point that he entered the arena. He couldn't identify the source of his confusion. Yet he knew from the moment that he stepped back there that something about the scenario was nonsensical. Something in this environment didn't add up. Standing here now, watching these two amateurs engage in a gladiatorial death match, he realized it for the first time. He understood why this bothered him on such a fundamental level.

He had witnessed an obscene number of deaths, most of them caused by his own hand. He had seen people expire in the most gruesome of ways, but he always knew why they died. He always understood the bargain they were trying to complete. Mothers protected babies. Fathers fought for sons. People struggled against the system to instill life for themselves or those they loved. People paid the ultimate sacrifice to ensure a life – a legitimate, licensed life – for those they cared for. Some people would pay any sort of price if it meant they could achieve the greatest of Centrian gifts – a Vitapass.

But here, in front of him now, he was watching two people engage in the most brutal of contests. They were two free, licensed, Vitapass-holding people. They were doing this so that one of them might achieve wealth. No matter which one lost, he would be a licensed man with all the benefits that come with such status in Centrian. One of these men would throw it all away because he could not otherwise realize the financial freedom he desired.

Pontius made a deal. He consummated a transaction with Chunk's parents guaranteeing him a Vitapass. Watching this spectacle before him, for the first time he wondered about the real value of that Vitapass. Many would kill for one. Some would pay millions for one. And yet, there were people in the dregs, like these two slugs before him, who would throw that Vitapass away. There were people, at base level or above, who were not feeling any particular gratitude for their licensed status. *If they risked such a precious gift without regard, then what was the value of the life for Chunk that he was trying so hard to deliver?*

Every violent act playing out in the pit below him made him question anew the value of that Vitapass. Every blow struck made him wonder if there was any point in finishing the transaction he agreed to. Chunk's parents were already dead. If completing this deal wouldn't provide the life for Chunk that his parent's envisioned, what was the point in so stubbornly pursuing the Vitapass?

The remainder of the fight played out before him like scenes in a hazy dream. Once he regained his footing, the glutton crashed back to the ground. He landed on his back and crushed the wiry combatant below him. The massive force crashing on the small fighter's chest finally caused him to release his grip. The glutton rolled to the side, leaving his opponent laying prone in the sawdust.

Pontius identified the look on the wiry fighter's face. The pained expression that peaked in visible pain with every new, slow breath was a clear sign that he had cracked multiple ribs. The glutton showed no urgent inclination to rise, but it didn't matter. The smaller fighter would not be getting up any time soon.

The crowd, having already reached a fever pitch, chanted in unison, *"Toti! Toti! Toti!"* Some were imploring the wiry one to rise, but Pontius knew this to be a lost cause. He only needed to wait for the glutton to regain his feet.

In slow, painful motions, the glutton did indeed rise again. His stand met with a thunderous roar and renewed chants of, *"Toti! Toti!"* After some moments to absorb the adulation, he reached down and grasped both feet of the smaller fighter. With great effort he began spinning his opponent through the sawdust. After several revolutions he gathered enough momentum to lift his opponent off the floor. He spun the wiry one higher and higher through continuous revolutions. When he felt he had gathered enough momentum, and when he believed that his good knee would stand no more, he flung his opponent into the steel wall of the pit. His opponent's head made a loud crack against the tempered steel.

Amidst raucous approval, he walked over to the limp frame of his opponent lying prone in the sawdust. It was apparent that there were still slow, pained breaths emanating from the victim. The glutton looked up to the top of the pit, catching the attention of the red jacket. He scrunched his shoulders, suggesting that he wasn't sure if his task was complete. The red jacket did not hesitate. He snarled and pointed an accusing finger back at the glutton.

"Toti!"

The glutton understood. He looked back at the once-frisky fighter and sidled next to his head. With little forethought, he dropped to the floor. He focused his entire weight on a protruding elbow that drove into the small fighter's cranium. It was finished.

Bedlam overtook the arena. The doors opened back to the front bar and the earlier scene repeated itself. They hoisted the glutton out of the pit. In an amazing feat of human engineering, they managed to carry him out of the enclave on the shoulders of those who had bet on him. They left the smaller fighter in the pit and the dogs descended. The half of the bettors on the wrong side walked sullenly back to the base-level streets. They returned to the drudgery of their lives.

Pontius did not linger. The reality of this gruesome match sobered his cloudy mind. His revelation during the fight was still fresh in his memory and he was anxious to return to Chunk and Moria with a new plan of action. He was intent to collect his winnings and leave this place as fast as possible.

To his surprise, he had no trouble receiving his money. Although the red-jacket was in no way cheery, he cleared enough profit on the fight that this payout was not something to fight over. He handed Pontius a new transfer card. It represented two million squalem – more money than Pontius had ever made in a single transaction in his entire life. He slid the card into his pocket, but the magnitude of this windfall did not register with him at all.

Back in the base-level streets, Pontius strode toward the first set of stairs he could find. He was now walking with a goal – a *purpose*. He needed to gather his colleagues before his next step.

Dozens of floors above, when he reached the first scaler terminal he convo'd Moria to ask her to assemble the crew. But as soon as Moria's voice echoed in his UNI he sensed her strain.

"Are you expecting workers?"

He stopped in his tracks. "*Workers*? No. Why? Is someone there?"

"There's a man at the door who says he needs to do a safety inspection on the alarms. Says he'll only be a moment then he'll be on his way."

His heartbeat quickened but he labored to keep his voice smooth and calm. "Listen to me very carefully. Do *not* let him in. Let *nobody* in. I will be there in fifteen minutes."

Chapter 10 – An Impractical Captive

When Caspian arrived, he made it no more than a half meter inside the living room before stopping dead in his tracks. He was already shocked to see the front door blasted open. Plasma charges left it ajar, forcing entrants to squeeze through the narrow space. But this was nothing compared to the scene inside.

Chunk lay against a mass of pillows on the couch and cooed at anyone who would listen. Moria lay sprawled against the other end of the couch, blood flowing from her left arm. Despite her obvious damage, she was oblivious to her own wounds and instead was staring with anger at the center of the room.

In the middle of the living room lay Tenarrin, hog tied with some kind of wire. He was face-down on the floor with his head angled toward the entryway. His breath labored and both eyes were almost swollen shut. A string of blood-mixed-with-mucous led from his mouth to a puddle accumulating below his head. He appeared to be missing several teeth. There were various kitchen utensils stuck into his body at odd locations.

Hovering over the captain was Pontius. He had just finished tying the bounds. He did so in such a way that any slight movement on Tenarrin's part would tighten their hold and drive the sharp wire deeper into his skin.

Caspian stood still, dumbfounded, with his mouth agape and his arms limp at his side. He might have stood there much longer if Kryx and Conti hadn't nudged him forward. They made their way through the same narrow entryway just blocked by Caspian.

On his was back to the apartment, Pontius convo'd Caspian and asked him to come immediately. He knew he would be needing a private transport and Caspian's cruiser was the only viable option for this. He explicitly told Caspian to come alone. He forced Caspian to repeat back over the convo that he would bring no one with him. He asked Caspian to confirm the importance of this condition.

Kryx walked into the room and moved to the side to allow for Conti's entry. Aside from the ever-present half-grin on his face, he gave no other outward indication of the situation. In fact, he seemed almost businesslike in his countenance.

Conti, however, was quite the opposite. Upon entry she released a loud gasp. She fell to her knees, staring straight into Tenarrin's face, searching for any sign that he was, or would be, alright.

Caspian's arrival led Pontius to stand up with a sense of relief. He was awaiting his friend. As soon as he saw the rest of the entourage pushing through, blind anger replaced his relief. He rushed across the room and grabbed the front of Caspian's coat with great force.

"I told you to come alone. You had to come *alone*! Why, for humanity, are these two here?!"

His last sentence lingered more in bewilderment than anger. It was imperative that Caspian not attract a crowd. Now that he already had, Pontius knew that there would be no un-seeing what they had now witnessed.

Caspian responded with a blank stare. His confusion was evident. He could recollect nothing to which Pontius was referring. Pontius stared back, driving his gaze through Caspian's eyeballs and into his brain. He searched for some hint of memory or recognition. Caspian was stupefyingly high.

In happier times this might have caused a great deal of amusement for Pontius. Caspian had destroyed so many of his neural pathways. He had become so jaded on conventional sensory stimulation. Traditional drugs were all but useless on him. Pontius had no natural memory of Caspian's last high. Neither did anyone else. This was a unique event – but these were not happier times.

"What exactly are you on?" Pontius could not hide his amazement.

Caspian thought for a long moment. He was still trying to remember the details of anything that had happened more than ten minutes ago. After some painful recollection of recent events, he began smiling and giggling and raised his finger to point at Kryx.

"You must try this stuff! He has the most amazing *stuff*!"

He said *stuff* as though this was the official name of the drug.

"I'm serious, Captain! I can't remember feeling so alive. Hell, I can't remember *feeling* anything before now. Kryx, good buddy – slide one of those over to my friend here!"

With those words, Caspian launched himself across the room. He almost tripped on the hogtied Tenarrin and plopped himself down on the couch between Chunk and Moria. While he was once shocked at the gravity of the situation in the apartment, he now seemed to have lost any realization of where he was. Kryx was not high, had no delusions about what he had stepped into, and did not take Caspian's urgings as an excuse to peddle his wares.

Pontius abandoned hope for any meaningful help from his friend. Instead, he went to his front door and began working to force it back into a closed position. He got it as closed as was possible given the level of plasma damage it had sustained. To no one in particular, he barked out a command to bring something that would block any remaining openings in the door. Without saying a word, Kryx complied. He headed into the bedroom to search for towels or blankets. They needed something to use as a makeshift barrier.

It was not until the apartment seemed secure that Kryx allowed himself the luxury of a query.

"Who, exactly, is that?" He pointed a long, bony finger toward the center of the room.

Pontius turned from the door and surveyed the center of the living room anew. The scene pained him, and it showed. He paused for a moment before responding, "That's my boss."

There was an awkward silence, filled only by the angry breathing of Moria and the slow, gurgled drooling of Tenarrin.

"Didn't get that promotion you were hoping for?"

Pontius ignored the ill-timed attempt at humor. Conti was rising back to her feet and beginning to recompose herself.

"Is he going to live?"

"I hope not." Moria spoke through her teeth with jarring vitriol. Pontius tried to ignore her reply.

"Yes, he'll live. He's received a sound and thorough beating, but I don't have any reason to believe his injuries are life threatening."

Conti's initial surprise was now giving way to indignation. She seemed somehow affronted by the situation.

"Why did you do this to him?"

Pontius released a chuckle and raised a finger to Moria. "I didn't do this to him. *She* did."

She was more than happy to pounce on the opening. "He came here to kill Chunk. When I wouldn't let him in he blasted through the door. He thought he could go straight for Chunk."

She raised her bloody arm and waved it in front of her like an exhibit for all to see.

"He thought he could dispense of me." The room answered her with nothing but more silence. "I thought better of it."

Pontius wasn't that surprised. He had known for millennia that Moria was not as mild-mannered as she often seemed. Her passions lurked well below the surface, but when they erupted they did so with great force. If Caspian were able to comprehend the situation, it would have flabbergasted him. He always dismissed her as a wilting flower. Conti had no real basis upon which to judge these actions. But Kryx saw them as in line with his assessment of her. He nodded in approval as he listened to her explanation.

Conti shot a glare at Kryx. Kryx volleyed it to Pontius. Pontius surveyed Moria, waiting for any sign that her adrenaline had subsided. Moria stared at Tenarrin's crippled mass. Caspian resumed staring at the hogtied captive, but it was unclear whether he understood what he was looking at.

Conti, still sounding annoyed, asked, "Why is he bound like this? He needs medical attention."

Pontius kept an eye on his boss and answered in a smooth, matter-of-fact tone, "He will have some questions to answer first. I can't afford to let him wander."

"Wander? Where in the hell is he going to wander while he's in that condition?"

"He's bound mentally as much as he is physically. If he were to complete a convo to the NCU, we'd be surrounded by authorities in minutes. I can't take any chances with him right now."

Kryx stood with his back against a far wall. He was upright in posture and he seemed to be calculating all the factors in the room before him. He was neither anxious nor pleased. He had the intensity of someone reverse engineering an intricate puzzle.

"This is a dangerous game you're playing. How do you intend to return this government operative to his rightful position without implicating yourself?"

The query didn't phase Pontius.

Kryx continued with his line of questioning. "Or implicating us?"

"The fact that he's here proves that the game began some time ago. Nothing that has occurred here this afternoon has made my life more or less dangerous."

Kryx waited for the answer to the most important part of his question – *how would they return Tenarrin?* Moments of silence ensued. This strengthened his suspicion that Pontius himself did not have any viable answer. The entire group swam in an awkward silence for a full five minutes. They heard nothing but the angry breathing of Moria, the happy gurgling of Chunk, and the sickening slurp of Tenarrin as he drew each painful breath.

Although he seemed calm on the outside, it was apparent that Kryx was far from comfortable. He resumed the agitated scratching of his neck and arms. His frantic gaze jumped from a random spectator in the room, to Tenarrin, to another spectator. He continued this process until he had cataloged every member of the room, then he repeated the cycle. He was unsure of the next step in this process, but he was aware that it lay with Pontius. After several more minutes of unwieldy silence, he could take no more.

"You convo'd Caspian because you require transport. Will your boss be making the trip with you?"

Kryx's voice was as soothing to Pontius as a sliver driven under the fingernail. Every syllable from Kryx's vapid mouth twisted the sliver and drove it deeper into the tissue. Perhaps most annoying of all was the fact that Pontius could not provide a logical answer. He was adrift without a proper plan. Anything he said now would further enforce this fact.

"He won't be going with us." The vague reply was all he could muster, but Kryx was never one to settle for vague replies.

"So you'll be leaving him here, like this, to report his condition to the entire hegemony of Centrian control?"

He did not acknowledge Kryx. He just kept staring at the center of the room. He never believed he would see Tenarrin like this and he couldn't have imagined that it would be by his own hand. He wasn't sure what his full plan of action would entail, but he knew it should include driving his fist deep between Kryx's eyes.

"I don't know where he'll end up. I won't let him die."

"If he's going to live, shouldn't you be working to get him to a clinic?"

The irony that Kryx, of all people, was the voice of reason and compassion in the room was not lost on anybody.

"He has some questions to answer first."

This declaration surprised and concerned both Kryx and Conti. They weren't sure how long it would take Tenarrin to recompose himself. They wondered what it would take to interrogate someone in this state. But they weren't sure that they wanted to be around for the festivities. As though responding to their worries, Tenarrin began to stir. He tried to open his eyes and strained his neck to look around at his captors.

Tenarrin's return to consciousness caught everyone's attention (except Caspian's). They watched with great interest. It was clear that he was struggling to focus. As he moved his neck through its limited range of motion, the subjects of his crippled gaze each shrank. They wanted to hide in an otherwise open and bright room. He could not move enough to see the couch behind him. But it only took limited movement for him to pivot his head to see first Kryx, then Conti, and then Pontius.

Tenarrin made several attempts to raise his head. He would make it a few centimeters off the floor, only to lose strength. His head would flop back onto the puddle accumulated beneath him. When he saw Kryx he had no discernible reaction, other than to further squint his bloated eyes and attempt harder to focus. When he saw Conti he caught her eye and held her gaze for several moments as though he was trying to compute her presence. By the time he made his way to survey Pontius, he had become exhausted by the effort required to twist his bounds.

It was clear from his reaction that this was the first time he had seen Pontius in the room. When the recognition was clear, he laid his head back on the floor and spoke through broken teeth, "Pontius. You're here, Pontius. You've saved me." Slow and painful breath punctuated each of his words.

Kryx and Conti watched Pontius. They expected him to reply in some meaningful way, but he stood, frozen, watching his captain wallow in pain.

"Pontius. That woman. That *bitch*. Did you kill her?"

With no warning and with brutal efficiency, Moria lept from the couch and launched a swift kick into his kidney. Having no idea that she sat behind him, and being unable to defend himself even if he had seen it coming, there was nothing for him to do. He absorbed the assault with a horrific grunt and a renewed round of gurgling. Kryx and Conti winced.

"Moria! Stop it!" Pontius flashed something quite unusual for him – pure anger. Seeing the strength of his admonishment, she retreated back to the couch and resolved to restrain herself. He stood for several moments, glaring at her, before he returned to a position in front of Tenarrin.

He knelt down before him, resting in the pool of blood, and brought his face almost to his level. He tapped his boss on the top of the head until he made a new attempt to open his eyes. Pontius came in close to his face and spoke in lower tones.

"She's still here. And I suggest you leave her out of this conversation if you want to leave this room alive." As he said this, he raised his head and looked back at Moria, assuring himself that she would not launch herself from the couch again.

"I know you're in pain, but we need to talk. I need you to be honest with me. If you're not honest with me, I can't guarantee that she stays on the couch. Do you understand?"

After a few more gurgled breaths, Tenarrin made a minuscule effort to nod his head. His eyes opened anew and he saw Pontius staring straight at him.

"Why are you here?"

His swollen eyes opened a little wider and he stared straight back at Pontius. He waited, as though Pontius might somehow relent in his request. But when it was clear that no such reprieve was en route, he began to chuckle from deep within his gut. As he did, each jolly convulsion racked his body in greater pain and he began to vacillate between misery and frivolity. After 30 seconds of this painful sequence he calmed down and renewed his gaze toward Pontius.

"You're harboring an *unlicensed*. You, of all people, have a fugitive. You, of all people, somehow felt that you could keep an *unlicensed* from the watchful eye of NCU."

Every utterance of *unlicensed* escaped his mouth as a muffled cacophony of spit, blood, and consonants. But Pontius understood every word. Even in Tenarrin's pitiful state, he recognized the scolding as a father scolds a child. There was nothing more ludicrous – nay, more shameful – than for an NCU officer caught raising an unlicensed human. He was now the drug dealer hooked on his own junk. He was the bookie who had become a degenerate gambler. All those who had known him would judge him as pitiful and deranged.

"You were the *star*, Pontius. You were the shining example of what NCU should be. You didn't cry when you dispatched those leaches. You had no second thoughts for the solemn duty with which you were entrusted. You were the most necessary of instruments in the grander landscape of Centrian glory."

Pontius, more anyone else in the room, understood the tone of his words. Although difficult to tell beneath his garbled speech, these events saddened Tenarrin. He spoke to Pontius as a coach speaking to a star athlete who has thrown away his talents for the pursuit of chemical highs and minor vices. He spoke with a genuine air of disbelief.

Tenarrin was an old soul. He was a tenured veteran long before Pontius was ever hired by NCU. He could have risen far above the rank of captain. Instead, he had hunkered down in his position because he thrived on the mentoring aspects of his job. He tutored Pontius on the nuances of NCU work. He taught him how to trace clues to find hidden babies. He taught him now to outsmart the witty parents who had the greatest of all stakes in his failure. He showed him how to find more children in less time with fewer resources. Of all the agents he had mentored, Pontius was, by far, his star pupil. It was not long before Pontius was outpacing anything that he had accomplished in his days on the beat.

Tenarrin's attention had not gone unnoticed. While Pontius had affection for almost no one in his working environment, he held deep respect for Tenarrin. He was cognizant of the contributions he had made to his career. There was no one in NCU that he trusted more.

"So you came here just to murder Chunk?"

There was a brief moment of confusion. Tenarrin had no idea who, or what, *Chunk* was. He also didn't understand the use of the word *murder*. It didn't take long for him to move past this incongruity.

"There is no baby here. There is no one to be killed or murdered here. There is just an unlicensed, invalid, and illegitimate human that must be eradicated. There is no other way. You, of all people, should know that."

Hearing this verbiage left a bad taste in Pontius's mouth. He had heard this approach articulated thousands of times before. He had heard it from every other member of the NCU and of Population Control in general. This was nothing more than a reaffirmation of everything he had worked for over more than a thousand years. And yet hearing those words now, uttered from the battered mouth of his former mentor, they took on an ugliness that was foreign to him. He couldn't identify anything wrong with the position. Yet he found it distasteful to hear the standard government protocol voiced so clearly, so succinctly.

There was also something wrong – something illogical – about Tenarrin's statement. Pontius strained to define the full extent of the non sequitur, but something was out of place in his mind.

"As I search my UNI I can find no time when you have taken it upon yourself to carry out an assignment. Why wasn't this assigned to someone else? How is it that the captain has been sent on such a routine duty?"

Again, painful convulsions racked Tenarrin's body. He found it impossible to suppress the pervasive effects of laughter.

"Routine? *Routine?!* What about this assignment is routine?"

The word routine spit forth from his mouth. Belabored emphasis accompanied it. These breaths mingled with random globules of fluid that spat in all directions onto the floor.

"I'm at the house of an NCU agent – our most decorated and accomplished agent. I am here to eliminate that vile thing playing on your couch – an NCU agent's couch – and you speak to me of routines? When is the last time you remember us having to bust one of our own? When was the grace of our office so besmirched by a traitor of your stature? We don't send out mere trainees or field agents to carry out this kind of assignment."

Everyone in the room now had their gaze locked not on Tenarrin, but on Pontius. Each of them understood the impact of these words, even if Pontius would not acknowledge their power. He remained kneeling by his mentor, perusing his wire knots and pondering the meaning of their presence. Even Caspian, in his chemical stupor, realized the serious attack now leveled against his friend.

The entire room remained in silence for several more minutes. Tenarrin, resigned to his condition, made no attempt to struggle against his bonds. He chose instead to rest his head back in the puddle and wait for the next move from his captor. The tragedy transfixed Kryx. Conti had never released her outward expression of shock. Moria became overwhelmed by the throbbing pain radiating throughout her arm. Caspian was uncertain that anything before him was actually happening. After several more minutes of tension, Pontius shattered the silence.

"What time is it?"

Everyone looked around in confusion, wondering if he directed the question at them. It was only after several more awkward moments that it became clear to everyone that Pontius was still talking to Tenarrin.

"What?"

"You heard me. What time is it?"

Tenarrin struggled with the question. Not only was it absurd, but it also illustrated his technical constraints. Pontius had injected a chemical distractor. It was an agent designed to cross the blood-brain barrier and send his UNI connections into overdrive. The resulting flood of nonsensical activity caused his brain to disregard all signals flowing to and from his UNI. This made the device unreachable. Without the aid of his lifelong mental computer, a simple question such as, "What time is it?" could be challenging. Having no clock or watch in his field of vision, he contemplated for a moment. He tried to access his natural memory to remember the time when he left he NCU office. After serious consideration, he deduced, "I think I left the office about an hour ago. That means that it should be somewhere around five o'clock."

Pontius nodded.

"You're close. It's 5:12."

Pontius looked around at the other inhabitants of the room. No one had a clue what he was driving at.

"The access log on my apartment shows you arriving almost 45 minutes ago."

The room remained frozen, with no one, least of all Tenarrin, understanding the point.

"When did you send me on that assignment? When did you send me to the Plethora plant?"

Tenarrin did not raise his head or re-open his eyes. He just rolled his head on the floor, unable to discern the path now pursued.

"I don't know. It was a while ago. It was this morning. It was late morning?" He was helpless to provide a more exact time.

"Correct. It was more than seven hours ago that you sent me on that mission."

Pontius raised his posture over the last several minutes. He now brought himself back down to Tenarrin's level. He ensured that their faces were almost even and waited for him to open his eyes. When Tenarrin acknowledged Pontius's renewed presence, the conversation continued.

"If there's any way that an agent can remove an unlicensed human with one or both of the parents gone, he will. No one ever goes into a assignment squaring off against a protector if he can avoid it."

Tenarrin knew what Pontius was driving at. He was not inclined to take the bait.

"You sent me on that assignment more than seven hours ago." He allowed the timeframe to linger on his tongue. It rolled off like a romantic language and he allowed it to hang in the air between his face and Tenarrin's grotesque visage. Tenarrin was still disinclined to speak. Pontius grew annoyed.

"You sent me on that assignment yourself. You had no doubt when I was gone and you knew that I'd be gone for hours. And yet you waited many hours before you came to to kill Chunk."

Again, silence.

"Any other agent, especially a veteran agent who taught me all the tricks of the trade, would have pounced shortly after I left. He would not have waited hours, knowing that every passing minute increases the likelihood that I could return."

Tenarrin said nothing, but his countenance transformed. He had now somehow managed to open his eyes quite wide and he was holding his head off the floor, steady and focused on Pontius. But he still offered no response.

"I was gone for hours – more hours than anyone would normally expect for such an assignment. When I did begin to return, at a time that was forecast to no one, then and only then did I hear that there is someone strange at my door. It makes no sense that you would allow me to wander half a day on this assignment, but then only strike minutes before I manage to return home."

Pontius was now speaking with force, staring all the while into Tenarrin's eyes.

"You're not simply here for another assignment – routine or not. You're not simply here to murder Chunk."

This turn in the conversation confused the others. Moria had no idea where this was leading. But Tenarrin became resigned, even as he held Pontius's gaze.

"I've been tracking you. I didn't know what was taking you so long to return home or why you had chosen your filthy route, but I knew that you were somewhere on base level. When you finally come back within range, it was time to complete my objective. I was going to eliminate the unlicensed, then wait in your apartment to eliminate you. Ideally, the entire transaction would have been completed in less than 30 minutes."

Moria was aghast but Pontius absorbed the information. When she heard their lives included in such a *transaction* she considered another attack. One look at Pontius's stolid face made her think otherwise. This did not shock him. He would have carried out the same assignment were the roles reversed. He consumed the information as one consumes a weather report.

"Harboring an unlicensed is not, in an of itself, a death sentence. Your words and your actions make it sound like you were resolved to kill me when you came here, even if I did not resist in any way?"

Tenarrin said nothing but nodded his head.

"Who gave the order?"

"No one, but Auditing has been investigating you now for more than a year. It's only a matter of time before they close in. I wanted to handle this myself, before you're outed in front of the entire NCU team. When Auditing finally sends the order, they're not going to send one man here to take you out. It will be excruciating, and it will be thorough. I didn't want you to go out like that."

Pontius allowed this to sink in. Auditing was responsible for rooting out corruption. Auditing handled the internal investigations of putative wrongdoing. A conviction from the Auditing department could lead to hundreds, or even thousands of years spent on a penal colony. In the most egregious of cases, Auditing had the power to mandate on-the-spot executions. They would send PC's own agents out into the field to dispose of the targeted offender. This only happened in the most heinous of cases.

Another several minutes passed before Kryx offered a matter-of-fact question. "What are you going to do with him?"

Pontius was not inclined to answer at once, but a half minute later Tenarrin looked at him and asked, "Aye. What are you going to do with me?"

Pontius replied by leaving the living room altogether. He came back in short order with a roll of packing tape in hand. He didn't wait for opinions or objections. He reached down and wrapped the tape around Tenarrin's head. It covered his mouth several times. This left nothing but Tenarrin's nose available for breathing. It also ended any viable alternative that he had left to communicate.

Conti protested. "Can he still breathe?"

Pontius looked back down at his boss and pondered the question. Without warning he lifted a boot and drove it down into Tenarrin's back. As he did so, his captive released a loud groan and a new mix of fluids flew from his nose. After the blow, Tenarrin sucked air back through his clogged nasal passageway.

"Yes."

Kryx motioned as if to provide some kind of commentary. Pontius was already making new plans and was not in the mood to solicit feedback. He swung around to Caspian and tried to gain his attention.

"Can you pilot? We're going to the islands. Can you get us to the islands?"

Pontius had been hoping that these last several minutes of sobriety had somehow worked their magic on his friend. Looking into his blank eyes he found this not to be the case. Caspian, while conscious, was not aware of his surroundings. Centuries ago, Pontius might have enjoyed the adrenaline rush of Caspian piloting in this state. He was now aware that a horrific crash with Chunk in his lap would be the ultimate betrayal of his word. Chunk's parents had purchased his life and that purchase did not include a fiery death at the hands of a drug-crazed thrill-seeker.

He began to survey the rest of the room, knowing that he himself had no knowledge of piloting. That was when he realized that there was another pilot in the room. Kryx gave a smug smile.

Pontius swallowed his pride and asked, "You can take us to the islands?"

"What islands are you searching for? We can reach Tyrian or Catillan within a few hours in Caspian's Nighthawk."

Tyrian and Catillan were the first two islands off the coast off Majorus. They were part of the greater archipelago of Centrian. Pontius had no desire to stay in the Centrian archipelago.

"Nay. We're going much farther than that. We're going to *the islands*."

Kryx was either confused or playing dumb. "Is there a specific destination in mind?"

"The last time you were here we discussed the islands – the tiny, far-strewn, and uncivilized colonies that rise from Oceanus all around the planet. I need to reach those."

"There are several hundred of those and they are in no centralized location. Are you expecting to visit all of them?"

"I'm not looking for an abandoned rock. There are some that are large enough to support some modicum of organized society? Some place with ample resources for an established hierarchy of civilization?"

Kryx gave this little thought. The answer was obvious to him.

"Then you're looking for Solis. It's an atoll on the other side of the planet. It supports a population of at least fifty thousand. Traders visit often. There is not a dish served in Centrian that does not contain some hint of flavor from those islands."

"That's perfect. How fast can we get there?"

Kryx shrugged his shoulders and performed some basic calculations.

"It's at least an eight hour journey. Depends somewhat upon our altitude. If we fly over the poles it will be faster, but the wind shear is much more dangerous."

Pontius shook his head.

"There is no reason to push for time. Once we're in the air and outside the bounds of Centrian, I have no reason to believe we'll be hassled. Do you have contacts there? I can't afford to jump blindly into that environment."

Kryx's hair pulsated with a renewed vigor as he pondered his most recent journey to Solis. His brow furrowed and he began shaking his head.

"I can drop you off but I will be mooring offshore. The bitch who runs that colony wants me dead."

Pontius couldn't help but think that this statement must apply to thousands of people in and outside of Centrian. It was of no surprise that Kryx could not be counted on for diplomacy.

There was a long silence while Pontius considered his options. He had never been outside Centrian and he did not know what to expect on these savage islands. He was uncomfortable with the prospect of dropping into such an alien landscape with no guide or translator.

"These islanders – what do you think they would make of a visitor such as myself?"

He hated counting on Kryx for such vital information but he felt that he had no choice. Kryx shrugged again. His papery skin pulled taught around his face as he smiled and considered the possibilities.

"If they're at war with each other – and they're often at war with each other – you will almost certainly be viewed as a spy. It doesn't matter which camp you reach first. Each one will see you as an agent of the other. If you are captured, you will be killed. And eaten.

"If they're at peace then you may find yourself able to negotiate in good faith, although their dialect is harsh on our ears and slow to comprehend. You may need to spend several days just establishing contacts. What happens after that is dependent upon your wits."

None of this rested peacefully on Pontius's ears. He knew not was he was targeting and he feared leading Chunk to a fate on some savage's dinner table. But he also felt as though he was out of options. Looking down upon his bound captain he knew that reinforcements would be here within hours. Although Tenarrin could not access his UNI, it was only a matter of time before agents arrived to investigate his whereabouts.

The myriad possibilities of this cannibalistic, alien society coursed through his brain. Caspian piped up with a random offering, "Dania!"

"Huh?" Pontius looked around in confusion, half expecting Dania to walk in the door. He assumed that Caspian was hallucinating.

"Dania's not here, Caspian. Go lay down."

"Nay. Dania can help. She travels to those islands – to Solis – several times a year. She damn near rules those islands."

This input stunned Pontius. First, Caspian's clear and coherent participation in the conversation amazed him. Second, the shear logic of this observation impressed him. Dania was one of the more prolific chefs of Centrian. Her restaurants earned renown for true flavor. They broke through the bland, seaweed-soaked fare offered by most of the other fishmongers on Majorus. The primary source of these flavors was her trips to the tiny islands dotting the planet. She searched for wild ingredients that made her food superior to anything dragged out of the sea.

"Of course. We need Dania. She is our ace in this drama."

Caspian sported a large, goofy grin. He amazed even himself by being able to contribute something meaningful to the situation. Kryx and Conti seemed unaffected, neither one of them knowing anything about Dania. They hadn't seen her since that night at Indiarium. Moria could not hide her look of disgust.

Pontius sprang to his feet in a flurry of activity. He began packing a bag. He had no idea what one should take when traveling to the islands, but he was certain that he would be gone for several days.

He also convo'd Dania. She was beyond pensive. She sensed in his voice that something terrible had happened and that he wasn't sharing most of the pertinent details. Nevertheless, she agreed to join the group.

Conti began wrapping Moria's arm. Over Moria's loud protests, everyone decided she would need to find a medical center. Her arm may need replacing. If left in its current condition it could turn gangrenous.

After this flurry of activity, Pontius began rounding up the crew to leave the apartment. He was almost ready to leave this place – for good – when Kryx placed a firm hand on his shoulder. Pontius spun around to address the query.

"And what happens to him? He's quite the impractical captive, don't you think?"

"We leave him here. I will contact NCU when we're clear of Centrian. They can come and collect him."

Kryx clicked his teeth and hissed a massive disapproval.

"And what then? He turns us all in? We are all now complicit in the assault of a prize NCU agent."

Pontius paused and looked around the room again at his colleagues. He understood Kryx to be correct and he was hoping to gloss over this issue with a hasty escape. Assaulting an NCU agent was one of the highest crimes. Robbery, rape, and even murder where treated with more mercy by Centrian judges. Those who had the nerve to assault PC employees paid a terrible price. The entire legal system held NCU agents in high esteem.

Even if one were not prosecuted by the Centrian authorities, the NCU department protected – and avenged – its own. Tenarrin may, at one time, have had great respect for Pontius, but this attack would not go unnoticed. When recovered, he would put out the word to all PC employees to execute Pontius and all his colleagues. It was conceivable that everyone in this room would be dead within a few months. Nevertheless, Pontius shook his head and tried to push this reality deep within his subconscious.

"We will be long gone. His short-term memory has been scrambled. He won't regain UNI access for at least another hour."

Pontius made another attempt to leave the apartment but Kryx broke in the other direction to the kitchen. The other members of the party, afraid to throw their lot with either side, sat motionless in their places. Pontius decided he must say something more.

"What choice do we have, Kryx? Do you know what the penalties are for killing an NCU agent? Everyone in this room will spend thousands of years in hard labor – if we're lucky. We leave this place. He remembers nothing. We call for assistance and the only one who's implicated is me, because he's found in my apartment. None of you have anything to worry about."

The strain in Pontius's voice was obvious. He didn't believe a word of what he was saying. There were too manner scanners, too many checkpoints, too many public records. The authorities would know who was in this room. It might take them a while to sort out the pieces, but NCU would have their revenge.

Caspian, regaining some level of consciousness, was now looking around the room. He wasn't sure what they were doing or how they had come here. But he knew that the hogtied and brutalized agent in the middle of the room could not be a good thing. Conti, while remaining stationary beside Moria, looked like a caged animal. She wanted to affect change but remained anchored to her spot in the room.

Pontius was about to launch into another round of pseudo-logic when Kryx flew out of the kitchen. He had the biggest knife he could find in his hand. Before anyone could compute the action about to take place, he plunged the knife deep into Tenarrin's back. This brought a guttural scream from Conti and a painful grunt from Tenarrin. Wanting to override any repairs the nanites could make, Kryx dug the knife through Tenarrin. He carved him like a turkey. Pontius stared on in disbelief, angry at the turn of events but unable to force himself to move.

The entire action took mere seconds. But seeing Kryx saw through the body like a butcher made it seem like 30 horrific minutes had passed. When finished, Kryx brandished the knife and stood over his victim. He had all the satisfaction of a big-game hunter who had taken down his prey with his bare hands.

The rage pulsing through Pontius's body would not escape, nor would it be witnessed by anyone else in the room. He was furious that Kryx had taken it upon himself to commit such a heinous murder and yet he was sadly relieved at the same time. Kryx was correct. The only chance that most of the people in this room had for maintaining a regular life would be if Tenarrin was dead. Without his testimony onlookers like Conti, Caspian - and yes, Kryx - had the best chance of escaping.

He stood arrow straight, his chest heaving with panicked breaths. His gaze alternated from the corpse, up to Kryx, then back to the corpse again. He could not believe that his captain was now lying butchered on his living room floor. This man had given so much of his time and energy to help Pontius in every way. Pontius became aware of a profound sense of numbness washing over every part of his being. He was physically numb – unaware of the position of his hands or feet – but he was also mentally numb. He could not bring himself to register any true emotion at the sight before him.

For his part, Kryx stood and stared at Pontius, the bloody knife still clenched in his wiry fingers. Conti sobbed in the corner. Caspian stared on in utter amazement, still wondering if what he just saw had happened. Moria showed no change in emotion. She was not happy with this turn of events. Yet she could not bring herself to feel pity for the man who had just an hour ago tried to kill both her and Chunk.

Abject shock pulsated throughout the room for several minutes. Pontius regained some level of composure. He shot a stern glance at Kryx and said, "Go wash up and let's all get the hell out of here. Now."

Chapter 11 – Savages

When Caspian awoke he was in a familiar place, but in an odd position. He was sitting in the back of his own cruiser. He wasn't sure if he had ever sat anywhere but the pilot's seat and it caused him to see his old familiar vehicle in a new light.

At some point during the flight from Pontius's apartment he blacked out. It wasn't that he was too drunk or too high to comprehend the situation around him. It was just that the sensory overload from Kryx's miracle drug overwhelmed him. The details were fuzzy. He remembered laughing hysterically, transitioning into fitful mourning, and then returning to laughter again. In a matter of hours he experienced not just his own sensations, but the thoughts and sensations of hundreds – even thousands – of people around him. By the time the whole crew reached the cruiser, Caspian fainted.

Kryx was sitting up front in the pilot's chair with Conti stationed beside him. He stared blankly and unmovingly over the oceanic horizon. He long ago cleared the point that required manual piloting over the Centrian skies. He sat erect. His confidence underscored his smug satisfaction with the events in the apartment.

Pontius sat next to him, enthralled by the scenery. Dania sat behind them both and her presence jarred him. He hadn't seen her since that night at Indiarium and he couldn't now fathom how she had come to rejoin their party. It seemed odd to add her to this unfolding drama and he wasn't sure who had recommended her presence.

He closed his eyes and tried to piece together the events of the last several hours. Every memory, every sensation, was still available to him. But they were nonsensical, jumbled like puzzle pieces spilled from the box. He remembered the apartment. He could see Kryx's satisfied smile. He could see Chunk cooing on the couch. More than anything, he kept coming back to the image of Tenarrin's butchered back flayed out on the living room floor.

"Moria. Where is Moria? Is she alright?"

Pontius explained they had dropped her off for medical attention, over her strident protestations. She was in no mortal danger, but he was certain that she would need a replacement arm. Before they parted she was already losing sensation in the limb. Tenarrin had torn it up quite well as she fought off his blows and protected the baby.

"Where is Chunk? Was he left with Moria?"

"No. He's sleeping behind Dania's seat. We're going to-"

And with that a sense of wonder overtook the cabin and any potential conversation ended. The cruiser was speeding toward the horizon – a horizon that now featured one of the rarest sights for a Centrian citizen: a sunrise.

Behind the cruiser the clouds of Centrian rose into the sky in giant, dark, and foreboding pinnacles. The ever-present twinkle of lightning played between those clouds. It illuminated the violent playgrounds of the Great Eye. But in front of them now those clouds were breaking and the brilliant rays of a white sun burst under the dissipating layer of gloom.

Most Torrenthians went months without ever seeing the sun. The planet was not covered in storms, but the islands of Centrian were. A stationary storm system – known as the Great Eye – camped over Centrian many thousands of years before the arrival of humans. Seeing a few rays of random sunshine was a powerful good luck charm in anyone's day. Seeing an actual sunrise or sunset was almost unheard of. The splendor of it now laid out before the Nighthawk's passengers was breathtaking. It even mesmerized Kryx.

The cabin was silent for a full 15 minutes as everyone assessed the panorama. The hum of the cruiser's engines served to further engulf the moment in a comforting layer of white noise. At one point Conti unconsciously lifted her hand toward the rising sun as though she could reach out and touch it.

Caspian leaned over and spoke to Pontius in a quiet, reverential tone, as much to preserve the moment as to conceal his words.

"I could *feel* it. I felt every part of it."

Pontius broke his attention from the horizon and gazed into Caspian's face, searching for clues. He wasn't sure if Caspian was still high.

"You could feel what?"

"I could feel Tenarrin. The knife plunged into my back. My organs screamed in alarm. My pulse raced – and then sputtered, and stopped. My body grew cold as my mind became disconnected from the shell of my frame."

Pontius was momentarily convinced that Caspian had lost his mind. But when he looked into Caspian's eyes he saw an earnestness that he could not remember experiencing in his friend. Caspian was quivering as he remembered the experience of Tenarrin's death.

Caspian's description would have appalled a stranger. There was no terror in his voice. He showed no concern over the taking of someone's life. It was as though Tenarrin's death meant nothing to him. But Pontius understood the raw significance of this moment. Caspian was neither saddened nor exhilarated by the death. Rather, he was ecstatic at having felt anything. He did not recall the sense of Tenarrin's pain with fear or skittishness. He reveled in it. He savored every memory now emblazoned in his brain of the gruesome events that had occurred.

Pontius said nothing but held Caspian's gaze for several moments more. There was now a look of contentment and wonder carved onto Caspian's face. He had never seen such an expression of ribald, hearty life on his friend.

"Where are we going?" asked Caspian.

Given the bizarre nature of these revelations, Pontius found it odd to hear him ask a logical question.

"We're going to the islands. I hope that we can find a good home for Chunk there."

This startled Caspian somewhat. It had the effect of softening his dazed look while he considered the tactical realities of that statement.

"Was Moria's Vitapass access restored?"

"No." Pontius knew where this was going.

"And you think that you can somehow acquire a Tombstone on those scattered islands?"

"Not exactly. From what Kryx tells me, most of those living out there are unlicensed anyway. Even if I could find someone there who is dying, they would have no Tombstone to sell me. Thus, I would still have no Vitapass for Chunk."

Caspian chewed on these words for a moment. He recognized the tectonic shift in Pontius's logic but he wanted to quantify it.

"Do you believe that there is someone out there-" and with this he motioned to the vast ocean sprawled out before them, "-who can somehow issue a Vitapass for Chunk?"

Pontius shook his head.

"This isn't about Vitapasses anymore," Pontius replied.

Caspian could see this coming, but he was still stunned.

"What about your grand commitment? What about the transaction that you still owe to his parents? I thought this was all about satisfying a barter gone wrong – about correcting the tragedy that occurred when Moria's system access was revoked?"

Pontius paused to organize his pending narrative.

"Have you ever seen a death match?"

"Ummm..." Caspian couldn't remember such a spectacle. He held a finger aloft while he searched his UNI.

"Oh, well, I guess I have. In fact, it appears that I used to bet on them frequently. But that was more than 900 years ago. They bore me now. Why?"

"Before I came back to the apartment, right before Tenarrin tried to kill Moria and Chunk, I was at base-level."

At the mere mention of base-level Caspian grimaced and shook his head. In all his 3,309 years of life he had never once set foot on base-level and he assumed that he never would.

"I saw one of those matches. I watched two men – two wretched, decrepit, desperate men – fight to the death so that some wealthy sponsor would get the loser's Vitapass and the winner would find himself a little richer for as long as the money holds out."

Caspian offered nothing but a blank stare.

"So...?"

"So think about that for a minute. I've been committed to that deal – to the deal that Chunk would get his Vitapass. It's the same deal I make with all of my clients. In return for a few moments of discomfort, I give their children *life.* I give them Vitapasses. No one else in NCU has the ability to offer such an amazing gift."

Caspian nodded but he still had no idea where this was going.

"But what if I'm wrong, Caspian? What if that gift is not the glorious gift I always believed it to be? I'm killing my former colleagues and ruining the career I've fought so many centuries for, all so that I can give that kid a Vitapass that he might end up throwing away in a death match someday."

Caspian interjected. "But what life is he going to have if he doesn't have a Vitapass?"

Pontius thought about this for a full half minute.

"I don't know. And I'm still trying to think of some way to get his Vitapass. But if a legal man – a licensed man – can still find himself in such abject misery that he is willing to risk his life, and his Vitapass, for a desperate shot at wealth, then is the Vitapass alone such a vaunted gift?"

This was not a rhetorical question. Pontius stared at his friend hoping for an answer. He received nothing but a shrug.

"I don't know, Captain."

Pontius shook his head and said, "Neither do I..." They both sat for a few minutes pondering the situation.

"Let me ask you this." Pontius now had a new avenue of attack. "If I could somehow give Chunk a life as a free man – a happy man – but he wouldn't have a Vitapass, or I could give him a life as a licensed man but he was miserable and ended up throwing it all away in a death match, which scenario do you believe would have made his parents happier?"

"Well, obviously, no parent wants to believe that their son will one day be participating in a death match on base-level." Caspian was seeing the point. But he still framed the scenario as being worse because it occurred on base-level. He didn't care that someone needlessly forfeited his life.

"Exactly. So one way or another, I must find a way to give Chunk that life. Chunk's parents weren't desperate for him to have a licensed, disconsolate life. They were desperate for him to have a happy, fulfilling life. They merely assumed that the Vitapass was a necessary ingredient in that. This is why they – or any of my other clients – would agree to the deal in the first place."

Pontius was smug, happy in his logic and feeling as though he just made a major point. Caspian chewed on the particulars for several more moments. He didn't quite understand the underlying premise.

"Then why don't you just bring him back to the Diaspori?" Caspian was puzzled, but Pontius frowned and began shaking his head.

"No. No, no, no. Those people are slaves. I won't sell him into a life of servitude to LiveLong."

"But you said those people, those 'slaves' as you refer to them, were happy. Isn't that now the point – to ensure that Chunk is happy? Even if he is unlicensed?"

Pontius was still shaking his head.

"Servitude is not happiness. It's ignorance. I won't do that to the boy." Pontius may have softened his understanding of the vaunted value of a Vitapass, but he still felt affronted by any suggestion of captivity. "A gilded cage is, nevertheless, still a cage."

Caspian didn't understand this line of reasoning, but he didn't feel strong enough to rail against it either. The descriptions he heard of the Diaspori were of happy, productive people. They enjoyed their lives and appreciated the corporation that made those lives possible. But he also knew from the tone in Pontius's voice that this was not an argument he would win – thus he didn't bother trying.

This conversation caught Dania's attention and she now leaned forward to hear the details. As she did, her long black hair dangled below her, swaying in a slow but steady rhythm. Her entry into the discussion had not gone unnoticed by Pontius. Nothing Dania did ever went unnoticed by Pontius.

***

Pontius married Dania three separate times. On each occasion, after hundreds of years of the standard married life, they grew distant and split. This happened with almost all couples who were not memoriae. But the central tenets of their attraction were still in place. Their network of mutual friends ensured that they were never too far from each other's influence.

Among people of standard memories, this was not an unusual. The limits of natural memory meant that even the best couples would come to see their partners more as roommates than as lovers. The platonic nature of the relationship would break down the aging romance. After divorce, and given enough time and space, if the two were still in casual contact it was not uncommon for a new cycle of attraction to arise between them. This happened once the record of their failed habitation was more of an academic fact than a guttural emotion. These on-again/off-again couples existed throughout the country, circling each other on elliptical orbits. They came in close, intimate contact for several hundred years. They alienated and drifted from each other for several hundred more years. Then they found themselves pulled inward to each other again.

It was more than 600 years since their last marriage. Both of them were feeling the renewed pull as their season of lust came back into full bloom. This led to snarky comments from Moria whenever they were in her presence, but neither of them cared much.

Dania held a vaunted position in Centrian as one of the foremost chefs. She operated several restaurants that catered to the planet's elite. In a world where every dish carried an undercurrent of fish oil, hers stood out as fresh and biting. They weren't drowned in the all-too-familiar flavors of Oceanus.

Her celebrity status came not just from her gastronomic creations. Many of her famous patrons wanted to rub shoulders with her. She had a beauty and a grace that beguiled men from all walks of life. Her business acumen challenged those who tried to dismiss her as a pretty face.

Her physical appearance was remarkable. But it was the manner in which she carried herself that hypnotized her cohorts. Her gait was smooth and efficient making her seem as though she was floating rather than walking. Her long ebony hair flowed and swayed as a single unit with a subtle sheen. The thin fingers of her hand led to slivery arms that were almost too long for her body. Those arms rocked back and forth as she walked as though she was wading to her destination. Her most stunning feature was her bright green eyes that shone like starlight from the canvas of her smooth olive skin.

Through their previous iterations, Pontius always felt he was "marrying up". He viewed her as out of his league – and she was, but she was always intrigued by his sheer force of will. More than anything, she admired the fact that when he put his mind to something, it happened. This was what caught her attention now in the cabin of the cruiser. She was quite unaccustomed to hearing him question any of his premises. His moral code was set many hundreds of years ago and she had never known anything to alter it.

***

From behind his seat, she placed a hand on his shoulder and commanded his attention with her emerald gaze.

"If captivity is such an issue, what do you hope to give that child on this island?"

He had pondering the same question from the moment they boarded the cruiser. Every thought had come back to this question. Without a clear answer in mind, he volleyed the query back to her.

"Honestly, I'm not sure. I just know that life on Centrian is nearly impossible without the validation of a Vitapass. Besides, these people – these savages – they are at least free to leave when they please, aye?"

She frowned as she considered the reality of this proposition.

"I suppose... they are free, in the same way that all of us are free to choose our path, our actions, our friends and acquaintances."

He nodded, relieved by this acknowledgment, but she wasn't finished.

"They are also free in the same way that every man on base-level is free. Even the Diaspori are *free* if they so choose to walk out the gates of LiveLong and confront the whole of Population Control. Is that the kind of freedom you're trying to grant to the child?"

He sat for a moment and stared back at the glowing horizon. The sky above them was now almost clear of cloud cover and the sun was rising over the ocean.

"But those people at base-level are miserable. They reside in squalor. They poison their mind to numb themselves against the pain of the present. They murder each other for a chance at something greater. And those people under LiveLong may look happy, but they're also brainwashed. They would no sooner leave that place than they would put a torch to the entire LiveLong Corporation. Both of these classes of individuals live in prisons of their own minds."

She nodded but she wasn't satisfied with the answer. She scanned his face for clues to his inner motivations.

"What do you know of the islands?"

This wasn't a trivial question. Pontius researched his targets with an intellectual determinism. Yet he could be haphazard in his approach to everyday crises. She had a hunch that he was operating in the same paradigm now. He curled his mouth and raised his eyebrows, confirming her suspicions.

"He tells me they are savages," he said, motioning toward Kryx in the pilot's chair. "War, disease, famine."

He paused, and she shot him an anxious glance to ask, "And...?"

"But I don't trust him. He speaks of those people with a vitriol that forces me to question his motives. Something happened there that soured him to these so-called savages."

She smiled, understanding his assessment.

"You've been there. Is Kryx correct? Are those people savages?"

She patted him on the back and sat upright, allowing her hair to fall over the front of her tunic.

"I think it's best if you see for yourself. We're almost there."

She motioned to the guidance system stationed above the cockpit. The outline of an island now made its way onto the outer edge of the screen and it was clear they would soon achieve their destination.

Fifteen minutes later he saw the outline of the island peaking over the horizon. At first it was a shimmering mirage, appearing and then evaporating against the roiling seas of Oceanus. As they came ever closer the island revealed itself. He sat forward in his chair, straining to obtain a better view of the approaching landmass.

As the isle grew larger in the passengers' view, so too did Dania's stature in the cabin. They were approaching an environment in which she was well versed – something no one else in the cruiser claimed. Knowing that she was on this trip for this experience, she now took it upon herself to assess the situation and assume command. She stood up and entered coordinates into the navigation system. She preferred the surety of a touchscreen interface to the more ephemeral connection via UNI. As she did, Kryx glanced back at her but offered no feedback. He rose to his feet, walked to the back of the cabin, and took the seat she had occupied for most of the journey.

As the island came into clearer view, Pontius also stood, agape at the sight. Where he had expected to see trees and huts, he instead saw structures. The units were modern in style and architecture. In fact, the structures covered the entirety of the island for as far as he could see. While none of them rose higher than several floors, they were otherwise similar to what one might find on Majorus.

The shore – where he had expected to see nothing but beach – was instead dominated by ships, warehouses, and ports. As he looked below the cruiser he saw a wide array of ships dotting the water. They ranged from tiny fishing boats to massive tankers. There were even helicopters and various cruisers zipping through the sky. The entire island was abuzz with activity and awash with development.

She was now in full command, monitoring communications that flashed across the main console. At several points, Pontius heard clear requests for landing codes coming from the communicator. Without thinking, she replied with the proper authorizations. She swiveled her chair and faced the passengers.

"We're cleared to dock at a vetting station a few hundred meters offshore. We will be met at the station by a security detail. *Leave all of the talking to me.*"

She had more to say, but she made it clear that she expected confirmation from everyone before continuing. Everyone, including Kryx, nodded in agreement.

"Once we are cleared for entry, it will be me, Pontius, and Chunk heading to the mainland. Pontius, leave all weapons here in the cruiser. Everyone else will wait here on the cruiser. Most importantly, Kryx – you are expected to stay right here at all times. Do not leave the vessel."

Pontius expected some kind of protest from Kryx, or from anyone else on board, but instead there was virtual silence. Kryx shrugged his shoulders, indicating that he was more than happy to stay on the cruiser. Conti and Caspian, although staring at the panorama before them, did not seem eager to experience any of it firsthand.

The vetting station was an artificial platform stationed off the coast of the island. It was octagonal and offered mooring for both sea vessels below and airships above. A scan of the coast revealed a series of these stations dotting the waters. Most of them had multiple docked vessels awaiting access to the mainland.

The vetting process was simple. Dania, Pontius, and Chunk exited the Nighthawk. They were escorted into the central processing depot in the middle of the platform. A few dozen motley traders filled the depot, awaiting their turn through customs. She did not bother with any of the queues. She glided to an express lane and nodded at the customs officer. He smiled in return and waved the three of them through. As they did so, they garnered many exasperated looks from the traders awaiting entry. Pontius caught many of their scowls as they walked past the processing queues.

"How long does it normally take to gain formal access to the island?"

"Days," she responded matter-of-factly.

After clearing customs they were led to a transport ferry that would take them to shore. The vessel was large enough to accommodate several dozen passengers, but the three of them were the only ones on board. It was autonomous and pre-programmed for the routine trip to the mainland.

She focused on the island, paying little attention to his befuddlement. From the moment he spotted the island his preconceived notions evaporated. The customs office only furthered his amazement. The agents manning the station dressed in modern fare. Their countenance was that of a proper government function. He felt as though he was gaining access not to a primitive island but to a sister nation of Centrian.

He leaned in close to whisper, as though he was afraid that his words would be overheard by angry islanders in the empty cabin.

"I thought this place was primitive."

She held her gaze on the approaching island but smirked as she responded, "And who told you that?"

"Kryx."

"And you believed him?"

He puzzled on that question for a moment. He didn't believe Kryx, but he didn't know what he believed.

"No."

"Don't mention his name on the mainland. He's well known here – and that's not a good thing."

"What exactly has he done?"

He wasn't sure that he wanted to know the answer, but he blurted out the question anyway.

"This is a prolific trading nation. Many of the things that you can't find on Centrian you can acquire here on Solis. But they don't take kindly to those who deal in smuggling and subterfuge. I bargain in good faith with these people, as do the thousands of traders that you see in the ships around us. Kryx bargains with cunning and deceit. He frequents the homes of smugglers and his agents would do anything they could to strip this island bare. The wars he refers to are the wars that take place between dueling factions of vagabonds. They are no more than mafia feuds."

None of this surprised Pontius. After several more minutes of watching the approach, he asked, "Do you know where we're going?"

She nodded.

"I'm taking you to see Vigoran. She is the chairman of the Ministry of Commerce and she has powerful contacts throughout Solis. If anyone can find a home for Chunk, it's her."

With the vessel about 50 meters from port, something frightening and wonderful overtook him. He felt as though a thousand screaming voices fell silent. The resulting quiet left him disoriented and nauseous. The sensation was so jarring and so sudden that he was unable to speak. He could do nothing more than gaze, dumbfounded, at Dania, desperate for some explanation.

She smiled knowingly and replied, "Your UNI has been disabled. They are banned here."

Regular visitors to Solis grew accustomed to this effect. In more than 1,800 years of life, he was without his UNI. It was as much a part of his brain as his prefrontal cortex or his medulla oblongata. Having it now so abruptly silenced for the first time in his long life was both exhilarating and terrifying all at the same time. UNIs developed millennia ago as memory storage devices. Constant software upgrades coupled with the brain's incredible ability to adapt. This meant they were now intertwined with all the natural, biological functions of the brain itself. For Centrian citizens the UNI long ago ceased to be mere hardware. It was now a cybernetic adjunct to one's own being.

When the vessel docked the automatic doors opened and several attendants came in to assist. He looked around knowing that it was time to disembark, but unable to move. He looked down at his arms and legs and they seemed to him like foreign, lifeless entities bolted to his frame. They ignored his commands and hung limp from his torso.

She scooped up Chunk with her left arm, realizing that he was not safe in Pontius's unstable grasp. With her right arm she began helping him to his feet. Attendants rushed in to his other side to stabilize him and guide him off the vessel. He stumbled off the ship and onto the docks, leaning first on Dania, then on one of the attendants, then back on Dania again.

The attendants guided him to a bench – one in a long series placed here for this purpose. It was clear to him that this was a common experience for new visitors to the island. Once the attendants left, she sat with him for a full half hour while he regained his bearings. She said nothing, bouncing Chunk on her knee. She occasionally surveyed his face to check on the status of his recovery. With each passing minute he felt the proper sensations returning to his limbs. When he was capable of standing on his own he nodded to her and gingerly rose to his feet. She hailed a taxi.

The ensuing ride was one of wonderment for Pontius. Everything that passed amazed him because it was modern and advanced, and also because it was not Centrian. This was a world of light. The bright sun shone down upon the buildings and left him with a permanent squint. The buildings themselves were modern but there were no skyscrapers. The tallest structure was no more than four or five stories. The roads bustled with activity. Foot traffic and vehicles abounded. It felt so foreign to him to be on base-level where that base-level was not a platform for filth and decay. Between every building and in every possible edifice sprouted trees, bushes, and all manner of flora. Flowers colonized every ledge, every platform, every horizontal space untouched by foot or vehicle. Larger inlets gave rise to trees that expanded so bountifully as to almost obscure the buildings behind them. The clothing was modern but much freer, lighter than anything he saw on Centrian. They favored brighter colors and they exposed more skin, but always in a tasteful manner.

Perhaps the most striking feature wasn't what he saw, but what he didn't see. Nowhere at the port or on any of the streets did he see a single dog. Not only were there no canine pets, there were no feral dogs roaming between the buildings. Their absence jarred him.

It was easy to spot the occasional Centrian trader making his way through this metropolis. Like Pontius, they all squinted and they were all overdressed. They lumbered about with a disorientation that exposed their UNI dependence. They all carried a dour expression.

Every so often he spotted people in the crowd who frightened him. They stooped over and walked in a halting fashion. Their skin fell from their frail bodies and their hair was a dull grey or, in a few cases, a brighter white. They looked unhealthy. He could not fathom the disease causing this condition that ran rampant throughout Solis. He wondered to himself if this disease was contagious. If he contracted it, he wondered if he would have time to return to Centrian for treatment.

After an hour of this commute the trio reached their destination. Exiting the cab, they stood before a large U-shaped building. It flanked an impressive courtyard, meticulously groomed with an immense garden. All around him, he became aware of the cacophonous drone of birds. They chirped and sang in such volume it was difficult to concentrate on anything else.

Dania took his hand, leading him through the garden and into the main foyer. Although there were people stationed in the foyer to guide visitors, she gave them no attention. She headed straight to the escalators and led him through the hallways to the chairman's office.

She strode into the office and Vigoran rose to greet her warmly. They shared a long embrace and gazed at each other with affection..

He found Vigoran unusual. She was attractive but not in a way he understood. Her build was athletic and he imagined that she must take part in some kind of racing activity. She wore a long skirt made of thousands of silvery strands hanging to the floor. As she strode forward to greet him, her legs broke through the strands and exposed wiry, muscular limbs. Her torso was long and her blouse stopped short of her waist, revealing an impressive array of washboard abs. Intricate tattoos covered her arms. They glowed and slowly transformed across her skin like shapes coalescing in a lava lamp. She sported a crop of short, straight, jet-black hair that leapt from her head. On any other person it may have seemed radical but on her it underscored the energy she infused into the room. Her hair carried prodigious streaks of grey, a fashion he never saw before.

Her face was beautiful but worn in a way he couldn't identify. Crow's feet adorned each eye and the skin beneath her chin sagged ever so slightly. While he found her intriguing, he couldn't help but wonder if she had borne some terrible tragedy in the recent past. He couldn't understand why someone with such natural beauty wore hardship so prominently on her face.

"Welcome, Pontius. I take it from your expression that you've never been to Solis before?"

She smiled at him. He was more than a bit embarrassed to be exuding ignorance. He nodded his head and tried to remove his gawking star. Grasping her hand in greeting, the power in her grip surprised him.

She motioned for them to take a seat on plush office. The broad, comfortable chairs were a welcome sensation. Although he hadn't walked much in hours, his legs were still weary as a side effect of his UNI disablement.

Vigoran pressed a button next to her chair and asked for drinks. Pontius shook his head. He explained that he wasn't sure if he could handle anything intoxicating at this point, but she laughed.

"We'll bring you fruit juice. No need to hold back on that."

He pondered this statement for a moment. He wasn't sure if he had ever tasted fruit juice, of any kind, and he couldn't query his UNI to check.

When the drinks arrived, he downed his juice. It had a sweetness he couldn't remember experiencing before. The film it left on his tongue was both tart and satisfying and he wished he had another glass.

Vigoran spent a full 30 minutes talking with Dania. It was clear they had known each other for some time and had much to catch up on. They did not ignore him but they weren't concerned with talking around him either. After they finished swapping tales of recent adventures, Vigoran turned her attention to him.

"So you have... a child." She said this while gesturing toward Chunk. "I have the impression that that this is not your child?"

He nodded.

"Where are his parents? Are they alive?"

He shook his head. He wasn't trying to be obtuse. Yet these simple gestures encapsulated all he wanted to explain about the situation.

"So you are now expected to care for this child?"

"Not exactly." He tried to leave the answer at that but it became clear that she expected elaboration. "His parents lost their lives trying to protect him. I made a commitment to them. In return for payment, I was to provide the boy with a Vitapass."

She furrowed her brow, trying to put together the pieces.

"And this payment. It was received in full?"

He nodded.

"You do realize, of course, that we have no Vitapasses here?"

"To be frank, my ability to supply Vitapasses has been interrupted. To be more frank, it might have been lost altogether. I'm not sure if I can ever fully deliver on the promise that was originally made, and I can't return the payment. So I'm trying to find a life for Chunk."

"Then why would you bring him here? What service do you expect to extract from the people of Solis?"

He wasn't comfortable with the tone of her questions but he had come too far to back out now.

"I came here hoping that I might find a suitable home for him."

She looked at him, then shot a gaze toward Dania, and then back to him again.

"There are unlicensed littered among the detritus of Centrian. One needn't travel to Solis to live without a Vitapass."

"You are technically correct, but the lives you speak of are pale comparisons of the life I would wish for my own child. It's certainly not the life his parents expected when they bargained for his Vitapass. If I can't give him an official, licensed existence on Centrian, it strikes me that he may be able to live a full and meaningful life here on Solis."

She fell into thought and he found himself dangling for a conclusion. Before she could give any answer he continued.

"There's much that I don't understand about this place, but there *are* unlicensed people living here, right?" A new thought had occurred to him. If everything he knew about the outer islands was wrong, then maybe there were no unlicensed souls living here after all.

She chuckled and relaxed a little in her seat.

"Most of the people here are, indeed, unlicensed. Some of them are refugees from the urban filth of Centrian. Many more are the free descendants of refugees who came decades, or even centuries, before. But there are only two ways to become a citizen of Solis. You are either born here or you migrate here of your own free will. We have a secret treaty with Centrian signed more than five millennia ago. It says that we will not engage in any smuggling of souls. We will not become a dumping ground for the unlicensed babies of Centrian. This treaty is a key component that keeps the bureaucratic pigs of Torrenth off our backs. If this boy, this *Chunk*, wants to live here he is free to do so as an adult. But he can't make that decision for decades."

With these words, the wind exited his sails. He was unaware of any treaty or any blockade in the trafficking of children. He didn't even understand the political motivations behind the treaty or what would happen to the island they broke it. He looked hard at her, but she was resolute in her statement. He shot a hopeful gaze to Dania, but her expression indicated that he was on his own. He looked back at Vigoran and wondered if she was about to escort them out. After several awkward minutes of her sipping her drink, he decided to try a Hail Mary. He leaned forward in his seat, telegraphing his earnestness, and stared straight into her eyes.

"There was more than a simple payment made for his Vitapass."

She gave him her full attention, but said nothing and raised her eyebrows as if to say, "Do explain." He swallowed hard and wrestled for the appropriate words. He could hear the din of bird songs rising outside the office.

"Chunk's mother agreed to subject herself to the most horrific of sexual defilements in return for that boy's future."

He continued to hold her gaze, hoping to receive some kind of positive response, but she continued her "Do go on." expression.

"His father was forced to witness this defilement as a condition of the deal."

Her face took on a dark countenance as she considered the reality of his words. She offered no direct response, preferring instead to force him through this confession.

"And once they had paid the ultimate price for Chunk's Vitapass, it came to pass that I could not deliver on my end of the bargain."

Dania looked out the window, trying her best to remove herself from these thoughts. Vigoran maintained her focus but she was not yet ready to speak. He felt caught in a play that would not end until he wrote the final act. After taking a moment to compose himself, he continued.

"When it became clear that they had been duped, his parents attacked me." The sound of birds outside the window had risen to a thunderous roar. "And I killed them both."

And with those words, the birds went silent. A muscular release allowed his torso to relax. All the foul air of Centrian, and Plethora, and base-level, escaped his lungs in one exultant sigh.

She continued sipping her drink but he was sure there was nothing left in her cup. She stared at the bottom of the container as though she had lost the last few drops of precious liquid.

Without looking up she asked, "And you want to wash yourself of these sins by depositing this orphan at our doorstep?"

"I'm not here for forgiveness. Think what you want of me, but that baby didn't deserve this fate. I can take him back to Centrian and he can wallow in the depths of base-level, but you and I know that he'll never make it back here to make his choice. He'll be dead. He'll be lucky if he survives the year. He's not just an unlicensed. He's an illegitimate child harbored by a fugitive NCU agent who's gone rogue. The entire force of Population Control will be hunting me, and him, like a pack of hungry dogs. They will bear down upon him as a show of force against anyone who thinks they can cheat the system."

"Then what makes you think they won't follow him here?"

"They would never expect me to bring him here. No one who understands me believes I would ever leave Centrian. The last scan they had on him came from the scaler platform outside my apartment. They might scour every tower on Majorus, but they have no reason to believe I'd take him off the grid."

She looked over to Dania. To his relief, Dania nodded. She didn't know how this drama was going to play out, but she knew his logic to be solid.

Vigoran rose and told them that she had to talk to a few people. She instructed them to stay here. The next 15 minutes were excruciating and awkward. Dania sat as stiff as a board and stared out at the glittering sun reflecting off the buildings. She could not bring herself to even look at him. She knew something had gone wrong – horribly wrong. But she didn't realize the extent of his depravity. She now felt more than a little embarrassed to participate in this murderous mess. He had no idea what to do so he also sat still in his seat and counted the minutes until Vigoran's return.

When the door opened again he felt a sense of relief, believing that Vigoran had returned with a verdict. Instead, he saw a young woman of some horrible deformity enter the room. She was overweight, which seemed even stranger on this tropical paradise. Her face had an unusual roundness and her eyes were mongoloid. Those eyes hid behind something he had only seen in textbooks – thick bottleneck glasses. Her tongue seemed a little too large for her mouth and made her breath heavy. As soon as she opened the door, Dania sprang to her feet and yelled, "Aylea!"

The young mutant responded with a gleeful, "Aunt Dania!" and she ran across the room, throwing her stubby arms around Dania's waste. He was in abject shock.

"What the hell is that?"

Paying no attention to his appalling response, Dania returned the hug with vigor and said, "This is Aylea! She's Vigoran's daughter."

The two of them finished a long embrace. Aylea started rambling about all the exciting things that happened in school since Dania's last visit. They were both oblivious to him. He made no attempt to hide his horror. His jaw slid down to his knees. They talked like giddy schoolgirls until he could contain himself no longer.

"What's *wrong* with it?"

Aylea, not understanding the basis of his question, paid no attention to him whatsoever. Dania, however, nudged her away. She faced Pontius, smiled at him, and said in a lower tone, "Pontius, she has a genetic disorder. It's called Down's Syndrome."

He struggled to make sense of this statement. He couldn't remember any *Down's Syndrome*. Then again, if he had learned about it in school that would have been more than 1,700 years ago and he had no recollection of it now. He couldn't remember ever seeing anyone like this. He couldn't ever remember seeing any kind of genetic disorder manifested in everyday people. Then again, he couldn't remember much of anything without his UNI. His natural memory could not process this information.

"Is this some disease? Do these conditions ravage the population of Solis?"

Dania didn't show her exasperation. His world was so different, and his access to it so removed, that she could not expect him to process this scenario. As such, she tried to be patient with him.

"No, silly, it's not a disease. It's a genetic condition. She was born with it."

She tried to resume her conversation with Aylea but he still needed help.

"So why don't they fix it?"

"It's in every one of her chromosomes, Pontius. What are they going to fix?"

"But I don't remember ever seeing someone like this on Centrian."

"Of course not. Those babies on Centrian are aborted. Some genetic conditions can be corrected in utero, assuming, of course, that your unborn child has a Vitapass waiting for it. If the condition cannot be corrected, the pregnancy is terminated by the state. You would normally know this. It's stored in your UNI."

Her words were logical but it still didn't make sense to him. He didn't understand how a monster like this walked the streets of an otherwise civilized society.

"Then why wouldn't they do the same thing here?"

She released a long sigh and walked next to him.

"You're not on Centrian anymore. They don't have nanites in the water supply. In fact, the nanites in your system were eradicated when we came ashore on that transport vessel. They don't sell or take Telomore. They don't have organ banks and they don't regenerate limbs."

This revelation smothered him like a steamroller.

"They don't have doctors? They don't have hospitals? Do they die miserable deaths whenever they catch the flu?"

"No. Of course not. Their medical facilities here are actually quite impressive. But they're not in the business of keeping people alive for millennia. They don't play god with the population. They don't decide who lives and who dies. They experience their lives with all the appreciation of someone who understands that they could be gone tomorrow."

When she realized that there were no more protests, she returned to the giggling teenager and he plunked back down in his chair. He wasn't sure what to make of any of this. He considered demanding that they return to the cruiser, but that seemed unwise. He wasn't sure if he could leave Chunk in this environment, but he didn't know of any other option. He felt trapped and alone in a far off land.

He also began to fear for his own safety. If he had no nanites in his system now, then what was happening to his 1,800-year-old organs? How fast would a body like his break down? How long could one even expect to live without their essential activity? And he was out of Telomore. This hadn't worried him in the slightest until now. Telomore was more ubiquitous on Centrian than rain. But if he didn't escape this island soon, how many more times could his cells split before they fell into senescence? Did he have months? Days? Hours? He had no idea.

His heart started to race and he could feel the initial signs of panic setting in when the door swung open again. Vigoran returned. With little fanfare she announced to everyone in the room, "You're very lucky. I've managed to call a special session of the Free Council. They will meet tomorrow night to consider Chunk's case for asylum. You can all stay at my house tonight."

Chapter 12 – A Council of Decay

Pontius awoke to find that he was still in a dream. The dark watery sky of Centrian was gone. In its place a warm comforting horizon glittered through his bedroom window. The windows were open and a cooling breeze washed over him. The air smelled of various tropical flowers and baked goods.

Waking to an open window and a gentle breeze was strange enough for this old veteran of the Great Eye. In Centrian, no one opened a window. Most windows didn't even open. The winds that ravage a building at an altitude of several hundred meters do not belong in one's home. Even without wind, the ever-present rain made outdoor access impractical. Citizens darted from one scaler platform to another and hopscotched across Majorus's many towers. A Centrian life was an indoor life.

He made his way to the and took his morning piss. The resulting shock was almost enough to make an entire mess of his host's quarters. His urine was almost black and disturbingly viscous. Dania had warned him about this – a natural side effect of the inert nanites flushed from his system. Yet it was still quite jarring to witness it firsthand.

Returning to the bedroom, he made a note of the accoutrements. When they arrived last night it was dark and he couldn't get a full sense of Vigoran's house or its furnishings. Now, in the blinding light of Solis he surveyed his surroundings.

The furniture, the flooring, even the walls themselves were formal, yet natural. Beige fabric covered the walls and gave the room a rustic feel. The furniture consisted of stained, polished wood. Nothing on Centrian was ever made of wood.

As he came down from his bedroom to the dining room he saw Dania and Vigoran munching on breakfast and discussing recent events. Chunk bounced on Vigoran's knee, so much so that he found it mildly alarming, but Chunk seemed happy so he said nothing. The dining room was more of a patio than a formal room and the generous breeze carried the heady aroma of food to his brain.

He said nothing as he sat down and perused the dishes. Vigoran greeted him with a warm smile but otherwise continued her conversation with her friend. The food arrayed on the table was unrecognizable. There were several baskets of fruit he could not identify. A series of dishes on one side of the table held various substances that looked like bread. A series of dishes on the other side contained different mushes. One was grainy, another contained tapioca-like bubbles, and a third was grey and smooth. It was only by watching the others that he understood to dip different breads into the mixtures. He also watched Dania and Vigoran to understand how to eat the fruits. They all required some kind of peeling or preparation he had not learned before.

At first he tried to nibble on the various offerings while he listened in on the women's conversation. The first bite to reach his mouth was a revelation, offering a pure joy of taste he had never experienced before. The second bite taken from another dish cemented his impression from the first. By the time he made a half dozen tastings he abandoned all pretense at civilized behavior. He sucked down the contents of each vessel. He looked up often to see if he was garnering unfavorable attention. But it became clear they were paying him little notice and he devolved into glorious gluttony. By the time Dania shot a casual glance back at him, he had emptied most of the containers on the table.

She shot him a knowing smile. "It's quite incredible, isn't it?"

His mouth was far too full to offer a formal response. He just nodded his head and tried to gather any remaining morsels that escaped to the outer reaches of his face.

Just about the time he completed his gorging, Aylea pounced into the room. Vigoran gave her a hug and told her to sit with them. He shot a guilty look toward the empty dishes. He wondered if he should have left something for Aylea, but no one seemed to notice that there was now little to eat.

Aylea sat next to him – a closeness that irritated him. He found himself scooting his chair away, a few inches at a time, to preserve some modicum of space between them. Despite Dania's logical explanation, he still feared that this disorder might somehow infect him.

Once it was clear that he could pillage no more of the breakfast offerings, Vigoran turned toward him.

"I will be leaving shortly. I have a great deal to prepare before tonight's asylum hearing. Dania will be leaving soon as well. She has some ingredients to acquire."

He nodded and looked to Dania.

"If you can just give me a few moments to wash up, I'll be ready to go."

Dania smiled and shook her head.

"I'm sorry. I must go alone. Some of my contacts are comfortable dealing with me and with me only. They wouldn't appreciate the presence of another city rat in their midst."

He was confused. "These ingredients you acquire here – they're available in a marketplace, right?"

She chuckled and shook her head again. "Solis offers some of the most exquisite tastes on Torrenth, but I can't satisfy my clientele with dishes that could be cooked up here on the main street. I'll be traveling throughout the island today."

In a whining tone that surprised even him, he asked, "But can't I just go along with you? I want to see more of this place. If Chunk has a chance to live here then I'd like to know the environment to which I'm consigning him."

Vigoran sprung to her feet, still participating in the conversation but ready to go on her way.

"Yes, that's exactly what Dania and I were thinking. That's why I've asked Aylea here to be your guide for the day."

Vigoran wore a proud smile of accomplishment, as though she had just solved a difficult and satisfying puzzle. Aylea threw her arms in the air and gave him a grand smile. He could not conceal his expression of horror.

"Oh, no, that won't be necessary. Look, if I can't join Dania I'm more than happy to simply explore on my own."

Vigoran exchanged a chagrined glance with Dania.

"Where are you going to eat?"

"Uhhh, there are restaurants on Solis, right?" He had no idea what she was getting at.

"And how do you propose to pay for that food?"

He cut off the retort in his throat before he could verbalize it. His only means of payment was to transfer squalem via UNI. He could not use his UNI, and he suspected there was no concept here of a transfer card.

"That's quite alright. This breakfast has me stuffed. I don't need to eat again this afternoon."

"So you'll be entirely on foot, because you can't pay for a taxi or public transportation. And where will you go? Which way is the port, Pontius?"

He searched his memory for anything, even a simple cardinal direction that would help him point toward the port. He had nothing.

"Where is the nearest shopping center?"

He still had nothing.

"From which buildings would you be barred without proper Solis identification? Do you even know?"

Again, he was speechless.

"You're in an alien world, as foreign to you as the surface of India. If you are arrested here, I won't be able to help you. If you become disoriented, you will have no way to contact us for directions. If you find yourself in need of something – anything – you will be adrift in a foreign sea."

She now leaned in to Pontius and gave him the stern look of a school teacher scolding an errant pupil. "Aylea will accompany you. She's quite helpful, and quite knowledgeable. You'll be surprised."

He shot a pleading glance to Dania but it was clear that she would be of no use in this fight. He considered just staying in the house all day. Then he pondered the prospect of staring at the walls for many hours with no UNI access and no way to communicate with the outside world. After several awkward moments in which Vigoran waited for his response, he dropped his head and nodded. Aylea released a squeal of happiness and Vigoran resumed her preparations to leave.

Minutes later, he found himself alone in the house with Aylea. She began talking to him but he couldn't understand half of what she said. Her slurred words could not penetrate his stubborn mind. He stared at her and nodded whenever it appeared that she expected a reply.

The awkward duo embarked an hour later. Dreading the company and still frustrated by Dania's abandonment, he took an inordinate amount of time to wash up. He considered slipping out a back door and taking off on his own. But Vigoran's stern stance made him wonder what might become of him if he disobeyed her command. After thinking on it long and hard during his shower, he decided that he would drag Aylea along with him. He would just say and do as little with her as necessary to get through the scenario.

A Dusk Forever Waning

When they left the house, she grabbed his hand and began dragging him forward. He snatched his hand back, making no attempt to conceal his disgust. But she was incorrigible. Every several steps, he found her clasping his hand again. This push-pull continued for more than a hundred meters before he acquiesced. Feeling defeated, he left his hand in hers and followed her lead down the street, grouchy all the way.

It took less than an hour for him to realize the wisdom in Vigoran's edict. As they walked down one street and then another, he was disoriented. He assumed it would be easy to wander through the local neighborhoods and make his way back home before it became too late. Yet now that they were out-and-about the surroundings bewildered him. It wasn't that anything in this environment was confusing. The streets of Solis ran in broad, straight, logical grids for easy travel. But with his UNI disabled he realized he couldn't maintain even the most rudimentary navigation. He wasn't sure how his UNI assisted in day-to-day travel. Yet it was clear that it was providing a deeper service than simple long-term storage. Streets they had already traversed looked new and strange to him. Once they had turned left, he couldn't believe that reversing and turning right led to their starting point. His disoriented mind shuffled the broader spatial relationships.

As he became aware of these cognitive difficulties, he wondered if there were other side effects of this impairment. He began to question the very nature of his "natural" memory. Tasks he attributed to his organic mind were now dysfunctional with his UNI disabled. He wondered what he was now capable of – good or bad – now that he was operating only on organic thought.

Although he would not admit it, Aylea made for an excellent guide. As she led him down numerous city streets she blurted out points of interest as they passed. She also threw out a continual stream of potential destinations. Most of these suggestions – shopping centers, parks, etc. - had little interest to him and he just shook his head in response. Occasionally, though, she would hit on something of real merit. In response he would nod his head – he was reticent to speak with her in any way - and she would change course.

En route to one of these locations he stopped and yanked her backward by the hand. She didn't understand his intention but he was not inclined to explain himself. Rather, he just stood for a full ten minutes and stared.

Across the street and separated by a rudimentary fence he saw a large elementary school in session. It was time for recess. Hundreds of children crawled like vermin over every square inch of playground equipment. They yelled. They cried. They laughed. The sounds came from all corners of the playground while harried assistants tried in vain to corral the children.

"Aylea?"

She was a little shocked. This was the first time he addressed her unprovoked.

"Aye?"

"This place. This is a school for all of Solis's children?"

She giggled and shook her head. "Of course not, Mr. Pontius. There are many schools like this one."

Without missing a beat, he shot back at her, "How many? How many schools like this are on Solis?"

She halted and wrestled with her reply. She wasn't good with numbers.

"I don't know. Maybe this much?" and she motioned toward all her fingers and all her toes.

He stood dumbfounded. Elementary schools didn't exist in Centrian. The birthrate was so low – and the licensed birthrate even lower – that there was no need for mass education. On the rare occasion when an authorized soul came into this world, education was a private matter for the parents to deal with. He could never remember seeing so many children in one place. He assumed this observation would stand even if he had restored UNI access.

When he had his fill he motioned for them to continue. While she resumed dragging him through the streets, he was deep in thought. He no longer had any natural memory of his own childhood. Yet it struck him that his childhood must have been like everyone else's childhood on Centrian – alone. There couldn't have been any time in his youth that he was able to play in an open schoolyard full of hundreds of playful peers. There were not several hundred school-age children in the entire nation at the time of his adolescence. That fact that was still valid today. He wondered about the effects of childhood isolation on a nation of now-ancient adults. He couldn't help but think that Chunk would be healthier in this environment.

He followed her through several more neighborhoods, not paying much attention to the surroundings. She babbled. She tried to tell him stories about the things she had done in these areas with friends or family members. He didn't care.

When they came to a corner store offering off-the-tree fruit juices, they stopped. She noticed he was sweating in the increasing midday heat of the island. She paid for his drink – just as she had to pay for anything they did. He found this profoundly humiliating but he didn't dare turn away the offer of a drink. He knew he was dehydrated.

The store stood on a slight hill. Given the island's low elevation this gave him an excellent view for more than a kilometer. As he looked in the distance, the rise of two- and three-story buildings punctured the horizon. In fact, he found it hard to see anything before him that looked like open forest. Several buildings in all directions were under construction. Development was booming.

"How many people live on Solis?"

He didn't expect her to have an answer. She surprised him by blurting out, "A million."

He smiled, wondering if this had somehow become rote knowledge for her.

"Can you show me how much a million is?"

Her round face contorted in concentration as she struggled with the parameters of such an answer.

"I don't know. Maybe this much?" and she motioned toward all her fingers and all her toes.

A Dusk Forever Waning

For the first time in her presence he laughed out loud and felt his posture relax. She had no concept of a million but she had memorized this small fact.

He sat on a bench outside the store and absorbed the ocean breeze while holding the cold drink against his forehead. He tried to do the math to determine how long it might be until Solis found itself in the same situation as Centrian. He didn't believe the island to be more than 30 or 40 square kilometers. Already the population built upward. They tested the limits of their ability to build outward. With no population controls they might only have four or five hundred years until the situation grew dire – maybe less. Nevertheless, the situation was not dire at the time being and it wasn't his immediate concern.

En route to a new destination, he again pulled her short and pointed to a building that required explanation. They stood across from a huge building made of gleaming white marble. It was the most audacious structure he had seen to-date on Solis. In no way did it blend with any of the other aesthetics on the island.

"What is that?"

"That's grandma!"

"What?"

"Come on!" And with that she dragged him to the brilliant structure.

A huge garden surrounded the building on all sides. The smells of that flora and the sounds of birds filling the trees made him feel like he had escaped the city. Stepping foot on the grounds had the odd effect of quieting all man-made noise from the street just beyond. As they came closer to the grand structure he made out many more details.

The building was five stories tall. It was not a traditional building in that it had open floors on all levels. Massive support columns supported the inner structure. People stood on all levels, stationary, but gesturing and moving in place. A grand archway marked the entrance to the building. Etched in its marble was, "Priori Terminus".

As they entered the ground floor he came face-to-face with these people. Seeing them up close it was clear they weren't people at all, but sophisticated projections – holograms. Each one moved and gestured, trying to speak to no one in particular. The distant holograms were silent to his ear, but as he walked in front of each one he heard the voice of that projection. Walking through the massive halls was like walking past a continual series of tour guides. Each told its own specific story to no one in particular.

She led him up several floors and passed a plethora of holograms. Living people joined the holograms. They engaged in real conversations with the specters. Once they reached the top floor the cooling wind dominated and the view of the entire island was splendid.

She parked in front of a hologram of a nondescript man who looked to have lived at least a thousand years ago. Pontius wasn't sure of her connection to this man. Before he could ask for clarification, she motioned from left to right across her body. As she did so, the hologram evaporated and reformed in the shape of a woman from about the same time. She made the motion again and the process repeated, this time with a new man materialized before them. She cycled through a menagerie of holograms and it became apparent to Pontius she was traversing her family tree.

With that realization he looked anew at the hundreds of holograms placed throughout this floor. He pondered the hundreds more placed on each floor below. Each station did not hold the hologram for a particular person, but instead was a docking station for the entire family tree. This meant that the building represented hundreds of thousands of dead souls.

After flipping through a massive stream of holograms, she perked up. She started reaching people she remembered. First she cried out, "Uncle Aian!" Then she yelled, "Aunt Flacian!" Every time she yelled a name, the hologram reacted in seeming recognition. They smiled at her and waved before she dismissed them with another arm gesture. When she reached her grandmother she lept up and down and squealed with delight. Her grandmother, in turn, smiled and said, "Hello, Aylea. Have you been doing well in your studies?"

"Yes, grandma, yes! Yesterday we learned about The Exodus."

The woman – young for a grandmother – nodded her head and renewed her loving gaze. For the next several minutes the two carried on a conversation – or a reasonable facsimile thereof. The holograms facilitated a degree of intelligent interaction. It was not only possible to gaze upon one's ancestors, but, to some extent, to talk to them as well. It was unclear to him whether she understood the distinction. In a rare moment of empathy on his part, he realized that it didn't matter. The site of her grandmother thrilled her. The "conversation" was quite satisfying to her. He stood by and observed while she indulged herself.

This continued for 20 minutes and Aylea seemed to lose her interest. She was still happy to be in the artificial presence of her grandmother, but she ran out of things to say. With the discussion dying, she grabbed his hand again. She asked about their next destination. He, too, was ready to leave, but he stepped forward to play with the gestural controls. It was an act of experimentation regarding the user interface.

With several swipes of his arm he managed to swap out the characters just as she had done. First, he found himself pulling up some of the same ancestors she had cycled through. Then, by reversing his motion, he pulled up new people. Satisfied that he understood the mechanics of the device, he was about to turn and leave when he made one more half-hearted swipe. The resulting change left an eerie fetus floating before him as though suspended in a test tube.

He looked at her and she turned her eyes downward, as though this was something she wasn't supposed to, or didn't care to, see.

"Do you know this child?"

She nodded but did not lift her head.

"Who is it?"

"That's my brother, Critus. Mom never had him."

He nodded in understanding then made another swipe, hoping to clear the disturbing image. But his next swipe brought forth a small baby. The baby was moving its arms and giggling but otherwise offered no speech. He might have left the situation at that, but he looked down and saw a very similar expression on her downward face.

"Aylea? Do you know this one, too?"

She nodded again and did not lift her head.

"Who is it?"

"That's my sister, Faria."

Not sure where this was going, he swiped again and confronted another baby. This time he looked to Aylea and asked, "And this? Who is this?"

"My brother, Coranus."

Sensing that he was treading on sensitive ground, he knelt down beside her. He asked in his most comforting tone, "How many dead siblings do you have?"

She did not answer but instead held up a hand with four extended fingers.

"That's an unusual number. How did they die?"

She just shrugged her shoulders and continued staring at her feet.

"You don't know how any of them died?"

She shook her head. It was apparent that he was stressing his guide. He didn't see this as productive. Yet the investigator in him made him curious about Vigoran's unique family history. He stood erect and was about to ask that they leave when he had an idea.

"How long ago did your grandmother die?"

"Last year."

With that he began swiping his way back to her grandmother's hologram. When she was redrawn before him he said, "Your daughter is Vigoran, correct?"

There was a visible pause. The artificial intelligence for these holograms was rudimentary by Centrian standards. After an awkward delay she said, "Aye."

"When did Vigoran come to Solis?"

Another delay ended with, "Sixteen years ago."

"Aylea, how old are you?"

She was clueless as to Pontius's cause and happy to hear a question that didn't refer to her deceased siblings. She replied, "Sixteen!"

He now turned back toward the hologram.

"What happened to Vigoran's other children?"

There was another long pause. He thought for a moment that the program might freeze, as the hologram was silent in computation. After several moments it replied. "Critus was aborted by the state after testing positive for Down's syndrome. Faria, Coranus, and Matrea were all executed by NCU agents."

With those words he froze. The unthinking hologram stared at him, awaiting a new question or direction that would never come. He didn't understand why he felt sick to his stomach. The hologram didn't care and Aylea didn't understand. And even if they did, what difference would it make? Her grandmother mouthed an explanation of Pontius's life for the last 1,700 years. Hearing it turned back at him now by this apparition did nothing to fix or to worsen his situation. Yet hearing this puzzle solved by the calculating words of the simulation's AI now made him regret having come here at all.

Aylea watched the events but was paying little attention to the particulars. Having heard all she wanted from her grandmother, she was anxious to leave this place and continue exploring. Without saying a word, he turned from the hologram and followed her out of the building.

Back on the bright city streets, his hunger nagged. With a tinge of embarrassment, he asked her if they could stop for lunch and she agreed.

The lunch consisted of another collection of fruits, breads, and sumptuous sauces. She chirped along, talking about all manner of life on Solis. He nodded as he consumed everything placed before him. He didn't feel that hungry when they entered the cafe. Yet the lunch, like the breakfast before, awakened a ravenous desire in him. It demanded more of the delicious cuisine.

As he gulped down his food, he tried in vain to forget the events of the Terminus. He wasn't sure if Vigoran knew who he was or what he did. He assumed that Dania had told her, but now wasn't so certain. As he observed Aylea talking on and on to no one in particular, he saw her in a new light. She was someone who otherwise would not have existed if her mother remained on Centrian.

The rest of the afternoon passed in a blur. She ferried him by corporate offices, docks, stadiums, theaters, universities, and all manner of government offices. They all displayed impressive architecture. They were all frequented by industrious individuals going about their business. The more he saw, felt, smelled, and tasted, the more he came to view this island as a paradise – as the anti-Centrian. Where Centrian was hot, humid, and rainy, Solis was warm yet breezy, bathed in glorious sunshine. Centrian suffocated like too many dogs crammed into a kennel. Solis still offered parks, trees, open streets, and space to live in comfort. Centrian cuisine drowned in the taste of fish oil. Solis offered an enticing array of fruits, vegetables, and delicious entrees. Even the countenance of the people here was cheerier. He couldn't help but wonder what his life might have been like if he had lived it here rather than on Centrian.

By the time they both returned to the house, Dania and Vigoran were waiting for them. Vigoran greeted them with a broad smile and asked with earnestness whether he enjoyed his tour of Solis. He nodded and offered a few cursory statements about the beauty of the island. Although she welcomed him back with warmth and hospitality, he now found it uncomfortable to look her in the eye. He wasn't sure if some aspect of his experience at the Terminus would come back to her. He wasn't eager to revisit that experience. They had no time to dwell on such matters.

The hearing would start soon and they had to make their way across Solis to the forum. The five of them hurried to the street and a driver ushered them into a waiting vehicle. Once they sat inside, Vigoran briefed him on the proceedings.

"This will appear to you as something like a trial. The Council will be judge and jurors, but Chunk will be represented by counsel who will be arguing the case for his asylum. There will also be an opposing council. You will not be allowed to participate in the proceeding or speak in any way. You have no legal standing here and if you interrupt the proceedings you will almost certainly jeopardize Chunk's case. Do you understand?"

Vigoran spoken in a matter-of-fact tone. She tried to explain the lay of the land for him, knowing he would be otherwise unfamiliar with the process. She looked to him for confirmation and he nodded.

When they arrived at the forum it was a bustle of activity. Men and women streamed in all directions through the central foyer. The foyer led to a grand hall. Chambers lined the hall on each side. Many meetings – many sessions – took place or were about to take place. Chunk's hearing was one of many official functions happening that night.

Vigoran escorted the party into one of these chambers. A large, elevated, semicircular table dominated the front of the room. Twelve figures sat at various stations on the semicircle but they sat back from the table itself. Each of them occupied a recessed enclave shrouded in darkness. The room itself was well lit but the lack of illumination in each enclave was striking. Each figure was visible only as a shadow, a nondescript entity indecipherable as man or woman, young or old.

In front of the semicircle stood three podiums. The one in the center was a singular speaking platform. Those on either side were primary stations for counsel. Behind the podiums were rows of seats for onlookers and participants in the trials. Aside from the shadowy figures and the counselors, the five of them were the only people in the room. The group shuffled into the first row of seating and waited for the proceedings to begin.

Pontius leaned over to Dania and whispered in her ear, "Who are the shadows?"

This annoyed her. Even a whisper in this library-like environment carried too far and drew too much attention. Yet she addressed his question.

"That is the Free Council. They will hear the case."

"Are they going to step into the light? Are they fugitives?"

"No. It is customary for the Council to be hidden during the proceedings. Their visage and their voices are cloaked during questioning so that no one knows from whom the objections are coming. When they deliver their ruling, they will reveal themselves en masse."

He tried to ponder the logic of this but he had no opportunity. Within seconds, they summoned Vigoran to the center podium. The proceedings began.

"Vigoran Armenius. You have requested a special session of the Free Council. Step forward and explain yourself."

The command was not spoken by a single voice, but by twelve voices acting in unison. More jarring was the fact that it was not twelve different voices. Rather, it was the same voice spoken from twelve different originating points. The voice itself was deep and booming. When the twelve spoke as one it resonated through the chamber as a chorus of cellos. It caused his chest cavity to vibrate like a drum.

She grabbed Chunk and strode forward to podium. He didn't focus on much of what she said, but rather how she said it. She explained in brief but powerful terms the gravity of Chunk's situation. She spoke smoothly but forcefully. While she did not invoke her own history, she gave the perspective of a mother who had faced the onslaught of Centrian's Population Control. She spoke for several minutes, knowing that it was not her place to make the legal argument for Chunk. Yet her words served as an effective springboard for the hearing. When she returned to her seat with Chunk on her lap she sat up and listened to the following arguments.

He tried to listen but it did not take long before the legal verbiage overtake him. On the right stood Chunk's counsel, a young man with obscenely good looks. When Pontius first saw him he feared that Chunk had drawn a bad lot. He assumed this pretty boy could not bring the substance required for a winning legal argument. When the counselor opened his mouth, Pontius knew he was dead wrong. The counselor's dashing looks coupled with elegant oratory and sharp wit. Pontius wasn't always sure about the legal argument at hand. Yet it was clear that Chunk's representative had strong footing.

This is not to say that opposing counsel was lacking. A brutish woman represented the state. She had thick eyebrows and scraggly black hair. He found himself wondering whether he could take her in a fight. He then realized that he didn't want to find out. What she lacked in outward appearance she more than made up in cogent thought. It was clear to him that asylum hearings must happen here on a fairly common basis. This woman seemed accustomed to arguing against any of them.

The hearing stretched on for hours. For long periods, he daydreamed. He was unable to follow the intricacies of the argument at hand. But then the booming voice of the twelve would come back. They asked questions and requested clarifications in unison. The effect dragged him back to the present and restored his attention.

He wondered if he was the only bored person in the room. Dania and Vigoran both listened to the rhetoric. Both counselors dove into the task at hand. Even Aylea seemed to be somehow following along. They debated international law, ancient treaties, legal precedent, and human rights. None of these held his attention.

At first he believed that he was missing something in their arguments. They talked and they talked but they came no closer to a resolution. Then he reached over and whispered to Vigoran, "Does this always take so long?"

Without averting her gaze from the Council she shook her head. Then she leaned over and answered, "Not at all. This is unusual."

For the first time, he realized he might understand more about the debate than he gave himself credit for. The arguments went round and round because they were stuck in a stalemate. The state's argument was irrefutable. Chunk's presence threatened international relations. It could threaten diplomacy and long-term stability. The defense's argument – that denying Chunk's appeal was tantamount to a death sentence – was also irrefutable. Even the questions levied by the Council seemed of no help in levering open a logical solution.

As this dance labored on he floated in and out of cognition. He was eager for a solution and he was starting to lose hope, but no amount of diligent attention on his part would speed this along. It was then that he heard his name mentioned for the first time.

From the booming concert of the twelve came the following question: "And what of Pontius?"

The question seemed to stun the counselors and left them at a loss for words. After collecting their wits, they both answered in unison, as though they were mimicking the twelve, "What *about* him?"

The Council did not hesitate to clarify.

"If the child's welfare is of such importance to him, is he prepared to care for him on Solis?"

There was another awkward pause as the participants looked to one another to find a response. He wasn't sure if he should answer. He began to rise when Vigoran placed her hand on his shoulder and guided him back into his seat. Sensing the need to clarify the scenario, she made an apologetic gesture and walked to the center podium.

"No-un. He is here merely as a steward. He is trying to deliver on a commitment that was made to the child's parents before they died."

"So this child – he is, essentially, a transaction?"

She looked back to him, somehow hoping he could provide a more palatable description of his motivations. But he only nodded to her. By his way of thinking, the description of Chunk as a transaction was a boon to the process. He believed that it strengthened his case.

Defeated, she turned back to the Council and said, "He is a city rat, like all the other city rats. He has made a commitment and he intends to stand by that commitment, but he does not care for the child."

There was a long silence in which everyone expected some kind of response from the twelve. Vigoran looked to the counselors who looked back to her and shrugged.

The Council was, in aggregate, confused. They could not understand someone dragging a baby to the other side of the world, only to drop it off and continue their degenerate life. They wanted to speak to Pontius but Solisan law forbade it.

"We would like to speak with Aylea."

The two counselors sat down behind their podiums. This turn of events perplexed them. Vigoran, though exasperated and confused, knew to do nothing else but comply.

At the mention of her name Aylea perked up. When her mother motioned for her she strolled to the podium and gave Vigoran a big hug. Vigoran whispered something in her ear and she nodded. Vigoran then stood to the side as though to signal that Aylea was available for the Council.

"Hello, Aylea."

"Hello!"

"You spent time with Pontius today, is that right?"

"Yes-un. I spent the whole day showing him Solis."

"And what kind of man is he?"

Pontius was both confused and alarmed. He didn't understand what any of this had to do with the case. He wasn't applying for asylum – Chunk was. He wasn't going to care for Chunk – some other foster family would. This struck him as ludicrous, made all the more so by the questioning of a mental mutant on his behalf.

Aylea looked down at her feet and then up to her mother. Vigoran nodded at her and smiled, encouraging her to speak her mind.

"He's an angry man with a great burden. He's lost and he doesn't know where to go."

There was a complete stillness in the room as everyone digested her words. Even Pontius had no idea how to react.

"Thank you for that." And with this acknowledgment Aylea smiled again. "Is this someone that you would want on your island?"

Aylea thought on this for a full minute and no one edged her to short-circuit the process. After giving it careful consideration, she replied, "We don't kill babies here and that's his job. So how could we have him on the island?"

While his exterior was stoic, his insides were screaming. His heart rate skyrocketed and a clammy sweat accumulated on his brow and in his palms. He wanted to run from the building but he feared doing anything that would jeopardize Chunk's case. As nonchalantly as he could, he moved his head around the room. He expected that at any moment a police force would burst into the chamber and arrest him. He surveyed Dania and Vigoran, expecting that either of them may acknowledge this moment. But neither turned their attention from the Council. He wanted a reaction – any reaction – that would give him a clue as to where this was heading. Even a look of scorn from Vigoran would have somehow made him feel more at ease. Instead, they continued as though he was not even in the room.

"The Council will adjourn for discussion. We will return with our ruling."

And with that, the shadowy figures evaporated from their enclaves. The counselors packed up their belongings and left, having done all that they came to do. Pontius's gaze darted around like a caged animal.

"What do we do now?"

Vigoran answered, "We wait."

The ensuing hour was the longest of his life. Dania and Vigoran retreated to a far corner of the chamber and talked amongst themselves. Aylea sat playing a video game. Chunk, having just eaten during the proceedings, was dozing on a bench next to Dania. Pontius sat by himself with no idea what he should do with himself.

Vigoran and Dania were just far enough away that he couldn't hear their conversation. This had the effect of convincing him that they were talking about him. He was certain that Vigoran was discussing ways to extract revenge against him. He wanted to ask her for some kind of forecast on the verdict. He didn't understand the strange turn it took at the end, or how this affected Chunk's future. Yet he didn't dare try to engage either of them. He was both afraid to talk to Vigoran or Dania and unwilling to sit by himself.

Without warning, doors opened behind the twelve enclaves. The Council returned, causing Vigoran to break off her discussion with Dania. A verdict was imminent – a verdict causing him to experience wheezing and tightness in his chest. Yet he now found himself unable to think about that verdict at all.

When the twelve returned, they did not do so in shadow. They were ready to provide a ruling. In accordance with Solisan custom, they revealed themselves and spoke as individuals. What he saw before him left him aghast.

The Council ranged in age from 60 to almost 100. There were six men and six women. These were some of the wisest and most respected souls on the island. They were all versed in the legal issues surrounding unlicensed refugees. The youngest and healthiest among them was, by Pontius's standards, decrepit. His flaccid skin hung from every narrow bone like sheets nailed to a wall. He only had a wispy trail of grey hair remaining on his head – a head covered in liver spots.

The other members fared worse. One of them required an automated breathing device that made loud noises and ferried air in and out of his lungs. Another member was a corpulent woman with no teeth and no natural eyebrows. She wore large bulbous ear rings that dragged her weary ear lobes down to her shoulders. Yet another member had teeth but they were black and brown, holding onto the gums by sheer force of will. The most disturbing image was that of a 70-year-old man who was in some state of recuperation. He was frail, even by the standards of the elderly. A nurse stood by his side with an IV hooked to an inordinate number of locations on his body. He was in a wheelchair and it was obvious that he did not have the strength to propel the device on his own.

A woman - the chairman - stood in the center of the semicircle. She stepped forward and looked at Pontius.

"It is the ruling of the Free Council that Chunk shall be granted asylum. He shall be assigned a foster home here on Solis and when he is of legal age he will be asked to affirm this choice which is now being made on his behalf. At that time, if he does not choose to stay he shall be ferried back to Centrian anonymously and allowed to live the rest of his days with the city rats."

Vigoran broke into a broad smile. Dania looked pleased. Aylea, reacting to her mother's joy, let out a small cheer. Pontius thought this was the end of the Council's work, but the chairman continued.

"As for Pontius, he shall be returned to his cruiser. He is heretofore exiled from Solis. If he ever returns to Solis or any of its sister islands, he is to be executed. He will be escorted to his vessel and forced to leave tonight."

Dania grabbed Chunk from Vigoran's arms and hoisted him in the air. Vigoran smiled and Aylea laughed with the others. Pontius rose to his feet and stared agape at the Council.

He wasn't sure what he was witnessing. The grotesque sight of these sickly people now brought the power of this place – this outlaw world – into full and clear focus for him. He had seen a few of these people shuffling through the streets of Solis. It never occurred to him that these diseased individuals were just old. How old, he wasn't sure, but staring at the monsters before him he now understood the future he was purchasing for Chunk.

"What is *wrong* with you?"

He blurted out this inappropriate comment to everyone and to no one. The council members, who were already starting to make their way out of the chamber, halted at the abrupt outburst. Vigoran froze. The chairman turned around and faced him.

"Excuse me?"

"I said, what is wrong with you?" His voice was now bolder and louder.

He understood, on some academic level, that Solisans lived shorter lives. He understood that they did not enjoy the virtual immortality of a Centrian. But none of this sunk into his stubborn mind until he saw this display of sickly, dying specters before him. He was sure he saw pictures of elderly people when he was in school, but he couldn't access any memory of them now. The people in front of him here were far more grotesque than he imagined the process to be. They looked feeble. They looked sick. They looked like death itself.

These people had barely lived. Now they withered away to the ravages of nature and time – ravages long ago conquered by civilized society. No amount of tasty food or beautiful weather could salve this fact. They were allowing their own citizenry to die in the most undignified of manners.

He grew annoyed. These cretins – these primitive animals – stood by and watched their own respected elders fade into oblivion. Yet they deigned to pass judgment on him. The situation struck him as ironic.

Vigoran raced over to him. She tugged on his arm and motioned for him to shut up, but he was focused on the monsters before him.

"Pontius! You have no legal standing here. We have to leave now!"

She grabbed his arm and tried to drag him from the chamber. Before she made any progress in her eviction the chair held up her hand and called out to Vigoran.

"Stop! If the rat wants to speak, let him speak. What so-called wrong are you implying in this Council?"

Dania joined the gesticulation, trying to quiet her friend, but he jumped at the chair's invitation.

"All of you! Look at you! You're decrepit. You're diseased. This is not a council of elders. This is a council of decay. The faster you run from the supposed horrors of Centrian, the faster you run into the gaping jaws of death. How old are you?"

The chair stared him down and answered, "I'm 82."

"Ha!" He yelled with a rude amusement. "I've a hundred years for each of your one and look at us. Let anyone hear compare the two of us. You look awful. What is *wrong* with you?"

The attention of the other elders was now riveted on him. Dania and Vigoran both sat down, shaking their heads and mourning his stupidity. The chair answered quietly, "I have late-stage cancer. I'm not long for this world."

"Cancer? You have cancer?! But we *cured* cancer! Millennia ago! Why would you allow cancer to ravage your bodies and Down's Syndrome to invalidate your children when we have cured this so long ago?"

Maybe he should have shut his mouth. He wasn't sure. But he knew that he wasn't stopping now. It was far too late. The chair was about to respond when he launched another volley.

"You cling to this island as your paradise. You deride the Centrians as *city rats*. But you allow your citizens to live tiny, abbreviated lives punctuated by the ravages of age, and disease, and disorders."

The chair now stiffened her stance and raised a long finger to him in accusation.

"Is that the only value you put on life? Is one's worth measured in years? And if so, why would you so willingly snuff out the lives of those who haven't even seen a single year? Are their lives expendable so you can tack a thousand more years onto your own? How many souls would you sell for the chance to enrich your own life? How many newborns have you *corrected* in your mindless service to the state?"

He launched a volley of spittle that fell inside the semicircle. As he did, the other ancient council members rose up as though they would attack him on the spot. Sensing a dangerous turn in the chamber's mood, Dania and Vigoran tried again to force him from the room.

"His parents," he pointed at Chunk now, "did not pay for a minuscule life of pain and pointless suffering. This is no paradise. This is a shallow and shameful compromise."

Although the members had removed themselves from the shadows of their enclaves, they now rose up and spoke again in unison. They shared a deep eerie voice that echoed throughout the chamber.

"Get out! Get out now! And take the rat-child with you. If you do not leave tonight you will both be dead by morning."

A sense of genuine dread filled Vigoran. She had never seen such a violent reaction from the Free Council and she had no doubt that their threats were valid. She grabbed his hand in hers and Aylea's in the other and removed them from the chamber.

As they fled from the building, he turned to Dania with a wry smile and said, "That went well."

Chapter 13 – Into the Pit

The warehouse bore an overwhelming aroma of sawdust, fish guts, and motor oil. The edifice was huge – more than a hundred meters in all directions – but Pontius could not see any of the far walls. The air was thick with smoke and his vision extended no more than a few dozen meters.

He surveyed the raucous crowd with anxiousness. Even in the diminished lighting he strained to scan faces – to identify any potential threats. Since escaping Solis he had been tense.   He was a refugee in his own land and he looked on even his closest of friends as potential liabilities. His head was on a swivel. He became aware of random conversations taking place between strangers. He was a nervous wreck.

The crowd in this enclosure was immense – far larger than he bargained for. The din of voices filled the massive building and rung in his ears. As the crowd filtered into the arena he found himself searching for someone, anyone, that he did not dislike on sight. The lower classes – the vast majority of the crowd – offended him due to their societal station. The upper classes offended him because he saw their smug, corrupt faces as part of the larger problem.

He scanned every face for danger. He wasn't sure what he was looking for. In some sense, every person in the arena represented potential trouble. Yet he knew that he didn't want to see anyone from NCU, or from PC, or from the broader Centrian authorities.

When the group had returned from Solis, he split up from Moria and Chunk and dropped into hiding. He wasn't sure of her status but he knew that he'd be a wanted man once they found Tenarrin's corpse in his living room. He spent several days lurking through the metropolis's murkier corridors. He felt he at least needed to investigate whether Moria had fallen into his fugitive status.

Not wanting to alert headquarters to his location with remote UNI searches, he decided to risk a personal trip to the PC offices. He had allies there and he was confident he could get in-and-out without tripping any alarms.

The initial phase of his intelligence gathering went as planned, even if the results were not to his liking. He managed to sneak into a colleague's office – a good friend named Furian whom he had worked alongside for 700 years. He used Furian as his proxy to perform queries in the system. As the two of them sat in the darkened office, he confirmed that he was now one of the nation's most wanted men. Moria was also under an arrest warrant for accessory to murder.

This guaranteed that she would never issue another Vitapass. It nailed shut the last hope he had to offer Chunk a legal, legitimate future. It sparked a furious bout of remorse. Working in PC was all that she had ever known. She shouldn't be in this. She didn't deserve to lose her livelihood – and her freedom – because of the vagaries of his side deals. But it would make no difference now whether he viewed her as an accessory or not. She was, for better or worse, ensnared in this drama. He assumed that their fates were inseparable for the foreseeable future.

A Dusk Forever Waning

Entering the PC headquarters was as fluid as he had hoped. He slithered into Furian's office without attracting any unwanted attention. He was in full disguise, ambling through the hallways as a janitor, and it was easy to reach his friend's location. Escaping the premises was a different story.

After Furian performed all the searches and provided all the favors that he could think to ask for, the two men embraced. They shared a goodbye which made it clear that they might never see each other again. He dropped back into character, pointed his head toward his feet, and slipped back into the hallway. He sought the nearest emergency exit that would remove him from this lion's den.

Before he could make his exit, a PC officer ran straight into him. She was convo'ing on her UNI and paying no attention to the pedestrian traffic in front of her. As she did, the two locked eyes and both of them stood upright in shock, staring at the other.

"Conti."

"Pontius."

The two stood there for maybe a half a minute. As they did, the rest of the pedestrians passed around them like a river flowing astride a boulder. No one else paid any attention to them. They were in their own world.

He looked her up and down. She was not dressed in the casual manner of the nightclub, or the cruiser, or his own apartment. She was now in PC attire, dressed as a senior officer. She returned the gaze. Not only was she simply shocked to see him, but it was clear to her that he was trying to pull off a disguise.

"You work here? You work in... PC?"

He could not suppress his confusion. He assumed what this meant, but he wasn't yet able to complete the puzzle.

"I work in Auditing."

"How-"

He cut himself off. His initial reaction was to deem this impossible. He presumed that he knew everyone working in PC throughout the entire country. Quick reflection made him realize he knew everyone working in the *Newborn Corrections Unit*, but not in the broader *Population Control*. He knew no one working in Auditing. Auditing was a reviled office. No one else in PC – and no one in NCU – ever wanted to socialize with the auditors. No one even wanted to be in their presence. They were pariahs and with that distinction, they were also anonymous.

The two stood staring at each other for another ten seconds, each unsure how to proceed. Finally, he blurted out, "Goodbye," and turned to flee. As he did, the spell broke and she began yelling for someone to apprehend him.

The element of surprise was in his favor. He turned and moved toward the exit. He was careful not to run but he walked as fast as possible without drawing undue attention. The other inhabitants of the hallway met Conti's cries with confusion. Most of these people were administrators like her. They were not equipped to arrest anyone and they were not interested in violence. By the time she managed to grab the attention of armed guards, he already had a huge head start and was far out of the building.

Nevertheless, he spent the rest of the week darting through all layers of Centrian society. He was certain he shook his pursuers hours ago, but he was now obsessed with hiding his trail. He spent half a day trudging through the filth of base-level, looking to get as far away from public scanners as possible. When he ascended back to the comforts of Centrian society, he spent several more days on the move. He relayed messages for Caspian, Moria, Telarus, and even Kryx through a handful of trusted intermediaries. Although he was no longer disconnected from his UNI as he had been on Solis, he was now, for many functional purposes, a man "off the grid".

The sheer size of the crowd caused his tensions to escalate. He couldn't be certain that anyone here was not a government agent, or worse yet, a bounty hunter. The bounty hunters were far more worrisome than anything the Centrian authorities could cook up.

When Kryx and Pontius arrived at the warehouse they were alone. The size of the facility surprised him. He expected something akin to the filthy yet intimate enclosure he witnessed at base-level. This was something grander. The warehouse had been converted for this purpose. The pit was well constructed and much larger. There was formal seating on all sides. Track lights shone a glaring spotlight into the empty pit. He wondered how many desperate men had met their fate in this single location.

"What the hell is this?" His voice was not loud but it echoed through the warehouse.

Kryx looked confused.

"Where else do you expect to fit twenty thousand spectators?"

"*Twenty thousand*? Why would there be so many people?"

Kryx shrugged.

"I don't question the demand. I merely connect the supply to that demand. The market does the rest."

This further confirmed what he already knew – that this was an awful idea. This was his last resort. It was a final desperate act. He knew it was wrong to trade a life in return for Chunk's Vitapass. No good could come of it. But when he fled Solis he was out of options. He knew of no other solution to fulfill his commitment.

Reaching out to Kryx to coordinate the event left him feeling slimy. Seeing the arena before him now put a pit in his stomach that would not dissipate. The transfer cards pilfered from Carian now fueled this unholy contest. Everything about it felt wrong.

This was shaping up to be an unmitigated disaster. He envisioned something like the spectacle he had seen on base-level. He imagined there would be a few hundred deranged bettors strung above a dusty pit in some forgotten backroom. It would be small. It would be discrete. It would be, for all intents and purposes, anonymous. The arena he now saw before him guaranteed that this event would be anything but.

He told himself that this number was boastful. He assumed that the actual attendance would be far smaller. He assumed that the huge arena would ring hollow with the deranged cries of a handful of bloodthirsty bettors. It didn't take him long to realize his folly.

Kryx and his attendant, Calon, spent about an hour readying things around the arena. Every few minutes Calon opened the main doors to allow entry to another attendant. Events of this magnitude required many helpers. There were bouncers — a great many bouncers — along with vendors, bookies, announcers, janitors, and whores. Upon entry, each one set about preparing some aspect of their eventual service.

Calon was a buzzing maelstrom of activity. He coordinated details with every person entering the arena. He convo'd and barked out instructions as the festivities began to take shape. Kryx was also involved but was much more disconnected. Calon was the puppet and Kryx was the overseeing master.

When the actual spectators started arriving, their numbers alarmed him. They came through in droves. They were not just the base-level scrubs saw in his previous match, although they made up a percentage of the spectators. Instead, the crowd was much more egalitarian.

By both dress and demeanor he could see the event would draw a much higher clientele. This amazed him, considering the brutal nature of what was about to happen. There were small-scale celebrities. There were women. There were politicians. There were even officers of the state.

This last fact had him in a panic. He withdrew to the farthest, darkest corner of the arena that he could find. He was paranoid that someone would recognize him and seize him. As more people streamed into the warehouse he found it ever hard to find any quiet corner.

When the arena was about half full, Calon made his way over to him. He held out his hand as a matter-of-fact gesture and said, "Transfer cards."

Pontius nodded and fished the cards out of his coat pocket. Rather than hand them to Calon, he instead held them for an awkward moment in his hand. He rubbed them together and ruminated on their importance. He had never expected to have them. He never assumed he would have the funds to sponsor his own death match. Now that Calon was requesting them so matter-of-factly, he questioned this course of action yet again.

Calon did not acknowledge the delay. He stood with his hand outstretched, refusing to relent. After several more moments Pontius dropped them into the open hand. Calon scanned them and gave a satisfied nod, then turned and walked away.

A rare moment of relief overcame Pontius when he saw Caspian approaching with Telarus. He didn't know why he wanted them there. He just did. Maybe he was wary of Kryx. Maybe he wanted someone next to him who wouldn't judge him in this endeavor. Regardless, he did not want to be party to this savage event alone.

"Aye, Captain!"

Caspian's greeting was goofy and inappropriate. In another environment this may have bothered Pontius, but given his overall level of anxiety he found it soothing. He smiled at his friend and grasped his hand.

Telarus greeted him as well. Although his expression was grimmer, it was clear to Pontius that he was here to offer his support.

"You know what I'm going to ask you."

Pontius nodded. He would expect nothing less of Telarus.

"You can still go back. You can still bring Chunk to the Diaspori."

"I know. And it's not going to happen."

This said it all. Telarus already knew his answer but he had to make the proposition anyway. He abandoned his frustration with the situation and decided to help Pontius in any way possible.

Pontius gazed beyond Caspian's shoulder, looking for someone else to arrive. Caspian understood the reference.

"She's not coming. She's angry."

Pontius furrowed his brow and nodded. He expected as much but he still held out hope that somehow Dania would come. When they fled Solis she was furious. She did not speak a word during the return journey and when they arrived in Centrian she departed without goodbyes. During the following week he made several attempts to reach out to her. She stonewalled him. Now, in the bowels of this foreboding environment, he wondered if he would ever see her again.

He may have sunk into an abyss of reflection if his attention wasn't torn away by the arrival of Moria and Chunk. His face became a melting pot of shock, anger, and bewilderment. He shot a desperate look to Caspian but Caspian just shrugged his shoulders as though the scenario was out of his control.

"Moria! What are you doing here? You must go. Now!"

She came in close to talk to him but he could not look her in the face. His eyes darted to-and-fro. He tried to determine if anyone in the growing crowd watched or paid them any undue attention. He cut off communication with Moria earlier in the week after his abrupt encounter with Conti. He asked everyone involved to not tell her anything of this event. He saw the presence of her and Chunk at this match both inappropriate and dangerous.

Paying no mind to his mental state, Moria came in close to him to speak.

"Pontius. Don't do this."

He was not interested in debating the efficacy of his plan. He was far more paranoid about the prospect that any of them — most of all, Chunk — could be seized.

"I am a wanted man. You are wanted now as well. If anyone here recognizes us, Chunk will be killed immediately. You and I will probably follow shortly thereafter."

His words affected her like water affects a stone. She chose to reiterate her message.

"Don't do this."

This exasperated him.

"What else would you have me do? Our futures are already written. But Chunk still has time. All he needs is a Vitapass. One simple Vitapass and he goes on to live thousands of years on his own terms. What else would you have me do?"

She shook her head in a mixture of anger and desperation.

"There are options. We can take him back to the Diaspori. They will still have him."

He shook his head but she was not finished.

"I spoke to Dania. She explained what happened on Solis. We can still bring Chunk back there. I know we can convince them to take him."

Anger rose in him. He was morally opposed to the "slavery" of a life spent with the Diaspori. Yet he was downright appalled that anyone would recommend an existence on Solis. Seeing those decrepit council members was more than he could bear.

"You weren't there. You didn't see those animals. They're dying. Every single one of them is dying in their own quiet way. They decay like rotten fruit and their days are numbered. Any one of them can be struck down tomorrow by some simple malady that was eradicated on Centrian millennia ago."

With her free hand she grabbed Pontius's and put it on Chunk's head. She stared at Pontius and waited for his anger to pass.

"Who is this about?"

This caught him off guard. It confused him.

"Are you trying to save Chunk? Or are you trying to save yourself?"

Caspian and Telarus were silent, transfixed. They both believed in the point she was now making but neither had the guts to confront him in such blunt terms.

"What are you talking about? I made a commit-"

"Yes, yes, yes – we all know about your glorious commitment. The Honorable Pontius made a promise and, by India, you're going to fulfill that promise."

She had taken on a mocking tone.

"There's no greater honor than defiling some poor woman and killing two innocent parents. That's an honor we should all hope to uphold."

This stunned him. She never spoke to him like this. Through many hundreds of years she was complicit in his activities. She knew the bargains made in return for the Vitapasses she issued. He was certain that she understood the magnanimity that both of them offered. Without their offer these children would die in front of their forlorn parents. With this offer, in return for a few moments of vague discomfort, those children achieved legitimate lives. She never questioned the arrangement. She never voiced any concerns. Her rebellion now baffled him.

"What else would you have me do? I've paid Calon. The arena is set. Most of the spectators are here. When this is all said and done, Chunk will have a Vitapass. I don't know what comes of us, but I know that he can be raised by somebody – anybody – and he will be able to live an official life. There's no turning back now."

His words were forceful but they lacked conviction. He wasn't trying to convince her. He was trying to convince himself.

"That's crap, and you know it. We could flee this place now. Telarus could find a way to get us back to LiveLong."

Telarus nodded but Pontius paid no attention.

"Or Caspian could get us back to his cruiser and we could find a way to get Chunk back to Solis."

Caspian nodded but Pontius was paying no attention. Seeing that Pontius was steeling his mind against her logic, she continued.

"Or you can consummate this grisly death match. You can trade one man's soul for another. You can extinguish one soul so that Chunk might live. What is it going to be?"

The tension in the group was palpable. Pontius believed she would continue with additional, desperate pleas. Yet it became apparent that she now awaited a verdict. He shot a glance to both Caspian and Telarus. Somehow he expected them to provide an escape from the current situation. They both returned nothing but grim expressions. He looked back to her again, hoping that he could leave the ball back in her court, but she was resolute. She was not moving, and neither were the others, until he had verbalized his final decision.

Not to avoid the situation, but to more accurately assess it, he took a step back and surveyed the growing crowd. This crowd did not have the savage feel he experienced in the cramped, base-level death match. The group here had something that bothered him much more – a festive sense of gaiety. Men laughed. Women smiled. People were convo'ing with their friends who were not so fortunate as to be present for such an event. Vendors made vibrant business of selling all manner of drugs, drinks, and general refreshments. If he did not already know what was about to happen, he might assume he was on the cusp of an acclaimed theatrical performance.

They may have stood there for many minutes more if Kryx hadn't made his way over. He wore an audacious red jacket imbued with many threads of different colors that gave it an iridescent quality in the dim light. Pontius recognized it as akin to the jacket worn by the bookie in the base-level death match. Kryx presented himself with a calm, business-like air and said, "We are about to begin."

Pontius held up his hand. This bothered Kryx because he understood it for what it was – an unnatural delay. Trying to conceal his annoyance, he flashed a disingenuous smile to the group and said, "Is there a problem?"

There was a full 60 second pause while Kryx waited.

"The Tombstone – the loser's Tombstone – must it be willed to me whereby I then need to give it to Chunk? Or can it be willed directly to Chunk?"

Pontius couldn't help but consider the fact that he might be dead by morning. All his possessions, including the newly-won Tombstone, might end up as property of the state.

Kryx did not reply but instead motioned for Calon to come over. When he reached the group, Kryx said, "I want you to ensure that the loser's Tombstone goes directly to this baby."

Calon saw this as unusual but he offered no resistance. He made several quick notes in his UNI and replied, "It is done."

Kryx smiled and nodded. Then he motioned to Pontius and said, "We are about to begin," while motioning for him to follow.

A Dusk Forever Waning

Pontius looked at his friends, nodded his head, and began following Kryx to the pit. As he did, Moria's lip began to quiver, not with sorrow but with anger. Caspian and Telarus, feeling that they should stay by their friend's side, followed some steps behind. Moria stood her ground. She watched as the three men walked off to the center of the arena.

The spectacle of the pit took Pontius by surprise. Dancers and musicians frolicked at various points around the rim. There were huge bleachers erected in a rough circular pattern all around the pit. The air was so thick and the bleachers were so high that he could not even see the upper rows. Multicolored lights raced around the arena. They turned everything blue, then green, then purple, then dark, and blue again. The cacophony of talk and laughter was so great as to rise up in a single voice of frivolity. Some people danced in their seats. Others gulped beverages and more chemicals. It felt like a dance club.

He proceeded to an ostentatious seat on the edge of the pit. He had no idea he would sit here but it was a place of honor for the fight's sponsor. When he sat down, the crowd greeted him with a loud roar of approval.

Thirty minutes ago he would have fought to avoid such a conspicuous placement but now he felt at ease. Knowing that the match's Tombstone would be willed to Chunk made him relax. With that Tombstone in hand, anyone caring for Chunk could walk into the PC offices and have a Vitapass issued. From there, Pontius's commitment would be complete. Even if spotted by authorities and executed right here in this very chair, he would fulfill his obligation. Pondering this truth gave him a relaxation he had not experienced in weeks.

Caspian and Telarus sat to either side of him and below him, like apostles. They sat on a broader platform designed to accommodate a sponsor with a much larger entourage. Yet the three of them sat there alone, conspicuous in their scarcity.

Much to his surprise, Kryx jumped down into the pit. He would have considered this to be impractical, as the pit was deep enough to cause a broken limb. But the prodigious rise of sawdust made it clear that the fall was cushioned. As Kryx reached the bottom it was the first time that Pontius saw the combatants.

Both were shockingly fit. One was tall with deep black skin. Even from afar, he noticed the incredible smoothness of his complexion. If it weren't for the sweat glistening on the fighter's skin it would have been hard to see the outline of his tone physique. He was so dark as to blend into whatever shadow was around him.

His opponent was also fit and somewhat shorter with a different skin color. He presumed him to be white, but it was difficult to know for certain. He had injected his skin with a thin sheen of silver. The effect, which had been stylish several hundred years ago, was not to make him shiny, like chrome. Rather, it gave him a silvery hue that made it difficult to determine his original color. The effect was all the more pronounced at the edge of any natural bulges – and his muscled physique provided an abundance of those.

A Dusk Forever Waning

Both men wore the singular garment he witnessed before. It was a white towel wrapped around their loins. It resembled a diaper. They wore nothing else – no clothing, no jewelry, no expressions.

Unlike the first match he witnessed, these men were standing, but they also seemed catatonic. As Kryx gesticulated around the pit, whipping the crowd into a frenzy, they stared in the other's direction. They weren't looking at each other, but rather, through each other. Each seemed as though he did not know or care where he was. They made no overt motions, nor did they acknowledge the crowd in any way.

He wondered what could have brought these two combatants to such a place in their lives. The base-level match presented two ugly examples of humanity. This made it quite plausible to imagine that they were willing to risk their lives. But these men below him now looked fit, capable, and even handsome. It was somewhat strange that such men would be willing to kill each other for a chance at riches. But when he thought about it for a few moments, he decided that he didn't care.

Kryx held court like a master showman. He yelled and motioned around the arena and as he did the crowd responded in kind. At times, Pontius tried to concentrate on the words but he drifted off after seconds. Everything in front of him – the pit, the fighters, the crowds – was a dream. He watched it as any other spectator, even though he knew he was much more of a participant than he cared to admit.

The entire presentation was far more professional than he expected. Kryx played off the dancers. The dancers played off the musicians. The musicians played off the lights. The crowd played off everything. It was shocking to see the extent of the choreography.

After an intolerable array of announcements, enticements, and cheers, Kryx began the show. He motioned for a rope and ascended out of the pit. This drew a cheer from the crowd. Kryx then made a show of thanking tonight's sponsor and twenty thousand people fixed their gaze on Pontius. This drew another cheer from the crowd. Kryx clapped his hands and all the music and dancing stopped. This drew a raucous cheer from the crowd. Then he yelled some unintelligible, blood-curdling call-to-action. The fighters began pacing. This drew a frenzied reaction from the crowd that made the bleachers shake and unsettled the sawdust at the floor of the pit. By the time Kryx started the match, the entire arena was a roiling sea of crazed sweaty humanity.

He came over to sit on the main platform off to the side of Pontius. Telarus was present, but as soon as the match started he made a point to look anywhere but into pit below. He didn't have the stomach to witness the gruesome rite. Caspian was all too happy to take in every aspect. Mesmerized by the melee, he found himself wishing that he were somehow in the pit with them. Kryx wasn't exactly watching the match. Once the process began he became a flurry of ongoing convos. He coordinated drugs, whores, drinks, and bets between various spectators and employees.

A Dusk Forever Waning

Telarus kept gazing back at his friend, expecting to see some kind of reaction. Pontius, however, was as catatonic as the fighters before the match. He sat in his seat, but he was not mentally present. Everything in the pit below felt like a bad movie, a forgettable Vaudevillian act. In other times he would be as sickened as Telarus at the spectacle but now his sole mental focus was on the Tombstone. One of these men would die in short order. One of these men would lose his Tombstone to Chunk. Chunk's caretakers could trade that Tombstone for a Vitapass. And he would fulfill his commitment. He repeatedly mouthed the words, "The commitment stands."

It was a good ten minutes into the fight before he realized Telarus was angling for his attention. It yanked him from his trance and annoyed him, but he showed none of it to his friend. Seeing Telarus's pending question, he leaned over so he could hear the query.

"What's next?"

He looked at Telarus, then into the pit, then back to Telarus again.

"What do you mean, *What's next?*"

"I mean, once the fight is over, what do you do?"

He didn't understand. The pointless nature of the question bothered him. He gave Telarus a dismissive smirk.

"Once the fight is over, it's done. I promised a Vitapass. I will deliver a Vitapass. The commitment is fulfilled. There is nothing to do after that."

Telarus nodded his head.

"Yes, yes, I understand all of that. You will have fulfilled your commitment. But what will you do after that?"

Telarus looked up at his friend. The blank stare returned by Pontius disturbed him.

"Pontius, you're now one of the planet's most wanted men. Where are you going to go? How are you going to live? You can't just go back to your apartment. You can't just report back for duty at NCU. What will you do?"

He was embarrassed to admit that he hadn't thought at all about these matters. In his drive to solve the overarching dilemma of Chunk, he gave no consideration to his own survival as a fugitive. If he evaded the authorities now, it was only so he could find a way to deliver that Vitapass. Everything since the day he killed Chunk's parents focused on this one central goal. In the completion of that goal, he threw his entire life aside. It was only now, with Telarus asking such a basic question, that he considered a life on the run.

He first pondered the tactical realities of immortality as it relates to wanted men. Anyone could elude the authorities, given enough cunning and effort, for a day, or a week, or a month. He was certain that people in the darker recesses of Centrian had been on the run for years, maybe even decades. *Given the infinite span of time and the immortality of Centrians, was it even possible to be a fugitive for an entire life?*

What did fugitives do? It was the first time he even pondered the question. He supposed that many of them fled to the outer islands, but he was afraid he had already burned that bridge. There were other islands, but as far as he knew they had the same problems – poor technology, no nanites, no Telomore, no medicine. If he was going to relegate himself to such a miserable existence, then he might as well hold out as long as he could here on Centrian. He preferred a few centuries on the lam in Centrian to a few short decades wasting away on a remote island and dying a premature death.

He also assumed that one could steal away for long periods of time on base-level. As distasteful as he found this possibility, it was nevertheless a possibility. But he knew that base-level was not a cure-all for those trying to avoid detection. Base-level was primitive, but not primitive in the way that the islands were primitive. It was not unheard of for law enforcement to make their way through base-level establishments. UNI tracking was still prevalent down there. Those subhumans still rose into the canopy of Centrian life if they wanted to enjoy such niceties as healthcare. A base-level existence would not be one that allowed for endless evasion from authorities.

It occurred to him for the first time in this drama that he was clueless as to his next step. He had no idea where he would live, how he would earn money, or what his future entailed. He could not see beyond the haze of this pit and this fight. The death match taking place before him now encapsulated the extent of his future knowledge.

After feeling this depressing conclusion well up inside him, he looked down to Telarus and said, "I don't know. I really don't know."

Telarus could only nod as he went back to looking everywhere in the arena but the pit.

With this unsettling idea now shoved to the back of his mind, he returned his dazed attention to the fight. The crowd answered each blow in the spirited match with glee. Although the fighters were in good shape, they were not trained as martial artists. This meant that they expended a lot of energy on unfruitful maneuvers. The crowd may have grown restless. But both men had a knack for landing a damaging blow just at the point when the action might have turned stale.

The fight continued for another ten minutes with both men managing, at best, to wear the other one out. They saved themselves with inordinate dances around the ring. Yet they were also intent on finishing the match in their favor. Bold take-down attempts and occasional flurries of hand-to-hand combat proliferated. It wasn't until the combatants had been at it for a full 30 minutes that one seemed to gain the advantage.

Silver grew tired. They were both on their feet and looking for an opportunity but it was clear that his knees were wobbly. Pontius was certain that Black saw this. Black's strikes became bolder and he searched for some kind of take-down, some kind of grappling position that would give him the advantage and leave him in a position to do serious damage. After several more minutes of this sparring, Black found the opening he sought.

Silver wandered a little too close to Black's range. With a technical acumen that stunned the crowd, Black delivered an epic spinning back kick. It caught Silver square in the face. The resulting smack echoed above the din of the onlookers. The roar of approval was exuberant.

Sensing blood, the entire arena sprang to its feet. Pontius could not have heard Telarus or Caspian, even if they had screamed in his ear. The crowd wanted action and they wanted it now.

"*Toti! Toti! Toti!*" The chant rang throughout the arena.

Not wanting to disappoint, Black sprung on his prone victim and wailed away. He pummeled Silver's face with wanton ferocity. At first Pontius was certain that Silver was unconscious and the fight would end soon. But as happened so often in these fights, two factors worked against Black.

The first was that Silver somehow managed to regain his wits and assume a protective pose. It wasn't a valiant defense. He couldn't stop all of the punishment raining down upon him. But any defense at all bought him precious time. He managed, even in the slightest way, to deflect some of the most damaging blows.

The second was that Black tired out. One of the tricky factors of hand-to-hand combat is that you'd better finish your opponent when you have a chance. Silver took the best his opponent could offer and was still alive to counter-punch. This left him better off than his aggressor.

Black stayed atop Silver and the man on the bottom seemed unable to remove him. However, Black now offered punches with precious little force behind them. Although Silver lacked the ability to remove his aggressor, he deflected all incoming blows. He gathered his energy while he plotted his next move.

They maintained this position for a few more minutes. The crowd expressed displeasure. It was apparent that Black would not yet be finishing the bout. Seemingly in response to their anger, Silver removed one of his arms that had been protecting his face. He used it to reach inside his diaper. His lack of protection meant that Black landed a few good punches, but Silver no longer cared.

From his diaper, Silver produced something small and metallic. It was almost concealed in his hand. Pontius wasn't even sure how many people in the crowd understood what was happening. He watched in horror as Silver pointed the device at his attacker and shot a blue bolt of lightning into Black's thigh. Black released a thunderous wail and lept off of his victim.

The reversal spurred Silver's adrenaline and he jumped to his feet. His bulbous, bloody face was now no impediment. He was armed and he was on the attack.

The spectators jumped to their feet again and screamed with delight. Everyone in attendance was overjoyed with this turn of events. Caspian was enthralled. Kryx cheered with the crowd. Pontius was disgusted.

He turned to Kryx and yelled above the din, "What is going on??"

Kryx did not turn to face him. He kept his attention riveted on the action in the pit.

"*Toti! Toti! Toti!*"

Silver lunged forward and struck his opponent with another electrical attack. The long arch of blue energy lept from his hand and found its mark in Black's chest. Black had no retort but to stumble backward into the far wall.

Pontius grabbed Kryx's shoulder and shook it. He had to get his attention.

"Is that allowed? Can they bring weapons into the pit?"

Silver started marching toward his stunned victim.

"Of course not." Kryx still fixated on the action below.

"So what happens now? How do we stop this?"

This illogical retort struck Kryx in such a way that he felt inclined to look to his sponsor.

"*Stop this?* How would you suggest we stop this?"

Silver closed the gap between him and his opponent.

"How? What does it matter how? The point is that he's cheating! He's armed. This isn't how the match should proceed. This is supposed to be a match of equals. A fair fight. An honest chance!"

Kryx turned to face Pontius.

"Just where do you think you are, *skylander*?"

The inflection in *skylander* caught Pontius off guard. He had only heard that before at base-level. He did not expect to hear it here from Kryx. Regardless of what he thought of Kryx, he did not see him as base-level. Kryx stared straight into his eyes and Pontius found it unsettling. His gaze darted from the pit, to Kryx, then to the pit again. He wasn't sure what to do next but he felt compelled to do something.

"This isn't-"

Kryx was having none of it and he grabbed Pontius by the front of his coat before he could complete his protest.

"*Toti* is a rite as old as Centrian itself. The match is set. The combat is engaged. The spectators have placed their bets. There is nothing," he placed a wicked emphasis on *nothing*, "that can be done now to stop the proceedings."

He now understood where Kryx was coming from. He cared not for rites or traditions. He cared not for honor or rules. He cared for the millions of squalem laid on this fight – millions of squalem that might need to be refunded if the fight were aborted.

Silver shot another bolt from his stunner and the energy coursing through his opponent forced his chest to arc upward in grotesque fashion. When the horrific energy subsided, Black rolled over, face first, into the sawdust and vomited.

"So this is it? Chunk's life is taken from whichever combatant is too stupid to smuggle in a weapon?"

"I don't care about your *Chunk*," Kryx sneered.

"Did no one frisk these men before they entered the ring?"

He knew that Kryx couldn't care less about the technical details. Yet he still felt compelled to find a hitch, a flaw, that would allow him to save face and correct this aberration of justice.

Silver jumped onto the dazed Black's back and began pummeling him from behind, even as Black continued to dry heave.

"The men proceed, naked, to a judge. He inspects them to ensure they are capable of combat. Their garments are provided by a neutral seamstress. Sometimes, men find ways around these controls..."

A Dusk Forever Waning

Even though he was yelling against the din of the crazed spectators, he still found a way to make this sound nonchalant. It struck Pontius that this was nothing more to Kryx than another day at the office.

"The black one is going to die! Doesn't that mean anything to you?"

Kryx was both angered and bewildered. He wanted Pontius to just shut up. Pontius brought nothing of substance to this conversation.

"One of them will die. One of them was always going to die. That much is the same. What difference does it make if the silver man lives or the black? Your equation is unchanged."

Pontius shook his head. He could not believe that anyone – even Kryx – could be so casual about such a central tenet of law, of honor. This was never the way it was supposed to be and he now had to find some way to make that clear. Thoughts of Chunk flashed through his mind. He couldn't bear the idea that Chunk's Vitapass would come at the cost of someone fighting honorably like Black. If Black was going to die, then he had already come to terms with that idea. But it couldn't happen like this, in such a blatant miscarriage of justice.

Perhaps sensing his angst, Kryx again looked into his face and spoke with a vicious clarity.

"This is your doing. You brought this about. You came to me with the transfer cards. You asked if I could arrange this. You set these wheels in motion. You can't recall the ferry when it's within reach of the far shore."

He looked around the arena. Wild spectators surrounded the pit, but every five meters or so stood one of Kryx's bouncers. They stood stoically, watching nothing.

Black gave up all pretense of defense and lay motionless on the ground. The cheater now stood up to wild approval from the crowd. Building up the cheers like a ringmaster, he waited until the din reached maximum volume. Then he launched a running kick into Black's side. It led to another round of heaving, this time punctuated by voluminous blood.

This would happen no fewer than three more times. On each occasion, Pontius reached new levels of panic. He sweated and his hands shook. He looked to Caspian but Caspian fixated on the bloodsport below. He looked to Telarus, but Telarus did not realize what was happening. Thus, he could not translate the pleading looks from his friend. He looked to Kryx, but Kryx stopped indulging his protests and now led the crowd in cheers of "*Toti! Toti! Toti!*"

Silver geared up for another blow, a blow that Pontius assumed would be fatal. He already saw that Black barely breathed. When Black did breath, blood spewed into the coagulating sawdust below. He had to do something and he had to do it now.

With no time for additional forethought, and with no official plan in place, he lept into the sawdust below. This action brought a stunned hush to the entire arena. Everyone, from the spectators to the whores to the bouncers to Silver stood in awe at the turn of events. No one had ever seen anything like it.

Caspian and Telarus rose to their feet. Caspian had no idea what this meant and was too engrossed to process the permutations of Pontius's action.

Telarus was under no such spell. He became nervous and defensive. He tried to take stock of all the potential obstacles in this huge enclosure.

Silver stood stunned. He knew Black was not quite dead yet, but he didn't understand if this meant that the match was somehow over. He looked between Pontius and the myriad of spectators above, wondering what he should do.

Pontius made no qualms about his intentions. He strode up to Silver and launched a vicious punch to his gut. It was so powerful that it raised Silver from the sawdust and knocked him backward. Silver was no match for Pontius if they were both at full strength. Pontius knew how to kill men with his bare hands and had to do it on numerous occasions. But in this current state Silver was even more of a sitting duck. Although he had adrenaline from walloping his opponent, he also just endured 30 minutes of brutal combat. If Black was now exhausted, Silver was not much better.

Pontius fell upon the now-prone Silver and snatched the stunner from his hand. He held it high for everyone to see, then crammed it deep into Silver's mouth, breaking numerous teeth in the process. Once lodged, he reached in a finger to trigger it. The resulting shock went straight to the back of Silver's throat and up through his brain stem.

Stunners were not considered lethal weapons. But this jolt straight to Silver's brain stem launched a violent series of convulsions through his entire body. He frothed at the mouth and choked on his own vomit. Before nature completed the process, Pontius stood up and drove a boot deep into Silver's face. The convulsions stopped and Silver was dead.

Flush with a sense of righteousness, Pontius stood erect and surveyed the carnage below him. Although Black breathed shallowly, Pontius was confident he would survive. He knew there would be no such salvation for the Silver scum. Satisfied with the results below him, he looked up to find twenty thousand silent and confused spectators.

The rabid environment of a few seconds ago transformed into abject shock. No one knew how to react. Few people in the arena even understood what this meant. *Had Black won? Had Pontius won? Would other warriors now jump into the pit? What did this mean for their bets?*

Kryx was under no such delusion. He knew what this meant. Millions of squalem in bets were now invalidated. The fees for the entire event – the venue, the staff, everything – would fall on his shoulders. He was ruined.

As Kryx stewed and cataloged his options, the crowd became restless. Whispers rolled into conversations that rolled into shouting that rolled into thinly-veiled rebellion. The bettors weren't sure what they had just seen, but they knew what they had *not* seen – an actionable result to their wagers.

It took mere seconds for the crowd to move from stunned silence to open rebellion. Anger hung thick in the air and it all rained down upon Pontius.

Telarus, seeing no viable option to extract Pontius, now jumped down into the pit. He drew a weapon – a weapon the bouncers had been unable to find upon entry – and brandished it at the angry crowd above. Caspian jumped into the pit as well. Telarus looked at Pontius in surprise. Pontius could only return the same confusion. Caspian had no weapon to brandish and he was as useful in a fight as paper mache.

The three of them instinctively formed an outward facing circle. They could not jump out of the pit and they could do nothing else to form an offensive. They felt helpless to do anything but wait for an onslaught.

And the onslaught did come. Kryx stood up and yelled with a booming voice, "Seize them!" Within seconds hundreds of turbulent staff and spectators poured over the edge and into the ring below.

Chapter 14 – Destination: Soltris

The first thing that grabbed Pontius was the cold. Cold was a foreign sensation for most Torrenthians. Base-level temperatures often reached 37 degrees Celsius. The thick atmosphere meant that even amongst the heights of the myriad towers, temperatures still lingered above 15 degrees. Air conditioning was always at a premium. But now a chill gale cut through his clothing. It numbed his extremities and pried under his closed eyelids.

Opening his eyes was alarming. Bright sunlight assaulted his vision. Cold wind dried his eyeballs. The inflammation of a prolonged beating ensured that he could open them by no more than a half centimeter. In this impaired state, he tried to survey the environment.

Even through his bruised eyes he realized he was high in the atmosphere. For as far as he could see, platforms hung in the distance. Thin, corrugated metal beams connected them. There were no moorings. The platforms, and even their metal connectors, floated between wispy clouds. It was a giant erector set in the sky and it stretched to the horizon. He was in skydock.

Skydock serviced the jump ships that ferried between the outer planets. Torrenth was the only habitable planet in this solar system. But they mined the outer planets for raw materials. This mining activity ensured a constant flow of ships bustling above Torrenth.

An endless stream of jump ships imported materials into skydock. The jump ships were not equipped to complete the journey to the planet's surface. Their cargo emptied at these grand platforms and proceeded to industrialized cruisers. The cruisers ferried it to various locations around Centrian.

The platforms themselves were open. They housed some small buildings and administrative offices. But they were otherwise exposed to the ravages of the lower atmosphere. In the distance, he saw many other platforms like this one. They were at various levels and some of them had workers scurrying about. Some of them were empty. But at this distance, those workers might as well have been a thousand kilometers away.

Turning his head painfully to his right, he saw Telarus slumped in another chair. He couldn't tell if Telarus was alive. In fact, he could only identify the person as Telarus due to the clothing and the thick crop of black hair. His face was hamburger – an unrecognizable mess of blood and tissue.

Seeing him made Pontius more aware of his own condition. They both sat in specialized chairs. They were not bound. There were no restraints. It seemed they could rise at any time. But he knew better.

The chairs were huge batteries. As long as one sat perfectly still on them, they were just chairs. Lifting an arm or a leg would trigger a massive electrical current throughout the body. The higher one lifted his arm or his leg, the greater the electrical charge. Depending upon the settings, it was rare that anyone could lift their hand more than a few centimeters off the chair. Doing so caused extreme agony.

Kryx and Calon were busy running to and fro. A small office building occupied one corner of the platform. Calon scuttled in and out of it every several minutes. Kryx spent more time attending the huge jump ship docked on the other side of the platform. They were both industrious in their work. They communicated little between each other. It appeared they were readying for a trip.

In front of the office building, about ten meters from Pontius, stood a large table. It was there for customs inspections. There were no goods on the table now. It held nothing but a small bundle. He recognized it immediately as Chunk.

This observation sent an instinctive spasm through his body. His muscles tensed and he struggled to rise. He wasn't sure what percentage of the agony resulted from the electricity or the pain already resident in his body. The current coursed through every muscle, every synapse. He pissed himself. His body screamed in exquisite pain. It was so intense that it took his breath away. He never experienced anything so intense.

Although he wanted to cry out, his clenched teeth allowed nothing but a guttural grunt. When he relaxed back into the chair he felt every ounce of his energy blow away in the gale winds. The struggle attracted Kryx's attention.

Kryx strode over to him and lorded over his chair. He closed his eyes but he knew Kryx was there. He could feel Kryx's presence. After several minutes spent breathing deeply and trying to collect his wits, he finally reopened his eyes.

Kryx stood like a statue and looked at him. He carried no expression. He wasn't staring at him. He was staring through him. He didn't know where this led.

"Yes?"

The word escaped his mouth in a muffled mess. His tongue lay crippled in his throat. The metallic taste of blood was constant. He wasn't sure how many teeth remained. Spit flew from his mouth even as he tried to pronounce this single word.

Kryx showed no emotion. He spoke with an evenness that was unnerving.

"I would have expected many things from you, but I never believed you would invalidate your word in the penultimate moment of that match."

The sentence had a jarring effect on him. It brought him back to the arena. He didn't know how long he'd been unconscious. He didn't even know exactly what transpired at the end of the match. He was only trying to gain his bearings on the here and now.

The chaos in the pit was a blur in his mind. He remembered watching the angry spectators flow over the walls of the pit. They came in waves and they wanted blood. Telarus transformed into a whirling combat machine. He shot with abandon and he fought with violence when shooting was no longer practical.

Caspian was predictably useless. But the image of him trying to fight remained emblazoned in his memory. He was so shocked to see his friend wading into the fray.

He couldn't recall how long he had lasted, nor the exact moment he succumbed. The three of them shot, punched, kicked, and bit whomever would come into range. But three men against hundreds leads to a quick end. He was certain they'd killed several – maybe more. Yet it only took minutes before the swarm engulfed them. The last thing he remembered was thinking to himself, "This is it," as the boots found his skull and he lay in the sawdust.

Even now, in this desperate situation, the memory of Silver came flooding back to him. It invoked a surge of anger. He ground his broken teeth and snarled at Kryx.

"My word? Are you speaking of honor? How dare you. You stood and watched as the silver one cheated. You would have let him take the other's life. You didn't care, as long as you were paid in full."

"As long as I was paid in full..." Kryx did not say these words with anger. Rather, he said them to himself as though trying to quantify their meaning. "It's amazing what people will allow to happen – as long as they're paid in full."

He closed his swollen eyes again. He laid his head back against the chair and began shivering. He offered no reply, so Kryx continued.

"How many women have you defiled? How many men have you degraded? How many parents were left sobbing on their living room floors, all so you could be paid in full?"

He felt a rush of shame mixing with his pain and agony. That shame was soon flushed out with indignation.

"I stand by my commitments. I honor my deals."

"Is there any honor to be had in a deal made under extreme duress? Is there anything those parents wouldn't agree to? You hold up your vaunted commitment as a badge of honor. But honor cannot be extracted. It can only be traded freely between equals."

"You know nothing of honor." He spoke with bitter vitriol. Kryx was unphased.

"Maybe. Maybe not. I do know that there is no honor between master and slave. There is no honor between jailer and convict. There is only power. There is only the ability of one person to force his will upon the other."

He did not care to humor his captor but he knew no other course of action. His anger welled within him and he had no other outlet.

"Don't paint us with the same brush. I offer people a *choice*."

Kryx loosed an involuntary laugh that carried surprising force, even in this wind-swept environment.

"A choice? You call that a choice? I know you." With this he leaned closer to him. "I know the *choice* you offer. It is no choice at all."

He turned his head, trying anything to avoid Kryx's presence. As he did, he caught another glimpse of Telarus.

"Is he alive?"

Kryx walked the few meters to Telarus's seat. He reached around the back of the chair and pushed something. Telarus's body sprung forward in an unnatural arc. Every muscle strained against his skin. He released a constant, grinding moan. Kryx held the button for ten seconds. When he released it, Telarus slumped back into the chair and his chest heaved as he gasped for air.

"Aye. He's alive."

He felt a pang of remorse. He could not have predicted this action, but he still regretted having asked the question. He turned his head away from Telarus. As he did, this brought Chunk back into his field of vision. For the first time, he realized that Chunk was alone.

"Where's Moria? Have you killed her?"

Kryx shook his head and shrugged.

"She was released. You don't care for her. I certainly don't care for her. I have no use for her."

The logic of this statement struck him. Kryx was correct. He no longer cared for Moria, and that may have been her salvation. If he loved Moria and Kryx knew it, he was certain she would be here now, sitting in another electrochair. Then a terrible thought crept into his brain.

"So release Chunk as well. What use could you possibly have for him?"

Kryx chuckled and shook his head.

"Don't be silly. You don't care about Moria. You can't say the same for that little rat."

Pontius experienced a wild mixture of panic, anger, and denial. What would Kryx do to a baby? How could he see Chunk as more than a transaction in Pontius's mind? What had he done to indicate anything more?

"I only care about the commitment to his parents. I only care that he receives the life they purchased for him."

This elicited an angry and maniacal response from Kryx. His calm demeanor disappeared. He felt affronted.

"Do you know what you get from NCU agents?"

He was no longer talking to Pontius. He yelled this over his shoulder to Calon, who was bustling about in the background. Without missing a beat, Calon replied, "Nay-un."

"You get LIES! They lie to your face. They offer you life while they kill your baby. They promise salvation while they fuck your wife. They believe in a code — a code built on suffering. And lies!"

"Yes-un." Calon did not stop preparations while offering this confirmation.

"Kryx! You have to listen to me. If you have something against me, then take it out on me. But that boy — he's just a pawn. He serves no purpose here. Send him back to Moria."

He wanted to move something — anything — to emphasize his point. He knew that any movement would bring back the searing electrical current. Kryx continued.

"There is no lower form on this planet than an NCU agent. There is no one he won't kill. There is nothing he won't do in the service of the state. And just when you think you understand him for the vile leach that he is, he wants to preach to you about honor!"

He no longer understood who Kryx was talking to. Calon had darted back into the office. Telarus was unconscious.

"Do you know how you reach an NCU agent? Do you know how you finally get through to him?"

With this, Kryx spun back around to Pontius and hovered over his battered face. Pontius was afraid to hear the conclusion.

"You must find something he cares about. Agents don't care much about themselves and they don't care much for others. But every once in a while, if you're lucky, you find something they do care about."

He turned around and started walking to the table holding Chunk. Without thinking, Pontius cried out.

"Kryx! Listen to me! I don't know what you think you're accomplishing but you can't do it with Chunk. If you want me to suffer then so be it. But don't impose this on an innocent child."

Kryx yelled. His voice boomed, even in the open air of the platform.

"Innocent? My children were innocent! The NCU cared not for their innocence. They dispatched their judgment with ruthless efficiency."

He was now standing over Chunk but staring at Pontius.

"Do I want you to suffer? Of course I do. And this boy is the most effective means to that end."

In one fluid motion, Kryx swiped the blanket off Chunk. This revealed a platform under the baby. It cradled him, but it was no natural device. It was a smaller version of the electrochair, made from the same material and having the same color. Pontius tried to scream but before he could complete the act Kryx applied the voltage.

Chunk released a blood-curdling scream. His infantile wails brought an involuntary wretch to Pontius's body. He tried to jerk free from his own chair. A paralyzing jolt seized his muscles and arched his back. His cries mixed with Chunk's in the bitter winds.

This process continued for excruciating minutes. Kryx applied the juice, released it after several seconds, then applied it again. Despite the agonizing results, he made repeated attempts to escape the chair. His most successful try saw his arm raised a mere 20 centimeters from the device before he could take the pain no longer. He believed he might faint.

This may have continued for some time if it weren't for the arrival of the cruiser. Vibrations hummed through the chair. A cruiser popped above the platform and began docking. This distracted Kryx and he turned to address the arrival. Pontius paid little attention. He was now weeping. His convulsive tears were less for his own pain and more for the constant wailing now released by Chunk. Pontius returned to silence with the removal of each jolt of electricity. But Chunk had no such composure. He screamed with the blind agony that only an infant can know.

Pontius had no idea what to make of the cruiser. He assumed this to be just another transaction for Kryx. He only hoped that the event would take a long time. He couldn't bear the thought of another jolt of electricity coursing through Chunk's tiny body. He needed to formulate some kind of plan.

He looked to Telarus, who was still unconscious. With Kryx distracted, he tried to call to his friend but there was no response. He had no idea what aid Telarus could provide, but he was desperate to find any course of action. Telarus's head bobbed slightly in his chair and Pontius believed he might be coming to. His hopes evaporated when he realized this was nothing more than the wind jostling his catatonic friend.

He played frantically with his own movements. He searched for a combination of slow or subtle motions that would escape the automatic response of the electrochair. Every time he believed himself to be making progress, the voltage would return and he would relax again into his prison.

Several men jumped out of the cruiser and consulted with Kryx. Calon stood behind them, listening and coordinating activities. They planned to unload something on the platform. After several minutes they hoisted a new electrochair out of the back of the cruiser. Caspian occupied the chair.

They carried him to a position next to Pontius. Seeing Caspian temporarily snapped him from his escape attempts. Caspian's appearance was amazing.

He looked nothing like Pontius or Telarus. Aside from a few scratches and bruises, he was otherwise normal. He wore a dumbfounded and goofy smile. Pontius instantly recognized the expression. He saw it in his apartment right before the slaughter of Tenarrin. Caspian was sky high.

With Caspian deposited next to Pontius, the men returned to the cruiser. They continued a discussion with Kryx. Kryx gesticulated to them and paid no attention to Pontius or Caspian.

"Caspian! How did you get out of the pit?"

Caspian gazed around at the open sky. He looked all around, trying to gain his bearings. It was clear that he had no idea where he was.

"What is this place?"

"We're in skydock."

A puzzled look shot across Caspian's face.

"Skydock? Why? Are we going somewhere?"

Pontius quickly became annoyed.

"It doesn't matter why we're here. I need you to concentrate. Your chair. Can you get out of your chair?"

Caspian looked at his chair, then at Pontius, then at his chair again. He understood the question but he wasn't certain how to move his limbs. Once he finally managed to piece together the necessary motor commands, he lifted his arm to a height of five centimeters. As he did, his body convulsed and his teeth involuntarily ground. He did not cry out. Nor did he display any signs of pain. Instead he just stared at Pontius in wide-eyed amazement. A wave of disappointment washed over Pontius and he relaxed back into his chair.

Caspian looked past Pontius to Telarus. The sight shocked him.

"What happened to Telarus? What's wrong with him?"

He was somewhat stunned at the ignorance in Caspian's voice.

"We were all in the pit. Do you remember being in the pit?"

He saw Caspian taking a mental inventory of the situation before nodding.

"We were attacked. Everyone rushed the pit. Do you remem-"

And he stopped. Caspian gazed around at his environment, his jaw agape. He realized there was no point in trying to recap events. Caspian was as useful in this situation as Telarus.

The cruiser exited the platform and Kryx returned to the group. Caspian shot him a broad smile. The incoherence of the gesture caught Kryx off guard. He looked to Pontius, as though he would find explanation there, but then decided to continue.

"So how long do we sit here watching you torture a baby?"

Pontius's voice held all the spite he could muster in his depleted state.

"We're not staying here. This is just the opening act. The jump ship is almost ready for take-off."

Calon's activities now made some degree of sense to Pontius. Preparing a jump ship for launch was labor intensive. Calon handled these preparations. Pontius was more worried about their destination.

Torrenth was the only habitable planet in this solar system. In fact, it was the only habitable planet reachable without spending centuries in deep space. The outer planets around Torrenth were rich in many natural resources and they were constantly mined. But those mining operations took place from tiny space stations orbiting around those planets. The planets themselves were inhospitable to human life.

"What does this accomplish, Kryx? You can kill us here."

"Who said I want to kill you? Killing you ends your pain and mine continues. I'm going to balance the scales. You're going to witness the pain I've experienced for many thousands of years."

As though to drive his point home, Kryx returned to the table. Fearing the worst, Pontius yelled out but it made no difference. Kryx resumed his pointless torture of Chunk.

He couldn't bear to watch. His watery eyes stared at the heavens. He tried in vain to block out the sounds of the boy's screams. He heard many babies' cries in his lifetime. He cared nothing about them. But this was the first time he'd experienced the unrelenting pain of a helpless baby screaming. It was an unsettling force he couldn't understand. It was a sound he never wanted to hear again.

After this continued for several more minutes he looked over to Caspian. Caspian's face lost none of its wonder, but he now wore a dark frown. He was aghast at the sight.

"Pontius. Why is he doing that?"

"He's trying to punish me by torturing Chunk."

The simplicity with which that phrase rolled of his tongue alarmed him. Caspian was still confused.

"He's torturing..." Caspian looked at Pontius, then at the baby, then at Pontius again. "...a *baby*??"

Pontius could do nothing but nod his head. He swung his head back and forth, crying and wishing that he could remove the horrific sound from his ears.

Caspian shocked himself with his own revulsion. He was a man who often took pleasure in the pain of others. But this was more barbaric than anything even he could imagine.

"How do we stop this?"

The stupidity of the question stunned Pontius. He returned a gaze to his friend and then nodded his head toward his chair.

"Do you have any suggestions?"

Caspian looked down at his chair and furrowed his brow. Pontius looked back at the sky.

For the next 30 minutes, each actor played his own solitary part. Kryx would apply just enough voltage to agonize the baby. Then he turned off the current and checked again with Calon regarding launch preparations. Pontius wallowed in his helplessness. Caspian commenced a series of escalating experiments.

The electrochair was a powerful captor. Properly tuned, it would not kill the victim. But it caused excruciating pain. The electricity didn't course haphazardly through the body. It trained on nerve centers. It sent pain receptors into overdrive. It was a pain that no normal man could withstand without surrendering completely to the device. Caspian was no normal man.

From the first time that Pontius asked him to test his bounds, Caspian found the feedback to be unpleasant, but not unwelcome. He lifted his hand and felt the current coursing through his body. As it did, his nerves fired and his sensory input revived. He was at once pained and exhilarated.

The first several times he tried this experiment he went from pleasure to indifference to outright pain. This happened in a matter of seconds. He would lay his hand back down, allow his nerve endings to calm down, and repeat the experiment. Each time he found himself able to lift his arm just a little further than he had before. After 20 minutes he lifted his arm upward at a 90 degree angle.

Pontius finally looked over to his friend in amazement. Caspian was waving at him and smiling. This dumbfounded Pontius. He had no idea what to do or say.

When the half hour passed Calon appeared to be nearing their departure. He came out of the open jump ship and walked back to the table. Chunk's screaming died down but he still cried pitifully. He threw his head from side to side, desperate for a soothing caress from anyone. Kryx smiled down to him and enabled the electricity again.

Kryx did not watch Chunk during these sessions. He watched Pontius. He locked his gaze upon him and delighted in every emotion that crossed his face. It was this last session that sent Caspian over the edge.

After more then 30 seconds it was apparent that Kryx wasn't turning off the juice. Chunk hardly had the strength to cry any longer but his tiny body continued to course with pain. Kryx watched Pontius sob and it overjoyed him.

Caspian lurched an arm off the chair. He was not impervious to the pain. At times the pain forced him to pause. He caught his breath and inventoried his surroundings. But it didn't stop him. He composed himself, steadied his muscles against the automatic convulsions, and continued rising.

Caspian reached full height. It was apparent that the electricity assaulted him in epic proportions. His arms and legs convulsed in unnatural arcs. His body spasmed violently. It was all he could do to stay upright.

By the time Pontius or Kryx even realized what was happening, Caspian was already exceeding the range of the chair. Pontius and Kryx were both stunned, neither believing what they were seeing. Caspian worked his way toward Pontius. Caspian sported a massive erection. He held an expression mixing joy with concentration. He felt something. He felt this so intensely. It was a rush of sensation he had not enjoyed for hundreds of years.

Kryx lept toward Pontius but it was too late. Caspian made a single move toward the back of Pontius's chair that disabled the device. Pontius tried to spring forward but was incapable of any spirited movement. He was unable to stand. Instead, he slumped forward and onto the platform, lying limp at the base of the chair. Kryx flew onto Pontius's chair screaming and flailing away. He was intent upon ending Pontius's life with his bare hands.

Caspian wanted to help Pontius when Calon jumped on his back. Calon had no idea what to do with such a position. He just knew that he must find some way to help his boss. Caspian was equally inept but he now had a rush of adrenaline like none he could remember. He grabbed the slight Calon from his shoulders and slammed him to the platform. Calon's breath forced out of his lungs as he crashed against the carbon surface.

There was no hesitation on Caspian's part. He reached down and grabbed Calon's foot with both hands. Calon flailed wildly but Caspian's grip was resolute. Caspian dragged him, kicking and screaming, to the edge of the platform and swung him over the edge. Calon's screams faded into oblivion as he fell into the clouds below.

Turning back to the center of the platform, Caspian saw Kryx pounding on his friend. He lowered his shoulder and began running, building up to full speed. By the time he reached his target, he exploded through Kryx with the force of a linebacker.

This blew Kryx away. He paid no attention to anything other than Pontius's bloody face. When the shoulder crashed into him he had no idea what had happened. Pontius was unable to provide any assistance.

Caspian did not focus on defeating Kryx. He doubted he could do so. Before Kryx could garner a full response, he lifted himself and re-enabled Pontius's chair. With Pontius now slumped forward, its electrical charge acted on no one.

Kryx rose to his feet and lunged at Caspian. Caspian made no attempt to parry the assault. Instead, he deftly pivoted, redirecting Kryx's momentum into the chair. Without realizing what he had just done, Kryx fell into the chair. He immediately tried to lunge forward, only to be wracked with the debilitating force of electricity.

Caspian strolled to the table and turned off the current to Chunk's device. He lifted the whimpering and exhausted child in his arms. He sat next to Pontius and listened to Kryx's endless stream of invectives. He was beyond excited. He had an expression of sheer joy. He placed an arm around Pontius.

"Are you OK?"

Pontius could do nothing but nod. Without saying a word, he lifted a finger and pointed at Telarus. He gave a questioning glance to Caspian.

Caspian walked over to Telarus and spent a few moments assessing his situation. He returned with a grim look.

"He's alive but he's not good. He's breathing shallowly. I don't know what to do for him. He'll die soon if we don't get him out of here."

"Convo the medics. Get them up here quick."

Caspian paused for a moment. He wasn't sure that Pontius understood what he was saying.

"Pontius, you're a wanted man now. If the authorities come here now they'll know who you are."

Pontius shook his head. This was not an argument he would lose.

"Save Telarus. We can't let him die."

Not entirely happy with the consequences, Caspian nonetheless initiated a convo. He asked them to send medical assistance. He was as vague as possible. He didn't want to alert them to a potential legal situation. He hoped the medics would come alone. With the convo complete, he sat back by Pontius. He started thinking Pontius would need medical attention as well.

"Come on, Captain. We need to get you into the office building while we wait. You and Chunk are freezing."

But Pontius was still shaking his head. He had plans to attend to. With great force of will he rose to his feet. The winds nearly blew over his wobbly stance but he was able to maintain stability by leaning into the prevailing gale.

"We're not done yet." He drew deep, labored breaths between each word. "Help me get him to the jump ship."

Caspian didn't know where this was leading but he felt he should obey. Pontius wanted Kryx – bound to his chair – dragged into the jump ship. The effort was significant. Pontius could do little but direct. With Caspian's adrenaline waning, his lack of physical prowess was damning. He dragged Kryx's chair awkwardly toward the waiting jump ship.

At the ship's cargo door the two men struggled to raise the chair inside. Pontius had little strength but Caspian couldn't do it alone. All the while, Kryx screamed every curse he could muster. Every so often he strained against the bounds of the chair and Pontius smiled as the pain coursed through his body.

After nearly five minutes of struggle, Kryx sat in the cargo hold. Caspian thought they might have finished the task, but Pontius motioned toward the cockpit.

With both of them in the cockpit, he asked, "This can launch on autopilot, right?"

Caspian nodded, still confused.

"Well, yes. This model can escape orbit in a fully automated role. But it will never be able to dock at its destination without the intervention of a human pilot."

Pontius shook his head again.

"Not my concern. Where is the ship's current destination?"

Caspian scanned the register.

"Golgoth. It's equipped to carry iron ore."

Pontius scanned his UNI, searching for some particular target unknown to Caspian.

"Can you reset the destination for Soltris?"

Caspian scanned the register to make the necessary adjustments. Then he stopped, grasping the illogical nature of the request.

"Captain, Soltris is a *star* – and not a particularly close one at that."

Pontius became impatient.

"Aye, I'm aware. Can you program it go to Soltris?"

"This isn't an interstellar ship. It only has provisions for a few weeks, maybe a month. It isn't equipped for deep space."

"Caspian, we're running out of time. The medics will be here soon. Can you program it to go to Soltris or not?"

Caspian furrowed his brow and stared back at the controls. As an aviator, this request was against his nature. He made a few notes in his UNI, referenced a few manuals, and returned with a verdict.

"Well, yes, I suppose it could be done."

"Good. Make it happen. As soon as you have the destination programmed, launch this thing."

"But it will never make it to its destination."

This last sentence was never heard by Pontius. He exited the jump ship with Chunk in his arms. Caspian began entering commands. At several points audio alarms sounded.

"Warning, destination invalid."

"Override," he stated.

"Confirmed."

"Warning, provisions invalid."

"Override," he stated.

"Confirmed."

"Warning, fuel insufficient."

"Override," he stated.

"Confirmed."

"Warning, life support insufficient."

"Override," he stated.

"Confirmed."

After several more minutes of fidgeting, the navigation system returned with a chirping confirmation.

"Coordinates locked. Destination: Soltris."

A Dusk Forever Waning

As Caspian exited the jump ship the thrusters were already warming up. On his way out he launched a single punch into the back of Kryx's head. The force from the punch lifted him out of his chair enough to reengage the electric shocks. Kryx gritted in agony. Exhaust poured across the platform, bathing everything in a chemical mist. Sixty seconds later the ship escaped the skydock.

The three of them didn't make it to the shelter of the administrative office before the medical cruisers arrived. Given that they were only medics, Pontius toyed with the idea that he might escape without notice. He would not have the chance to find out. He collapsed just as he was leading the doctors to Telarus.

Chapter 15 – The Bowery Butcher

Conti was in her usual flurry of convo'ing activity. She had been talking all day. She talked all day, every day. This tended to make her oblivious to outside activity. Today she could not remain oblivious. Returning to her office, Caspian waited for her patiently.

As she closed the door and turned around, she noticed him for the first time. She didn't know what to say. He smiled at her. She did not return the gesture. After a long, awkward pause, she finally said, "Caspian..."

The two had not spoken since Pontius exposed her as a PC agent. Caspian almost always ignored good advice. Yet he wasn't dumb enough to keep her acquaintance given the drama that swirled around Pontius, Moria, and Chunk. It was three weeks since their last conversation. She assumed she would never see or hear from him again.

"Aye, Dame Conti!" His air was goofy and inappropriate.

"What are you doing here?"

She locked her office door and sat down. Her movements were cautious, as though she expected Caspian to pounce across the desk. Despite the silly smile on his face, Caspian maintained a relaxed posture. He did nothing to support her apprehension.

"I believe that you and I have a mutual interest."

"You know where is he, don't you? Are you harboring him? You realize that you will be implicated in his crimes if you don't reveal his location?"

Her questions flowed forth without forethought. She didn't believe him to be harboring Pontius. The authorities were monitoring Caspian like a hawk. They weren't able to tie him to Pontius. Yet she felt the need to blurt out these thoughts now that she was sitting across from him in her office.

"I don't know where he is, but I know how to communicate with him."

She leaned forward over her desk to accentuate her next statement.

"Don't be a fool. You need to turn him in. He's the most wanted man in Centrian. You can't hide behind some shield, pretending that you don't know where he is. When we find him, you'll be dragged down in this whole mess. You'll be convicted as an accomplice. You'll pay an unnecessary price for his crimes. There's no reason for you to be caught in all of this."

Her words did not affect him. He listened politely as she made her plea. He cared not. Threats of implication or conviction were completely lost on him. He understood the substance of her words but he did not listen to their specifics.

"Did you fuck me just to get closer to Pontius?"

The question caught her completely off guard. She didn't expect anything like this from him and she wasn't sure what to say. Caspian wasn't the type to care about love or commitment or affection. He fucked men, whores, drug addicts, androids, and animals. His sexual conquests were nothing but pawns in his quest for pleasure. What difference did it make if she was using him to reach her target?

She sat in silence and offered no reply, so he continued.

"Was I a means in your investigation?"

She thought that ignoring him would force him to move on, but now she realized that he expected an answer. She wasn't sure what to say. She targeted him when she wanted to gather more intelligence on Pontius. She failed to catch Pontius's attention so she instead tried to latch onto someone in his inner circle. Yet like so many other moths drawn to the light of a rich and powerful playboy, she had a natural attraction to Caspian.

"I don't know."

This was the best she could offer. He nodded and pondered those words for a moment. Their honesty seemed to satisfy him and he moved on.

"So I believe you'd like to find our friend."

She wasn't sure where he was going with this.

"Are you here to turn him in?"

"I'm here to dictate terms."

The word *dictate* left an unsavory residue in her mind.

"What are you talking about? A fugitive is in no position to dictate anything."

"Perhaps." He sat back and relaxed, forcing her to wait on his next words. "But I believe you have a media problem."

The acknowledgment of this fact stung her. All of Population Control was on pins and needles.

When the medics rescued Telarus from skydock, Caspian managed to whisk Pontius away. His quick thinking saved his friend. Every skydock platform came equipped with an escape pod used in case of fire or other emergencies. Caspian bundled Pontius and Chunk into the pod and the three of them floated down to the surface far below. It was only minutes after their departure that the Centrian Guard arrived on the platform en masse. By the time the Guard realized what had happened, they had already landed. They melted into the base-level underworld.

None of this would have much bothered PC were it not for the fact that Kryx had alerted numerous media outlets to the drama. He hadn't just planned to torture Pontius in some far off space base. He wanted to embarrass the NCU on a national scale. With this in mind, he led reporters to uncover the whole story of Malorus, Torrenthia, and Tenarrin.

The ensuing media storm was an existential crisis for NCU. The government always went to great lengths to bury any hint of impropriety in Population Control. It was hard enough to maintain public sentiment. After all, they facilitated the extermination of babies. It was almost impossible to quell unrest if citizens viewed the government as corrupt. The federal authorities did anything in their power to hide any crimes committed by NCU agents.

Now Pontius's story screamed across all public news outlets. They dubbed him the Bowery Butcher. Urban legends exaggerated the confirmed facts. What started off as the investigation of a corrupt NCU agent blossomed into hyperbolic tales of cannibalism and ritual sacrifice. Pontius wasn't just a criminal. He was a demon of the highest order.

Conti furrowed her brow and frowned.

"The media problem has already occurred. Is our *Butcher* going to erase the minds of all the Centrians who now see PC as the diseased arm of a totalitarian state?"

He placed his hands together at the fingertips. He enjoyed the advantage he hadn't yet communicated.

"Pontius can't erase anyone's mind. But he can ensure that they don't see anything more than the tragedy that is currently racing through the news outlets."

She didn't know what this meant. She wasn't sure if she wanted to know what it meant. She stared at him for a long moment before replying, trying to gain a better read on his intentions.

"What do you mean by *anything more*?"

Caspian was about to hold court. His smile widened. It turned from goofy to calculating before her eyes.

"You can't honestly believe that this is the only act of depravity he's committed? You can't think that this is the first time he's sullied the hallowed name of NCU?"

She frowned and considered these words before replying.

"No, of course not. He's a sick bastard. I know he's been doing this sort of thing for centuries. That's why I was assigned to this case. Auditing has been tracking him for a long time. What difference does any of that make? We don't need to convict him of every crime. The single crime he committed with Chunk's parents is heinous enough to put him on a penal colony for eternity. We don't need to dredge up every detail of every incident to ruin him."

"You don't need to dredge up every detail, but the media would be happy to."

"The media doesn't have every detail, nor will they. They can fabricate ridiculous stories of ritualistic depravity, but the educated citizens can see the hyperbole. The media hounds have created their own fairy tales of PC corruption before and they'll do it again."

"Do you really *know* how Pontius goes about his assignments? Have you heard any eye-witness accounts of his process?"

She paused again. This line of questioning made her uncomfortable.

"What do you mean? I know the crap he pulls with his victims. I know he forces them to do all manner of disgusting acts. I know that Moria illegally issues his Vitapasses."

Caspian slowly shook his head while maintaining his smile.

"You're missing the central point. He records *everything*."

This stunned her. She didn't know this. She tried in vain to hide its impact.

"He *records* it?"

It was a rhetorical question. She had no reason to doubt it but she couldn't believe that someone wanted to keep these visions for posterity.

"He has a library that encompasses thousands of assignments. They stretch back for more than fifteen hundred years. He can illustrate every act of corruption in which he's participated since he joined NCU."

This repulsed her. She could easily fathom killing these unlicensed vermin. It was the guiding mission behind Population Control. Everyone in that building felt they were performing a valued and essential service for the nation. But she couldn't imagine why someone would want to record these actions for posterity. A garbage manage doesn't photograph the garbage before it's taken to the dump. An abortionist doesn't record a fetus before it's disposed of. *Why would an agent want to reflect on these individual engagements? Especially when some of them stretched far beyond anyone's natural memory?*

"So he's more deranged than even I gave him credit for. He really *is* the Bowery Butcher. It makes no difference here in Auditing. Whether he's recorded a single act of corruption or a thousand, he's still committed horrific crimes. We already have the evidence necessary to send him away – and we will."

"I have no doubt that you'll send him away. The question becomes, how much collateral damage will be incurred by PC?"

A tinge of anger now rose in Conti. She wouldn't be hostage to some animal who was threatening to go public.

"He's not the first mass murderer in history, nor will he be the last. If he chooses to release that footage it will only solidify public opinion that he should suffer for thousands of years."

Caspian did not reply verbally. Rather, he began transmitting a stream of images to her UNI. Within seconds she was drinking from the waterhose of Pontius's past. He completed thousands of assignments. Yet it became immediately clear that Caspian wasn't just transmitting all of them.

Every image that flashed into her brain was the record of assignments Pontius completed in tandem. While NCU agents completed many assignments solo, it was not uncommon for them to work in pairs or even in larger teams. It all depended upon the tactics the particular situation. Most assignments called for a single agent but there were times that required an entire group.

For the next several minutes Conti endured the awful montage. What she witnessed was not simply the crimes of Pontius, but of dozens of other NCU agents. She saw supervisors, veterans, and trainees taking bribes and abusing victims. She understood, for the first time in her life, that a death sentence over someone's baby offered these agents the most terrible kind of leverage.

Caspian offered no interruption. The montage continued unabated for a full 15 minutes. The display wasn't restricted to current NCU employees. Many of the more decorated agents had graduated to grander positions. The videos included corporate leaders, politicians, and even one individual who had gone on to achieve celebrity. Some of these people were even known to her. It was like watching surveillance footage of her own family committing crimes against humanity.

When the montage ended they both sat in silence. She didn't know what to say and he was in no mood to force the conversation. She stared at him, trying to guess his intentions. The images tore through her but she was still unsure of his motives.

"Releasing this footage will not save him."

A Dusk Forever Waning

The smile evaporated off his face. He replied in a stoic voice.

"Nothing will save him. His fate was sealed the moment he decided not to kill Chunk in that apartment. If he had just killed that single unlicensed, he probably continues happily making his deals for thousands of years."

Her voice now took on a pleading air.

"He can't blackmail his way out of this. If we had seen this footage a month ago, maybe this whole thing just goes away. But once Kryx leaked this to the media, it tied our hands. You can release this footage to the world if you want, but the public is already clamoring for justice. They want to see the Bowery Butcher brought to trial. And quite frankly, PC has no choice but to prosecute him. If we can't show the world that he has been scrubbed from our department they will never have faith in another PC operation again."

She paused but Caspian just nodded in return. He didn't argue with her. He allowed her to connect the dots.

"If you release this now, it drags down dozens of other prominent figures. It causes a worldwide crisis. *But it doesn't save Pontius.* You have to listen to me. Not even these images can save him now. He's a public pariah. No one in the government will sign off on his acquittal."

"He doesn't want acquittal."

Those words sat in the room like a white elephant. He said nothing else, allowing them to sink in.

"What are his terms?"

Her voice was cold and stark. She first assumed that Pontius was trying to blackmail himself to freedom. With this possibility now taken off the table, a potential new direction intrigued her. Yet she was also skeptical. She could not see any scenario in which this worked out for Pontius.

Caspian sat up straight in his chair. He affected a lawyerly air. Having reached this point in the conversation pleased him. Yet he determined to address it in a professional manner.

"First, Moria is to be reinstated at PC. She is to be cleared of all charges."

Conti had to restrain herself in her seat. She was incensed.

"What? She has enabled every step of his depravity! She is the supplier and he is the pusher. This will never fly!"

He was unphased. He held a finger aloft to indicate pause.

"No one outside this office knows about Moria. They know of the Bowery Butcher. They know about the heroic fight of Tenarrin. They know about the tragic loss of Malorus and Torrenthia. But no in the general public has any clue who Moria is. There is no reason for her to go down with this ship."

"That is *never* going to-"

"Second, Chunk is to be issued a Vitapass. He will be allowed to live as a free soul devoid of any harassment from PC."

Conti was now beside herself.

"Excuse me?! We absolve his co-conspirator then we allow an unlicensed vermin to live? This will not-"

A Dusk Forever Waning

"In return for these concessions, Pontius will not release any UNI footage to the media."

"That's not going to-"

"Pontius will surrender to the authorities. Once in their care, as you know, his UNI can be erased, ensuring that no one will *ever* see that footage again."

She was now quiet.

"He will plead guilty to the murders or Malorus and Torrenthia. He will plead guilty to her forced degradation before her death. In fact, he will plead guilty to anything you choose to charge him with. You can charge him with any of his crimes from centuries past, although that would require acknowledging them in a public court. He will plead guilty to any of the crimes of his colleagues. You can do whatever you wish with him. You can crucify him with all the sins of this world, so long as Moria's is reinstated and Chunk receives his Vitapass. If you refuse any of these terms all of the videos will be released to all major media outlets tomorrow at noon."

He finished. He allowed a self-satisfied smirk to cross his lips while maintaining his gaze on Conti. She stared into her desktop and tried to compute the consequences of these terms. She was silent for a full five minutes. He did nothing to break the silence.

"So he surrenders himself?"

"Aye."

"And he pleads guilty?"

"Aye."

"And those images go no further?"

"Aye."

"But this doesn't save him."

She was perplexed. She was still trying to calculate how Pontius believed he could escape.

"He knows that. This isn't about him."

A light clicked on in her head. She narrowed her gaze and became suspicious.

"Those images – they could exist anywhere. He could have copied them to a thousand locations. They could be in the media's hands right now. This is just a ploy to save Moria's and Chunk's necks before he takes down the whole fucking machine."

He leaned forward and placed his hand on the desk as though he were tamping down an unruly child.

"Let's be realistic. Pontius is many things but he is no idiot. The videos are held in escrow. If you renege on your deal, they will all be released. If you release Moria or if you kill Chunk, PC will be reviled across Centrian. Every person with grid access will see those videos."

She felt vindicated. She had snuffed out the ruse.

"But if they are released without cause – if you hold up your end of the bargain and you are betrayed – we all know that Moria and Chunk will be killed. He would not allow those videos to be released knowing that it would end Chunk's life.

He's traveled to the bowels of LiveLong, through the death matches of base-level, to the chaotic islands of Solis, just to find a life for that damn kid. You were beside him during some of this journey. You saw it for yourself. If you accept the terms, do you really think he'd betray you, knowing it would lead to Chunk's death?"

Another bout of silence overtook the room. He just smiled and stared at her. She was deep in thought. Everything Caspian told her made sense but she didn't want to admit it. She didn't want to accept this deal. She wanted to storm out of this room and announce to the world that she captured the Bowery Butcher. She just wanted to make him pay for his crimes. She had no desire to shield his sniveling little co-conspirator. That woman had so brazenly reissued Vitapasses outside of government guidelines. She had no desire to reward Pontius's depravity by granting a Vitapass to that filthy baby. She wanted to find some grander solution but none was forthcoming.

"The terms are accepted. As soon as he surrenders, Moria will be reinstated and Chunk will get his Vitapass."

"Nay." He shook his head and maintained his grin. "Moria is reinstated *now*, and Chunk gets his Vitapass *now*, or the whole deal is off."

Conti fought hard to suppress the incredulous anger as it welled up within her.

"What? He needs to bring himself in before I can authorize any kind of deal. Besides, there is no magic button I can push to make this happen. These things take time."

"Bullshit. Don't play coy with me, Dame Conti. Moria's access *can* be restored in minutes if you want it so. Once her access is restored, Moria herself can issue the Vitapass. It's that simple."

This flabbergasted her. A rage of thoughts and actions battled in her mind for supremacy. She wanted to smack him. She wanted to call security and have him thrown out. She wanted to have him arrested for attempting to blackmail a government officer. She wanted to spit in his face.

She blurted out a series of non-words and half-words. She struggled to put together a coherent thought, let alone a cogent argument. Caspian's audacity offended her on a professional level. The fact that she used to fuck him only made it worse. Every time she was ready to throw him from the office she kept returning to the thought of those videos.

Against her better judgment, she blurted out, "I have to coordinate with some of the other officers. This could take a while."

"I can wait."

He sat back in his chair and lifted a steaming cup of Caffeinate to his lips. She hadn't noticed the cup before. *Had he brought it with him?* She wasn't sure.

Although she communicated her need to *coordinate*, she sat for some time just staring at him in befuddlement. Despite the completion of the deal, she somehow believed he would just go away if she stared at him in anger for long enough. This did not happen. He just kept sipping and smiling. After ten more minutes of this awkward arrangement. she rose and left the room.

For the next two hours she completed a series of conversations. Some of them were convo's. Others took place with officers summoned into her office. While Caspian watched she tried to explain the incredible nature of the situation to several different individuals. Most of them were her superiors. She was a woman of significant authority. Yet even she did not have the sole power to reinstate an employee under investigation for corruption.

Several of the other officers gazed in amazement at Caspian as she explained the situation. Caspian smiled and nodded at them, but said nothing. He already said all he had come to say.

With the two of them alone again in the room, Conti felt exasperated. She did not raise her head. She was looking down into her lap.

"It's done. Moria has been reinstated."

He released a joyous laugh and threw the empty Caffeinate cup behind him.

"Excellent! Excuse me for a moment."

He initiated a convo to Moria.

"Conti tells me that you've been reinstated."

Moria's response was more emotion than words. Her joy came through in her squeal.

"Conti's really sorry for the way you've been treated. I'm sure she'll be coming by your office personally to apologize in a few days."

Conti gripped the sides of her chair and bit her lip.

"I need you to check your remote access, right now."

"Of course."

There was a pause while Moria fiddled with UNI commands.

"I'm in! I'm in!"

"Good. Now for the most important part. Is Chunk with you now?"

"Yes, he's right here."

"Good. See if you can give that little beast a Vitapass."

There was a long pause. He listened as she checked various data. Not having been through this, he had no idea how long the process took. He kept his smile on Conti. After several minutes he heard a wail of joy.

"It's done! It's done, Caspian! He has a Vitapass. Chunk has his Vitapass!"

"Thank you, Moria." And with that he abruptly cut the convo.

He rose to indicate that his work here was done. He gave Conti an exaggerated and flourishing bow. She was not amused. She felt stung by the deal and his demeanor. She wanted so much to kick him in the testicles.

"Pontius will arrive here before midnight to surrender himself. If he is not here by then, I would encourage you to have Moria and Chunk killed."

When he reached the door he turned to give her one last look.

"Fuck you, Caspian."

"Aye, you did that already. And it was lame."

And with that he exited the office and skipped out of the PC headquarters.

Chapter 16 – An Eternal Sun

Pontius sat in the open-air cabin of the transport ship. It cruised above the ocean surface at a mere altitude of a hundred meters. Bright sun and gale wind buffeted his harsh features. His long blonde hair would have blown to and fro in the wind, if he still had any hair. His head and his mind were bare. He still carried his natural memories from the last 400 years or so, but they wiped clean everything beyond that.

The passengers around him were exactly the motley lot one would imagine in a prison transport ship. A few of them whimpered quietly to themselves, shaken by the prospect of an immortal life spent in hard labor. Most of them just stared straight ahead. They were hard men, unbending against life's realities on Centrian. There was no reason for them to change course now, even in the face of this grim future.

He considered himself quite lucky. Most of the prison colonies existed in off-world mines. The laborers lived for thousands of years in stifling environments maintained only by high-technology life support. There was no wind or sun or natural world in which they could breathe fresh air. Pontius drew his lot on the polar island of Tynan. It was a land of eternal sun. It was a land where he would toil outdoors in the elements sucking in all that Torrenth could throw at him. It was an environment he welcomed.

The long journey across the ocean afforded him many hours to reflect. He regretted not being able to see Telarus before his departure. He was still receiving serious medical care. He regretted not seeing Dania. She refused to see him one last time, even though she understood the future he faced.

Moria was much more stoic than he expected. With Chunk still in her arms, she gave him a long hug. She said little. He expected her to cry or otherwise break down. Instead, she stood quietly and kept Chunk facing toward him. He wasn't sure what she wanted to accomplish. She just seemed intent on giving Chunk as much face time with Pontius as possible.

Caspian was another matter altogether. He became extremely agitated as his departure grew nearer. He babbled almost incoherently. He kept trying to give him small tokens of their time together. He even tried to give him his Priori necklace. Pontius found it all to be silly. He would be stripped of all possessions soon. There was no point in accepting anything from anyone else.

The trial was an exercise in kangaroo justice. The press was in high attendance. They laid the Bowery Butcher low for all Centrian to see. They charged him with so many crimes that he stopped counting. He instructed his counsel to remain silent. He offered no counterarguments. He gave no defense. His appointed lawyer did nothing more than acquiesce to a handful of cursory motions.

At first, the lawyer worked hard to present a stern defense. Pontius undermined this approach when he scolded the lawyer and told him to sit down and shut up. He didn't want anything to threaten the deal for Chunk's Vitapass.

A Dusk Forever Waning

The trial lasted for four hours. Petty theft trials took longer. The jury deliberated for fifteen minutes. When they read the verdict – guilty on all counts – it was broadcast live across the UNIs of every Centrian citizen.

The sentence was a foregone conclusion. Pontius would spend the rest of his life in hard labor in a penal colony chosen at random. The term *for the rest of his life* was not meant in a natural sense. Authorities force-fed Telomore to inmates. They received a full complement of nanites. Organ farms provided replacements for any failing body parts. Constant supervision ensured their ongoing safety. It was much harder to die on a penal colony than in the general population of Centrian. Some prisoners had already logged more than 8,000 years of hard labor.

While unable to speak with Telarus before his departure, he knew that all videos were safely in escrow. No one but Telarus could release them. He knew, beyond any doubt, that Telarus would never release them unless someone betrayed the terms of the deal. As long as Moria and Chunk were safe, those videos would never see the light of day.

One of the whimpering idiots sat directly next to him. The guy looked like a businessman, even with his head shaved and his prison garments. He cried for the last several hours. His pity party interrupted Pontius's thoughts. He looked over to the desperate man.

"Shut the fuck up."

It surprised him that the man complied. Everyone sat in eletrochairs – the same chairs that imprisoned him on the skydock platform. No one could rise or move any part of their body other than their head. Yet the sniveling prisoner choked down his sorrow and grew silent.

His thoughts strayed to the penal colony. He heard nothing but the worst. Sadistic guards corralled a violent population condemned to an eternity of painful labor. Rumors of escape floated through the population, but no one truly believed them. No one could confirm a successful flight from the colonies. They were the embodiment of purgatory.

The faces of the prisoners reflected every aspect of this truth. None of them knew what they were in for. Prisoners weren't assigned to these colonies on a temporary basis. Once a sentence condemned you here, you were here forever. Everyone on the transport pondered an endless future spent in back-breaking work. Hellish conditions would dominate that work.

He was the only soul on the vehicle in good spirits. He carried a sense of pride – a sense of accomplishment. The gentle smirk on his face was unbroken. It did not leave when the transport guard beat him for no apparent reason. It did not leave him when he realized he would never see Dania again. It did not leave him even as he saw the imposing shore of Tynan crest on the horizon.

Even from a distance he spied the frantic activity of slaves whipped into motion. Great scaffolds rose into the sky, buffeted by tiny souls dragging supplies behind them. The closer they came, the more he could see the land itself teaming with prisoners who flowed through the work sites like ants. Watcher drones hovered over all activity and shot random charges of punishment into the crowds below.

Nothing in this panorama broke his concentration. He pictured Malorus and Torrenthia. He knew they would be so proud of him. He thought of Moria. He knew she would cherish a life as Chunk's mother. Most of all, he thought of Chunk.

The commitment stood. He delivered the Vitapass he promised to Chunk's parents. He did not sell Chunk into the slavery of LiveLong's undercity. He did not condemn Chunk to a painful and abbreviated life on Soltris. Although he temporarily faltered in his morals at the death match, ultimately he didn't allow Chunk's life to be purchased by a dishonorable cheater like Silver.

Watching the bright sun pound down on Tynan filled him with hope. He knew the world was one that Chunk could conquer. It didn't matter whether Chunk chose to follow his footsteps in NCU or aspired to far greater ends. Everything Chunk would accomplish was made possible by his fortitude. He fulfilled his destiny to grant life where none should have existed. He thought about all that Chunk might achieve one day, and he smiled.